BY THE RIVER SO SWORN

By

K.R. Carnegie

Dedicated To Dad & Mum

Thanks for the Dragons

LET IT BE KNOWN ACROSS ALL OF MIR

On This Day, The 09th Of November 1107 MD (*Magi Domina)*

On The World Of Mir, Centre Of Creation

In Sight Of All Magi

The Children Of Our God Cronus

Assembled In The Heart Of The River, Holiest Temple of Magic

The Codeci Oratorium,

In The City Of The Sea Wizard, The Seat of Merlin

Terrastra, Jewel Of The West, Last Light At The Edge Of Mir

This Concord Has Been Proposed And Ratified By This Assembly

Henceforth And Forever, It Has Been Thus Decided

By The Guardians Of The Concord, The Aurum Council

On Behalf And For The Betterment Of All People Of Mir

Whether They Be Magi, Commoner, or Anathema,

All Beneath The Magi Shall Be Bound To The Concord

Bound By An Oath Sworn Between All Honourable Nations:

Blessed Concord Shall Be Forever More

For Cronus Has So Blessed Magi

In Turn Magi Have So Blessed Mir

And Woe Unto They Who Would Break Faith With The Blessed

By The River So Sworn

Hello?

THE CONCORD

1. NO MAGUS SHALL PRACTICE NECROMANCY
2. NO MAGUS SHALL PRACTICE DEMONOLOGY
3. NO MAGUS WILL SUFFER ANATHEMA TO LIVE
4. NO COMMON IS TO HOLD POLITICAL OFFICE, EITHER BY VOTE, APPOINTMENT OR CONTIGENCY
5. NO COMMON IS TO OPERATE ANY LANDED BUSINESS WITHOUT EXPLICIT APPROVAL OF THE LOCAL MAGOCRATIC GOVERNING BODY
6. NO COMMON IS TO HAVE FREEDOM OF MOVEMENT BETWEEN NATIONS WITHOUT EXPLICIT AUTHORIZATION FROM THE MAGOCRACTIC GOVERNING BODY OF THEIR PLACE OF BIRTH
7. TERRASTRA WILL REMAIN SOVEREIGN, FREE OF ALLEGIANCE, FEALTY OR SUBJUGATION
8. TERRASTRA IS TO BE GOVERNED BY THE HIGH COUNCIL OF THE LYCEUM IN PERPETUITY
9. TERRASTRA WILL REMAIN NEUTRAL GROUND, OPEN TO ALL MAGI UNDER THE CONCORD, FOR THE BETTERMENT OF ALL MAGOCRATIC NATIONS
10. THE WEST IS FORBIDDEN, FOR THERE LIES THE EDGE, AND THE END OF ALL THINGS

UNUM MIR UNUM MAGI

BY THE RIVER SO SWORN

Chapter One

The Rogue and The Scrivener

Plinius pried the large dusty tome from one of his hiding places, flicking through the crinkled pages frantically. Finding the page he sought, he hastily tore it from the bindings and stuffed it into his robes. Tossing the rest of the book onto the hearth, he grimaced as the centuries old knowledge it contained burst into white flames.

White flames? I think not. Black flames.

Oh! Cronus be good!

Hello.

You're here!

It appears I am. To whom am I speaking? Oh, by chance do you happen to know my name?

It's working! Ah, hello!

Hello? What is happening?

HELLO?

Prologue

The Narrator & The Voice

Hello, ser!

What in the bloody hells!? We were just in a bookstore- and now… Where the hell are we?

Hello ser; ah, again, ser. Ahem. My apologies, you just startled me is all. Some of us weren't sure if this was going to work. I was worried you wouldn't come, and you showed up in the first paragraph. Right at the beginning! Threw me for a spell.

I can see that! Chapter One, and now we're in the Prologue! I know enough to know that's backwards. And my name is apparently Plinius? And you're… Narrator? That's a stupid name. Curious, I know my name now, though I didn't a moment before. How does that make sense? What in bloody hells is going on? I can't see you- where are you? Bloody hells, I can't even see me! What in the Edge is going on!? Everything is white, and then these words pop up, and then… I see… Why can I see these words?

Plinius, please. Yes. Your name is Plinius. Plinius Scrivener. Focus your attention on the words. This is a story. A story being written at this very moment while we talk! I would love it if you stayed and gave me your opinion as we go. Can I continue? Is it ok if I tell this story?

I don't know… I was… where was I? I was aware, but only just, and it felt like the span of an age- like an eternity! And then -BAM- I was in a bookstore- NO! It was my bookstore! But… everything seems… fuzzy? Muddled. Muddy. A story, you say. A proper novel. Do I want you to continue, you asked? Well, I suppose that depends on what kind of story it is. I like adventures. Whodunits. Fantasy and science fiction. Romances…

Wait, what did you say there? I can barely read it.

It doesn't matter. I enjoy just about everything in fact.

Is that so? That's good! I think you will enjoy this story. It has a bit of everything and something for everyone.

A story, eh. How does any of this make any sense? All I see is… white nothing? Then the words. But when you described the bookstore… it was so vivid? I swear to Cronus, I was there! But… that was years ago… right? But I was just there!

Well of course the bookstore makes sense. It is only natural you remember it. This is, in fact, your story, Plinius.

My story? How intriguing, seeing as how I cannot remember a single thing, I get the sense I am a humble man. How am I worthy of such a story?

Oh, trust me, you are worthy, friend.

But HOW then? How is this happening?

Well… that is complicated.

Well make it uncomplicated.

The easiest explanation for now is, well, magic.

Magic?

Surely you haven't forgotten about the River.

The River. Of course not. It is beyond forgetting. It is not like forgetting one's own mother- that I have done seemingly easily. Do you know my mother? The River is all things. How could I ever forget.

So, magic! That explains it. And I suppose the only way to end the spell is…

Finishing the story.

Of course. It's so cliché it borders on becoming a classic. So, it is to be a story, eh? A biography too… not my usual cup of tea. They have the tendency to be too dreary and self-indulgent, in my humble opinion. I hope that isn't what we're getting here.

More of an adventure, really.

Comedy or tragedy?

We can decide that at the end of the story.

I suppose I have no choice but to take your word for it. Well then. Perhaps if we continue along with the story the truth of this matter will be made apparent. I do seem to be recollecting as we go. Please proceed.

Thank you! This is good. The truth will be made clear, and the truth is that you can trust me.

Mm-hmm.

Again, thank you for listening. Reading? Never mind. Please, feel free to offer insight as we go.

Oh, I shan't intrude. I've never been a big talker. A very private magus I am. Or was? Will this… will it… hurt?

No! No, it shouldn't. It's ok. Focus on me, Plinius. Relax, and enjoy the story. Let's continue and you just jump in when you feel like it. This is probably just as confusing for whoever is reading this

Sorry. I mean there's a good chance that we'll all be

Things will be clearer as we move along.

Wait, what was that?

What was what? Nothing. It was nothing. Let's just-

Oh no! Not so fast! You were saying something about reading? Then you disappeared! Do you have any idea how long you were gone? Do you know who you are talking to? I am a Magus of the… the Sixth circle! Eighth? Eighth circle! I am not some gullible common that will swallow your lies wholesale. You were saying something, and then there was this… this… pause? Break? What is the word?

Void?

Yes! A void! Just so.

Ok, what was that?

It was nothing.

You just did it again!

No, I didn't.

Yes, you did!

You must be joking.

Ok, yes. Sorry Plinius. When I disappear like that, I am conferring with my associates. I just had to step away from the story for a second. That was the pause. It doesn't mean I'm gone, ok?

Associates? What associates? Who are they? Who in the bloody hells are you? I can't even see you, and you ask me to trust you? I assume you're the writer of this book.

Well, sort of. It's kind of-

Let me guess- complicated?

Yes.

You're reading this, aren't you? Or writing it? Out with it!

I swear, you better get back here right NOW!

So, I'm trapped in a book? The Edge take me!

Please Pliny, it's ok. I'm a friend, and I'm sure everything you have forgotten will come back to you if we continue with the story. Are you ok if we proceed?

Pliny? That name is what… what…

That is what?

That is what my friends called me. Isn't it?

Ah, yes. Your nickname. You didn't remember your nickname?

Oh… another name…

Oh?

An… an… Ana… damn it! It's so hard to focus. I can't remember gremlin shit! Circles above!

But you remembered your favourite books back there.

Did I? Well, yes. I suppose I did. Hmmm. Do you suppose it was due to you pulling me into the bookstore with your tale? Favourite books, bookstore. Get it? That there's some association with where the story goes? Jogging loose memories? Hello? Hello?

Sorry Plinius, just stepped away for a second.

Plinius, are you there? Shit, did we just lose him?

Plinius?

Grandmagus?

Not so nice to be left in a blank void, is it?

Fine. Point taken.

I will accept that as an apology. Please keep the vanishings to a minimum. Now, will you tell me to whom I am addressing? Are you a magus?

No, I am not one of the magi. Maybe I am though. Kind of. Not really.

Well, that is just deliciously, evasively curious. Then what manner of magic is this? Surely not demonology.

That story is a long one, Plinius. Much longer than your story. How about we focus on yours for now?

A long story, eh? Well, I am sorry. Whatever magic this is, I will not be party to anything that breaks the Concord.

You remember the Concord?

Remember the Concord! Ha! How could I forget the most important document in magino! Mirysh!- history? The bedrock of Magocratic society, written by the Aurum Circle themselves? Do I remember! Anyways, it was a few pages ago, right before you showed up and plopped me down in my bookstore.

Wait, so you were here before I started reading? And there were words?

Yes, some title or something. It was all rather dreadfully confusing, and I was as turned around as a dolphin chasing its flipper, and I cannot remember for the life of me what it said or where I was. Seeing the Concord brought me back though! Like a life preserver in a tempest- straightened things right up. And then you showed up.

Interesting.

So, to recap, you say this is my story? And how is it you know my story anyways?

Do you really want me to give away the ending right at the beginning?

You nasty devil! You know I can't resist a good story, don't you? I didn't know I couldn't either, until just now, if that makes sense! Wait… is that what's going on here? You lure me in with the promise of a story, and then…

Then?

You follow it up with something nefarious no doubt.

Oh, give me a break. Nefarious?

Assume my identity! Steal my artifacts! Or maybe you will trap me in a pocket dimension, like a genie or djinn! Or infect me with a spell plague, or the pox,· or ceremorphosis! Perhaps you are here to steal my kidneys! Maybe you will ruin my credit and leave me beggared. Or turn me into a sleeper agent, activated on command to enact your dreadful schemes!

Good to see you still have your imagination.

I am being earnestly serious! I am making educated deductions based on the air.

The air?

You have the air of a villain about you.

That's ridiculous.

As ridiculous as you talking to me through a book? This whole situation is ridiculous.

You're being ridiculous. I'm not here to do anything but help.

Or kidnap me for my knowledge! Or ransom me back to the Empire! The… Empire…

I swear on our friendship that there is nothing nefarious going on here.

Whatever that promise is worth. So, no spoiling the ending then. Before we proceed- you know my name, but I am still at a loss as to what I should call you.

Oh… Ah. It's back there in the prologue title, I guess. Narrator. You can call me Narrator?

Narrator? With a question mark? It sounds like you're asking for my approval. Then no. It's immensely unimaginative, cliché and stupid. I will not be party to mediocrity, especially if this is an accounting of yours truly. Narrator is a terrible name.

Fine! Objection noted. Bloody hells! Just give us a bloody name ye big baby so we can move this along!

Plinius?

Plinius?

I am not a baby. I am a grandmagus.

Hey, come on now. I'm sorry I called you a baby. Please, give me whatever name you want.

Ok. I will call you… Tabitha.

Prologue

Tabitha & Plinius

Seriously?

I am not in the habit of changing my mind, Tabitha. If we are such great friends, you would know that. Tabitha.

My name is not Tabitha.

Why can't it be Tabitha?

Tabitha… Tabitha is like- it's a cat's name!

Names can be anything. Use your imagination. Don't be so narrowminded.

Me? ME!? Narrowminded? Oh, Cronus be good, that is rich!

What's that supposed to mean?

If you let me continue with the story you would find out.

You are very coy. I find it annoying. Very well, Tabitha. I give you leave to continue. Continue.

My name is not Tabitha. Please change it.

Fine! This one time I will change my mind, as a show of good faith on my part.

I name you, ye who are nameless! You are the reader of the first word, the singer of the first song, the movement of the first dance. Since the time behind all beginning, to the last light, I mark you. Thus, I name you Talespinner.

Very dramatic.

Tales when I am feeling chummy.

Prologue

Old Chum Tales & Plinius

Good to see you haven't lost your sense of humour, magus. This is starting to make me nauseous.

I don't think the name is THAT bad.

Not the name! The whipping around back to the start of the prologue. It's putting things all out of order. It's very… disconcerting.

Oh. I understand. My apologies. Ah, look! The title says you're my old chum!

Well, that part is true at least.

Truly? Are we friends?

Yes. We have been since the beginning.

I don't remember any friends. Why should I believe you?

You will believe by the end, I promise. What do you have to lose?

Plinius?

I will conditionally agree to an extension of formal cordiality between us, until you give me a reason to withdraw said olive branch.

Same old Plinius.

Same old Tales. I presume. Let us continue, Talespinner. Only because, to be honest, I fail to see an alternative option. I do believe I have all the time in the world.

Chapter One

The Scrivener & The Rogue

Plinius pried the large dusty tome from one of his hiding places, flicking through the crinkled pages frantically. Finding the page he sought, he hastily tore it from the bindings and stuffed it into his robes. Tossing the rest of the book into the hearth, he grimaced as the centuries old knowledge it contained burst into black flames.

You already read this part.

"We really do not have the time for this. Go get your quills, and then we need to leave!"

The heat was becoming unbearable in the closed confines of the tiny bookstore. What was originally a quite spacious town home on the Street of Sighs had slowly, over an indeterminate but lengthy amount of time, transformed into a cloistered warren of literature. Towering stacks of musky tomes teetered precariously as the magus hustled between the stacks; entire walls of thick leatherbound texts that had been untouched for decades exploded into whirling clouds of white dust and debris as they came crashing down.

The magus' mouth dropped open, his short brown and white beard working up and down as silently as a fish. The magus was gangly and tall, with untamed, neglected hair bristling in all directions. The wrinkles around his eyes gave the appearance of a magus exiting his early adulthood, but as with all magi you never could tell. He rounded on the swarthier, handsomer, younger man. *Hey now!* His eyes squinted in accusation. The man met his gaze with his own unworried stare while yawning wide and loudly.

"No time? No time?" An edge of hysteria was creeping into the magus' voice. "And who is to fault for that, I wonder?" The magus desperately tried to retain his grip on the half dozen books in his hand, only to spill them out over the floor. He wildly kicked out with his foot to block some from rolling into the quickly expanding flames, failing miserably. "Anatoli, you could have come sooner! Could have WARNED me sooner!"

Oh, Blessed Concord. Anatoli. He was my friend.

"I came when I found out, not a moment before or after," replied Anatoli in an even and measured voice. Plinius prickled at his tone. *Oh my, the nerve. I think I am recalling how much I hate him.*

"I am so very happy for your sense of punctuality," retorted Plinius. "It is good to know that coming here and ruining my life is going so precisely to schedule."

"Me? *I* ruined *your* life?" Anatoli scoffed. He lifted the small white porcelain cup he held and took a long sip, his wispy moustache dipping into the cup and coming up glistening as it dripped down his bare chin. Turning away from the dirty window, he waved his hand dismissively. "Was I the one with a hundred little secrets? Hmmm?" He turned his eyes back towards the window. "*Da*, you have made your own bed on this one, Pliny."

Plinius stomped his foot bitterly. Hooking his high starched collar with his finger, he tried in vain to loosen the grip his grey robe had on his sweat-stained neck. The heat was making him even more irritated than he already was with the disruption to his day. Muttering a few words, he turned his hand in a motion of memorized movements he had diligently learned long ago. His perspiration ceased and his body temperature returned to normal. Anatoli arched an eyebrow expectantly at the magus. Plinius bristled. Coming up short with a proper retort, the magus responded by sticking his tongue out before promptly turning his back on the rogue.

The cramped conditions of his small bookshop were normally quite cool and cosy and much to his liking. The hazy air of dust. The rows and rows of bound knowledge, windows into history, committed to page eternal, old friends one and all. The muted sounds of the cities boisterous hustle and toil blissfully kept at bay by his large and locked oak door. Plinius had been burning scrolls, parchments, and tomes for the better part of half an hour. The frenetic pace in which he added fuel to the blazing fire had turned his once homey bookstore into a furnace and downright inhospitable.

Anatoli was calm as ever as he peered out the dirty window that faced the main street. Leaning casually against a bookcase packed with antique elvish literature, Anatoli was dressed as usual in a loose-fitting white linen shirt buttoned halfway, a rather dashing leather vest in the northern style and green trousers tucked into knee high leather boots of cracked worn leather. His hair was full, dark, and tumbled down from his head in curls. He looked as if he had stopped in for a polite how-do-you-do or maybe a cup of southern caf. Plinius would have preferred that to barging in and upending his world. Plinius could not decide which irked him more- his friend's calm demeanour or the fires heat.

Running his finger down the pane of glass, Anatoli brought his finger to his lips and blew away a blizzard of dust. "Cronus' balls, *moy drug*. When was the last time you opened these drapes?"

Plinius waved a hand at him as he dumped an armful of books into a large iron cauldron, the legs of which were fashioned in the likeness of dragon claws. He muttered a few words and a ball of flame shot from his open palm into the cauldron, causing the books within to explode into a fountain of charred pages. Paying no attention to the rain of embers, he reached under the cauldron, muttering a simple spell. A compartment clicked open in one of the clawed legs. The magus began pulling out far more paper than could have possibly fit in the hole and tossed them into the fire.

"I think I see their banners turning onto your street," warned Anatoli in his most pleasant voice, picking his nose as he peered out the window and yawned. "They should be here in, oh, no more than half an hour, given the foot traffic this morning. Mayhap even more- you know how heavy those manacles can be to carry around."

Plinius let out a small eek and begun a furious attempt at opening a locked drawer on his desk. After the third unsuccessful try at finding the right key, Plinius swore and pointed at the obstinate desk. Muttering an incantation under his breath, a silky ribbon of blue flame shot forth from the tip of his finger and upon contact with the drawer, a shower of charred wood and soot erupted outwards showering the room with chunks of debris. Reaching inside, extra careful to not let his skin touch the still smouldering embers, Plinius grabbed the stack of scrolls and tossed them into the hearth as well.

"Nice trick Pliny," said Anatoli, shaking his head. "Why do you not just burn the whole place down and be done with it?"

Plinius rounded on Anatoli, his finger now pointing accusingly with just a hint of menace.

"Mayhap I should, you- you- rogue! What is a charge of arson added on top of violation of the Concord? Mayhap they will bloody hang me after they burn me at the bloody stake!" *Me, violate the Blessed Concord? Preposterous. I thought you said this was non-fiction.*

Anatoli rolled his eyes. "You are such a dramatic. You should consider joining the theatre."

Bounding over to very high bookcase, Plinius scrambled up a ladder two rungs at a time and started heaving books off the top shelf towards the fire. Priceless copies went into the flames, and some one-of-a-kind originals as well. Such tomes as Veneficus Logain's *Thoughts on The River,* Dan'Els *The Death of a People,* and a genuine handwritten *Codexus Maldaemonicon* bound in some sort of pale leather went sprawling across the room, the latter making it into the fire and not so much burning as vanishing in a cloud of oily smoke. Anatoli chuckled as no more than one out of every five came anywhere near the target. In his haste there was a lot of collateral damage, most of it inconsequential. A couple of cheap calendars, never opened, with the three hills of Terrastra under the year 1410 MD on the cover incinerated instantly.

"Maybe I will! Maybe I will!" Plinius frantically bobbled his head in sarcastic agreement, not even watching what he was tossing or where it was landing. "Change my name, flee to some Cronus forsaken shithole and rut in the mud with the other makeup plastered simps with-" Plinius caught himself short. He could feel his face redden, this time no fault of the heat. He glanced furtively at Anatoli, who regarded him with an arched bushy black eyebrow.

I'm sure it was an accident. Terrible, terrible word to call a common. There's a difference, you know. Between a commoner and a simp.

"Ah… sorry. That was- I mean to say," Plinius fumbled for the right words.

"No offense taken," Anatoli waved his hand dismissively again.

"Truly Anatoli, I- I am just out of sorts today. I would never-"

"*Da, da,* I know Pliny, drop it. I've been called worse, eh?"

"I have had plenty of common friends, you know that do you not-"

"Please just for Cronus' sake hurry the bloody nine hells up! Did you grab your quills? Hurry!" Plinius recoiled slightly at the impatience and aggressiveness- he had never seen Anatoli like this. The rogue exhaled slowly.

"We should have been away as soon as I got here," he chided himself. "Just, please, Plinius. The quills. Hurry."

Despite this plea for haste, Anatoli seemed incredibly casual as he went and topped up his cup. He stepped over the grandmagus as Plinius dropped to the ground, using a butterknife to stab at a gap in the floor.

After a minute, Plinius grabbed a small green book hidden under the now mangled floorboard and hesitated a moment before shoving it into the bag slung around his shoulder. "I cannot just leave! I need to destroy the reagent pouch in my bedroom, along with the -oh, gremlin shit. I just remembered my copy of *Codex MalDemo*-"

Anatoli had appeared behind him so silently and swiftly Pliny nearly fell over. Anatoli adroitly shot out a hand and steadied his friend gently. "Pliny- there is no sense in destroying anything. It is over for you. Whether they find what they are looking for or not is no longer a matter to concern yourself with," Anatoli smiled weakly at the magus. "You know how the Empire operates. You have been accused, and after a short and demonstrably unfair trial, you will be found guilty; innocent or not. Then it's the rope for you, *moy drug.*"

"Nonsense!" Plinius protested. "If I can just get rid of- I can explain- if there is nothing for the Empire to discover, I can work this out! Why are they even here? This is Terrastra! I don't understand, they have no jurisdiction here-"

Anatoli shook his head. "No Pliny. You have been locked away in here for too long. The Empire has been slowly sweeping away any resistance to their rule in Terrastra. It is nearly over. Now hurry up and let us be away." He turned back towards the window, peering into the distance. "Oh! I think I can see their halberds now. Do you suppose it's magic that gets them so shiny?"

The traffic was often thick on the Street of Sighs in the morning-

Woah! Woah, woah, woah. What happened?

Sorry?

Where are we now? What happened?

Oh, we just went back to a point before. You know, a place before where we were in the story. It is a, ah, a flashback.

How confusing. Why not just tell it in order?

I wish I knew. I'm just reading what pops up on the page as my hand writes it.

So, the spell is some form of auto-writing? That must mean you are a magus!

It's more complicated than that.

What is- the spell or what you are?

Both.

I would feel a lot better about this if you were a little more forthcoming.

We're in this together, so I suggest we just enjoy the story. I doubt this will be the only flashback, so just go with it. If you want your memory back, then this next part must be important.

Fine. But I don't care for it. It feels dizzy and disruptive, despite dealing with desired data from days long dead.

Really?

What?

The alliteration?

I like alliteration. My apologies for adding some flair.

The traffic was often thick on Hill Street even this early in the pre-dawn twilight. The throngs of merchants, daytalers, stevedores, porters, shore hands and citizens at large were busy about their morning, and the sea of humanity made for slow going. Anyone- regardless of social class, race, circle, or Imperial warrant- trying to make their way in the business park at this hour was in for a wait, as sure as the sun set at the Edge of Mir. The twilling of blue and white birds among the boughs of towering maples lining the Street of Sighs was quickly drowned out by the growing clamour of barking voices and clank and clatter of wheels along a finely red-bricked road. Friends stopped in the middle of the road, shouting gaily at each other in happy greeting, while in equal measure total strangers cursed them to the hells for getting in their way. On both sides of the road stretched buildings as tall as storm giants, four stories or more, white-washed stone buildings with living roofs of green grass, spell wrought in the days of old by the magi who first discovered the Sapphire Falls and the bay-side canyon it had carved. Those who had come to the western edge of the world with Merlin and William the Lyon in search of freedom.

Up and down the street, doors opened as magi and commoner alike met the rising day. Golemists directed their common labourers, straining under gigantic balls of clay. Tattooists sat on stools, their talents parading across their own skins, flowing along their flesh in an orgiastic riot of moving colour. Numerous magi sold their services as wardists, salubrists, allomancers and diviners. Each and every one of them specialists in their major circle of magic. This set them apart from each other. The thing that bound them all was that each and every one of them was also learned in the school of scrivening, the magic of creation and recreation. Through this knowledge of scrivening they made a comfortable living through their primary school of magic. These hundreds of amateur scriveners made up not even half of the magical services available along the Street of Sighs.

The lion's share of magi dealt with the purest form of scrivening, the art of scrollwork. Spells on demand, the tool and weapon of the magi that had made possible their spread and dominance across the continent of Mir.

It truly cannot be overstated how fundamentally important scrivening is as the bedrock of modern Magocratic society.

How so, ser?

A student of the 1st circle, with the right scroll in his hand, could be as powerful as an archmagus. For instance! A salubrist of the eighth circle could only bring freshly dead corpses back to life if they were in the same room. And then only maybe once or twice a day-that kind of draw from the River is incredibly draining.

I had a friend once… long story short, we nearly lost him because the salubrist was so drained.

It was the great limiter. A tired magus is no magus at all.

And scrivening changed all of that.

Yes. The discovery of scrivening made it possible for that same magus to duplicate his spell for a fraction of the effort. I won't go into the technical aspects of it, but essentially, you're using yourself as a conduit. The spell is now viable in any situation. A powerful scrivener with the right knowledge and acumen is an invaluable resource to a community, making it possible for thousands of lesser magi to wield the greatest of magic powers heretofore denied to them through their own inherent lack of ability and worth. Terrastra had thousands of scriveners.

Terrans, traders and tourists would come to the Street of Sighs throughout the day, browsing for the scroll that would solve their problems. Without fail all their needs were met. Cantrip scrolls could be found by the thousands, simple spell scrolls for starting a fire or cleansing water. Even commoners could use those, if taught some rudimentary letters. But the scrolls for Magi? It felt like there was no boundary. Reshaping your home, freezing meat for storage, healing a wound, traveling, cooking, entertainment. Want to talk to your dog? Go for a flight? Conjure a feast, or kill a beast? Clean your house or become a mouse? *Sleep for hours or bring spring showers!* All this and more could be found for sometimes as little as a few silver pieces. The art of drawing from the River of magic and binding it for later use had been the most monumental and pivotal development in magical society since the creation of the spell light or create food.

Create food is a myth.

Get out of here.

Edge take me if I'm lying!

Scrivening was in modern times, by the largest of margins, the principal school of magic practiced in all of Mir. Most magi never moved past earning their red robe- the mark of a 1st circle 'student' or 'primori'. This granted magi the control not only to utilize spell scrolls but to scribe their own cantrips. Consequently, the red robed 'primori' absolutely mobbed the Street of Sighs. From the foot of the road near Drake Bay to its head near the Lyceum Way, a tide of crimson with ink-stained fingers dominated the busiest road in all Terrastra. The most popular and respected scrivener in town could be found closest to the top of the street, her business in a breathtaking building of the most modern and gaudy geomorphic design that begged you to notice its wealth. She was a scrivener of adequate talent, but even she had only reached the blue robe of a 5th circle Superior. As far as anyone knew, that was as good as scroll making got in Terrastra outside of the Lyceum.

About midway on the street, however, there stood a non-descript building. A heavy oak door and windows with thick and dusty burgundy curtains drawn tight had remained shut for nearly as long a time as anyone living in the vicinity could remember. No sign hung to identify it as a business, no children playing on the porch marked it a family home. So as such it had remained a mostly quiet and ignored oddity to its neighbours for decades. Any inquiries at the door from the curious were met with stoney silence from an implacable oak door. Stories about the house, rumoured to have once been a bookstore, had been passed around by the neighbours that had come and gone. Their children believed a ghost haunted it, a popular theory for over twenty years.

The closest anyone ever came to finding out the truth was a man by the name of Henter Chang, a rather wealthy merchant from Xeijpang looking to expand into the Terrastran market. Upon seeing the forlorn house, he knew he had to have it. His quest took him to the Hall of Records at the Lyceum, a search through the archives for a deed or title, certain he could make an acceptable offer to whoever owned the property. Henter was promptly dropped into a bureaucracy so labyrinthian that some people say he is still searching in the basement of the Lyceum.

Nowadays, whispers about the house persisted. As of late, the newest rumour was of a man seen leaving in the dead of night under cloak and hood. Talk abounded- mostly salacious trash or crackpot conspiracy theories. The truth, if they knew, would have been a resounding disappointment. *Hey!*

Plinius Scrivener- *that's me!*- Grandmagi of the Eighth Circle- *wait, when is this?*- alumnus cum laude of the Lyceum, accredited Scrivener, master Wordbinder and- *As Anatoli would say, 'a possessor of some neat tricks'*- and up until this morning, though he didn't yet know it, bookstore proprietor and very well-respected gentleman to the very, very few who knew him- *my correspondence list had been formidable once upon a time*- looked out from the upper window of his home, his bookstore. He turned away and sniffed dismissively as the outside world rolled awake and reared itself, rising like the revolting rodent it was. *Nice.*

It was not that Plinius disliked his home, the jewel of the western shore, the grand city-state of Terrastra. It was, in his scholarly opinion, the most civilized and enlightened place on the continent, a direct result of its autonomy being assured in the Concord. It was a place where a magus could be left well alone and with that came opportunity for someone in his line of work. The Terrastran authority was a little less draconian in its citizens lives compared to, say, the Empire or Xeijpang. *That's the understatement of the century.* In those regards he liked it very much. If only it was not so busy, so teeming with life, and all the noise and smells that came along with that. Plinius prized his solitude. Despite all that he was comfortable in his little nook, his little slice of life carved out in the heart of all the chaos of city living.

His routine had been unchanged for some time now *-surely not that long! I can be a dynamic and exciting fellow* - and that suited Plinius just fine. He had woken up on time, right on schedule, precisely an hour before the dawn sun crested the eastern hill. If he had lived in the common slums on the eastern slopes, it would have been well into morning as far as daylight hours went. The shadow from the lowest hill in the southeast of the city denied the suns reach to the trade district of Terrastra for roughly five hours compared to the rest of the city, the only exception being Shadowside west of the Highhill and the near eternal gloom of the Tradebasin.

Plinius shuffled over to an ostentatious lounging chaise of dwarven design, picking up and putting on the wool undershirt and grey robe he had been wearing yesterday. A quick sniff of the armpits and a baneful eye on the splotchy ink stains along the sleeves made him momentarily reconsider. Deciding that taking the robe back off would be too much of a hassle he instead muttered a simple incantation, and the robe instantly became as if it was freshly laundered. *It's not lazy if it's magic.* A scent of lemon and geraniums infused the air. Satisfied, he slipped on a pair of leather moccasins and made his way downstairs, humming as he went.

A few more muttered words and a pleasant little fire sprang to life in the hearth near the back of the bookstore. The fire in the hearth flickered, a feebly glowing bed of embers giving off a miserly light. The dim light draped the room in long jagged shadows stretching out from behind the stacks of books and rows of free-standing shelving. Curios were crammed around any space not taken up by books. Polished yellow skulls of various creatures stared at Plinius from their bottomless black eyes. Taxidermized creatures both monstrous and natural hung or perched or piled up in any space not blocked by bookcases or reserved for traveling around the hoard. A few crystal balls were piled in the corner, a small pyramid rising above a plethora of idols. *Some idols were genuine; most were fakes.*

The magus walked through his house on narrow pathways through the valleys between mountains of books and other treasures accumulated over a long life. Looking around the pre-dawn gloom the magus tsked in annoyance. "Oh, this will not do."

Plinius repeated the spell he had already cast. Four large, frosted glass balls suspended from the ceiling by black chain flared to life. Like miniature suns, they provided a blanket of comfortable light that pushed the shadows into the corners of the voluminous room that took up the first two stories of his home. Reaching into a cupboard along the back wall, he took out a small pot and a sachet of dried leaves. After another few words to fill the pot halfway with water, he placed it on a stovetop to boil. After a minute of staring into nothing he cursed quietly and muttered a few words to conjure a fire in the stoves belly. While waiting for the water to boil, he wandered around, adjusting a stack of books here, flipping through another there. He made a move towards the front door, as if to unlock it. *I remember having this feeling, this thought. Why not open the store for business today? It had been quite some time since I had unlocked the door for an actual day's business. 'Today will be the day' I would say. The whim would usually come and go quickly.* He froze a few steps short, his hand stretched out towards the door, trembling. After a moment he shook his head, turning around. *The world could always wait a bit longer. There was always another project to tinker with, or another spell to modify, or another scroll to perfect. I was happy in my studies. I didn't need anything else.*

Finished with his daily ablutions, Plinius whistled a melody, jaunting across the room to his workspace. Shelves strained in long sagging curves under the weight of inks, powders, writing implements, various waxes, rubber seals- not to mention the prodigious quantity of loose blank paper. Loose paper could be found within arm's reach at any place in Plinius' home, some of it blank but most of it riddled in scrawls and random thoughts that at first glance could only come from either a magus of great genius or a mad man. Only a small population of Mir was literate, and the amount of paper available in his bookstore would be unbelievable to even most magi. The most important of pages were piled in stacks of thousands anywhere they could fit on the shelves, most of them long, long forgotten. The shelves buttressed a large, angled drafting table of solid yellow pine. Stretched out and held in place by two thin iron bars on a sliding vertical rail, an unfurled scroll waited patiently for its artist to return and complete it. He settled onto his stool, conjured by himself personally to fit the contours of his body perfectly. It had once had a cushion, but that was long gone, rotted to nothing with the passage of time. The seat was now just smooth concave wood, an indentation matching his backside furrowed into it from extensive use. As the pot heated and his caf steeped, he set to work.

The inscription on the waiting scroll was nearly finished from a late-night surge of boredom during the wee hours, and for one of Plinius' talent was rather simple and rote. *Barely a test of my skills; barely a chore really.* Unbidden a smile creased along his lips. He grabbed a fresh quill from a small rack above the table. Each quill was unique- some of incredibly rare pedigree. He thought his most beautiful one was a golden quill with iridescent emerald feathers ending in fiery red tips. *Cockatrice feather.* His hand rested on a slim jet-black quill with downy feathers that rippled gently from a non-existent wind. *That one was used… for certain spells.* Changing his mind, he picked up a plain looking quill of white and grey. *My favourite. From a western gull. One of millions but special all the same.*

Plying his fingers across the tops of the ink jars, he settled on a jar filled near to the brim with what looked like at first glance a thick black ink. On further inspection one could see twinkling speckles of diamond-light pulsing through the darkness. Plinius barked the word '*Hand!*' with a quick snap of his wrist and a floating, almost translucent hand of nebulous blue materialized out of thin air, a framework of tiny stars floating throughout, as if the hand was a tiny galaxy. The hand picked up the ink jar before floating up to the top of the drafting table. Placing it on the upper ledge, it pulled the topper cork out of the jar with a *pop!* Hand rolled the cork across its knuckles before flicking it onto a side table where it came to rest perfectly. The fingers wiggled in satisfaction. Hand then faced its palm towards its master, tiny stars on the palm rearranging into a question mark. The grandmagus did not spare it a look, waving a lazy hand in dismissal. Its thankless job complete, the hand vanished but not before extending a particular digit towards the oblivious magus. *Cheeky. Hand was always in a mood.* Plinius ran the tip of the quill across his lips. Quick as a swooping falcon, his hand reached up and dipped the tip of the quill into the ink. *Oh yes, here comes the good stuff.*

His vision narrowed as darkness crept into the room. The sounds outside dulled to an inaudible mumble. The crackling fire became a distant whisper. The walls closed in, and his world shrunk to the size of the parchment. The ink touched the scroll, and his senses exploded as the entire cosmos revealed themselves to him. He could not see but felt the entirety of creation. A torrent of life, of energy, channelled through him- through the soles of his feet, the tip of his head, on the tip of his tongue and pit of his stomach, bursting and beating in time with his beating heart- a rush of flowing magic, the fundamental River coursing through the universe. With a thought made easier by talent, time, and tenacity, he bent the River by the force of his will into his hands. The power travelled through his fingers, connecting through the quill, his very will the implement he wielded to focus the magic, infusing the ink. Then his work truly began.

As his hand began to move, the world went quiet. Then he could hear the thundering chant of the spell in his ears, a chorus of disembodied voices from a distant place singing the ancient words that would reshape the magic of the River into what he desired. Although he made no sound but the scribbling scratches of the quill, the ink was his voice, his power, his magnificent skill entwining with the River that nourished the world. Through his skill he made the River pour its essence into the scroll. *It is a rapturous feeling. Nothing compares.*

And then the voices ceased. The world crept back in. The fire crackled. A shouted greeting on the street was met with muffled laughter. The pot bubbled merrily. A bird tweeted shrilly. Everything had come back into focus, and Plinius looked down at his work. He grinned and nodded his head, satisfied. The words on the scroll shimmered in otherworldly light, a twinkling aurora emanating from the magic ink. He was pleased with what he had finished, what he had created. A simple spell, but the intense joy that filled Plinius whenever he completed a scroll buoyed his soul.

A not rather loud knock on the front door startled him so much he jumped in his seat. "Shit!" he swore as he smashed his knee into the underside of the drafting table. The jar resting on top of the table wobbled and sloshed out, covering the left half of the newly finished scroll with dark ink. Dismayed, Plinius tore the soiled scroll off the table. Plinius let out a small cry of dismay that quickly turned to irritation.

"Who in the bloody hells is knocking on my door at this hour," he asked no one in particular, as the knocking resumed. Even though this was the first time someone had knocked on his door in quite some time, Plinius was quite miffed with the audacity of someone calling without sending a message spell first. *Tap-tap-taptaptap-tap.*

Plinius had half a mind to ignore the knocking. He dabbed at the scroll with the sleeve of his robe. It only served to smear the ink and stain his cuffs. It very quickly became clear that this was a losing battle. *Can't use a cleansing spell either, it'll destroy the ink underneath as well.* The words that had shimmered slowly dulled until they looked no different from a scroll a common could produce. Plinius scowled as he crumpled the parchment into a ball and tossed it in a nearby wastebasket that promptly incinerated it.

Tap-tap-taptaptap-tap.

Huffing himself up as he stormed towards the door, Plinius cast a simple defensive shield on himself. Contorting his hand in a precise manner the bolt, despite no outwards means of disengaging, slid back within the door with a thud. Swinging it open he began to launch into a tirade of justified annoyance.

"Now see here!" He tried to say in his most imperious voice.

Plinius blinked a few times, staring out into the street before he could let his thoughts catch up to the situation. The first few rays of sunlight were beginning to peak down over the southern hill. His eyes darted quickly around his doorstep, seeing no one. *Probably a prank by some common child.* A surprised looking neighbour, an antiquities dealer from across the street taking his dog out for a shit, raised a hand slowly in greeting as they made eye contact. He might have called a greeting to the magus, but Plinius glowered and quickly retreated, slamming the door shut.

The nerve of some people.

Plinius turned away from the door, flicking his hand back and locking the door behind him. He had taken two strides towards the stove when a dapper man materialized before him while simultaneously yelling "BOO!"

Plinius screamed and shot his hand outwards in reaction. A coil of pink energy snapped into reality with a pop and coiled around the man like a giant snake, trapping him thoroughly. The man let out a large oomph as the air was forced out of his lungs. "Pliny! Stop! It's me! Stop!" he croaked.

"Blessed Concord," Plinius swore. "Anatoli, you rogue, you scared me half to death!"

"Grrk," choked out Anatoli.

"Oh! Sorry!" Plinius dispelled his spell instantly, and the pink rope disappeared as if it had never existed.

Anatoli flopped to the ground, his back landing in a pile of books that spilled over the pathway. "Oof. *Spasebo, moy drug.*"

Plinius took a moment before rounding on Anatoli. Finding his voice, he began to move towards the man sitting on his floor, who was rubbing his sides gently while wincing. "Anatoli! Do you realize what you have done!? Now is not the time for a visit!"

"Caf?" Anatoli asked, bouncing up and taking a few short strides towards the stove. Plinius hurried up to follow. Turning abruptly, Anatoli had a smile so wide it caught Plinius short, and it took all the magus' meagre reflexes not to crash into him.

"Nonsense Pliny! Nonsense. Now is the perfect time to pay a visit. This is how you greet your old *droug* Anatoli? How long has it been?"

"Ah," Plinius thought about it, "An actual visit? Not just picking up, ah, packages? A year or two, maybe. I do not keep the time as well as used to. Busy, you know. Studies, research, and all that." He looked at the man, tsking and shaking his head. "Yup, magus business. Very consuming stuff, I assure you."

"Too long a time between friends, I say," Anatoli nodded, "The perfect day for a visit."

Plinius looked at him dubiously. "Perfect? I dare say not. Why, you just interrupted a delicate scribing that-"

"I do say perfect my good friend," interjected Anatoli, "I would dare say you will be quite glad I have come by today when all is said and done. We have ourselves a busy day. Is that kofe I smell?"

"No!" Plinius voice raised shrilly. "I mean, yes! It is *caf*," he emphasised the pronunciation, speaking from the top of his throat, "It's over on the hearth, please, help yourself-"

"*Spasebo*, thank you, Pliny, I will do just that."

Plinius nodded agreeably as the rogue stepped past him before catching himself. "No! Yes! I mean no, today is not the perfect day for a visit. I have much to do, much to do," Plinius pointed at the wastebasket still smouldering with flakes of ash in a vain attempt to direct Anatoli's attention, who was much more interested in scouring the cupboard. "Look! Your savage assault on my door caused me to upset delicate scrollwork- quite delicate in fact."

"The only thing delicate here is you, Pliny," Anatoli said, his voice echoing out of the cupboard.

Plinius gritted his teeth. "How many times do I have to tell you? I am not delicate! My *work* is delicate, Anatoli. Your impromptu visit has ruined a good many weeks work. My client will be most upset. Most upset. I simply cannot afford your distractions today."

Anatoli slammed the cupboard door, causing Pliny to jump again. "By the bloody hells Pliny, where do you keep your cups?"

"Over there, in the upper- no, you brain-addled dolt! Here let me- wait, no! Stop confusing me!" Plinius threw up his hands. "I am very busy today. Anatoli, you must go!"

Anatoli let out a small 'aha' of victory as he grabbed two small porcelain cups down from the upper cupboard.

"Careful with those!" Plinius wringed his hands. *That is fine Imperial porcelain. Very rare.*

"Your client? What clients, Pliny? I am your only client, you gregarious old hermit. You are right, though. I must go. Not now, but soon. Very soon. Sooner the better! And you with me," he told Plinius, looking up at him as he gingerly ladled the steaming aromatic liquid from the pot into the cups. "Careful, it is quite hot."

"What?" Plinius asked curiously, his eyes searching Anatoli's face, his hand absently taking the cup that was offered to him. "For what reason in all of Mir would I have to leave my home? I am not going anywhere- not today, or tomorrow, or anytime soon. So that begs the question as to what in the bloody hells are you prattling on about?" He lifted the cup to his lips and quickly set the cup down as the bitter brown liquid scalded his upper lip. "Bloody hells that is hot!"

Anatoli smiled at him in a way that put Plinius ill at ease as the rogue swaggered across the room. With his open hand he yanked on the curtain and drew it back, casting natural light into a room that had nearly forgotten its touch. A billion motes of dust danced along the invading shafts of light. He peered between the black iron bars and out the mud encrusted windows. The rising sun slanted half of his face in light. Turning back around towards Plinius he leaned against a bookcase that ultimately held despite it shifting backwards a frightening degree with his weight. He took a few tentative sips from the cup.

"Ooo, that's good," he muttered, "Look, Pliny, let me put it this way. Do you want the good news or the bad news?"

Plinius' eyes narrowed. He had known Anatoli of Tsarusska for what seemed to him a short time but had in fact been a dozen years now. In that time, he had earned a modicum of trust from Plinius that some would see as beggarly but for those that knew better would be considered most generous. Despite that trust, Plinius also knew that Anatoli rarely if ever brought good news unexpectedly. If things were running smoothly in their… partnership, the overwhelming majority of correspondence between them had been via message or voidcrow. Plinius deduced that because a house call was very out of the ordinary, especially at this time of day, that the bad news would have to be pretty bad.

"Good news for who? You or me?"

"Both of us! Good news for both of us," Anatoli nodded his head emphatically. He picked up a book resting on the windowsill, giving it a cursory glance and frown before throwing it on a pile.

"Is that so…" Plinius replied doubtfully.

Anatoli gave a sharp affirmative nod.

"And the bad news?" Plinius asked hesitantly, rubbing his beard.

"Oh, that is all for you *moy droug*," replied Anatoli generously. "But it is of no bother, once you hear the good news."

Plinius bit his bottom lip. He took a thoughtful sip of his caf and tutted at its heat. He muttered a phrase and dipped his finger in the caf, cooling it a few degrees. He felt like cold water was trickling down his spine. "Very well then, you have piqued my curiosity. Once again. Let us put the cart before the horse this time. What is the good news?"

"You, my good friend," Anatoli intoned, adopting an exaggerated Terrastran accent, "are coming with me on a quest!" Anatoli threw out his arms, splashing some of his caf on the window, and smiled.

Plinius' frowned. "A quest? Like Marcus Gaul? Or those Wayfarer fools at that sad, ridiculous guild? Preposterous."

Anatoli's smile dropped for a split second before doubling in its original geniality. "Ah, no foolishness here, my most excellent grandmagus. All the arrangements have been made by yours truly, all needs have been looked after by our most excellent sponsors, all we need to do is but be along our way. One foot in front of another as it were, and we will be just so." He gestured excitedly towards the door.

Plinius looked down his nose at the man. "Anatoli, I appreciate your jokes, I truly do," he said with a complete lack of appreciation. "This is not one of your better ones. How truly absurd. I cannot begin to fathom what the punchline will possibly be."

"No punchline. No joke."

Plinius stepped towards the man, their eyes locked, his lips pursed.

"Seriously!" Anatoli made a holy gesture with his hand.

"This is not funny, Anatoli," said Plinius.

"Of course not. The funny part is the bad news."

Plinius gave a sharp bark of a laugh. "Go on then, let us hear this bad news so we can put this morning's joviality to rest, and I can get on with my very busy day." Plinius felt like taking a nap. He sipped on the caf, drawing in a mouthful, finally satisfied with its temperature.

"You are to be arrested by the lictors today on charges of violating the Concord!"

Plinius nodded absent-mindedly for a second before spitting his caf halfway across the room. Anatoli attempted to sidestep the shower and was mostly successful. He picked up a loose page and wiped some incidental spray off his vest. Plinius stared dumbly at Anatoli.

"Oh, this is a good one. Arrested, you say?" He asked.

"*Da*," he confirmed in Tsarusskan.

"For…" his voice trailed away. His gaze wandered to a large dragon skull mounted above the hearth. He absently noted the unique curve where the orbit met the naris. *Oh! Yes! Look at that! Black dragons and blue dragons share a common ancestor, undoubtedly. Huh.* He looked back towards Anatoli.

"For… what was it?" Anatoli did not respond, instead waving his hand towards him in an encouraging manner.

"Concord violation," Plinius finished in a distant voice.

"Amongst other charges I would imagine. *Da*."

"Other charges."

"*Da,* other charges. You know what I mean."

Plinius sipped his caf thoughtfully. "Such as?"

"Does it matter? Those Imperials are creative types. You would know better than I."

For a moment Plinius stood there staring blankly at Anatoli. The rogue accepted this good naturedly, having known Plinius for near on a dozen years and used to his ways. *We were old friends then, were we?* Plinius hmphed. "Very well then, I concede good man. Well played. What is the joke?"

Anatoli sighed. "You, again with the jokes! No jokes I told you, and still, here you are bringing up jokes. Plinius, I mean it," he placed a hand on the magus' shoulder, "There is no joke here. I am being serious."

Plinius was tired of this game. "This is not funny, Tsarusskan."

Anatoli did not drop his smile. "No, no I suppose it is not. No need to get nasty, though. I am as terran as you."

"Point taken," Plinius agreed. He squinted at the man, swishing some of the caf in his mouth. He swallowed. "Not one of your best jokes."

"You keep using that word. The Magistracy is most likely mustering the lictors as we speak. Word has it they were originally going to make a night-time arrest, but Heuronicus decided a daylight arrest would have more of a, what did he call it?" He flourished his fingers in the air as if sprinkling salt. "Impact on the filthy commoners."

"The Magistracy? Heuronicus? Who in the bloody hells is that? What in the Blessed Concord are you talking about? The lictors? Aha!" Plinius beamed in triumph. "That makes no sense. If this is true, why would it not be the militia making the arrest? The lictors? Ha! The Iron Cohort has no jurisdiction here." Plinius smiled, quite smug. "Poorly crafted joke my friend."

Anatoli gave him a look Plinius did not appreciate. "If you say joke again, I will slap you."

Plinius smirked.

"No jurisdiction?" Anatoli shook his head. "Cronus save us, Pliny, sometimes I forget what a complete recluse you are. Have you not heard of the Accord Compromise?"

"Concord Compromise? What the in the Blessed Concord are you talking about?"

"Edge take me," Anatoli sighed. "Not Concord. Accord. The treaty of appeasement. Signed by William Lyon before his death."

"Wait? What about the Lyon? The Lord Regent is dead?"

Anatoli rubbed his temples with his palms. "Yes, Plinius. The Lyon has been dead for oh, about five years now. During the last imperial expansion towards Terrastra, a large contingent of the Codeci voted to let the Empire annex us. Not enough to make it come to pass, but enough to alarm the Lyceum. The Accord Compromise gave the Empire the right to erect a dozen churches to Cronus in the Tradebasin and Lowhill, implement duty tax coming in from the Imperial highway, but most importantly it gave them authority to enforce the Concord in Terrastra."

Plinius was becoming increasingly flustered. "What are you going on about? What the hells do churches have to do with anything? Anatoli, this is preposterous. Lyon dead? The Empire in Terrastra? What silly gremlin shit are you trying to convince me of?"

"Surely you know of the Hall of Staffs?"

Plinius snorted derisively. "The Imperial embassy? The Simon House? That ancient pile of logs? What of it?"

Anatoli shook his head again. "It has not been an embassy for five years, and the old Simon House was replaced even earlier than that. Now it is the citadel of the Magistracy, and gaol for the Magocracies enemies. The Iron Cohort has been garrisoned there since last autumn, right across the square from the Lyceum, its eye constantly watching." Anatoli took a step back and looked at Plinius with a queer expression. *It looks like pity.* "Plinius, how long do you think it has been since you last left the bookstore?"

Plinius' scratched his neck. "Ah. What happens to be the date?"

"June 25th, 1499."

"Ah. Well… then. Hmph." Plinius mouth worked as he did some math in his head, "I suppose it has been roughly… six years?"

"Six years."

"Well, if you count buying some flavoured ice treats. If you mean actually heading out beyond view of my porch?" His lips worked wordlessly as he did the math in his head.

Anatoli waited patiently, his eyes darting to the now covered window only a couple of times. "Pliny…" he entreated.

"Ah," Plinius said, his attention switching back to his friend. "We met in what… 1487? So then… it has been… oh… seventeen years. No! Eighteen."

Anatoli looked at the magus, then said a word in Tsarusskan that Plinius did not understand. "Well, Pliny my friend, today you are leaving your bookstore, and going a bit further than a passing ice-fruit peddler's cart. It is either that or a one-way trip to the Hall of Staffs. Or the Exchange, and you know what that means."

Plinius felt woozy. His face felt flush. The enormity of what Anatoli was telling him was beginning to sink in.

"But… but… there must be some mistake. The Hall of Staffs? The Exchange?" He felt weak in the knees. *I can sense a memory… of rope? And an elf? I had never been to the Exchange. Or had I?* "I would never deal in necro- the mere thought is, ah, abhorrent-"

Anatoli dropped the smile and snorted. "Oh, *now* who is telling jokes? Both our necks are deep in it."

Plinius looked at the rogue and a hundred thoughts thundered through his mind at once. *Scrolls penned with a black quill. Bags with hidden bottoms passed in the shadow of his stoop to a young Tsarusskan.* He dropped his cup. The priceless Imperial porcelain shattered on the floor. The dregs of his drink slowly soaked up into some loose parchment scattered across the floor. His eyes darted from Anatoli to the window, to the door, back to Anatoli, and then to a dozen concealed compartments around the bookstore.

"Blessed Concord. BLOODY HELLS!" Plinius was shaking now. "What in Cronus' name am I going to do!"

"I told you," Anatoli replied cheerfully, taking another sip of his caf. "We are going on a quest!"

Plinius pushed Anatoli aside to get a look out the window. *Ugh, I feel sick. I'm just going to take a moment.* Just as the rogue had described, a slow-moving procession was cutting through a sea of red robes, lictors draped in mail and boiled leather marching down the Midhill, a tall banner emblazoned with the iconic crossed sword and staff symbol of the Magocratic Empire blowing in the ocean breeze coming up from the west. *The Gladia Virgum.* Lumbering in their wake was a raised platform pulled by two oxen, two large lumber posts sticking up like a tuning fork with thick manacles dangling from large rings at the top. The large axes known to be carried by the lictors glinted in the climbing sun and served as a better motivation for the mass of people in their way to quickly move to the side. Even then, the thick morning traffic impeded them as they made their way with purpose down the street, inching closer to the bookstore with every passing second.

Plinius let out a tortured groan as he stumbled back away from the window, bumping up against his desk and slightly bruising his lower back. Rubbing his eyes, a pained groan escaped his throat as a sad wheeze. He waved his hand weakly in an intricate manner, picking up a sprig of thyme resting on the table. The smell of storms and sound of whispers infused the room for a heartbeat and the glass of the front window turned black and opaque, shutting out the morning light.

Anatoli turned, an exasperated look on his face. "Pliny! Now why would you do that? I was enjoying the view."

Plinius could feel the blood rushing to his head. He shot the man a venomous look. "I am so glad you are enjoying yourself. Can I get you more caf? Flag down the passing ice peddler? Perhaps send out for some biscuits or some baked cheese and nuts?"

"Another cup of *kofe*," he smirked as he pronounced the word, "would be just the thing I think."

Plinius' teeth grated. "Were you not just saying we needed to be away? Now you have time for another round of refreshment?"

"We have plenty of time for refreshments now, *moy drug*. Can you conjure me up some scones?"

"Create food is a myth," said Plinius, not able to help himself.

"For the both of us, I am afraid time has run out. The time we needed to be away has passed. However," said Anatoli, strolling over to the hearth," Thank the Blessed Concord there is still plenty of time for one of us to get away,"

"Then- oh, Cronus!" Plinius began to shake. He quickly whispered a cantrip and Hand shimmered into existence. "Go and get my grimoire, Hand. NOW, HAND!"

The hand splayed its fingers out in surprise. It shook an irate finger at him before bunching into a fist and flying off upstairs, narrowly missing the magus' head as it went.

Plinius turned and began to run around the bookstore frantically, stopping midstride to grab books and scrolls, throwing four in the fire for each one he shoved in his bag. "I will throw myself on the mercy of the- what did you call it? The Magistracy. The Empire can be merciful. I have never set a foot out of line before. I have paid my taxes; I have made charitable donations! Anonymously, but I can tell them it was me. I am a model citizen! I have never dodged the census! Well, perhaps a few times. When was the last one? They cannot have much evidence, there is no way. I've been very careful in my dealings with your people Anatoli-"

"My people?" Anatoli interjected sourly, looking up from the pot as he poured himself more caf. "Now I have been insulted twice."

Plinius threw his hands up. "Oh, you know what I mean. Do not take false offense. What I am saying though is I think I can get out of this. I will make amends to this Magistracy, and the Lyceum council will protect me, I am sure they will. Maybe not as much when Archmagi Lyon was still alive- are you sure he's dead? Don't look at me like that! I have friends on the council- Orillia, Iselda, are they still alive? That old fat enchanter with the stinking weasel familiar- what is his name? Doric? Domeric? The one you brought here."

"Donric?" Anatoli suggested.

"YES! Donric, I did that favour for him with the-"

"The wraith?" Anatoli arched a bushy eyebrow.

"Yes! The wraith!" Plinius nodded excitedly.

"You are going to use that as leverage? While being charged with Concord violation?"

Plinius' face dropped for a second, then he looked up at Anatoli hopefully. "Money! I have money. I can buy my way out of this!"

Anatoli shook his head. "Money leaves a trail, *moy droug*. You try that route; you will wind up with more charges. Not that it matters, da? Either way you will burn. Anathema." Anatoli pulled a finger across his throat while making a grrk sound.

Plinius collapsed in his chair. His shoulders sagged and he rubbed his eyes again with his fists.

"I could appeal to the Emperor…" Plinius began but was cut short with a look from Anatoli that killed that thought in the cradle. He could feel his stomach constricting into a knot as despair took hold. He turned abruptly and retched into the cauldron, sputtering the flames.

"I am done for," he cried quietly, wiping bile from his lip.

Anatoli let out an exasperated sigh. "Have you not listened to a word I have said? The good news, remember? We are going on a quest! There will be no Imperial executions in the Exchange today."

Plinius looked up to him with doubting and exasperated eyes. "You said we were out of time."

"Da, that is what I said. For *both* of us to run." His tone was as if he was speaking to a child, and even in his agitated state Plinius felt a flash of annoyance at being talked down to. "The plan has changed a little, due to you being you, but as in all things I have anticipated this."

"You have?"

"*Da*, I have. Your good friend Anatoli will distract the nefarious and dastardly lictors of the Iron Cohort, while you make your way to the rendezvous."

"The rendezvous?"

"Yes! Our great quest begins now!" Anatoli looked down at him and screwed up his face. "That is what you are going to wear? You have nothing warmer? Especially get rid of the whites at least, you'll stick out like a sore thumb."

"Warmer? In the middle of summer?"

"I'm sure we can get you a coat. Quick, throw on some traveling clothes! Nothing that will indicate your status."

Plinius clucked his teeth. "Travelling clothes? Travelling clothes? And what exactly in Cronus' name are travelling clothes? Blessed Concord, Anatoli, do I look like a tailor to you?"

Anatoli rubbed his temples with the balls of his hands. "What do you have then?"

Plinius jumped up, running upstairs, a little pleased to have a course of action. As he bounded up the steps, Hand nearly collided with him as the spectral appendage came flying down, a large sack in his hand. "Out of the way, stupid!" Plinius cried. Hand stopped completely as the magus skipped past him, taking the steps two at a time. Dropping the sack unceremoniously so that it bounced nosily down the stairs, Hand gave his master another one finger salute before zipping over to restack the books Anatoli had knocked over.

Anatoli walked over and scooped up the bag that Hand had dumped on the floor. Anatoli chewed on his lip, looking at the mouth of the closed bag. *He's going to open it. I'll bet you a buck.* After a moment of thought the rogue whispered *'why not'* and plunged his hand in the bag. *Told you.* When he withdrew it, he clutched a thick tome with a red leather cover, clasped closed with a mithril chain inlaid with various stones. Although he knew it contained an immeasurable amount of power, in his hands it felt like nothing more than a common book. Shrugging, he placed it back in the sack.

After a moment Plinius came back down with a burgundy dress robe of wool with a simple rope cinch. He held it up in his arms for Anatoli to see.

Anatoli sighed. "You have nothing but robes, do you, Pliny?"

Plinius huffed. "They are comfortable and suit my needs."

Anatoli waved impatiently now.

"Hurry! Hurry, put it on, it'll have to do. Do you have everything? Did you grab your quills?" he asked urgently.

"Oh! My quills! Thank you for reminding me," said Plinius as he began to change, doffing his grandmagi robe and folding it very carefully as Anatoli tapped his foot with increasing annoyance. Plinius opened the medium sized bag hanging from his waist and easily put the large robe in despite its bulk being nearly twice the size. Snapping his fingers and holding out his palm in an imperious manner, Anatoli threw the bag at the magus who juggled it between his hands before getting it a hold of it. That too went down into the smaller bag. He then slowly walked over to his drafting table. He placed a hand on it reverently. *I was saying goodbye.* Grabbing first his gull quill along with another plain sparrow one, he then grabbed the cockatrice quill, his quill from a dwarven rockbeak, and a quill of hammered gold. The grandmagus hesitated for a moment before he snatched the black quill as well. Deposting them all in the bag, he looked around the bookstore. "Oh! I should also get my-"

"Edge take you Pliny, enough! Enough with the delaying! You must be away now, or I fear it truly will be too late. You know the fountain of Merlin? In the mid-market?"

"Yes…"

"Good, head out of your bolthole- do not give *me* that look, I am not a fool," Anatoli began to shoo the grandmagus to the backwall of his bookstore. Plinius ducked around him and scooped up the bag holding his grimoire. "As it is, I know a great deal more than you suppose I do- and take the alleyway north to the Street of Flasks. Stay out of sight. Tell no one who you are. Head directly to the midmarket. Do you understand?"

"What!?" Plinius tightened the rope around his waist, a look of incredulity on his face. "Head *towards* the Hall of Staffs? Have you lost your mind?"

"ENOUGH!" Anatoli's voice took on a hard edge, the command in it enough to kill Plinius' protests on his lips. He had never heard Anatoli speak this way and directed at him. "Trust me, Pliny, trust *me* as you never have before. Proceed up Midhill to the market. You will find a Coptician there, about this tall," he held up a hand, "with black hair and an olive complexion. Tell him *our mutual friend from Vokgorod has a package for us.* Then he will respond 'You will need to pay the duty'. He will bring you the rest of the way."

"Rest of the way? To where!? Just let *me* know where we are heading, and I can cast a spell that will-"

"NO MAGIC! Absolutely no magic. We cannot take the chance that they may have a detect spell ongoing. They will be on you like a bear on a beehive if you so much as fart a spell."

Plinius began to protest. "Anatoli, now see here, I cannot-"

"Pliny! Alley- Flasks- Market- Merlin- Coptician," Anatoli listed. "Repeat it!"

"Alley- Flasks- Marker- Merlin- Coptician. Now, Anatoli, I really think we should reconsider our course of action here. This all seems very hasty."

Anatoli shook his head, as a heavy rapping cracked against the oaken front door. Both men looked towards it, then back at each other. Anatoli smiled a ghastly wound of a smile. "Well, there is the Empire, knocking on your door. Off with you! I will see you soon! Now go!"

Chapter Two

Plinius & Pots

Anatoli's push sent Plinius sprawling into the alley, tripping over the hem of his robe. Flinging his arms out he caught himself on a small tower of crates stacked up against the opposite wall, some sort of glass inside jingling as they rocked against his weight. Plinius rounded on him just in time to hear Anatoli whisper "Remember- the market! Be quiet as a mouse, *da?*"

He took a step forward. "Now wait a minute Ana-"

He found himself facing a brick wall. Plinius couldn't help but admire the craftmanship of his bolthole- no seam or crack betrayed the slightest hint that the back of his shop was anything but a normal wall of red brick. He had a fleeting thought to cast the spell of opening to march back in and give Anatoli a piece of his mind. *Would serve the man right. Treating a magus like that.* He faltered as he lifted his hand up, a slight distaste creeping up his throat. With a quick shake of his head, he turned to survey his new surroundings. That was when the smell hit him.

The alley. I don't quite remember it looking so... filthy. In truth, I don't think I remember it at all. Except those pots over there- I wonder why those are calling to me? Something hidden in my mind... Interesting.

His nostrils puckered up in revolt as a foul smell found access through his mouth. The smell was more of a living thing, coating his tongue and travelling up backwards through his throat. His body instantly rebelled, gagging and convulsing so badly he could not get the words of a spell out to dispel the filth around him. *Doubtful prestidigitation would clean this area anyway. This environment is positively infused with a surfeit of pollution most foul.* At that moment Hand materialized through the wall, wagging their finger at Plinius in admonishment, presumably for being left behind. Hand stopped short, questioning what in the nine hells its master was doing. Plinius pointed at his mouth and nose frantically, and Hand drooped in resignation. Cupping itself, Hand covered Plinius' mouth like a mask, serving as a filter for the putrid air.

"Ahh," Plinius sighed with relief, "Hand. Turn invisible. I most assuredly look ridiculous."

Once that distraction was under control and Plinius regained some of his composure, he took a studied look around. He first noticed that this side of the building row did not seem as straight and orderly as the front facing onto the street. The buildings seemed to curve in, like two steepled hands so that the edges of the roofs could not have been more than a few feet apart. Looking up the hill, the walls rose higher and higher, the Midhill of Terrastra looming over him like a haphazard urban waterfall of stone, wood, and metal. Looking the other way towards the harbour, a garden of roofs spread out lower and lower towards Drake Bay, a sparkling pool of sapphire water beyond them, with the western strait on the horizon, leading to the ocean beyond.

No windows adorned the buildings backing out onto the alley- just small hinged wooden hatches spaced out up and down the walls. As Plinius noted them, he gasped out loud in disgust as one slid open and a large arm upturned a silver pot and deposited a putrid rainbow of filth on the alleyway below. Large steel doors with no handles were placed seemingly at random intervals, but elsewise it was just an unending smooth stonewall as far as the eye could see in an uninterrupted wall. The only thing that indicated a change from one building to another was the spacing of the doors. Graffiti in a riot of colours ranging from fresh and decidedly anti-Imperial to the older, flaky, and less political proved the only decoration along the white stone walls. The morning sun had not risen quite high enough, leaving the lower alley shrouded in grey twilit gloom while the roof edges glinted high above him. *Were the buildings on my street always this tall?*

His nose crinkled, its defences crumbling in the face of continuous onslaught. He held a sleeve up to his mouth. A few scattered newssheets tumbled in the slight breeze billowing between the buildings. A pile of soiled rags clumped in a mound next to the crates of glass bottles he had crashed into. Plinius gagged at a nearby collection of bedpans in varying sizes and of various materials stacked in a tiny pyramid giving off a foul odour. Plinius could easily make out the din from the Street of Sighs despite it being on the other side of the long row of buildings. A little stream of foul liquid meandered downhill along the alley, pooling in little alien ecosystems here and there where the alley levelled out. One of these puddles, a viscous jelly of some greenish lumps, pooled on the side of his building as insects hovered lazily above it.

Plinius looked up and down the alley, realizing he had been standing there gawking when he should be getting away from there as fast as possible. Plinius strained his ears. *I thought I could hear them; the lictors breaking in while I sat there helpless.* Plinius made a conscious effort to slow his breathing. *An old mantra I learned from... I don't remember. I can picture him though; I think he was a teacher of mine? Steady breaths, steady mind. Great way to get a hold of yourself.* A melodious laugh echoed from somewhere, but the tight confines of the alley made it seem as if it could be coming from anywhere. Looking up hillside the alley branched off into two different directions, with the right side sharply curving away. He thought of the collection of maps he had on the other side of the wall- surely one of them had a map of the alleyways on them. He could solve his dilemma easily if he had time and the right ingredients. *Damn straight.* His hands began to tremble, and an oily feeling began to grow from somewhere in the pit of his stomach. Plinius could feel a headache beginning to swell behind his eyes.

"G'day!"

Plinius froze in tableau, his fright paralyzing him. Paralyzed except for his bladder, the urge to answer the call of nature growing fierce. His eyes darted frantically up and down the alley. No one was in sight. Looking up he saw a large crow perched on the edge of the roof. The bird cocked its head and stared at him with one beady eye.

"Hello?" he asked warily.

"Hullo! Down here, ser!"

Plinius looked down at an outstretched hand attached to a great beaming grin. A face peeked out from a short, matted, oily beard below two big eyes framed by eyebrows like one thick red caterpillar. What he had mistook as a pile of rags was in fact a rather dishevelled looking dwarf. Standing up, the dwarf was no taller than Plinius' waist. The dwarf wore a threadbare cloth shirt, soiled linen pants and a ratty knapsack fit for the trash. The clothing covered a slight frame that looked odd on a dwarf. *The children of the mountain are almost all universally overweight, or what they call 'Th' Bigguns'. City dwarves, if I recall correctly, are on average 10% lighter in mass than their ancestral underworld cousins.* Plinius deduced from the state of the dwarf that he was someone quite accustomed to habituating under filthy rags. Plinius recoiled from the dwarf's outstretched hand, withdrawing it back into his sleeve. The dwarf's smile faltered for an instant but quickly regained its intense amiability as he lowered his hand.

"Ah, well, no offense taken ser," said the dwarf agreeably, "I's is not havin' a chance to wash my hands today. And given my line of work, it'd probably be best to settle for a smile and nod by way of greeting."

It had been so long since Plinius had spoken to a stranger he found his mouth refusing to open. It had been nearly two decades since he had last had to make small talk, and it seemed the skill had completely abandoned him. *What do strangers talk about? Politics? Religion?* The dwarf was talking but Plinius barely heard a word as he struggled to think of something to say. *Is this what people do? Look at this little fellow go! He just will not stop talking! Do people just up and talk to strangers on the street, or alley as it were? I can see why I never left the bookstore.* The dwarf was not talking now, looking up at the grandmagus expectantly. *Oh crap. What did he say? Did you hear? Come on, past me! Say something!* He desperately tried to recall his time at the Lyceum, when his silver tongue could effortlessly argue a thesis with a magus four circles above him. The grandmagus blurted out the first thing that came to mind.

"Nice weather currently, eh?" asked Plinius haltingly.

Blessed Concord. That's the best I could come up with.

Either by sheer luck, divine providence, or the dwarf's tact, Plinius' answer seemed to be an acceptable one. The dwarf did not miss a beat. "Ye be tellin' me, ser. I started th' day up by th' Sapphires, and by Cronus, I says to myself 'oh she's gonna be an ugly day' on account of the fog rollin' down off th' pool. 'Foggy pool the rain will rule' Da always says t' me. Da aint always right tho'. As ye can see! Ain't a drop o' rain t' be seen. Soon as th' sun done come up, that thar fog went an' burned right up! 'Summer suns mean burnt bums' Da says. Gonna be a hot one, eh, ser?"

Plinius stared at the dwarf, then nodded slowly. He searched again for what to say that could get him out of this conversation. "Ah, yes, well… I must be off, terribly busy day and all that."

"Say, ser, where did ye come from? I's just been sitting down for a spell, closing th' ole' peepers and such for a quick nap, before getting to thar pots, then- poof!- ye was standing there just like so. Then -poof!- that fancy glove pops up and covers ye mouth and disappears! Is it still there? Did ye use some sort of spell? Ye are a mage ain't ye boy-o?"

"Magus," corrected Plinius off-handedly. Plinius glanced up and down the alley, despite his previous hesitancy inside his bookstore, and he was eager to be away. *But which way to go?*

"The robes always give it away. 'Mages' robes be thar uniform' Da says. Dunno reckon ever see'n ye out back here before now, not that I reckon at all. Are ye in need of Pot's pots services? Ye mage types always seem keen fer us wee folk to take care o' yar pots and I's be the boy-o always willin' to take on more customers if it suits ye. Ye needs that is. I dinnae clean suit-suits. Just pots."

Plinius had not the slightest notion what the dwarf was blabbering about. "Pots?" he asked. "Ink pots? I have no time for business- I mean, I have business. Not with you! I must be off," Plinius began to take a step towards the high hill.

"Oh! Ha! HA!" the dwarf chortled. "No, ha, no ser, not ink pots," he picked up one of the chamber pots and held it up towards Plinius. A foul liquid accompanied by some sort of pulpy substance sloshed around inside. "Chamber pots! I's collects them along the alleys and takes 'em down to th' harbour fer a good scoo-urin'. Like Da says, 'ye always have the capacity to take on more customers on account of yar stella' work ethic boy-o!' So, ye be interested?"

Plinius recoiled in obvious horror. What the dwarf said was true- most magi deemed the mundane chores like cleaning beneath them and often retained staff to take care of such things. Plinius had no such aversion to menial labour- what chores he could handle by himself he gladly let Hand take care of. The very thought of having others in his home, doing the cooking and cleaning, was ghastly to him. *What a bothersome dwarf.* A loud clattering bang accompanied by a chorus of screams and jeers echoed over from the street. Plinius bit his lip. The dwarf looked over, as if trying to see the street through the walls, a puzzled expression crossing his face. A suspicion began to fester in Plinius' mind.

"Why are you delaying me, dwarf?" said Plinius accusingly. "As I said, I am on business and must be away." Turning his back on the dwarf he began to walk uphill towards the rising sun, now peeking over the eastern rooftops.

"Oh, my apologies, ser," the dwarf was hurrying alongside him, his short legs pumping furiously to keep up with Plinius' long strides. "I's dinnae mean to delay ye, just tryin' to be friendly is all."

"Well, yes, thank you then," sneered Plinius. "Good day then." Plinius stopped at the fork in the alley, hesitating as he looked down each way before him. The path to the right smelt worse than the other, but the left way seemed less sticky and kept parallel along the Street of Sighs.

"I must say, quite a shock seein' ye ova' 'ere in th' alley," continued the dwarf merrily as he nimbly hopped over a puddle of thick black ooze. "Never run into more of ye finer folk this side of the row. Da says that 'the alleys were fer dwarfs and what few elves that be left 'round', and he usually has th' right of it, y'know. Oh, I's say thar on-a given day, I see one human out o' maybe forty of us older races. And nevah a mage! Da never said anything 'bout meetin' no mage in th' alley, on account o' it never happenin' I reckon. Nope, th' alleys were made fer us lesser folk. 'Out o' sight, out o' mind, out o' trouble' Da says. Th' way most mages like."

Plinius stopped abruptly, letting out a loud harumph. "Really, dwarf, that is offensive. I assure you as one of the *magi* myself, we have no compunction with laying eyes on dwarf or elf. I would demand an apology, but instead I will suggest you be out upon your business. Why do you insist on pestering me?"

"I dinnae mean to be pesterin' ser. Nope, no pesterin' 'ere," the dwarf held up both hands, "Like I's said, I's just bein' friendly is all. Didn'a mean to cause no offense."

"A little *too* friendly, perhaps!" Plinius jabbed a pointed finger into his chest, stooping over to reach, trying his best to look intimidating, "Are you with them? Are you? Who are you with! Answer me!"

The dwarf scrunched his face, his thick eyebrow taking on the aspect of a big furry caterpillar. "Beg yar pardon?"

"Do not play the fool with me dwarf!" Plinius raised to his full height, completely forgetting Anatoli's advice of being circumspect. He contorted his fingers into a pattern ingrained in his muscle memory, and a purple stream of the River spread from his fingertips until it coated him in a pale aura. It was like flexing and holding a muscle in his mind, but one he had exercised a million times and could now do so with the barest of conscious thought. As the spell began to take hold, the dwarf craned his neck upwards as Plinius doubled in size. The air darkened behind him as his voice raised to a booming rumble. *Thaumaturgy- and three active effects besides! A simple spell, very common first spell for a pueri. It's all an illusion, a trick of the vict- er, targets mind. To multi-cast three effects with one invocation? Colour me impressed with, well, myself! The spell works well on the beggars when you want to be left alone.* "You are with them; admit it!"

The dwarf craned his neck so that he was nearly looking straight up. "Now, now, no need for ye to get testy. I's swear on Cronus ser, I's 'aven't the foggiest idea what ye mean. Who be them?"

"Bloody hells you don't! If you do not go about your way, I will- I will- turn you into a frog! Yes. A frog!" Plinius eyed him menacingly, his arms held up bent like a mantis, his fingers hooked like terrifying claws before him as he made a cooing sound in his throat.

Whether the dwarf was fazed by this it was hard to tell. *He is positively terrified. It is obvious.* His one eye rose, one side of his eyebrow raising with it. As he took a step back, his hands held up with the palms facing Plinius. "Ok, ok, no need to be getting' all bothered. Sorry ta' bother ye."

Plinius harumphed smugly. *Impudent dwarf.* "Off with you then." Plinius turned and began walking briskly up the hill. "The Street of Flasks then," he muttered quietly to himself, "This way. Edge take me! Where the hell do I go!? I must be away the lictors think to look back here."

"You talkin' bout the Horts?" Plinius could hear spit hitting the ground behind him. "What's going on up by the Flasks?"

Plinius stopped dead in his tracks, whirling back on the dwarf. "Aha! You've slipped up now, my rancid little fellow!" He raised his hand in a clenched fist of triumph, shaking it boldly at the sky. "You admit it with your own treacherous tongue!"

The dwarf had his arms folded across his chest, a look of profound disgust on his face. "What I'd'mit ta is thar Horts can all be burned in the bloody hells, Cronus take 'em all. And as for the Street of Flasks, well…"

Plinius wagged his finger furiously as he shook his head. "No, no, how could you know where I was headed? I had not said a word about my destination," the magus stopped short as the dwarf pointed at his mouth and held his hands up to his ears.

"What?" asked the grandmagus, the dwarf still hearing it under the booming volume from the thaumaturgy spell. Closing his eyes, he pinched his nose and silently dropped the subconscious concentration he had been maintaining to retain his connection to the River. His voice returned to normal as his illusory size shrunk and the alley around him returned to its normal morning shade. He could feel his face reddening.

"Dwarf," Plinius began through gritted teeth at slightly less than normal volume, "I would kindly ask you to turn around, head to the harbour with your urine-stained crap buckets, and kindly forget you ever saw me. Now." Plinius turned with an air of final dismissal.

"Yar going the wrong way, mage."

Plinius turned back, staring at the dwarf with a tight frown.

"Yar going to the Street of Flasks ye say?"

Plinius glanced over his shoulder down the alley. A large purplish grey rat was scurrying down into a hole in the wall, struggling to pull a headless bird along with it. He looked back and nodded at the dwarf.

"Up or down?" asked the dwarf, rubbing his beard, smearing some brown paste-like substance through it.

Plinius hesitated a moment.

"Up. The midmarket."

"Well then ye don't want to be headin' thar way, boy-o."

A rumbling crash from the bookstore, loud enough to be heard through the stone wall, caused both to jump back a step. Powdered dust tinkled down as the wall shifted a fraction. The dwarf looked at the magus with alarm. As the blood drained from his face, Plinius bounced his gaze from the dwarf to the bolthole and back to the dwarf. He wringed his hands.

"You, ah, don't say?"

"Yes, ser, magus, ser. If ye go thar way, it'll take ye right back 'round to the Sighs. And a judgin' by that commotion jus' now, I reckon ye dinnae wan' t'be headin' thar way."

Plinius let out a sigh through his nose. He could feel Hand shiver in irritation. "Ah, well, then. So which way should I, ah, be heading?"

The dwarf smiled. "This way, ser. Follow me." The dwarf turned and began marching in the opposite direction, heading towards the harbour.

Plinius hurried to follow, settling in a brisk walk aside the dwarf as he jogged ahead. A new smell wafted across the alley, like woodsmoke but more acidotic. He swore as he had to sidestep a large puddle, hiking his robe up and exposing his pale and bony legs. "But the Street of Flasks is uphill!"

"Yeppers," agreed the dwarf, "But th' alleys this close to the harbour all take th' edge of the shore. Quickest way is to cut back 'cross down here," the dwarf turned so quickly into a recessed offshoot of the main alley that Plinius had to catch himself and back up a few steps to follow. *I didn't even see the side alley there.* He caught up to the dwarf mid-sentence. "-and this will lead us to behind Bayview, another quick cut and it'll be almost a straight shot up to the Flasks and then Midmarket!"

Plinius cast a side eye at the dwarf, trying but failing to dispense of his suspicion. "Beg my pardon, dwarf, but why are you helping *me*?"

The dwarf let out a hearty laugh that echoed off the walls. "Well, two reasons, if ye must know. If th' Horts are lookin' fer ye, then that usually is a good enough reason for me kin and boy-os. Let's just say that us *less human* folk donna' exactly hold tight with them Imperial bastards. But I ain't one of them dwarfs that'll only help other commoners. No ser, Da taught I's better than thar ye ken. You dinnae seem to be with th' Horts, so thar means yar a Terran, just like me, eh? So I will help ye, even if ye be a mage." *Again, with the insults.* The dwarf gave Plinius a congenial smile.

Plinius huffed at the slur as he kept stride. "Watch your tongue. I am a grandmagus, not a mage."

"Same thing ain't it?"

"It most assuredly is not!"

Plinius winced as his foot splashed into a puddle, cringing as a tepid warmth spread through his sock. "Enough with 'ser' and 'mage'. You may call me Plinius. You keep saying that word- Horts. Is that another word for the lictors?"

"Yer a quick one are ye?" Pots teased. *Awfully familiar. Apparently, manners disappeared from the hoi poli while I was otherwise busy with my studies.* "Horts, ye get it? Iron Cohort? Cohort- Hort! Is what e'ryone calls 'em. Da says he was the first to coin th' term, sometime back around the ole Lyon's funeral. Said it to ol' Heury's face he did."

"Yes, yes, your 'da' and such," Plinius mimicked the dwarfs low Terrastran accent, not kindly while visions of torture in the Hall of Staffs danced in his head. "What is the second?"

"Second?" Pots questioned.

"Second reason for your assistance."

"Oh yah! Thar second reason be an easy one," the dwarf's eyes twinkled, and a shrewd grin Plinius did not particularly care for spread across his face. "Money! Maybe some food, eh? I's awful hungry and scourin' pans ain't pay what it used t'. Back in th' day, Da says we used t' live like kings under the Lowhill! We scoured every pot in th' city, cleaned the latrines in th' Lyceum, and-"

Plinius interrupted with a sharp, barking laugh. "How presumptuous! What money or food do you think I could possibly have to give you?" The dwarf stopped in his tracks so abruptly that Plinius once again overshot him with his long stride. He took the spontaneous break as an opportunity to rest his aching legs, leaning up against the wall and desperately fanning himself with his hat. *Terrastran summers are dreadfully humid.* The dwarf stood still; his hands planted firmly on his hips. Instead of wheezing and heaving like the winded magus, the dwarf had not even broken a sweat.

"Oh, ye know. Thar mage money. Kind of money one could spend if he wasn' locked up in th' Hall of Staffs. If ye dinnae 'ave it, well, we can 'ave it yar way and part 'ere, eh?"

Plinius looked up and down the alley, the image of lictors bearing chains popping into his head. He gave the dwarf a sour but resigned grin. "Very well," he gasped between breaths, "If money is what you want, then money is what you shall get. But I will retain your services until my affairs are in order, and you shan't see a penny before then."

"Deal!" agreed the dwarf, promptly spitting in his hand and holding it out to Plinius. Plinius' face contorted in utter disgust. Before he could react, Hand became opaque, revealing himself and firmly clasped their new guide's hand. The dwarf laughed in delight. "I's be taking thar as a yes! Deal, boy-o!"

Hand hovered between them, giving the dwarf a thumbs up. *I regret every improvement I made to that cantrip.*

"A floatin' 'and! I canna believe it!" hollered the dwarf, slapping his knee. "I canna wait t' tell Da!"

Plinius gritted his teeth, dismissing Hand with a thought. The floating Hand vanished promptly. The dwarf let out a disappointed 'ohhh' and shot the magus a disappointed look.

"You better be worth it dwarf."

The dwarf resumed his slight jog and Plinius strode alongside, keeping up this time.

"Enough of callin' me dwarf," the dwarf said, peering up at Plinius with a sideways glance. "We have names y'know. You can call me Pots."

"Very well. For what it is worth, thank you, dwarf," Plinius coughed. "Apologies. Thank you, Pots."

How interesting. I don't think I ever had a dwarf acquaintance before then. Don't think I ever had talked to one before then either. Different social circles. You understand.

Pots gave Plinius an appraising look and a slight nod as they hurried down the alley. "Huh. Ain't no mage ever called I's by *me* name before."

"Is that so?" replied Plinius, not really listening. "Pots, may I ask you a question?"

"Of course, mage."

"Magus. My name is Plinius. When referring to me, please address me by my name, or my title of Grandmagus. No! Actually, don't call me that! Just Plinius."

"Why d'ye nah wan' me t' call ye grandmage?"

"Grandmagus! And don't say it!"

Pots pursed his lips. "If ye tryin' to not look like a mage, ye might wanna ditch them robes."

Plinius nodded tersely. "Yes, yes, I know."

"So what's yar question?"

"Pardon me?" asked Plinius, confused.

"Ye said ye had a question fer me?" Pots laughed as he kicked some sort of carcass into a corner as he ran by.

"Oh, yes! It's just that I am still having difficulty understanding your motivation in this. My question is thus- why in the world would you help *me*?" wondered Plinius, stressing the word would. "If you hate Imperials so much, and knew I was a magus…"

"Ah, donna mind that, I knews ye was a good one," said Pots.

"A good one? A good one what?"

"A good mage."

"Magus. What do you mean?"

"Thar be wha' I said! I knew ye was a good one on account of ye threatening to turn me into a frog," answered Pots as if it was completely obvious.

"Pardon me?" Plinius was confused. "Me threatening to polymorph you proved I was, I quote, 'a good one'?" *That accent is terrible, why am I doing it?* "Is that something else this Da says?"

Pots shook his head sadly.

"Nae, boy-o. Everyone knows ain't no mage making people frogs. A regular mage would h' just killed me."

Chapter Three

The Boys & Boy

The smoke was clearly visible from the Midmarket, although the fire itself could not be seen from Plinius' lofty vantage. Wringing the hem of his robe, his pale and bony legs exposed below the knee, he knew without a doubt the source of the fire. A loose paper caught on an updraft rocked back and forth, fluttering in the air past his face. Thousands of papers, most of them singed or outright burning, fell like snowflakes from a rare winter storm across the city. A thick, roiling column of angry black smoke rose in sharp contrast against the few castle-like clouds blowing in off the western ocean. The column was an angry scar across the blue of the western morning sky that could be seen for kilometres around. *My poor bookstore.* Plinius felt tears welling up, as he silently swore that the Iron Cohort would pay for what they had done to his home.

They had circumvented most of the Midhill through twisting and turning alleys. It had not taken long for Plinius to become completely lost. Despite living in Terrastra for his entire adult life, he had never ventured further within its walled confines than was necessary for the furtherance of his studies. The alleys that Pots had taken him down could have been on the far side of the moon for all he knew, each one looking nearly identical to the last. The only difference he could notice was the varied hue and humour of the various streams of waste spilling into the open-air sewer he was running through. *I wonder if you could correlate any useful data of certain neighbourhoods with the quality of their waste.* Not just the alleys but whole sections of town were unknown to his feet, large voids that he was only passingly aware of if some prior history had forced him to turn his gifts towards them. In those cases, he knew them down to the finest detail.

"This way, Plinius. This way!" Pots would call out merrily every time Plinius began to lag and fall behind. *It wasn't my fault; there was a lot to be curious about.* His eyes would catch sight of some interesting building or creature, and he would slow down until the dwarf admonished him. "Stop sight-seeing! Ye'd think ya 'ad nevah been 'ere before boy-o!"

Why can't I picture the city?
You can't?
I really can't, beyond the Street of Sighs and the Lyceum and now these filthy alleys.

Those I can remember vividly. The rest of the city… something about hills? And a waterfall?

Waterfalls. More than one. The Sapphire Falls.

Oh… could you describe it a little bit more?

Yes, I think that would be ok. I'll try my best.

The City of Terrastra, founded in 720 MD by the wizard Merlin, largely considered the greatest of all Wizards, the Father of Modern Magic, Kingmaker, The Sea Wizard, Father Time, renowned recluse, and, if you believed the Emperor's propagandists, a raging asshole and maniac. With his apprentice William the Lyon, they had journeyed west with a company of eleven adventurers who would one day become known as the Wayfarers. They set out from Aliston on the east shore of the great Marelocus, the inland sea. Heading west into the wilds of Mir, they marched into the unknown, centuries before the signing of the Concord. After months of gruelling travel and countless hardships, they came across a wide, circular, and terraced valley abutting the Western Ocean. A large lake teeming with fish occupied the northeast corner of the valley, fed by the relentless, roaring deluge of three waterfalls that glittered in the setting sun like a million sparkling gems. The lake emptied into a swift river churning with white froth, disappearing into a lush jungle of ferns, vines, and towering redwoods. The river briefly reappeared again as it dropped from the terraces three times until emptying out in a deep turquoise bay encircled by a high cliff like a natural break wall. A narrow strait broke the circular escarpment, providing access from the bay to the wide western ocean beyond. Three severe hills jutted up like fists from among the verdant green carpet of the rainforest. Merlin chose the highest and largest of the three hills for his new home.

It is said that Merlin and William raised his tower at the top of the Midhill in a single day- the tower that the Lyceum would build up around over the centuries. Even now the tower stood in the heart of the Lyceum, locked and lonely for nearly a century. It is said that the Wayfarers, for their fair and loyal service in escorting them to their new home, were granted ownership of the Lowhill, but in their respect for the Sea Wizard took only the peak. Their hall still stood high above the bustling southern part of the city, fading and nearly forgotten. It is said that the magi came in greater and greater numbers to learn at the foot of the greatest wizard to ever live, and they chose Northhill to build their own towers and villas in pale imitation. The city of Terrastra grew up around these hills, until they themselves disappeared under a blanket of urban sprawl and vertical construction. And so, the city prospered and grew over the centuries, one of Merlin's eyes always looking west.

Terrastra was the city of the west and the West- literally and metaphorically. The city stood on the westernmost point of land on the continent of Callista, a strategically located and valuable trading port between the Empire to the east, Tsarusska to the north, Kanta to the south, and ships coming all the way around the far south Cape Maul from Xeijpang.

There was a well-known commoner joke about the city's location. It was so chosen because it was the furthest Merlin could get away from the Emperor and still stay in Mir. I didn't say it was a good joke.

There was some truth to that joke. It had always been rumoured that Merlin's flight from Aliston into the west had been due to the growing jealousy of the Emperor. This common perception gave rise to Terrastra as being seen apart and opposite the Empire. Where in the settled lands of the east order and security were paramount, Terrastra was seen as a place of independent thought and freedom of expression. A refuge for those that chafed under the Empire's restrictions. In this way did the idea of Terrastra grow, the western bastion of freedom a lone hero in defiance of the Empire's growing hegemony.

The other cities of the world were greater than Terrastra in many respects. Grand Aliston, capital of the Empire and seat of the Emperor, perched where the black pebble shores of the inland Marelocus Sea met the ancient Mimir mountains, outshone Terrastra in splendour and strength. Sprawling Kanta in its riot of colours, beating heart of the southern savannahs, surpassed it in population and diversity. Only Nozomi, the half-submerged fortress city of Xeijpang, it's titanic forges burning hot in their murky underwater smithies, rivalled Terrastra in craftsmanship and culture. It was said that even Vokgorod put Terrastra to shame in the quality of its scrivening, but that was hearsay from the few traders brave enough to venture into the haunted expanse that was Tsarusska. The city of Terrastra was second best in everything except what counted most. Terrastra was envied by its sister-cities, for nowhere in the whole world of Mir was a city where magic was so powerfully concentrated.

The Codeci Oratorium. The High Congress of the Magi.

You can remember the Codeci?

I am starting to remember. Thank you, Tales.

You're welcome Plinius. Anything you wanted to add?

Just that there's no way Tsarusska has better scrivening.

Plinius had to admit that he did not really know the city he had been living in for over a century. For quite some time, Plinius had found that if a route did not take him from his home (a home which until today was ostensibly a bookshop, and now a raging inferno) to the Lyceum and back, Plinius had no care to stray afield from the most direct route to his given destination. Why bother when all he needed was so close at hand? Why go out and seek out when his hard work had given him the ability to be self-sufficient in his home?

Why waste time that could be better spent unravelling the mysteries of the River. In those days I truly wanted not. I had practically everything. Everything I needed. It was all right at hand. Not because it was given to me- because I had earned it, through hard work and study. I had earned my solitude. My craft was all that mattered. At that time, at least. I am not sure if I agree with that now? Or do I?

"This… place has changed."

Pots looked up at the magus. "Has it now, ser? I's never been up here before, so I's rightly cannae tell ye one way or 'nother. I's saws a paintin' once of 'ole Merlin there, thar be 'bout it. It were a drawin' Da had, did it himself 'e did, on th' day he saved th' ole sea wizard's life!"

Plinius was looking appreciatively at the statuesque fountain of Merlin dominating the centre of the market. "Yes, Pots, the fountain remains the same as always. This though," he waved an arm towards the south where the market stretched out into a large plaza teeming with people, "This is much, much bigger than the last time I was here."

"Aye, is it?" Pots asked, his face scrunching up in thought. "Nah, that cannae be right. They built up the plaza, oh, thirty or so years ago or so, when *me* was jus' a babe. Da told me so. Ain't nothing much change since then, eh?"

Plinius was quiet as he ruminated on that. He could not believe it had been that long since he had made the trek up to the Lyceum. *It had been that long. What a recluse I was. I can remember flashes of the Lyceum, and all of them are tinged with a warmth that buoys my heart. I can't fathom why I would have stayed away.*

"So now what, ser?" Pots asked, uncomfortable with the silence.

"We are supposed to be meeting my contact, a Coptician, near the fountain. Here, take this," Plinius reached into his bag and pulled out a couple of gold coins stamped with the face of William Lyon on one side and the triskelion of Merlin on the reverse. He handed them to Pots saying, "Go by the fountain and keep an eye out. Do the merchants still sell mush & pig? Buy us a couple, this should cover it."

Pots eyes widened as the coins were pressed into his hands. *That was probably more coin than Pots had ever held in his life.* "Aye ser! But ye be handing I's way, way too much, ser. A few lyons should do it, I's dinnae need skelions!"

"No worries about that Pots. Just bring back the change."

Pots hesitated for a moment, looking at the magus strangely. Whatever he was thinking, he quickly shook his head and hurried off into the market, leaving Plinius with his thoughts. The Midhill Plaza was still familiar, but so much had changed that it had Plinius feeling unnerved.

The three hills of Terrastra each boasted their own main market. These markets served as the foci for commerce in each district dominated by their respective hill. Highly specialized, smaller markets served individual neighbourhoods, but the Northmarket, Midmarket and Exchange were the dominate places of business for the Northhill, Midhill and Lowhill respectively. All three were teeming with sundry items, but even then, each market took on unique characteristics in how they served and catered to the range of needs for the citizens of the cosmopolitan city. Plinius could not recall ever having visited the other two markets- the Northmarket and the Exchange.

The Northmarket sat high on the north hill of Terrastra across from the Cathedral of Cronus, the towering edifice to the one true God of Mir. It was only vaguely like the church he remembered from his younger days. *I think I remember Anatoli saying something about a renovation.* The Magistracy had poured a good deal of money into Terrastra to renovate the cathedral, increasing the size of its two large bell towers with twisted obsidian and ivory buttresses and expanded towers, raising them further to the heavens. They had also gone about replacing every window with multi-hued depictions of the Great Blessing, the creation myth of Mir, in iron bound stained glass. It was nestled among the gleaming marble villas of the great magi of the city, whether they be from strong legacy bloodlines or those who had earned their station through merit within the Lyceum. It was the only market in the city closed off to the general citizenry- strict signs warned that commoners without a magi writ were forbidden from entering the market. One better have a good reason to be there, or the militia would see you dumped down in the Tradebasin with only a few lumps to show for the trip. Plinius had been told that the finest wares and wonders from across the wide breadth of Mir could be found there at exorbitant prices. Plinius had lived a quiet life, a life of comfortable pleasure, and the reasons for him to visit the Northern market could be counted on a closed fist.

Plinius turned on the bench he was sitting on. The south-eastern crescent of, and to his mind, the lesser half of Terrastra, spread out before and below him. *That's not true! I think all Terrastra is wonderful.* The southern edge of the Midmarket jutted out from the Midhill like a table mushroom, built up over the years on top of hundreds of buildings that dotted the hillside like a child's building blocks. Over the decades the plaza had expanded as the city itself expanded, outwards and skywards, the wide half circle of its southern perimeter now ending at a railing and a plunging drop some hundred meters to the shadowy ground below. The Street of Flasks came up on the western side, the eastern side the Street of Sways, like two arms rising from the lower city, two big arms that encircled the Midmarket in embrace, both streets intersecting with Lyceum Way at the northern edge.

The Lyceum Way extended in a straight line upwards to the hill's zenith where it came to an abrupt split, splitting like a large Y at an expansive park. *How many times had I walked that street?* One side lead into the grounds of the Lyceum, the oldest building in all Terrastra, its polished walls of gleaming granite veined with gems rising high until splitting into half a dozen fluted towers, giving it the look of a regal crown perched atop the Midhill. A figurative beacon of light that was visible from leagues around, it was the finest centre for education, research, and knowledge in all of Mir. Magi from all over Mir came to study at the feet of the Archmagi of the Lyceum.

The other road led to one of the newest buildings in all Terrastra, one vastly changed from the simple house that used to sit in its place. A foreboding gate of black onyx set into high black iron walls of spell forged metal was undoubtedly designed to intimidate, and it succeeded. Parapets of spiked blue crystals ringed the walls like the teeth of a gigantic beast howling at the heavens. A singular large drum tower of the same smooth onyx stood like an unburnt candle, rising windowless from within those implacable walls. The tower was adorned with almost comically large red pennants bearing the crossed staff and sword, the Gladia Virgum, of the Magocratic Empire. They snapped furiously in the wind, slapping off the side of the tower. Where the Lyceum looked warm and inviting, the Hall of Staffs gave the opposite effect. It perched above the city like a great, hungry gargoyle, ready to swoop down and take into its jaws anything unfortunate enough to be noticed. Plinius tore his gaze quickly away from it in hopes it had not noticed him.

Plinius turned, looking inwards at the market's most famous and dominate feature. The fountain of Merlin stood in the centre of the Midmarket, effectively marking the split between the market stalls of the western hemisphere, the park of the southern hemisphere and the wide-open plaza of mosaic tiles in the eastern. Plinius took interest as a large crowd had gathered around an orange-clad 2nd circle disciple giving a speech from atop a large stone, the mosaic patterns spiralling out from the stone and a dozen like it. It had been a tradition since time immemorial for students to practice speechifying at the Midmarket Speaking Stones, on any topic they deemed worthy. The art of magic and politics, philosophy and history, anything really could be discussed here and find an educated audience atop a plinth, each one surrounded by ringed benches. Plinius had never indulged himself, public speaking not being high on his list of things to master. *I very well could if I wanted to.*

One of the current speakers was a woman of younger years, but as for any magi, looks and age could be deceiving. She constantly pushed her long ginger hair out of her face as she wildly gesticulated at the sizable crowd. She was of short stature and stood on a wooden crate placed on top of the stone so that she could be seen over the heads of other students. A half dozen or so of her fellow students stood around her in a protective half circle facing outwards, nodding in agreement, and clapping their hands in booming flourishes of sparks whenever she emphasized a point. Her voice carried and echoed off the walls of the Midhill rising behind the market, determined and bold with the fiery enthusiasm of youth. Given the size of the crowd, it was evident her word was garnering some interest, Plinius' not the least among them.

"And so, I say that Terrans must stick up for fellow Terrans! It does not matter your height, the shape of your ears, the abilities you possess! We are all children of Cronus! The Magistracy is here to serve the interests of the

Empire- not Terrastra! The Emperor does not care for us!" Plinius could not hide his surprise as a chorus of boos and cheers swelled up from the crowd. A rotten head of cabbage thrown at the speaker burned to ash as one of her protecters incinerated it with flame from an outstretched hand. She teetered precariously on top of the rickety box before some helpful hands helped steady her. A finely dressed merchant accused of throwing the produce was promptly confronted and roundly beaten upon by half dozen students before he fled the plaza.

The woman was unfazed. "See how they resort to violence to silence us? It will always be those who benefit from the insidious Imperium and its lapdogs. Yes, the Iron Cohort! They are who strike first at their master's whim. An ill-thrown cabbage is the least of their methods- in fact we should applaud that fine gentleman for showing restraint! We have all seen the smoke pouring up from downhill" -she pointed in Plinius' general direction at the column of smoke billowing behind him- "word is that the Imperial dogs prowling the city burned an innocent bookseller for no more than the crime of possessing knowledge that the Empire finds unsavoury!"

"I heard it was a dark wizard from Tsarusska, practicing necromancy!" yelled a preening voice from the crowd.

"Lies! All lies I tell you. They lie so they can say they did it in the name of the Concord, they did it by the blessing of the Accord, but we are given no recourse for their overreach or when they make a mistake! Burned to the ground for valuing knowledge!" Angry mutters circulated the crowd. *An appeal to knowledge always works with the Lyceum crowd.*

"The Magistracy is here to slowly infect this city with the sickness that is Empire!" she screamed indignantly, many voices in the crowd agreeing, "They are slowly binding us further to the Aurum Circle and its perverted view of the Concord. We all know what they have done! They broke down William Lyon, they forced him to sign the Accord, and then they murdered him!" Even more upset and hostile voices rumbled through the crowd. "They wish to chain our dwarven, our elven, our goliath, our demonkin cousins and eliminate or enslave them." That line was greeted with a muted response from the crowd.

"To breakdown our liberties and replace it with the subservient security of the Magocracy! To press us under the boot of Iron Cohort oppression! I say better to live as a free Terran than a slave to the Empire!" Resounding cheers roared back at her, yet Plinius could still pick out many who were frowning or arguing quietly with others.

A slave to the Empire? That is hardly the Empire I remember. I find it hard to believe the High Council would ever let the Magocracy get a real foothold here. When the Empire had taken Thessalonia, Bashtalem, Coptica, a good two dozen more inconsequential lesser nations and city-states into their arms- but never Terrastra. Terrastra is protected. It's right there in the Concord!

Plinius snorted. He shook his head condescendingly at the ignorance of youth and the folly of naïve rebellious behaviour. He nodded his head wisely at his own self-assuredness. Plinius knew his history. Terrastra would never be consumed by the Empire; of that he was certain. *I concur with, well, myself.*

Turning his attention back to the market, his stomach protested loudly as the smell of cooking meat mixed with the fragrant melange of exotic spices wafted across the terrace. *Oh my, those smells are intoxicating. I'm not hungry though… do I eat still?* The market boasted a dozen of a dozen stalls offering anything the denizens of Terrastra could desire, yet the bulk of selection catered to the students and masters of the Lyceum. Magi in the pale pink robes of apprentices known as pueri hurried and haggled along the market with long lists prepared by their masters for upcoming lessons and/or private research. Plinius felt a faint smile creep on his lips, his present hardships forgotten as he remembered doing the same so many years ago.

"Mind if we join you?"

Plinius nearly jumped from the bench, his hands halfway up and the words of a reactionary defensive spell on his lips. The faces of two young students smiled down at him. A young burly man in ill-fitted apprentice robes the colour of salmon meat had asked the question. Next to him, a lithe woman in red robes inscribed with runes along the hems indicated she was a 1st circle initiate of the School of Salubrity. They looked at him expectantly, dripping skewers folded in wax cloth clutched in their hands. "What?" he answered dumbly.

"May we... join you?" the man repeated, a puzzled look on his face.

Plinius palms began to sweat. "Please go away." He said, not looking at him.

"Ah, excuse me? You're sitting alone on the bench. Can't we-"

"No. Away with you."

"Come on Jerathan, let's go over to another seat."

"Wait a minute, Theresa," the man pointed a finger in Plinius' face, "Look at me! We're from the Lyceum! How about you go away you common-"

"I say!" Plinius' face screwed up into one of profound distaste and fury. "Can you see I am attempting to enjoy a day about town? Have manners fallen so far at the Lyceum? This is a terrible breach of protocol, and I for one am disgusted with your lack of respect!"

They're looking at him- at me- like I'm crazy!

The woman looked concerned. "Are you ok? Ser?"

Plinius huffed. "Ser? SER? I am a Grand Scrivener! You will address *me* as Grandmagi!"

The man was getting annoyed. "Now see here- we haven't the foggiest idea who you are- and we are both at the Lyceum as well as children of the court in Aliston. YOU are a Grand Scrivener? Ha! I do believe I would have remembered meeting you at some point. My father is the head enchanter in

Aliston!"

Plinius eyed the boy imperiously.

"Head enchanter you say. So, your father is Magi Hastings?" *Hastings… overweight fellow. Big moustache. Laughs at his own jokes.*

The man's face became wary. "Yes. How did you know…"

"Ah yes, I can see the resemblance now. Truth be told I thought you were lying. How did I know? Be quiet and observe, pueri."

Plinius set his face in his best annoyed scowl. Extending his right arm out from his sleeve, the students' eyes glanced down at the pale tattooed skin. Plinius willed the magic into his arm, like tensing a muscle. Energy began to crackle between the hairs of his arm in tiny bolts. Runes and sigils began to glow with a faint, wavery light.

Magical tattoos were common amongst all magi, and it was a time-honoured tradition to get the 'Codeci' tattooed on one's arm as they progressed through their mastery of the River. Each chain of symbols was comprised in concentric circles. First the inner rune, the simple rune for the letter P, or pueri, the apprentice. It was done in simple black ink and was done immediately after the successful casting of your first spell for a master of the Lyceum. It was usually a simple, easily repeatable cantrip. *Oh! I remember- mine was create light.*

Once one ring on the magus' arm had fully illuminated, the next ring would light with the corresponding sigils representing each successive circle. A fiery red, the 1st circle, the student. Orange like a sunset was the colour of the 2nd circle, the disciple. 3rd circle, the senior, a canary yellow. The 4th circle was considered the jump from "childhood" to "adulthood" in the magi community- the apostoli, a shimmering green in a hundred blooming and fading shades. This was followed by the superior (cerulean blue) and veneficus (indigo purple) at the 5th and 6th. The students' eyes grew wide with surprise as the 7th circle on Plinius' arm lit, and fear showed up as the 8th circle lit. Pearl white and ghost grey; magi and grandmagi. The last two circles on his arm remained empty and unlit. *The penultimate one, the black of the archmagi, perhaps someday to be mine; the last one, not unless heaven and earth moved in mysterious ways. The one beyond that… impossible.*

The one beyond?

Yes. The mythical 11th circle.

I was unaware there was one.

Yes, there is! I'm sure my memory is right about this one. It… Edge take me! I can't remember, it's like trying to grab an eel. Go on, go on. I'll think about it.

The male student's face was as red as his companion's 1st circle robes. He glanced back up at Plinius face for a moment then quickly aimed his gaze down at his shoes, seemingly near tears.

"Your father is a good man," Plinius said sternly but gently. "I corresponded with him some years back regarding the transitive properties of fossilized bone. Send him my regards. Now off with you." Plinius dismissed them with a turn of his head.

"Sorry to have bothered you, Grandmagi, Master Scrivener, ser. Emperor Eternal!" Plinius had stopped listening at that point, waving a dismissive hand. The students backed away, slowly at first and then in a hurried gait back towards the interior of the plaza.

That man certainly was rude. The Lyceum is a place for refined people. In my day that lout would never have made it past his pueri. Plinius thought he should go and check in at the Lyceum once this whole mess was sorted out. He still had friends there. It had been a long while since he had stopped to visit his old teachers, now peers. *The last time I visited was 1472, the week of that freak snowstorm… I remember because all those children were upset when I melted all the snow. So, it had been about 27 years.*

The southern quarter of the market, where Plinius now sat, was reserved for a wide-open plaza bereft of stalls. The plaza had been funded by the magi at the Lyceum- prior to its construction, the students of the Lyceum would take their lunches, breaks and dinners in the hallways and open study halls of the Lyceum itself. This had proved to be altogether too much of a distraction to most of the magi- Plinius knew all too well the dangers of sharing a meal with a person and the penchant they had to devolve into frivolity- and given the delicate nature of some of the experiments conducted at the Lyceum, the magi decided that an alternate place for their students to conduct their social excursions seemed a worthwhile investment.

The plaza's centre was dominated by a large fountain wrought of veined granite and copper. It had been transmuted and fashioned by the enchanters of the Lyceum. Plinius, as a matter of professional respect, begrudgingly accepted the craftmanship and skill of the enchanters who had fashioned it. Standing nearly ten meters tall from the base was a statue of Merlin posing heroically. *That iconic hat and beard combo. The classic ideal of a magus.* An outstretched arm clutched an orb from which water poured into the fountain below in a steady torrent. Plinius had been told once by Anatoli that the enchanters had bound an elemental in the orb. *How would a commoner know that for certain? He probably made it up.* The cost of running the piping necessary for the same effect would have proven to be extraordinarily costly and invasive so why settle for common tricks when magic would suffice? Despite the decades of weathering a normal statue would have suffered in similar circumstances, the copper and granite looked as smooth and new as the day it was made. Not so much as a single pit or patina marred the sublime craftmanship that magic could achieve. So lifelike was the statue that at any moment it seemed that if it had the mind to it could step down and leave.

The edge of the plaza was ringed with rows of benches in front of fullered columns of white marble. Potted palms facing out over the city, offering a breath-taking view and place to rest and reflect. In between the fountain and the precipitous edge, rows of tables in concentric circles were packed with people. Students and merchants, citizens and tradespeople, magi and common, the hardworking backbone of the city. It was the most likely location in all Terrastra where you could find magi and common thoroughly intermixed. Laughter and shouting infused the plaza and Plinius watched two students, arms linked with each other as their free hands clutched folded fried dough with fruit filling, finding a place for an early lunch or perhaps a late breakfast. They walked up to a table where a group of what must be acquaintances welcomed them excitedly. Plinius turned away, his smile vanishing.

I forgot how breath-taking the view is from here. Plinius deliberately kept his gaze away from the westward side of the city, keeping the smoke from out of his sightline. The southern half of Terrastra laid out before him, dominated by the Lowhill rising like a great tower from the sprawling, towering slums built up around its edges. The Exchange, the main market for commoners and foreign trade, peaked out from around the southern edge of the hill, a hazy cloud of dust and white smoke. *A noisy, dirty place. Horrible.* Sandwiched tight within the shadows between the Midhill and Lowhill was an over developed canyon of near perpetual gloom. Glow globes illuminated an area home to the scores of differing trades suited to the commons who called Terrastra home.

The smithies could be heard from even here, the tanneries could be smelt, the wheelwrights could be seen, the masons were everywhere, and the coopers were near the misty banks of the Sapphires at the northern escarpment. *They are probably cooping as we speak.* Those were the only commoner professions Plinius could recall, but he was sure there were many more hidden down there. The chaotic sprawl spread out south until devolving into the packed dockside tenements that housed the labour necessary to make such mundane professions viable. A long brown waterway bisected the space between the hills. Three large bridges had been spell-wrought from the bedrock to facilitate traffic across the canal, pulled up from the rock far beneath the city. At least that was the purpose.

All three bridges were packed with traffic. They served the wagons and coaches that were desperate enough to traverse the most direct path into the heart of the city. Traffic that penetrated this deep into the city moved at a snail's pace, a combination of the horde of Terrans living in such tight quarters and the limited visibility from being down in the murk. Always on the forefront of ingenuity, the commoners had erected dozens of haphazard bridges made of rickety wood to serve the voluminous pedestrian traffic.

The steep slope of the Lowhill above them was so packed and developed with homes and walkways piled one on top of each other that none of the natural hill itself could be seen. Hundreds of dingy, blotchy, whitewashed buildings created a sheer cliff rising high into the sky more than a kilometre. Even more, smaller wattle hovels hung onto these more structurally sound homes like barnacles on a hull. People scurried like mice among large switchback staircases and the long winding road that circled upwards to the top. Near the top of the Lowhill stood buildings that had been raised by common hands more than half a millennium ago. They were buildings built by commoner Terrans, those whose skill and effort rose them a fraction above the mud and misery that surrounded them. Plinius felt tired just looking at it, imagining the sheer effort it must take to eke a living out on the Lowhill. *Thank Cronus for magic. If I was a common, I would probably just go and die.*

The buildings at the zenith of the hill were a swollen mass with roofs of hammered copper that gleamed in the morning light between the chunky green swathes of aging patina. *The mercantile guilds of Terrastra. Little better than beggars.* Prominent amongst them was a large but simple stone building, a round drum of a tower devoid of decoration but for a single flag atop a poll rising from its centre. *The Wayfarer's Guild…* Plinius thoughts turned to Anatoli briefly, which then turned to his bookshop, which then turned back to frustration and anger. His stomach growled.

Plinius gazed around the plaza. He thought irritably about how if he could just summon Hand, this would go much easier. Anatoli had said no magic though. *So, a commoner knows better than us? I suppose so since Pots has been leading me around by the nose, despite me living here at the least fifty years longer.* As if summoned at the thought, Pots came rushing up to the magus.

"Plinius, gran- uh, ah ser!"

Plinius snapped his head around as if on a swivel, his nerves on edge. Grabbing the dwarf by the collar, accidentally grabbing a fistful of beard hair, Plinius pulled him down onto the bench beside him. "Quiet you fool!" He hissed through gritted teeth. "Do not use my name! What is the matter with you! We need to be discreet!"

The dwarf at least had the good grace to blush. His already ruddy cheeks turned crimson. "Ah, aye, that is a good point ye have. Worry not, ain't see sign o' a Hort anywhere abouts. Here's yar skewer, and yar change, boy-o."

Pots handed Plinius a waxed paper, folded to hold the juicy kebab of seared button mushroom and charred pork. The portion was more meagre than Plinius had remembered, and he grimaced in dismay as the dwarf handed him his change. "That is all? How much did this cost, Pots?"

Pots shrugged. "I ain't never been good wit' numbers, ser. Ain't never had much need fer 'em. Da always says thar bloody Empire has been jackin' the costs comin' in from the incontinent."

"Do you mean continent?"

"Thar wha' I said!"

Plinius pushed the coins in the palm of his hand around. "I am sure the merchant charged a fair price. This is Terrastra after all, not some Kantanian dirt market. I am just surprised that the cost has risen so drastically. A month ago, I had similar items dropped off at my bookstore; it was half the price!"

The magus took a bite of his skewer- at least that was still as good as he remembered it. Sighing, Plinius glared at the dwarf expectantly.

"No sign of thar, or any, Coptician," shrugged Pots. Plinius fidgeted with his leg, feeling his anxiety grow.

Plinius' paranoia had grown steadily worse since they arrived at the Midmarket. Too many people, too noisy, too open a space and too many ways for the agents of the Magistracy to hide and spring upon him unawares. Letting that paranoia guide him, Plinius had decided to let the dwarf be his eyes as he sat away from the crowd. He was beginning to regret that decision.

"What use are you?" asked Plinius pointedly.

The dwarf scoffed. "I reckon I's been plenty useful. Got ye this far ain't I?"

"Oh, yes, my deepest thanks." Plinius scrunched his shirt into his hands, the knuckles turning white. "What was I thinking? I was a fool to come here. The Magistracy sits behind my back, and I wait like a fool for them to come and arrest me on their very doorstep!"

"Well, maybe this is th' best place to be. Only an idiot would go near the 'all of Staffs if the Magistracy was out to get 'em, eh?" Pots offered helpfully.

Plinius fixed him with a withering stare. "Right," he said, his teeth grinding against each other, "Only an idiot."

"Exactly!" Pots beamed cheerfully. "'*Be where they want ye and they'll never find ye'*, Da always says. Ye are probably safe. Wan' I's th' get ye another skewer?" He asked as he chewed, his mouth stuffed full of the juicy skewer meat.

Plinius pensively took a slight bite of mushroom. "No. I want you to do as I asked and find this contact. This Coptician who will help us. Curse Anatoli and his cryptic descriptions! The sooner we find this person the sooner we are away, and the sooner we are away the better."

Pots' frown made him look like a kicked puppy. "I dinnae see the harm in 'avin' a full belly is all. I can do both, eh."

Plinius' irritation was at a bowling point. *Don't you mean boiling point?* He had visions of throwing the dwarf over the terrace and scoring points for whoever or whatever he knocked down below. *Leave the terrible puns to me.* Who was this dwarf to argue? "If you cannot be helpful than I think it best if you return to your alleyways."

Pots hand shot out and grabbed Plinius sleeve. *The affrontery!* Plinius mouth dropped open, a vicious rebuke of the dwarf's impropriety dying on his lips as he saw the worry on Pots face. Plinius felt like ice water had poured down his spine. "What? What is it, Pots?"

The dwarf's eyes darted from Plinius, to behind him, and back again. "Lictors," he hissed through his teeth. "Quick, we best move."

Plinius felt frozen with fear but let the dwarf pull him by the arm until he was on his feet. Glancing sideways he saw two imposing figures walking the perimeter of the plaza. Both lictors wore black breastplates emblazoned with the Gladia Virgum of the Magistracy, announcing their allegiance as if there could be any doubt. Their blue trousers tucked into high leather boots, matching the blue sleeved tunics tucked into gloves of plate and chain. Plinius choked on his breath, terror filling his chest. Their hard faces framed by coal scuttle helmets frightened him, but not as much as the hatchets hanging loosely from loops around their waists.

"Le's go, Plinius! Come, now!" the dwarf tugged at the magus' sleeve. Every instinct was telling Plinius to run, to dart away as quick as a hare, but his muscles would not listen. "We need t' go, now!"

Plinius, a surge of adrenaline flooding his body, bypassed his fear. He quickly and clumsily stumbled away from the benches, putting as much distance between them as they could as quickly as possible. He followed the dwarf as dumbly and docile as a sheep. Pots strode purposefully towards the interior of the plaza. He could hear one of the lictors behind him tell a joke in an Alistonian accent. They pushed their way into a crowd of students.

"Little furtha', this way, this way, 'scuse me, 'scuse me," Pots murmured, his eyes downcast.

Plinius could feel his skin crawling as a sharp tightness began constricting his stomach. The warm sun was beating down on him, he was aware of the heat, knew it was there, but all he could feel was a cold sweat leaking down his back as his body began trembling with tiny tremors. *It is too much for the poor man. For me.* The noise of the crowd was washing over him like a tidal wave. The shrill laughter. The pungent odours. A blurry mural of faces swimming across his vision, laughing and smiling and frowning and jeering and screaming. *It's too much!* The entire world began pressing down on him, the immensity of it overwhelming. He was drowning.

Plinius closed his eyes, muttering. Runes memorized long ago flashed into his consciousness as he recited the words, replacing everything else. He became acutely aware of his own breathing, letting it become an anchor. He stretched out and the River revealed itself. An iridescent rainbow ribbon of pure magic flowed around him. The anchor kept him steady, feeling the currents of the River flow through and around him. *In… and out. In… and out.* He stood for a moment transfixed. First the universe, then Mir, then Terrastra, then the plaza, shrinking and shrinking until they existed in a single point of time, the space between his breaths. The River sang with his beating heart. He opened his eyes.

The anxiety was gone. For the moment.

He had fallen behind. The packed crowd of the plaza spread out before him, the statue of Merlin watching over them like a shepherd over his flock. He had lost track of Pots. He stole a quick glance over his shoulder. One of the two lictors lounged lazily against the terrace railing, listening while the other moved his hands animatedly in the retelling of some no doubt gruesome anecdote. Turning back, he intently scanned the crowd, his effort at keeping the lid on the tempest within slowly giving away.

"Hey! What do you think you're doing? I am talking to you, disgusting bitty!"

"My apologies, master," Plinius could hear Pots. A crowd of students had gathered a few tables over- the dwarf had not gone far at all. Plinius began marching towards them as he heard the dwarf continue his apologies.

"Beggin' yer pardon."

"Beggin yer pardon?" the voice replied in the exaggerated voice. Sniggers accompanied his own braying laughter. "Is that what you said? You brushed up against my robe, you filthy blockhead, and now my lunch is ruined. It is ruined! DO you know what that word means, simp? Do you know how much this robe cost? Do you know how much meat costs nowadays?"

"No, ser. I ain't know. Sorry, ser."

"Ain't is not a word, dwarf," The student said patronizingly. His nose crinkled. "Edge take me! What is that smell? Have you pissed yourself, simp?" The students' companions laughed cruelly as they joined in.

"Hey dwarf!"

"Where's the rest of you, bitty?"

"Filthy simp."

Pots smiled stupidly as he continued with muttered apologies, making sure not to raise his eyes from the flagstones. It looked like the dwarf had inadvertently bumped into a student and caused a slight accident with his lunch, evidenced by the red saucy stain across the student's robe. The students began to circle, pueri one and all, closing off any way forward for the dwarf in an implacable wall of pale pink cloth. Insult and abuse rained down on him, culminating in one of the more brazen students dumping a lukewarm cup of caf over his head. All the while Pots stood there smiling, his face frozen into a mask of neutrality learned from a life among magi. Plinius became aware that he was tightly clenching his fists. Pots looked up at that moment and his and Plinius' eyes connected.

Plinius could feel an intense heat rise into his throat. All thoughts of caution and control vanished in an instant. In a few short strides he was upon them, his arms raising upwards and with a few quick words and a large *whoosh* the group was forced by a sharp wind away from the cowering dwarf, sending a couple of the students sprawling on their backsides. The lead apprentice turned angrily towards Plinius but stopped immediately at the sight of Plinius' face.

"What is the meaning of this?" No need for simple cantrips this time- Plinius laced each word with as much menace as he could muster, bringing to bear the full weight of authority being a grandmagi granted him. Plinius himself was surprised at his own tone. *I'm surprised too!*

"I- I- uh," the apprentice stammered. He seemed terribly confused, his face alternating between bewildered and angry. His eyes darted like a rat, beady and frantic, trying to find something, anything, to help explain the sudden appearance of this angry man. His compatriots were slowly backing away.

"Answer me, boy." Plinius eyes flashed.

"Nothing," The apprentice replied petulantly. One of the other apprentices stepped up to the young man and whispered in his ear. Plinius felt a tremble in his knees as he recognized the boy that had asked to sit with him earlier. *Cronus! Bloody hell!*

"Oh, Cronus, bloody hells," the previously haughty bully spluttered quietly as the pueri scurried away.

"Excuse me?"

"I am sorry, Master- er, Grandmagus." The apprentice's eyes would not meet Plinius' eyes. "We were just having some fun is all. It's just a bitty-"

"A what?"

"A bitty-"

"What in the Blessed Concord is a bitty?"

"Y'know," whined the student, "Just a simp!"

"Just a simp?" repeated Plinius, not even attempting to conceal the loathing he had for the word. The conversation at the nearby tables petered out as the plaza-goers began to take notice of something far more interesting than their meals.

The apprentice, perhaps in vain hope, perhaps just because of a life full of never being called to account, mistook Plinius' tone. "Yes, exactly! Just a dirty simp-"

"Boy." Plinius voice grew very quiet. "If I were you, I would think on the merits of my next words, and then choose which ones to speak very, very carefully. I question you- where do we live?"

The apprentice looked up at the magus dumbly. "Uh?"

"Uh?" Plinius imitated. "The city of Uh? Answer *me*!"

"Terrastra! Grandmagus! Ser!" He hurriedly added. The apprentice winced as if his answer was incorrect.

"Correct. And is Terrastra not still the free city?"

The boys mouth worked up and down like a fish gasping out of water. "Uh… uh…"

"Uh again? Uh? Out with it boy!"

"Yes! Yes, master. B-but the Magistracy!"

"The Magistracy nothing!" hissed Plinius. The grandmagus paid no mind to the few mutterings and gasps from round him. "Is this what passes for Terrastran hospitality nowadays? The city of peace? Is it now acceptable to bully commoners in the middle of the day?"

"Bully?" protested the pueri, regaining some courage, "I'm no bully! Why are you so bent out of shape? It's just a simp."

An equal response of gasps and snickers spread through the crowd at the use of the slur.

Plinius could feel the anger boiling up inside him.

The apprentice glanced around for help again, but the only help forthcoming came from an unexpected source. "Plinius!" whispered Pots through tight lips, his eyes terrified. "Our friends are, ah, the uh… we needs t' go!"

Plinius quickly glanced over his shoulder. The lictors had stopped talking and were staring with interest at the scene playing out. Despite the overwhelming urge to soil his pants, Plinius rounded back onto the apprentice.

"Apologize to him. Now!"

"Plinius- it's alright- we need to go!"

Plinius was adamant. "Apologize!"

The apprentice looked down at Pots. "Sorry," he said, unapologetically.

Plinius seethed. With a quick flick of his fingers, the dripping caf lifted off the dwarf and struck like a driving rain across the robe and face of the apprentice. A flash of anger crossed the apprentice's face but was quickly and wisely masked as a titter of laughter rippled through the crowd and quickly became a tidal wave. "Today is your lucky day, boy," Plinius whispered to the pueri, unheard by the crowd over the mocking laughter, "I hope you have learned something."

Pushing past the still shaking apprentice, Plinius grabbed Pots by the shoulders and hurriedly began making their way towards the fountain. Plinius dared not look back towards the lictors.

"Welp, thar was something," Pots said, slightly astonished. "Wha' were ye sayin' bout being discreet?"

"Oh, shut up," Plinius replied tersely. Reaching the far side of the fountain, Plinius peaked past Merlin's legs and through the cascading water. The lictors had joined the group of apprentices and Plinius could see the now soiled pueri pointing towards them as the taller lictor crossed his arms. The momentary satisfaction the magus had felt was quickly evaporating.

"Hello."

Plinius and Pots looked over and saw a lanky, wiry boy relaxing, a serene and unworried expression on his face. *Who is this child?* He seemed very young to Plinius. *Surely this… boy, cannot be our contact.* He was sitting idly with crossed legs on the edge of the fountain. His skin was the tanned olive common to the Coptic people of the Marelocus and it glistened in the morning sun, contrasting with the tattered grass green shirt hanging loosely off his bony frame. He reached into the olive cargo pants he wore- a style favoured by the tradesmen of the Lowhill- and pulled out a sad looking pear from which he took a great bite. A curly mop of short black hair came down just above his wideset ears.

Plinius stared at the boy, his wits racing to catch up with him. "Huh?"

The boy stood up abruptly, shoving the half-eaten pear back into his pocket. "We really don't be having the time for this."

The deep bass of the boy's voice belied his reedy frame. He tapped his foot expectantly, his eyes rolling at Plinius.

Great, another impudent common.

"You truly be bad at this. He said you would most likely be late. Then here you be coming, goofing off with some students. *Al-Qadim Alish!"* he swore in Coptic. Please, now, there being something you wish to ask me…"

Plinius blinked. *What did Anatoli say again?* "Our mutual friend from Vokgorod has a package for us?" he asked haltingly.

The boy sighed. "Good enough. 'You will need to pay the duty'. Let us be going, quick, before we be making acquaintance with the inside of the Hall of Staffs. Follow me."

Plinius stole one last quick glance at the Lyceum and the Hall of Staffs as they moved towards the Street of Sways. A foreboding feeling bloomed somewhere deep within him. A single page, slightly charred around the edges, fluttered past him on the wind. It carried over the plaza, twirling madly as it buffeted along the wind until it plunged out of sight over the terrace railing. Plinius fought back tears, the adrenaline still running him hot. He kept his head down as they exited the plaza. Meanwhile, under the untiring gaze of Merlin, two lictors strode around the fountain with their eyes intently searching the crowd.

Chapter Four

The Centurion & The Cohort

Long shadows cast by the Lowhill draped the Tradebasin in smoky gloom.

Plinius felt exposed despite the perpetual twilight of this strange neighbourhood. "I really think we should get moving," Plinius muttered, more to himself than anyone else.

"Oh ho, so now you want to be moving?" The Coptician asked sarcastically in his baritone, melodic voice. They crouched in the deep darkness of a side alley, far from the soft light of the nearest glow globe. Perhaps once open to the road, the alley was now separated, for some reason in the past a common mason had decided to erect a barrier here. The boy was bent over, his face pressed up against a hole in the wall. He never moved his eye from the surreptitious view of the chaotic torrent of Terrans roiling up and down Tumbledown Boulevard- the main street on the upper west side of the canal in the Tradebasin. "You were content to sit around back at your fancy market," continued the boy, "How about you be doing *me* a favour and wait quietly now."

Plinius bristled at being talked down to by a boy. Biting down on the inside of his cheek, he remained quiet despite having a few choice words he wanted to share. The sing-song voices of a half dozen young girls echoed down the alley from the opening nearly fifty metres away, chanting in a droning rhythm as they swung a long rope, taking turns jumping in-between. *I can barely make out what they're singing… something about a tin-can?* It was made all the worse by the encouraging smile and pat on the shoulder Pots was giving him.

"Are you at least going to tell us your name, boy?" asked Plinius in a demanding tone.

"Boy?" replied the boy derisively, "No. No names. I will be getting you where you need to go, then you can forget about *me*. If you must be having something, then be calling *me* just that. Boy."

"Fine, Boy. And where exactly are we going?"

"Be quiet, mage. I be trying to think."

Mage. How inappropriate, especially from one so young. How young is this imp? All

Copticians always look so young. He definitely doesn't act like a child. Plinius felt completely and totally out of his depth.

The Tradebasin derived its name from two defining features. Originally this area had been known just as the Basin- nestled between the Midhill and Lowhill, it sloped gently from the northeast down to the Bay of Drakes in the southwest. A long river poured into the Basin from the grouping of waterfalls called the Sapphires along the northern escarpment that separated Terrastra from the lands beyond. The river then cut an aedifactioneer-

I always thought I would have made a great aedifactioneer, but the school of elementalism was too loud for me. All those explosions, and dirt, and dust. Yuck. You see, Tales, the urge to create was always in me! Even from a young age. So, when elementalism become too... exciting for me, I naturally drifted towards scrivening.

Why not enchanting?

With these arms? You do realize enchanting usually involves a lot of hammering. Thanks, but no thanks.

A canal shaped by aedifactioneers cut straight down towards the harbour. Over the centuries, sewers, pipes, sluiceways, and spillways had been built above and around it. One on top of another, with very little thought or planning beyond whatever the immediate need was at the time, all designed to empty the cities sizable liquid expulsion into the canal. It was currently estimated that over two-thirds of the city's sewage, rainwater, effluence, runoff, and spillage made its way through the Tradebasin. In turn, the locals had given it the charming local nickname of the Runs. *It smells like gremlin shit.*

The former part of the name, the Trade part, came from the professions that inhabited this part of the city. It was estimated that commoners outnumbered magi in Terrastra nearly ten to one in the last census- *1440?-* that was taken in 1492 MD. *Ah. I think I missed that one.* Most of the city's common tradespeople worked daily in the gloom and noise of the Tradebasin. Blacksmiths hammered out steel on the Street of Nails, which ran closest to the ridge that encircled Terrastra, the better to serve the barracks and the militia garrison of Terrastra along the outer escarpment wall of the city. Carpenters and stonemasons, tanners and beltmakers, dyers and wheelwrights choked the edges of the Runs all the way down to the harbour, their labour echoing across the water and the bouquet of rancid smells created a miasmic cloud that infused the Tradebasin with a signature smell rarely experienced by any of the magi in the city.

On the side of the Runs closer to the Midhill, finished goods were created in staggering quantities for use by the citizens of Terrastra, with more besides exported to the rest of Mir. Weavers of yarn, silk cloth and wicker; cordwainers nailing and stitching together boots, shoes, sandals, and slippers; glassmakers and painters, ropemakers and chandlers, potters, and fletchers;

artisans of every and all material imaginable toiling with nothing but sweat, hands and tools. It made Plinius feel sweaty just thinking of the sheer exertion of it all. *It all sounds rather tiring, doesn't it?*

On the opposite side of the Runs closer to Lowhill, the largest section of the Tradebasin by far was home to the tens of thousands of commons toiling away to make sure the city did not go hungry. There were butchers, bakers, grocers, and bottlers. Fishmongers with their loud braying swarmed near the docks as the longshoremen hauled in the early morning catch. Glass gardens stuck out from the hillside like reflective thorns as cultivators trimmed and pruned through-out their greenhouses. Brewers sat in their massive halls near the base of the hill, wagons laden with casks perpetually moving in and out day and night, slow and weighty as they went out, yesterday's casks light and drained as they came back in. A city's worth of food passed through the Tradebasin every day, enough to supply nearly half a million mouths clamouring to be fed.

And most numerous of all the commoners that toiled beneath the magi on their lofty hills were the porters, scrambling like mad ants across the length of the Tradebasin. They were hauling cargo endlessly at all hours. *Porters' feet never sleep, as they used to say.*

In every city across Mir (excluding Nozomi with its Mir-famous canals and elemental barges) wagons were the chosen conveyance due to their common-operated logistical expediency. In Terrastra you could hire a wagon to transport a merchant's goods across the city, so long as they were content with moving at a glacial pace. Long ago the magi had conjured a trio of stone bridges that extended the main thoroughfares across the Runs, yet as the city grew, they had proven to be bottlenecks, turning the main crossings into nightmarishly viscous chokepoints of sluggish inaction. Naturally, a work-around was quickly discovered by the commoners. A porter using one of the dozens of hastily and sloppily common-created plankways across the Runs could quickly move across the Runs- so much so that for an overwhelming majority of businesses, it was much quicker to hire porters to make a dozen trips across the 'Ricketys' then wait on one full load driven by a teamster. They were precarious and a local game had developed where the citizens of the Tradebasin bet on porters making the crossing successfully or not. This game was especially popular during the fall storms, when the Sapphires would rage and the flood of water coming down the Runs would wash away almost all of the Ricketys. Still, this proved to be the work-around to the congestion, and a result completely from commoner ingenuity. *They have their moments.* The magi were content with this arrangement, although they often mused where the commoners were getting all the wood from. *Stealing it no doubt.*

Goods were moved at an acceptable speed for the businesses trying to operate, all thanks to the porters. Today however, with the added traffic of patrolling lictors and displaced commons fleeing from the spreading Midhill fire, the press of stinking urban life was unimaginable to Plinius, with the accompanying shouting and jockeying of wagons, carts and porters devolving into a thrashing riot. It left Plinius aghast and desperately yearning for the quiet solitude of his bookstore, and eminently thankful for the stone barrier between him and the rampant pandemonium of daily life in the Tradebasin.

"What are we waiting for?" Impatience was beginning to get the better of Plinius. The only light in the recess of the alleyway was cast from the sources of light atop the high poles lining the adjacent street. Darkness was a constant companion during much of the day in the Tradebasin, cast by the shadow of the soaring and sheer hills bordering the narrow district. This necessitated the assistance of magical lighting- enchanted globes of dim light hung from tall iron posts on all the major streets. It had come at a great cost from the magi of the Lyceum- Plinius had heard that the merchants were still paying off the debt.

Boy turned and looked at Plinius with a placid expression. "We are waiting for the right time."

Plinius frowned. "Alright then. Why are we waiting?"

"We are waiting because I say we wait."

Shrill girlish laughter from down the alley drew Plinius' attention. The rope had tripped one of the girls and pulled her down, giggling madly as she tried to untangle herself from the rope much to the other girls' delight. It delayed the game for a few seconds before they were once again singing their rhyme. *I am the... Helloman? Haloman? Is that what they're saying? I think I know this one...*

Plinius motioned towards the exit of the alley. "Were putting those innocent girls in danger! What if the lictors were to come, hmm? Do you want their lives on your hands?"

Boy shook his head. "That be commendable, mage. My heart be warmed that you be the one magus alive to give a gremlin shit about commoners' lives. Do not be worrying about them- they have their job, I have mine. You have yours. Now be quiet." He turned back to the hole.

"Their job? Your job? My job?" queried Plinius in a way that was reminiscent of a cawing gull and not in the remotest way what one would call quiet. *Who is writing this crap?* "What in the Blessed Concord is my job?"

Boy let out a sharp sigh and turned back towards the grandmagus. "Mage-"

"*Magus,*" interjected Plinius in the most professorial tone he could muster and stressing the word, "You will use my title when addressing myself. Or Grandmagus. Wait! Don't call me that. Call me ser. Plinius is also acceptable."

"*Plinius,*" said Boy through gritted teeth, "First of all, stop saying *Blessed Concord.* You might as well be shouting 'look over here, I am some weird old powerful mage- magus.

Second, my job. My job was to be sitting at a fountain in the insufferable Midmarket and be keeping my eye out for a magus that, if things do not be going according to plan, will show up and be needing me to take you to a backup rendezvous point. So that is what I be doing.

Third, your job. Your job is to not draw attention to yourself. No magic, no outbursts, no defending some dwarves honour," he said the last part while thumbing towards Pots who grinned broadly, "Just be a good mage and worry 'bout nothing while us commoners get the dirty work done. As usual."

"Now see here-"

"No! No be seeing here. The fourth and final rule is to be quiet! Shut up! No talking!"

Plinius seethed, his lips pressed tight together. Boy and the magus stared at each other defiantly, an invisible contest of wills being waged between them. Neither was going to give in- the Coptician presumably due to a need to retain control of a volatile situation, the grandmagus because he was too stubborn to back down. *Blessed Concord. You make me sound like an ass.*

"Cannae I still talk?" asked Pots timidly.

Plinius and Boy both closed their eyes at the same time, a mirror image as their hands pinched the bridge of their nose and rubbed it in an exasperated manner. With their eyes closed, neither saw the symmetry at play. The Coptician released his nose first, Pots question going unanswered.

"You want to know why we be waiting? Well, why don't you be having a look yourself?" he gestured towards the small hole in the mortar of the wall he had been viewing the street through.

"Fine then. I will." He scooted over as the boy moved out of the way, carefully and gingerly bending over to spy through the hole. Plinius hissed a sharp intake of breath as he saw what Boy had been keeping an eye on. A half dozen lictors lounged on the other side of the wall, standing in the middle of the street. The denizens of Terrastra went about their business under their ever-watchful gaze. For the most part they seemed unconcerned about what was going on about them- one of them was leaning against the wall of a cobbler's shop and for all the world looked to be fast asleep. "Are we waiting for them to leave? Should we not just take a different route?"

"Yes. No." The boy had picked up a handful of loose pebbles and was trying to throw them in a rusted pail further back in the alley. "They will be moving on eventually. That will be giving us our opening. Keep watching. Say what you be seeing."

Plinius frowned and turned back to his tiny window into the street. He pressed his eye up to the hole, damned to the hells if he was going to be patronized. As Boy continued tossing, the sound of the pebbles skipped across the cobblestones. It almost sounded like the sound of the clinking pebbles was keeping in time with their cadence. *It's clearer now! Listen-*

I am the
hollow man
Shiny, empty, a man tin-can

"Is that a centurion?" asked Plinius.

Damn it! I can't hear the rest. Shut up Plinius!

Plinius eyes strained at the motion beyond the spyhole. Plinius found it rather interesting that it was not unlike watching the River. A deluge of mayhem with a beautiful natural motion, nonetheless. A torrent of people desperate to get to their destinations. Carts jostled and thrashed, their drivers yelling profanity and vulgar encouragement at anyone foolish enough to impede their movements. Impediments were in ready supply. Porters strained with muscles covered in sheen sweat, wheelbarrows and backpacks and laden with bags across long poles full of stone or tools or marble or food. Bespectacled common scribes- *Blessed Concord, look how cute they are-* lesser versions of scriveners, marching determinedly to destinations unknown with ledgers clutched to their chests. Snorting draft horses stamped their feet in indignation anytime they came to a breaking halt due to the congestion, registering their displeasure with steaming piles of dung that were promptly trampled by uncaring and otherwise occupied feet. It made Plinius' head spin and he gave it a shake, trying to focus beyond the general mayhem to whatever it was that the boy had noticed.

These people are as dissimilar to magi as one could possibly be. Plinius observed how varied the people he saw were. He noticed a group of a half a dozen dwarves whipping a bundle-laden donkey who had decided at that moment to stop in the middle of the road. He chuckled to himself as they struggled to get the braying donkey moving. Most of the foot traffic passed by without a glance as a growing train of carts began to backup, noisily and colourfully letting the dwarves know what they thought of this delay. After a few minutes of vain attempts, a woman stepped forward and spoke to the dwarves. Not being able to hear them from this distance, all Plinius could do was surmise help had been offered at the wild gesticulations of the dwarves with their pleading faces. Plinius eyes widened with surprise.

Oh, that's not a human woman at all!

Dropping her hood back revealed a haughty face of high cheekbones, aquiline nose, arched brow, and chilling eyes. Most telling of all was her long, upswept, and pointed ears. The elf placed a hand on the donkey and bent over, her mouth close to the ass' ear, and after a moment the dwarves were on their way with a docile and compliant pack-beast.

"There is an elf maiden out there!" Plinius said wonderingly.

Plink! "Is that so? And you be amazed by this?"

Plinius turned to look at the boy, frowning. "I would not say amazed. Just a little surprised is all."

"Surprised?" asked Pots curiously, his intense attention not turning away from the pail. Flicking a stone, it sailed wildly off the mark and missed the pail by an embarrassing margin.

"Well, yes," Plinius replied. "They are practically extinct."

The boy nodded his head. "Yes, that they be," he agreed, a hint of sadness colouring his voice. "But there still be a large amount of them in Terrastra. A couple thousand at least."

"What! Truly?" Plinius was surprised. *Funny to think, I had never seen an elf in person until then.* No elf had ever come into his bookstore or sought out his trade. Not that anyone else ever came in his bookstore, but that was beside the point. As he thought about it for a moment, he realized that until he ran into Pots earlier, he had never seen a dwarf in or near his store either. "I was unaware."

The boy barked a sharp laugh. Plinius could feel his face warm. "What is so funny?"

"Nothing," answered Boy. Plink! "Just that the only reason there be so many elves in Terrastra is thanks to the magi."

Plinius blood ran cold, as he wondered how much this young man knew of the truth. *About what?* "What do you mean?"

"The Empire," murmured Pots, his latest pebble the worst throw yet.

Boy nodded. "With the destruction and annexation of Sil'Dorin, the Magocrats be giving them a simple choice. Leave or die. So, they left, and now be living in slum tenements along the Sapphires." This was said with no emotion that Plinius could detect.

"When did that happen?" asked Plinius, afraid of the answer.

"Before I was born," answered Boy.

"Me too," chimed in Pots.

"Oh," Plinius replied, "I had… not noticed." Boy shrugged.

"I just be supposing a magus would have to look down first to notice any common." The dwarf snorted a laugh that quickly changed to a clearing of his throat as he caught sight of Plinius looking at him.

Plinius bristled, turning his attention back to the hole in the fence. He inhaled sharply and his breath caught in his throat.

A large lictor fully encased in plate armour was standing over the elf in the middle of the road, an implacable wall of steel festooned with a billowing blue cape snapping around his plate-clad legs. The Gladia Virgum emblazoned the front of his breastplate in burnished copper that caught the ghostly light from the glow globes. Nearly two heads and a half taller than the elf- who was not short to begin with- the lictor was an imposing tower of a man. Armoured head to toe in polished steel, a blood red tabard with black bordering hung from his chest like a grand hall tapestry, the silver gauntlet of the Iron Cohort declaring his loyalties. A bronze galea mask dropped across his face had vent-tails like rows of spikes, making it look like the grinning jaw of a hungry predator. Through the openings a black scarf wrapped around his face hid any features. He wielded a large great sword in one hand with his arm outstretched, the tip planted firmly on the ground as the fullered blade reflected the ghostly light of the glow globes. In his other hand he had a sheet of paper which he thrust aggressively under the elf's nose.

One dozen lictors encircled her, while two dozen hands rested on weapons. The traffic edged its way slowly around the group, not a single word of vulgar encouragement to shove off to be heard. The elf shook her head, and whatever was said next by the steel giant, the other lictors cackled in response. A few moments later, the lictor chopped his hand down in a dismissive fashion and the elf made a not unhasty yet still serene exit in the opposite direction of where she had been going a moment earlier.

Plinius was nearly choking on his fear as the squad of lictors sauntered up to the wall blocking the mouth of the alley. *Choking on fear? That's overdoing it a bit, I think.* All that separated him from soldiers of the Iron Cohort, his hunters, was a wall of stone. Plinius felt like a weight of molten rock had dropped into his stomach. He had the overwhelming urge to void his bladder. He was conscious of his breathing. The giant lictor sat down on a barrel, leaning back onto the wall and Plinius was sure for a moment that it would explode backwards in a shower of pebbles as it took his weight. It shifted ever so slightly for a moment, then miraculously held. Plinius dared not breath, even in quiet relief. Looking back in the hole, he was slightly disappointed to find the view blocked.

"Did ya see that stupid elf bitch's face?" chortled a heavily accented and shrill voice. A chorus of laughter followed. "I tell you; this might be the worst posting in the entire Empire, but it does have its perks."

"You mean outside the Empire," answered a feminine voice.

"Whatever, you know what I mean."

"Making the miserable even more miserable, that's worth it to you, Weasel?" Asked another woman. Plinius shivered, the hairs on the back of his neck standing on end. The woman's voice was like air escaping an ancient tomb, quiet and foreboding, a timbre that brought up feelings of hopelessness and dread.

"This is the worst posting I have ever had, and I did a stint up in the Sil'Dorin camps. At least there nobody gave a rat's ass what you did to them knife-ears. Here I just swim in my own damn sweat all day while having to watch this Terrastran scum strut around like they're just as good as *me!* I got to find my entertainment where I can, and if picking on a few common sluts makes the day pass a little faster, what's so wrong with that? Even the Terrans despise their filth, and that's saying something considering what absolute bleeding hearts they are. I've busted my ass for the Emperor. I've earned my fun. What's the point in being on the winning side otherwise? Also, not my fault they make it hard on themselves."

"They make it easy, do they?" The woman did not sound convinced, or maybe she was just disinterested. Plinius found it hard to tell without being able to see her face.

"Course they do. The whole of Mir makes it easy. The Empire because they shit on 'em, and those that get shit on like to turn around and fling that shit right back at the Empire. Lucky for us, we get caught in the middle."

"So that gives us the right to harass them? I saw what your hands were doing earlier. Mayhap you're just a lecherous little gremlin."

"A compliment! Why thank you, Venem." A few snickers. "Bloody hells it gives us the right. The Empire is the winner here, and I shit on this Terran scum for making our job harder than it has to be. The council of robed bastards up in their cushy white tower can take a few lessons from the Emperor- ya hafta put a common in their place. Else they all get queer ideas about being equal to us. And if you need help understanding why that's a terrible idea, well, go head over to the Exchange this afternoon."

"Equal to us?" Venem laughed. "We're not even equal to them, you mouthy fool. Or did you get white robes when I wasn't looking? If you need proof of how little you matter to the magi, feel free to try and shop in Northmarket."

The lictors broke out in laughter before abruptly stopping.

"Gutter trash the lot of 'em." The giant spoke from his chest, a menacing rumble like an earthquake. "Bloody shame they weren't wiped clean from the face of Mir the first time."

"When yer right, yer right. The Centurion knows what I'm talkin' about," said Weasel, quick to agree, encouraged. "Can't trust 'em at all. Elf, dwarf, halfling, don't make no difference. If you aint human-"

"'If you aint human?'" The Centurion growled from somewhere deep in his expansive chest, the reverberation vibrating the wall.

"Oh, ah," stammered Weasel. "Sorry, Centurion, sorry, what I meant to say is- humans, you know, ah." His voice trailed off.

The other lictors began to laugh and pile on.

"Yah, Weasel? What's that?"

"If you ain't human what?"

"Edge take you Weasel; you never know when to shut up."

"I meant no offence, Centurion." All bravado had gone out of Weasel like dirty water from a bilge. "All's I'm saying is there's US and there's THEM."

The Centurion grunted. "You are correct on that account, lictor." He shifted his weight and the wall rocked back like it was being hit by a spring storm wind. Plinius grabbed his nose desperately to protect it from the shower of dust, fighting desperately to not sneeze. He leant back down slowly to the spyhole as he noticed the centurion's move had uncovered it once again. "A more helpful populace would be beneficial in this instance."

"Yes, exactly," concurred Weasel quickly and eagerly. "If these Terran's knew what was good for them they'd be helping us to find this mage. But good luck wishing for that."

Plinius froze, not daring to even breath. Once again, his instincts screamed out for him to run, run away as fast as he could. Turning his head so very carefully, Plinius looked back to see Pots squatting alone.

Boy was gone.

Pots opened his mouth to say something but immediately thought better of it, choosing to shrug instead, pointing his thumb back over his back. The girls continued their game as before, but no sign of Boy was evident. *The boy ran away… no, that doesn't make sense. He had a job!* Plinius could not decide if he was angrier at him for leaving, or just jealous for having got away.

"What's so special about this mage, anyways?" purred a woman. The woman- Venem, Plinius remembered from the voice- held up a piece of paper from a pouch of leaflets hanging from her belt. "Doesn't look like much to me. What a waste of paper."

Weasel snatched the paper from her hand, happy to steer the conversation. "You're right there, Ven. A fugitive scrivener? Please. What's the worst he can do? Write us a mean letter? Ha! Don't see what all the fuss is about."

The Centurion moved so quickly it took all of Plinius' resolve not to react in shock. The goliath's hand snapped forward like a viper. The giant centurion remained stock still except for his arm as he backhanded Weasel across the face with his heavy armoured gauntlet, sending the wiry man sprawling in the mud. The rest of the lictors straightened up immediately in an imitation of parade readiness as the Centurion rose to his feet.

"It is not for you to question the will of the magi, lictor. I will have no break in discipline under my command. The Iron Cohort is unbending, unbreakable. The Hall has seen fit to turn out the garrison to apprehend this enemy of the Emperor, and his will shall be carried out unquestioningly." The Centurions head turned, the black pools of the bronze galea encompassing the rest of the CONTUBERNIUMS under his command. "Is that clear?"

"Yes, Centurion!"

"Get up, Lictor."

Weasel picked himself up off the ground, blood trickling from his mouth, down his chin and matting the scraggly beard bristling from his chin. "My apologies, Centurion. I meant no disrespect to you, the Century, the Cohort, the Legion, the Hall, or the Emperor."

Waving a hand, the Centurion dipped his head towards the contrite lictor. "Irrelevant. You will be on scouring duty after our patrol for your lapse in good judgment." One of the lictors pointed up into the sky, drawing the Centurions attention. Swooping down on silent wings, a bird in the shape of a crow but made of what looked like shimmering liquid bronze perched onto the Centurions shoulder. Plinius was familiar with the creature, having seen it's like many times before flitting through the skies. It was a voidcrow, a construct thought up by the enchanters of the Magocracy to relay orders and information literally as the crow flies. The iridescent breast of the facsimile pulsed with an indigo light hidden within swirling mist. The Centurion cocked his head as the bird perched on his shoulder, its beak leaning into the giant's helmeted ear, as the message was relayed. After a moment the voidcrow seemed to fold in on itself and disappeared back to the River from whence it came, its mission complete. "Let us make haste down towards the docks. The fugitive has been spotted trying to leave on a frigate heading to Nozomi. Venem, Wetzel, take rear guard. Marcus, Gaius, take point. Move out."

As the lictors moved away at a brisk but disciplined pace, Plinius felt the knot in his stomach loosen a little. Venem chided Weasel with a clicking tongue. Weasel wiped his mouth with his sleeve as he stared with barely hidden contempt at the Centurion as he strode away. "You really need to learn to watch your mouth, Weasel."

Weasel wiped mud off his breastplate with one hand as he crushed the leaflet in his other. His face scowled at the Centurions back. "Fucking ogre. Who does he think he is?"

Venem patted Weasel on the back. "Your commanding officer, stupid. If you don't watch it, he'll string you up at moment's notice without a hint of remorse. Don't forget what he is."

Weasel scoffed. "For now. All these subhuman maggots will get what's coming to them eventually." Plinius froze as he tossed the crumpled leaflet over the wall.

"Weasel, did you actually serve up in the camps," asked Venem softly.

"Aye," spat Weasel, "Hutchinson camp."

Venem whistled. "Nasty place."

"It wasn't so bad. Let's go before I step in it any further. Scouring duty! Shit!"

As the lictors marched away, Plinius discovered he had been holding his breath. Pots had reached over and picked up the leaflet and smoothed it out on his tummy. Frowning, he turned to show it to Plinius.

"They didn' get yer eyes quite right, but it ain't thar bad a drawin'," Pots eyes scanned the rest of the paper, then looked quizzically at the magus. "I's dinnae know letters- what exactly did ye do, Plinius?"

Plinius snatched the paper out of the dwarf's hands, and with dismay he looked down at his own face plastered below a large bold script that declared WANTED. The picture was drawn by a mensetist, a magus skilled in the recreation of a person's memories as art. The Plinius looking up at him had a thicker brow, sallower cheeks, wormy lips, and a menacing scowl. Below the picture listed various crimes against the Concord and the Magistracy and a meagre reward for information concerning his whereabouts. Plinius tore the paper up in a fit of pique and let the scraps of paper drop from his fingers in a flurry as he sat down. Pots looked at him for a moment before shrugging and returning to his game of flicking pebbles.

Plink. Plinius found himself studying the dwarf, numerous questions running through his head. The silence between them stretched for a few minutes, until Plinius could not stand it anymore.

"Dwarf," began Plinius.

"'Uman," replied Pots.

Plinius inhaled sharply and exhaled slowly. "Pots," he began again, "I was wondering if I could pose an inquiry."

"Huh?" asked Pots.

"Can I ask you a question?"

"Oh!" exclaimed the dwarf, pleasantly surprised. "Yeh, sure, *me* boy-o! Ask away!"

"Back there- in the midmarket- when those, ah, students were accosting you," started Plinius gingerly.

"Oh, yah, mm-hmm mm-hmmm," remembered Pots.

"Does that thing, ah, happen often?"

Pots sat back, a thoughtful look on his face. "Like, getting' caf dumped on *me?* Nae, that dinnae 'appenin' all thar often. Usually it's a kick in th' bum, or some poop flung on ye." The dwarf shrugged. "Y'know, jus' the normal stuff. No big deal-o."

"Blessed Concord!"

"Beg yeh pardon? Bleating concourse? W'at's a blasted conch cord?"

Plinius could not have been more shocked if the Emperor had shown up with Merlin for a game of Minions of Dublain. *Minions of Dublain! What a great game! I've read the rulebook cover to cover more times than I can count. Never had anyone to play with though… unless you count Hand.*

"Pots… you do not know… what the Blessed Concord is?"

Pots scratched his head. "Cannae say I's 'ave, boy-o. Is it an Imperial thing?"

Plinius shook his head in response, muttering some choice words about the state of education in Terrastra. Pots went back to throwing his pebbles, cheering happily when the next one hit home. Plinius lost himself in thought. The girls singing their haunting melody echoed down the alley. *Hollow Man… Hollow Man…*

Boy returned shy of a half an hour later. Plinius stood up and did his best to loom over the youth, trying to do his best impression of the Centurion. "How nice of you to return! Where in the bloody hells did you go to?"

"We be having a clear path forward now," the boy's face stretched into a beaming grin that Plinius could not help but find incredibly endearing if not a little annoying. "A helpful citizen has let the lictors know a certain fugitive has been spotted near Drake Bay attempting to board a ship."

Plinius frowned. Pots let out a huge laugh which he quickly stifled and patted the boy on the back as he beamed. "Well done boy-o!"

"Yes. Ah, well. Very good." Plinius did his best to straighten out his robe. "We should get going then. Let us move out."

The boy arced an eyebrow. "Oh yes, let us do that Master Magus. Follow me, stay close and try not to look like a certain someone on every wanted poster from here to the Northhill." The boy walked away without a second look behind him. Pots followed quickly after, motioning the grandmagus excitedly to come along. Plinius took up the rear, scowling.

As they approached the exit to the alley, Plinius slowed for a moment as they passed the skipping girls. *Oh good! Let's listen closely.* Their smiling faces belied their words.

I am the
Hollow Man
Shiny, empty, a man tin-can
When you sleep
I then creep
As I caress the shadows deep
It's you I follow
Your dream I swallow
Maybe then, I won't be hollow

Plinius shuddered as he ran past, as if ghostly fingers had just caressed him down his spine. One of the girls, a small waif with dirty blonde hair wearing a sackcloth dress, smiled and waved as they ran by. Plinius found himself responding in kind automatically. *A simple gesture. Random kindness, even this small, always lifted my heart.* The girl covered her mouth with her elbow as her smile twisted into a hacking coughing fit. The other girls resumed their rhyme as the boy, the magus and the dwarf ran into the murky fog that had started to spill down from the upper Sapphires, a mix of water vapour and various soot and ashes belched from the multitudinous industries crammed into the Tradebasin. Shadows shifted and cavorted alongside them as Plinius followed Pots and the dwarf followed Boy. A loud splashing sound nearby startled Plinius, who hurried his pace.

The glow globes were like buoys on a murky sea, points of light strung in a line that guided their way. *Not entirely sure what street this is… maybe Baskins? That density of the smog… it's thick, but I don't smell any shit, so we must be pretty high above the Runs. I'm going to guess we're on Ross St.* Boy dodged between the points of light, weaving, bobbing between the illuminated beacons. They were not on a main street for long, a course of action of which Plinius heartily approved of at the time.

The fog was so thick down here that Plinius nearly missed them turning into a side passage. He hesitated at the mouth, a stone staircase disappearing after a few steps down into an impenetrable darkness. He looked around, his fear holding his feet in place. *I'm sure I was merely being cautious. I am a grandmagus. I do not get scared.* He so desperately wished to cast light and see what the forbidding passage held. He did a double take as the fog twisted along the street, twirling like a dancer on a tall wooden glow post, the light scattering across it in a kaleidoscope of shapes. A pale face with black pools for eyes reared up in the smog, a malign spectre that Plinius cowered before. A pitiful whimper escaped from his throat as he turned, fleeing after Boy and Pots into the darkness. *Jumping at shadows. That is embarrassing. Perhaps fear had, ever so slightly, grasped me in its clutches.*

"Plinius?" whispered the darkness from somewhere ahead as he very, very carefully stepped down an invisible staircase blindly.

"Boy? Where are you?" asked Plinius, a tremble in his throat. *A tremble? Barely a tremor.*

"What do you mean? I'm right here!"

"It's pitch black in here!" *I can't see shit either!*

"Oh, shit… I be forgetting," swore Boy.

"Ferget wha'?" asked Pots in a hushed tone.

"Our esteemed friend here be having no dark vision."

A rustling sound and a hand reached out, folding itself into Plinius palm firmly. Plinius flinched back from the contact, but the Boy's handhold remained firm. Plinius relaxed. *Preposterous. We are a grandmagus! As if a commoner could provide any sort of comfort. Laughable.* Plinius relaxed, if just a little bit, and mostly due to his own mastery of his emotions. *That's better.*

"Relax, grandmagus," said Boy calmly, "I be right here. Follow me, we will be out of this little stygioque soon."

Stygioque! How strange for him to use that word! I'd expect it from an academic, not from a commoner.

Why not from a commoner?

Well, you know. They're not very educated.

Is that so. Every commoner is dumb?

Don't put words into my mouth. I think most commoners are intelligent. Intelligence and education are two vastly different things though. You would know this, were you as intelligent AND educated as I.

Oh, please then, Plinius, could you educate me?

Naturally, Tales. To share knowledge is the will of the River. I would be happy to share my wealth of knowledge with you. I have met ignorant savants and I have met educated morons. Ignorant morons are plenty across Mir, and educated savants are sadly in slim supply, even in Terrastra. I am but one of a handful in Terrastra.

There's that Pliny humility.

I am humble! It's not boastful to state facts. It would be dishonest to downplay my inherent gifts.

Hoo boy. Whatever, just get to the point.

Don't rush me. Here, let me take a page out of your book, and I *will tell* you *a story. There is an ore called ripanulite. It has the unique properties to nullify the River in its proximity. Nasty stuff, it was-*

Stop. I know what ripanulite is.

Do you? Curious and curiouser. Well good, it makes this story easier to impart if I do not have to explain everything.

Bully for you.

Bully? Indeed, bully! Ok, where was I?

One day an archmagus from Aliston was making a pilgrimage to the holy Codeci Oratorium in Terrastra. All he had upon him were the clothes on his back and a large sack of rare tomes from the Imperial Archives on loan to the Lyceum. After a while, staring at the passing landscape full of commoners lazing around in wheatfields and rutting in orchards proved uninteresting, so the Archmagi cast a spell to automate his motion while he could study some of his tomes.

This proved so successful, the archmagus managed to read two whole books before his spell came to an abrupt halt- it would seem that during his repast, the archmagi had steered off course into a wetland teeming with ripanulite. With utter dismay he found himself wet up to the knees, a large, deep and fast-moving river ahead, an obstacle in his path. As luck would have it, a local common man came passing by in a flat pole boat.

Commoner to the rescue!

Don't interrupt.

"My good fellow," called the archmagus, "any chance you could kindly take me across the river?"

"Sure can," drawled the man.

As they proceeded towards the river, the archmagus settled down and opened another book to past the time. Soon the archmagus became impatient, asking the boatman how long it would be.

"I aint know suh, aints got nope idea," replied the man.

Now that is offensive.

"Blessed Concord!" exclaimed the archmagus, "Have you no education good ser? Your grammar is atrocious. Did you not attend school?"

The boatman spit over the side. "Nope. Aint had nope need for nope school."

What is with the 'nopes'? Do people actually say that? I'm assuming it means no?

The archmagus sniffed at him, going back to his book.

"Then I dare say you've wasted your life, my good ser."

As they approached the centre of the river, a large storm came crashing down upon them. As the boat took on more water, it began to sink.

"We's gonna have to swim!" yelled the boatman.

"I don't know how to swim!" replied the archmagus in a panic.

"Well, looks like you've just wasted your life then!"

Is that it?
Yes.
Kind of a downer, isn't it?
Do you get the point?
Nope.
Be serious please.
That you like to make up stories that never, ever happened?
Nope! I mean, no! It's a parable, moron.
I get that. The moral alludes me.
Think on it. It doesn't matter if it was true or not.
Can I continue with the actual story?
Fine.

They came to a stop, and Plinius squeezed Boy's hand reflexively.

"Just a moment, mage," whispered Boy, "There be a stash around here somewhere. Ah!"

"Magus," corrected Plinius absently.

Still completely blind, Plinius strained his ears to listen to what was happening. A grinding vibration of heavy stone being moved followed by the clicking of a lock being opened. Boy made a tiny noise of pleased discovery.

"Here, put this on. Be handing the robe when you be done."

Plinius fumbled in the dark, accepting the bundle of clothes passed to him by Boy. Taking off his robe, he opened the small bag at his waist and stuffed it within, meeting no resistance despite their disparate sizes. He pulled on linen pants that were too loose and donned a wool sweater that itched his chest terribly.

"These don't fit all that well," said Plinius to Boy, or at least where he thought he was standing.

"Don't worry, it won't be long now until I be getting you where we be going."

They continued long enough for Plinius to become completely disoriented. All he knew for certain was that they were going downhill, but whether that was southwards, eastwards, or westwards he could not tell. For the umpteenth time that day Plinius's inner monologue turned to a monotonous dirge of sorrowful self-pity. *Can you blame the poor guy? He- we- me? I was terribly out of my element. I had never experienced such conditions in my life. It's fine to have some pity; I had never had it so rough.* His anxiety was making him near delirious- a few times he had to stifle a scream, either from something brushing up against his leg, or a strange chittering coming from some invisible side tunnel. The air quality grew more and more repulsive each step they took, as well as the sound of rushing water growing louder and louder by the second.

The world lit up from impenetrable darkness to shadowy gloom as they finally stepped out of the winding paths of the warren into a vast gorge. Plinius could make out windows, staircases, one room homes grafted onto derelict buildings, patches and repairs and structural additions all done with reclaimed materials. Columns stained with smoke over the centuries, pulleys and clotheslines, flags, downspouts, gargoyles, graffiti, water towers, glow globes; all this and more looked as if it had been thrown at the east and west slopes of the valley to see what would stick. This continued for centuries until the Tradebasin had become an urban canyon. Each side was a towering escarpment, jumbled collages that bordered this kilometre wide space. They soared upwards towards the sky at an angle just shy of a true ninety degrees, disappearing into a haze of light and smoke thousands of metres in the air. That air, despite still being quite foul, was clearer down here visually than when they were nearer the forges, more of a light mist than a smog. The source of the howling water was now evident, as Plinius looked down and ahead of him with growing, horrified disgust.

Chapter Five

The Runs & Ruins

Water churned and frothed as it made its way down the Runs, a constant flow of black, brown, green, and yellow oily water moving down the wide channel that cut through the city all the way towards Drake Bay. Plinius could not decide what was more offensive, the beating his ears were taking from the roaring water or the assault on his nostrils. *Cronus be good, I thought the alleyway was bad.* The alley was like a ladies perfumed parlour compared to the rank aqueduct of fetid filth that now coursed before him.

"Edge take me! It's horrible!"

"Yes, it be," agreed Boy, "Your first time running the Runs?"

"Running? Excuse me?"

Boy nodded his head downstream towards a group of people queueing where the edge of the paved street ended in a steep drop to the splashing water below. Each of them was in the process of readying themselves and each other, checking clasps and tightening buckles on the large packs they all wore across their backs. The porters nearest the end of the line looked tense and focused, awaiting their turn.

As they made there way over, the relief Plinius had at leaving the claustrophobia of the dark tunnel was replaced with a growing anxiety as he watched what they were now lining up for. His slippered foot mere centimetres away from the edge, he leaned over ever so slightly and peeked below. A fifteen-metre drop ended in the most disgusting churning soup of waste that the poor pampered magus had ever laid eyes on. A wave of nausea and vertigo washed over him, and he placed a hand on Pots shoulder to steady himself. He gagged with abject horror and revulsion as he spied a dead body circling through the current, crashing into a floating wheel-less wheelbarrow, all the while being swarmed by at least a hundred and fifty heads of rotting cabbage. *It seems we have found the city's garbage chute. Wait, is it on fire?* What Plinius at first mistook for thick clouds of smoke were in fact swarms of fat, hairy runflies, billions of them, literally swarming down in the trench, so thick in some places that Plinius could not see and make out what had so garnered their interest. This continued for as far as the eye could see in both directions. The Runs cut through the middle of the city from northeast to southwest, splitting it in twain. All Plinius saw was an infected and polluted aorta running through the heart of the city.

"But… but…" stammered Plinius.

Boy, tightening his belt and checking his pockets, looked up at the magus. "But what, mage?"

"I knew what this was… the Runs. But I never uh, had the chance to come this close before. From the Lyceum it always looked so… beautiful. Like a ribbon…" he trailed off, his eyes fixating on the body as it tumbled down a drop and out of sight.

Plinius snapped out of his trance and found Boy looking at him appraisingly. The magus' face reddened with a shame that had been hiding somewhere within him. Boy reached out a hand and squeezed Plinius' shoulder.

"It do be unfortunate- the rains be making the Runs run dirty, as the commoners be saying. Usually there's a hundred or so bridges here, but the rains be making things run fast. Don't be worrying though, ser," reassured Boy, "There be nothing to it. Thousands of people be doing it every day. I chose this one on purpose- this be the Cockatrice. One of the easier, more popular crossings. Not like those."

He pointed further down the Runs, running down all the way to Drake Bay. Plinius could see a dozen more much smaller and narrower bridges made of what looked like sticks from up here. As he watched, a person far in the distance vanished. Plinius could not tell if they had fallen or if it was just a trick of his eye.

"Are you serious?" asked Plinius incredulously, "What about that looks easy!?"

"Well, you be seeing now," he said, inclining his head to the front of the line.

Plinius turned as a young man stepped up to the bridge.

A roar of cheers rose above the sound of the Runs. Plinius looked up in surprise, noticing for the first time the thousands of onlookers. They crowded on balconies and crudely built mezzanines. A large hole in a part of the western wall looked as if it had been blasted in by a large explosion, the recess exposing a ribcage of a grandstand brimming with raucous commoners cheering wildly. A large platform jutted out from the western wall all the way to the edge where the crossing started. Atop the platform, a large group of men and women congregated around a large purple illusion of betting odds hovering above their heads. Money was being thrown around as bets were placed with a separate group of rather fierce looking characters. *That one- the one with the bowler hat. She undoubtedly has orcish blood in her veins! Look at the prominent jaw, the musculature. I truly can't believe it. I thought they had been…*

Been what?

Nothing. I cannot remember.

"What are all these people doing?" asked Plinius.

"Ye nevah watched the runners?" exclaimed Pots disbelievingly, "Best game to watch in all'a Terrastra!"

"Game?" Plinius was confused. *Confused? Pish-posh. I think you're editorializing.*

"People be watching the porters run the Cockatrice," explained Boy, "Runs Running, they be calling it. Only when she's running dirty. Commoners, even some magi, be coming down here to be betting on the runners. Very, very popular game. There's other bridges that run it, but this is by far the most popular."

"I see that it is popular. There is a lot of people here, Boy," said Plinius in a careful hush, low enough for the people waiting in line with them could not overhear, "Maybe a less… visible route… might be in our best interest?"

"I be having considered that already," admitted Boy, "But I be believing this is our best bet. I be needing to get you to your destination, and this be the safest, quickest way to cross. Time be of the essence. Just be keeping your head down, and do not be drawing attention to yourself."

"If time is of the essence," began Plinius, casually as he could, "I have a certain scroll in…" Plinius trailed off, Boy's expression telling him what he thought of that idea.

Plinius tried to wrestle his paranoia down, but now he felt as if people were watching him. Looking around at the quality of character around him, Plinius began to tremble involuntarily.

A tired and sweaty looking magus in tattered pink robes sat on an overturned milkcrate near the bet takers. *Look at this pathetic wretch. No wonder he never moved past the pink robe- a magus needs to have pride in his appearance.* A burly looking dwarf with metal studs pierced through his brow stood over him, an axe dangling from a rope around his waist, peaking out from behind black facial hair oiled and braided into a long and voluminous beard. A frail and diminutive man with pale thin skin and wet spaghetti-like hair madly scribbled on a slate with a piece of chalk, stopping only to peek into a magnifying scope in front of him, the viewfinder fixed on the spot where the next porter waited for his turn across the Runs. As the next man stepped up onto the landing platform, the wiry man wrote down a new number, handing it to the weary magus. With a heavy sigh, the dishevelled pueri read the slate and pulled out a small scroll from a pouch on the ground next to his foot. Incanting the spell, the scroll disintegrated into purple dust and the illusion above him changed to the new updated odds. The crowd went into a betting frenzy. *The thought of the River being used in such a base manner turns my stomach.*

The porter that had stepped up onto the landing platform reached out as the runner from the other side came bounding over the bridge. A helping hand was proffered, and they grasped hands as the incoming runner finished the final stretch. The porter who had arrived stopped and took a quick breath and wiped his forehead. He then proceeded to run off into the warren of side streets Plinius had just emerged from.

The crowd cheered and Plinius turned his attention back to the runner. He was a smallish Xeijpangian man, no more than a metre and a half in height, but the burden on his back soared to well over an extra metre above that. A quick glance at the odds said the crowd did not see a successful crossing in his future.

A chant began to echo across the urban canyon.

"Rickety! Rickety! Rickety!"

"What are they saying?" wondered Plinius aloud.

"Rickety," answered Pot eagerly, excited to know something the grandmagus did not, "Jus' a tradition, y'know. Is jus' what we call the woody bridges. Gets th' people in th' game! Da says he coined th' term back in th' day, on accounts of how rickety th' bridges cannae be, ye ken?"

Plinius nodded, not seeing the point, nor believing the outlandish claim about the dwarf's 'Da', which Plinius had deduced by this point was the dwarven version of father. *Well that's obvious, isn't it?* This was the fourth possible translation for the word 'Da' that Plinius had hypothesized since meeting Pots in the alley, but the one he felt most confident about. *Edge take me.*

Children swarmed out of the warrens at the call of the crowd, as if someone had kicked an anthill. They joined in the chant with sing song cherubic voices. They crowded the edge of the Runs, dangling their feet over the sides in rows like doves on a tree branch. The chant died suddenly, a hush falling over the crowd as the porter took his first step onto the Cockatrice.

The Cockatrice was a bridge made of toothpicks and string. Swaying planks twenty centimetres wide and three metres long hung from hemp ropes dangling from a long ancient chain that was attached on the west-wall, somewhere so high up Plinius had trouble seeing where it began. The iron chain ended halfway across the Runs (a quarter of a kilometre Plinius estimated) at an old, crumbling, wet, mossy spire of mortar and stone rising from the thrashing viscous trash-syrup, looking like an ear of corn that been sloppily gnawed to the cob. The shape of the chain was like a slender curved neck that resembled the letter 'J'. Trash had caught on the debris at the base of the tower and had formed a small island, spreading out towards the eastern side of the Run, the only point down in the trench of relative calm as far as the eye could see. An excess of wooden logs made up the supports for the second half of the bridge, sticking out like quills from the roiling trash below. It looked stable enough to walk on, mostly due to the contrast of the fast-moving water on the opposite side of the tower. Taken as a whole, Plinius had to admit the bridge's name was apropos. *If I squint a little and fuzz it up, it most definitely takes the shape of its namesake! Commoners can be so clever.*

The bridge planks swung back and forth like a metronome, and the porter started to not so much run as dance across the first part of the Cockatrice. The ancient iron chain soaring above him was made of links the size of an ogre, metre thick tempered pure iron, forged in an eon past by the forge-masters of ancient Kharza-Lok, greatest of the fabled Twelve Mountain Forges of Dwarvenkind, gifted to the city of Terrastra as a symbol of eternal friendship, and there was no doubt in Plinius' mind that it would snap as soon as he stepped onto the crossing. *You never know. These things happen.* It showered orange snow down onto the runner as the rope loops sawed into the rusty outer layer of the chain. Each step he took set the planks swinging, and it was only with excellent timing that he could save himself from a wet ending. He bounded along the planks, maintaining his balance by steadily continuing forward at what Plinius was certain was a reckless pace.

The children along the Runs gasped as the porter's foot skidded on one of the planks, his arm cartwheeling as he tried to grab one of the ropes suspending the plank he had slipped on. He had just barely managed to grab it and regain his footing when he was off again, easily crossing the next few planks and reaching the halfway point over the raging waters. A round of applause and a few words of encouragement rained down on him from the gallery of people spectating. The children near Plinius set his nerves on edge with their delighted squealing.

"Well, that's the hard part done, right? Doesn't look that bad," said Plinius.

"A skellion says he takes a dip," wagered Boy.

"Seriously? Not an elf's chance in Aliston," guffawed Plinius. A few of the other porters in line shot him dirty looks at the idiom he had chosen, but Plinius did not notice. *I noticed.*

"I accept your challenge, Boy,"

The porter took a breath and adjusted the straps on his shoulder as he eyed the long sinuous and branching path of planks stretching from pole to pole. *Is this what passes for commoner engineering? What a deathtrap.* The wood used was from a variety of sources, different types, colours, stains and cuts all present. Some looked as if they had been there for decades, others might have been slapped up and hammered in this morning. The porter stepped out onto the first plank tentatively. Unlike the first part of the Cockatrice, the porter took a steady and measured gait as he worked his way across the rickety bridge, his feet picking his path carefully while his eyes were fixed not on the other side, nor at his feet, but rather upstream, furiously scanning the surface.

"Ox!" yelled a voice in dire warning, the urgency echoing back and forth across the Runs, carrying clearly by pure luck across the water.

The porter froze as a thousand rapt faces leaned forward while holding their breath. Plinius was confused for a moment as to what was transpiring, until Pots pointed a finger and yelled out.

"Spotted!" he screamed excitedly. A gasp rippled through the crowd as they followed the dwarf's finger.

Plinius was a step behind, trying to process what was happening in real time. Then he saw it- a bloated carcass of what Pots said was an ox. It rolled like a barrel bounding downhill, flipping, and flopping, a wrecking ball of bone and thick rotting meat as it was bashed along by the current's relentless push. With a dawning realization Plinius began to see the peril the porter was in.

"He's going to fall!" yelled out Plinius.

Some of the crowd around him broke out into laughter. One voice yelled out "Here's hoping!"

Plinius looked back at the ox carcass, barrelling down towards the Cockatrice and the porter. The porter hesitated, and that sealed his fate.

If he had started moving at the first warning, or waited for a transfer, he could have made it.

Excuse me?

Classic Mendoza defence. Remember? From the world cup against Vokgorod?

Against Vokgorod? What the bloody hell are you talking about?

I... Run Running? The NRRL. Great sport.

Sport? Why are you talking about hunting? Plinius, are you ok?

I'm just fine. I just get... flashes? Memories get kind of jumbled here and there. Sorry, I did not intend to cause a disruption. I apologize for the intrusion.

Oh... ah, thanks, Plinius.

The ox stampeded through the trash marsh, nothing in its way slowing it down even slightly. The surface Plinius had thought was sturdy was just an illusion- the undercurrent strong as the rest of the Runs. The porter tried at the last moment to save himself, jumping in a wild, desperate attempt to an adjacent plank. The ox crashed into the poles with an ear-rending blast. The plank bridge he had been standing on did not stand a chance. The pole snapped in two, tumbling down into the runs and dragging another pole down with it. The porter, having missed his target by a foot, smacked face first into the corner of the plank. His limp body plummeted into the water below as a chorus of jeers accompanied it.

"Cronus save me," choked Plinius.

"It was, ah, his first day," said Boy, "You'll be fine."

"It's my first day!"

"Good! You will be having beginner's luck then."

"I suspect that is not true, Boy," said Plinius.

"He sucked, Pliny, dinnae worry 'bout it," said Pots with a dismissive jerking motion.

"What do you know about it?" said Plinius acidly.

"A bit, thar's fer sure," replied Pots genially, "I've run th' Cockatrice, oh, a dozen times at least. The smaller ricketies at least a hundred times."

Plinius stared at the dwarf as if he had just sprouted wings. He looked at

Boy for his take and was doubly surprised to see him nod his head slightly after a moment's consideration. *Well, it's not that surprising. Pots isn't… the freshest mandrake in the reagent jar if you catch my drift. I imagine his fundamental bestial desire for self-preservation is suitably tampered to a degree that it makes this activity seem like jolly good fun.*

"This is absolute madness! Why would anyone do this!?"

"Magi are an impatient lot," explained Boy, "These porters are undoubtedly carrying scrolls, reagents, alchemical equipment, artifacts, and such. High risk, high reward."

Plinius did not answer, although feeling personally aggrieved by Boy's comment.

The bowler wearing woman stomped up towards the line of porters waiting to cross, easily a full head taller than the next tallest person. She bellowed at them in a teasing voice, "Alright then me boy-os, who be up fer a little Run Running? Winner goes home with quarter of the take!" She walked down the line, inspecting and goading them into volunteering for the next round of the game. Most of the men and women ignored her or declined as indifferently as they could. As she walked up to Plinius, she started to laugh.

"Oi! Looker this 'ere guppy!" she chortled, "Ye be the definition of a longshot, kutty. Ye make it 'cross, we'll be rich as Alistonians."

"Kutty," said Boy, stepping up beside Plinius, "Slang for a greenhorn. A newbie. Fresh fish."

The woman started howling with laughter. "Edge take me, you bastard! Oh-"

"Not interested in running, miss," barked Boy, surprising Plinius with its severity. The woman did not miss a beat.

"Nor would I take ye, kutty," teased the woman, slapping him on the back with a sly wink, "Too scrawny for me likings, boy-o."

One of the other men behind them in line finally spoke up. The woman grabbed his hand and lifted his arm high in the air. The crowd cheered as the runner's face and the opening odds bloomed above the pueri, who was wincing as he took a swig from a small flask.

"What was that?" asked Plinius.

"It was nothing," replied Boy.

"It most certainly was not nothing. Do you know that lady?"

Boy's jaw clenched. "Forget it, mage."

Plinius chewed his lip. "Magus. Why don't we take one of the three bigger bridges? The stone ones?"

A cry of boos and cheers went up as the runner from the opposite side missed a step on the swaying planks. His fall did not even make a splash, his body folding backwards into a taco as it broke on a passing log. Plinius' dry throat hurt as he tried to swallow.

Boy looked to all the world as if he were waiting in line for soup. "That would not be good. When the Runs are running, the bridges be the home for turtles. We would be sitting ducks. Not to mention at least two centuries worth of soldiers split between the three will be checking all traffic. I won't be herding you like a sheep to the lictors. We be needing to be wolves. One pack. You be needing to trust me, Plinius."

Plinius stared at him with tight lips. "I'm uncertain," began Plinius, "if you are being serious or mocking me."

"Mocking you!" exclaimed Boy, completely sincerely, "What would be giving you that idea?"

"That was a lot of animal cliches at once."

"I suppose it was," agreed Boy, "I like animals."

"I do as well," concurred Plinius awkwardly, "but nonetheless, I still must protest over this course of action."

"Duly noted. Plinius- trust me."

Plinius sniffed. "I trust Anatoli. He sent me to you. That is the extent of my trust in you."

Boy shrugged at this. "I will do my job. You do yours."

The line inched forward every five minutes or so as the next runner began his run once the way was cleared, each side taking turns one for one. For the most part a small fraction did not make it. Plinius was very impressed when an elven porter made the Run across, gliding as if on air and not once appearing to be in any sort of danger. He did not grab the waiting runner's hand, nor was one offered. Without breaking stride, the elf bounded off the bridge and onto the pavement, running off as a few muttered words along the lines of "knife-ear scab" rang out weakly in his wake.

"Shit!"

Plinius looked up at Boy in alarm. With a nod of his head, Boy motioned back upstream towards the northeast. Plinius turned and his hopes sank.

A glinting centipede of steel marched inexorably downhill towards them. Two dozen soldiers of the Empire, either halberds held high, or hatchets clenched in their hands. At the head was the unmistakable gigantic stature, easily identifiable even from this distance, of the centurion from earlier. Walking close beside him was a blue-robed superior. *He is channelling- I can see the River shimmering around him.*

Plinius turned in a panic to Boy. "We are undone!"

"Calm down, Plinius," suggested Boy urgently, "Let me think."

"Think!?" screamed Plinius, and the other runners and spectators started to turn towards them as they noticed the commotion. Boy motioned emphatically at him to quiet down, but Plinius was becoming manic. His hand pulled open his pouch and began rooting around. "I have a scroll here, that will take care-"

"No! Cronus damn it!" Plinius was taken aback by Boy's frustration. "How many times do I have to tell you? Do not be using no magic! We need to go. Now!" Boy began to push Plinius and Pots up onto the platform, the mention of magic setting everyone within earshot muttering.

The runner coming from the east-side almost tripped up at his confusion at seeing three men waiting for them. Boy pulled him off and pushed him firmly out of their way.

"Ok then," he said, pulling the grandmagus and the dwarf into a huddle, "Pots, you are going to be leading, ok? Show the mage here how it be done. Plinius, you will go next, and I will be right behind you. No magic!"

"I heard you the first time," snapped Plinius grumpily, then his voice cracked, "Boy, Pots, I don't think I can do this."

"You can, and you will," said Boy, his voice hard as the iron chain dangling above them.

"Ye cannae do it, Plinius, ser!" said Pots reassuringly, giving Plinius a small punch on the shoulder, "Yer a mage! Ye can do anything!"

Plinius laughed, not as hollowly as he meant to. "Magus, Pots. Thank you for the vote of confidence in my abilities; if only what you say were so," he patted the dwarf on his back, "but I thank you for the encouragement nonetheless."

As their heads were pressed together in conversation, the stout black-haired dwarf from the platform walked up to them, putting his hands on his hips with his fingers massaging the peened bronze pommel of his axe. "Eh! What in the bleedin' hells is goin' on here, kutty? Ye holdin' up the game, boy-o's," He glanced at Pots, giving him a respectful nod as they exchanged some words of honoured clan greeting in dwarvish.

Boy crouched down at the edge of the platform, speaking earnestly with the rough-looking dwarf. "Dunger, I'm porting a package. We need to get across before our crow-friends get here."

The dwarf, Dunger, turned and saw the lictors and centurion pushing their way towards the Cockatrice. The dwarf growled and spit on the ground. "Well, ain't this a predictable change of entertainment. I was boring myself stupid watchin' the kutties," he cocked one eye back up to Boy, "We got it. Terrastran strong, brother."

"Terrastran strong," sighed Boy in relief, "Thank you, Dunger. Meet us at home later."

The black bearded dwarf nodded and ran back towards his gang of gamblers. The efficiency and speed at which Dunger, the thin man, the pueri, the half-orc and the rest disappeared into the nearby Warrens was astonishing. *They've clearly had experience running from the law.*

"Pots, go, now!" commanded Boy.

The smiling dwarf did not hesitate, walking out on to the platform as if he was going for a leisurely walk. His feet never missed a plank, his body never shifted or jerked to maintain balance. Before Plinius knew it, his diminutive companion was across to the centre tower.

"Edge take me!" whispered Plinius, his voice cracking.

"See? It be as easy as a morning stroll," said Boy confidently, "Off you go!"

"What!" blubbered Plinius, looking down as the corpse of some animal was dashed against the wall of the Runs, exploding into a stew of viscera. "I- I- I- can't! There- there's no way!" Plinius felt tears welling up in his eyes.

Boy grabbed him by the shoulders, looking into his eyes.

"Plinius," he said, and Plinius for the first time in his life stopped himself and truly listened to a common, "You can do this. You must do this. I know you can. The alternative is to die, mage."

"Magus," whispered Plinius.

"Magus. Grandmagus," emphasized Boy, "You can do this. Commoners do it every day. Can you not be rising to the challenge that a common be doing each and every day?" he asked this, and at any other time a regular magi would probably incinerate him for the implication. Plinius only felt grateful. "The first step is the hardest," Boy continued, "But I believe you can do it. But if my belief in you be not enough motivation, feel free to look north."

Plinius followed his direction. The lictors disciplined lines had slightly fallen apart but were still making forward ground. The children that had been raptly attentive to the game along the Runs had stood up en masse and mobbed the soldiers as if this had been rehearsed to perfection, pawing at their waists, begging for spare lyons or skellions. It was like the sucking muck of a bog, clinging to their legs and slowing their advance to a crawl.

"Now!" urged Boy. Plinius bit his lip, blinked his eyes, prayed to Cronus, and took his first step onto the Cockatrice. Everything around him dampened to background noise, and despite the overwhelming fear gripping his heart, his focus narrowed in scope to the half-kilometre path ahead of him. *Here we go.*

The swaying planks were far more stable than Plinius would have assumed from his spectating. He transferred his weight in full to the first plank, and it swung out slightly, his weight realigning the planks centre of balance. His arms stretched out above his head; his grip taut on the support ropes that held up the swinging planks. *Edge take me! Plinius don't look down!* The plank rocked back and forth, feeling entirely too precarious for Plinius liking. He bit his tongue hard, a desperate attempt to focus his mind. He could hear Boy dimly encouraging him to move, but Plinius' body refused to move at anything but its own pace.

Another step forward. Then another. *Oh, this doesn't seem so bad.* Plinius confidence grew with each step he took. Pots was already at the midpoint tower, looking back at Plinius while wildly gesticulating his limbs in encouragement.

One in front of the other, old boy. Plinius, unlike the runners before him, moved forward on each plank with steady determination and carefully placed steps. He did not lose a handgrip on the ropes once. *Three points of contact! Slow and steady! He's doing it! This is commoners' cake! Go Plinius!*

Plinius' foot slipped, his toes not finding purchase on the plank before him, swinging erratically from a chance breeze. He could dimly hear the crowd gasp and jeer as his body went almost horizontal, his other foot still pushing hard against the previous foothold which swung backwards when his weight fully transferred to his back foot. A dozen spells that could remedy the situation flicked through his mind, all easily incanted for one of Plinius' skill. In a moment of supreme physical will that until now had remained dormant his entire life, Plinius' arms burned with exertion as he forced himself to stay upright. He took a deep breath to steady himself, his face looking down at the swirling waters and roiling clouds of flies.

A moment's thought and he envisioned a way out of his predicament. Tightening his grip on the support ropes he lifted his foot. The crowd gasped as Plinius dangled above the Runs, the plank swinging back to a neutral position below him. No sooner than it did, Plinius dropped his feet and sprang forward, sailing through the air to rest stably on the next plank like a cat. He could not help but feel a little pride rear up in his heart as the Runs exploded in cheers. *If they had known I was one of the magi, they would have booed until I split my skull open on the trash below.*

A few more careful steps, and Plinius gladly grasped Pot's outstretched hand as he haltingly made his way across the final stretch of the iron chain walkway.

"Way t' go ser! I knew ye could do it!" cheered Pots as he pounded the magus on the back. Plinius smiled at the dwarf, looking back towards the side they had just left from, his smile faltering at what he saw.

The lictors had evidently grown tired of the youthful impediment in their path. Even from a quarter kilometre away Plinius could see the lictors forcibly clearing the children out of the way with the pommels of their weapons. The wailing of injured children echoed across the water, quickly drowned out by the angry screams of the commoners, all interest in the Runs running forgotten.

Boy reached the centre tower. The old platform of crumbled stone and thick timber was barely large enough to have all three of them occupying it at the same time.

"I could destroy the bridge behind us with a word," offered Plinius.

"No!" both of his compatriots replied at the same time.

"You be wanting to confirm their suspicions?" demanded Boy, "They will know exactly who you are the moment you dip a finger in the River!"

"Ye can't blow up the Cockatrice!" lamented Pots, "It's fun!"

"Fine, I know, it was just a suggestion," grumbled Plinius, desperately trying to maintain a modicum of distance between his body and the others. This proved futile on the crowded landing.

"Pots, go now!" commanded Boy.

The dwarf, to his credit, did not balk or hesitate at the order. Plinius would later swear that the dwarf had chosen his path completely at random, while Pots would say it was his inherent skill and instinct that led him across so easily. The truth, regardless of whether Plinius or Pots was correct, was that the simple pot cleaning dwarf would cross the ricketies of the Cockatrice in record time. If anyone had been paying attention to Pots instead of the chaos erupting around them at that moment, it would have been a

runnings record that could have stood for nearly a century. Unfortunately for Pots, no one was watching.

What the people of the Tradebasin were watching was the Iron Cohort unleashed upon them. It was standard practice for any Imperial force in Terrastra to steer well clear of the Tradebasin, it being decided by the Hall a long time before that the situation was untenable along the Runs. Any attempted enforcement among the dregs of unenforceable commoners was an unwise allocation of resources. This day, however, a manhunt for a certain magus had pushed the lictors into places they had never been ordered or bothered to patrol before. This was, not that anyone present cared for the fact, the first time a company of lictors had approached anywhere near the Cockatrice in the years since the signing of the Compromise.

It was a perfect recipe for disaster.

The riot began as Pots stepped onto the rickety. While he was leaving the mid-way tower, one of the more zealous lictors decided that the crowd had become too hostile. Lashing out his hatchet, the lictor split the skull open of a teenage boy who had merely been pushed into his path by happenstance. His father, who had taken a day off from working in a tannery to bring his son to the Runnings, immediately lost all sanity and pounced on the lictor with tooth and nail, his rage bolstered by the fury of a freshly grieving parent.

Escalation quickly followed.

As the bereaved father sunk his teeth into the lictor's cheek, the Iron Cohort dropped pretence. Unlimbering their weapons, a calm descended on the disciplined soldiers.

The crowd froze in shock for a moment before exploding into pandemonium. Bottles and stones rained down on the lictors as the children scattered towards the warrens. A large gargoyle struck an unfortunate lictor like a meteor, crushing him to a paste inside his compacted armour while chunks of stone exploded outwards, injuring a further half a dozen other Imperials. The much larger crowd of commoners ran forward as one, weapons both martial and makeshift materializing in their hands as they rushed the lictors.

They never stood a chance.

The lictors could not be stopped. At a bellowing command from the centurion the soldiers reformed around their injured comrades, every second soldier using their shields to create an overlapping armoured roof over their heads. With methodical steps the well-armed, armoured, and trained soldiers of the Empire pushed forward to the Cockatrice with a steady and unstoppable momentum, might and magic combined to swipe away the meagre resistance before them. The centurion strode at the vanguard like a force of nature, reaping a harvest of flesh and bone as he pushed forward to the bridge. His blue-robed companion shot forth bolts of purple lightning from the palm of his hand, frying commoners where they stood as it chained from one person to another, jumping from knife-blades to belt buckles to chains and hammers and pitchforks.

The River weeps. The power of the magi… it is so much more than just a weapon.

Shadowy figures wielding bows appeared in the cracks and windows along the west wall, firing scattered arrows down that struck with vibrating twangs into the skyward shields. *Look how ineffectual arrows are compared to the magus' magic. They haven't felled a single foe with their sticks.* Abruptly the arrows ceased, and some of the lictors laughed at the commoners' ineffectual attack. It was then that they realized something was wrong.

While Pots was reaching the halfway point of the ricketies, three green glass wine bottles plummeted from the heavens. Each was a falling star, thick black smoke pouring from the burning rags shoved into their stems. The lictors were so preoccupied with reaching the platform that they did not realize what was happening until too late. All three bottles smashed unerringly into the lictors upraised shields, breaking open and spreading a flood of flame that ignited the tube-arrows.

The potion that had been poured carefully and gingerly stoppered into each tube had begun seeping through the cracks from the impact on the lictors' shields. The potion, which had been purchased from an indebted 'alchemist' that had mysteriously died soon after, exploded at the slightest touch of flame. If they had known the 'alchemist' had in fact been an expelled pueri meddling with scrolls beyond his ability, and if that pueri had known that the scrolls he had stolen from the Lyceum to brew the potions had not been the fireball scrolls he thought they were, and knew and related to his buyers that they were experimentally enhanced firewall spells, they might have been a bit more conservative in how many tube-arrows they had rained down on the lictors. *Then again, they may not have.*

The ensuing explosion was catastrophic.

Lictors caught in the centre of the blast never felt a thing, disappearing as an erupting geyser of flame, stone, and charred armour presaged a hailstorm of flaming chunks falling everywhere Plinius could see. The lictors at the edge of the impact were blasted in away, the concussive force strong enough to send them flying off their feet. Only the centurion maintained his ground, merely having to reposition his feet to maintain his balance as he weathered the shockwave like an implacable boulder. Glass windows and glow globes shattered for kilometres up and down the Runs. The lictors closest to the river of sewage, still screaming and engulfed in magical flame, went crashing into the fetid water below. The swarms of flies they passed through lit on fire; the water they crashed into lit on fire; the garbage passing by the spreading magical flamewall lit on fire, the current carrying it quickly along the Runs. The ricketies in the distance were eager recipients of the cleansing flame. Plinius watched them erupt in conflagrations for only a moment before they disappeared behind a firestorm.

The denizens of the Tradebasin watched on in horror as the runflies, in a mad and instinctual frenzy, flew upwards in their millions, a flaming swarm rampaging, driven by the fundamental, primordial fear of burning to death. *A fear that all living things possesses.* Pots had reached the other side of the bridge as the Cockatrice's ricketies, infused with all manner of solvents and chemicals from decades of pollution, greedily accepted the fire's kiss. Everything they crashed into became a raging inferno within seconds.

Plinius' throat stung as he tried to breath, the heat unbearable. Thick, sodden wooden beams that had propped up the tower for decades exploded outwards as pockets of water hiding within flash boiled. He shied away behind a weathered crenelation as the Cockatrice became a flaming effigy of its namesake. The flames consuming the ricketies rose higher and higher, the dwarf disappearing behind a rearing chicken-snake. Orange and yellow feathers of flaming plumage as tall as the tower Plinius and Boy were now trapped upon puffing up across the entire eastside of the river. The iron chain, slick with all manner of countless failed alchemistic agents and carelessly discarded effervescent reagents, had a mane of oily black smoke billowing from its hissing, pitch-dripping neck. The grandstand that had been packed with people was now the mouth of hell, desperate people jumping to their deaths to flee the inferno. A magus, glowing with a yellow light, floated unscathed from the fire, rising serenely upwards as commoners dashed off the pavement far below him.

The runflies, sizzling and popping, crashed into Plinius and Boy, their clothes catching fire instantly. Boy began to scream as he and Plinius desperately, futilely tried to bat out the fire spreading up his sleeve.

The grandmagus made the only choice left to him. Taking a deep breath, he calmly placed a hand on his companion.

Plinius opened himself up to the River and unleashed a deluge. Revelling in the surge of life and power that enveloped his being, Plinius yelled the words of the spell. It washed down his arm and through his hand, all magical fire immediately dispelling from both magus and man. Instead of gratitude Boy had an alarmed look on his face.

"I said no magic!"

"What else could I have done?" cried Plinius, "You- we were going to die!"

Boy turned around, shielding his eyes as he scanned the now ruined landing.

The blue-robed Imperial superior had regained his wits from the blast and was dispelling as much of the fire as he could from among the lictors, while the centurion had not ceased in cutting down anyone within his reach. At the very moment Plinius cast his spell, the Imperial magus turned immediately, facing the mid-point tower in shocked surprise. Even from this distance, with all the pandemonium erupting around them, Plinius could clearly make out what he was yelling.

"CENTURION! HE'S HERE! HE'S HERE!"

A loud siren began to wail, then another, until the entire Tradebasin was frantic with a screaming chorus of alarm. Whether this was due to the spreading fire or the magus detecting the fugitive grandmagus' presence, Plinius could not tell. The centurion turned and spotted his prey. With a roar greater than a lion's, the goliath warrior pointed his sword at Plinius.

"BRING ME THE MAGE! DEAD OR ALIVE!"

Lictors armed with crossbows ran forward, kneeling and taking aim. Plinius lifted a hand, and a lens-like wall of blue energy sprang to life in front of them, the bolts meant for them bouncing harmlessly off from the shield. The blue-robed superior joined the assault, sending his own bolts across the Runs, these ones not commoner wood but razor-sharp javelins of ice flung from his fingertips. *Frostbolt. Simple pueri spell but incredibly effective. I managed to modify one in scroll form to chill meat for preservation.* They shattered against the shield, but Plinius could feel the added stress from the magus' attacks. Holding out his free hand, he waited for the right moment. The Imperial magus held out both hands, attempting to overwhelm the grandmagus with a double cast of the spell. Two frozen missiles in parallel streaked towards him, and Plinius smiled. Turning his hand palm outward, he spoke the spell for frostbolt in reverse. The loud twanging sound banded across the Runs as the twinned frostbolt, in the blink of an eye, flipped and hurtled backwards towards the blue magus. The superior gasped and dove out of the way as the frostbolts slammed back into the platform, instantly coating it in a ten-centimetre-thick sheet of ice. The attacking lictors sprawled and tripped over themselves as they slipped and slid along the pristine ice, the few managing to still get shots off careening wildly off target. Plinius saw his opportunity and seized it.

"Grab my hand!" screamed Plinius over the deafening crackle of the inferno. Something in the tower shifted with a loud crunch, causing it to lurch violently sideways. Plinius lost his footing. His arms flailed wildly as he tried to regain his balance, but he could feel himself tipping back off the ledge. Boy's hand shot out, grasping the grandmagus by the forearm. The instant he made contact, Plinius closed his eyes and whispered a word.

In a flash they vanished, reappearing on the eastern side of the Tradebasin.

An avalanche of stone sent fountains of flaming brown water skywards in massive geysers as half of the old tower sheared off into the runs. The other half, miraculously mostly unscathed up to this point, teetered for a moment, until the large chain began to groan. The weight pulled the tower forward, the flaming chain swinging back towards the west-wall. With a rending snap the chain broke free, sending the remnants of the tower crashing into the water below. The chain moved as if in slow motion. Lictor and commoner alike fleeing in panic out of its inevitable path. When the chain struck the edge of the aqueduct, the sound could be heard across the entire city. It sliced like a knife through cheese, obliterating everything in its path, the ground where they had waited evaporated into dust and gravel, the platform where the betting had taken place was demolished, its flaming timbers blasting out in every direction from the force. Like daggers they burst through the wall in a plethora of places, spreading the insatiable flames of the firewall spell and doubling its size. The chain did not stop on contact, cutting a channel from the Runs to the west wall. It finally came to a grinding stop against it, dangling straight down, a flaming candle spreading the fire hundreds of metres in the air. The demonic flames cast the Runs in a hellish light. Burning oranges, flaming reds and brilliant yellows danced like chaotic imps on the underside of the cancerous clouds, black as sackcloth, spewing forth from the choking Tradebasin. This was not the worst of it.

The now decapitated Cockatrice had cut a wide and deep channel for the Runs water to flood into. The magically infused fire eagerly seized on the opportunity to flood down into the cellars and lower levels of the westside Tradebasin. Fire spread literally like rushing water, doubling the size of the fire in moments as unsuspecting, shocked citizens downhill found themselves simultaneously drowning and/or immolating. Dust and smoke smothered the air, Plinius' worldview shrinking to the size of his immediate surroundings.

Pots ran over to them, grabbing Plinius in an unwelcome hug that the magus did not have the strength currently to resist.

"Cronus' nuts! Me Da will nevah believe this, boy-o! Pliny thar was 'mazin'!"

He's not wrong; that was damn amazing. His grammar is atrocious, but this dwarf is no fool, I think. This story is getting exciting. I can't wait to see what heroic thing I do next.

Boy and Plinius disentangled from each other and stood up. Boy was trying to catch his breath, steadying himself on Pots shoulder. He met Plinius' eyes.

"You be saving my life, magus," panted Boy. Plinius could not help but notice the tinge of wonder in his voice.

"Ah," said Plinius sheepishly, trying to sound modest, "It was nothing. We need to get out of here!"

Boy nodded, regaining his composure. He started walking and Pots and

Plinius followed in step. "We are close now. Let us hope we can give them the slip. We know they are scrying you- No more magic! Let them search like commoner."

"Yes, I promise, unless I absolutely need to," replied Plinius, as sincerely as he could. *Magic saved their lives! It would be so much easier.*

The three ran as the magical fire engulfed the Tradebasin.

Chapter Six

Drinks & Dwarves

The barmaid leaned over, an ample decolletage presented as she put the three mugs of lukewarm ale before them. *Does anyone find that kind of garishness attractive? You would have to be a singular kind of fool to be drawn in by that overt titillation.*

Plinius eyed the drink, creamy foam spilling over the mottled grey edge of the pewter tankard. Pots gladly accepted it, his gaze firmly locked to the wench's heaving bosom as he tilted the mug towards his mouth. Boy murmured his thanks before pulling the beverage towards him, swirling the contents under an appraising eye. After a moment's reflection, he took a generous swig. A slight wince manifested around the corners of his mouth, but only noticeable if someone was intently watching. *Like me. It didn't kill him at least.*

The barmaid placed a hand on Plinius' shoulder, a warm smile beaming down at him. "Anything else hon?"

"Urk," croaked Plinius, his eyes darting down to her hand, his face going red.

"That be fine, thank you," said Boy, a small grin forming on his lips.

The barmaid's gaze lingered on Plinius for a moment, making him increasingly uncomfortable as it remained fixed on him. Then she flashed a very wide smile at him before turning and walking away.

"Me thinks she be liking you, you handsome devil you," laughed Boy teasingly.

"Shut up," replied Plinius, blushing. He began to intensely study the tankard before him.

Plinius' awareness of fermented barley beverages came from a purely academic interest- certain schools of magic relied heavily on the properties of alcohol to effect certain conditions. *Very useful as a catalyst in alchemical reactions. Archmagi Flamel was a wizard when it came to developing and refining the applications of alcohol.* Anatoli had also provided ample and unwarranted anecdotes on plentiful occasions concerning its effects, both positive and negative. With abject worry and morbid curiosity, the grandmagus lifted the mug to his mouth. Then he paused.

"And you just drink it," he asked.

Pots laughed. "Nah, ye just rent it." A couple of nearby tables demurely chuckled in agreement. Plinius did not get the joke.

After a second of deliberation, Plinius took a timid sip. He swished it around and swallowed. He began coughing into his sleeve in a painful hack, his eyes watering. "Ale," he croaked. "Delightful."

"Straight from Cronus' table," Pots said contentedly, smacking his lips after draining his cup in a gulp. He looked around for the barmaid, who had beat a hasty retreat from their table after plopping down their drinks. *The reek from Pots will have that effect.*

"When I said to be blending in, I didn't mean to be getting drunk, dwarf," said the boy jokingly, slouching in his chair while absently flipping a coin.

It looks like a sound strategy to me.

The charming location his streetwise guide had brought him to was easily the dirtiest place he had ever set foot in. He frowned as he lifted one of his legs, flapping his hand across the sole of his shoe to dislodge the dirt he had picked up from the floor. *An unpaved floor. Inside. Edge take me.* Plinius had no idea that rooms could become so filthy. That anything could be this filthy. That was including the recent alleys he had made acquaintance with since becoming a fugitive.

Not a fugitive! Falsely accused businessman would be more accurate. Defamed saint. Framed angel. Dare I say it? Icon for our time. Hero for the downtrodden.

You can't be serious.

May I remind you that this is my story. I sincerely doubt that I'm the villain in this.

The only thing dirtier than the tavern itself was the sour bartender serving drinks behind the bar. The only thing dirtier than him were his patrons. The only thing dirtier than the patrons was Pots. Even then, it was a close call.

"You know," the grandmagus said, keeping his voice low. "I could have this place cleaner than the Codeci Oratorium in the blink of an eye."

"No magic," the boy said in a voice that brooked no argument. "We be seriously pushing our luck."

"I did what had to be done back at the bridge," sniffed Plinius.

Boy nodded in understanding. "I be knowing that Plinius. And I be grateful for it. But going forward- no magic! It be too dangerous."

Plinius threw up his hands. "I wasn't going to do it; I'm just saying I could."

Boy flipped the coin high into the air, catching it deftly as it came back down between his pinkie finger and thumb. "Very impressive. Now remember rule four and be quiet. Pretend to be a common. Like we discussed."

Plinius scowled, crossing his arms sulkily and slouching back in his seat. *How dare he speak in such a tone to me.* "I can tell you're a friend of Anatoli's."

Boy laughed, deep and from the belly. "I be taking that as a compliment."

"It wasn't meant to be," spat back Plinius half-heartedly. *It was hard to fight with someone so quick to laugh. It was one of the reasons I got along with Anatoli to begin with. Always quick with a joke, my friend. You must admit though, Boy does have an exceptionally warm laugh.*

"Where is that barmaid?" asked Pots, staring sadly into his empty mug, amber foam fingers trailing down the stained-glass mug.

Plinius glanced around. Hunched backs and hushed conversations occupied the two dozen or so tables in the murky dimness of the low ceiling tavern. The tavern was tucked away in a cellar underneath a grocery shoppe, the smell of raw cut produce and rotting leaves drafting down through creaking floorboards in the air. *Not the most pleasant of smells, but unquestionably preferable to the Runs.* It was cool and dank in the tavern this close to the bay, on the Upper Bay Promenade a few blocks south and below the Tradebasin. The regular clientele of common sailors, stevedores and labourers that composed the quiet day crowd; a stark contrast to the raucous mayhem that would occupy the tavern a scant few hours after sundown. For the time being the shiftless dregs of Terrastra were content to stare into their mugs, letting the outside world move on without them.

Plinius was fairly enraptured with his current environs, enjoying the rest after the mayhem they had fled. *So common! How novel!* He admired the fieldstone walls and rushes on the bare dirt floor. An unlevelled square oaken bar was centred in the middle of the room, encircling a large pitted and pebbled stone support wall. The wall was bedecked in shelving, holding up a plethora of bottles, a muted rainbow of glossy colours. A few small windows along the street-side wall let in the most meagre light through cloudy, grime encrusted glass, but it was sufficient to lift the basement a few degrees above lighting one would consider generous in a punitive dungeon setting. Other than the entrance they had come in through, there were two other egresses from the large main room they currently sat in. One had a door with a sign reading EMPLOYEES ONLY, and one was a short hallway with a rusted iron sign that bore a vulgar ideogram of a large man urinating in a hole. Further beyond that promising invitation, Plinius could make out a large table dominating the backroom, various implements hanging from the far wall alongside a numbered chalkboard. "Boy," Plinius asked the bored youth, who arched an inquisitive eyebrow at him. "Is this decor typical of a common tavern?"

Boy shrugged. "I be supposing so. I do not frequent such establishments regularly, so you be asking the wrong person."

Plinius smacked his forehead. "Of course! I apologize for my daftness. You are far too young to be frequenting such establishments."

"How old do you think I be?" the boy paused, holding the coin in his closed fist, looking at the magus. "Why you be asking about the tavern anyways?"

Plinius shook his head. "Not old, and no reason really. It is the first time I have been in an establishment of this sort. I do believe it is the first time I have ever been in a common constructed building as well. It is all rather quaint, is it not?"

Boy looked sceptical. "You be telling me that you have never been in a bar before now? Never been in a house, or stable, or-"

Plinius nodded. "That is correct; I have only lived in three places in my life, each one of them spellwrought."

Boy gave him a dirty look. "I do not live in a stable."

"I believe it," said Pots off handedly as he tried licking the last drops out of his overturned mug.

"You said you think this place," he twirled his finger in the air, "be quaint?"

"Well, mayhap not the best choice of words. You must understand this is all rather new to me. I just find it all rather fascinating!"

The boy looked around with exaggerated interest. "Oh, yes! Truly fascinating!"

Plinius frowned. "I'm serious. It all looks so… rustic? Basic? Plain? Disostentatious? Wait, that's not a word. Oh, do not look at me thusly, my words are not proffered in insult. This business has a certain common charm to it. I can see why the- what do you call them? Morons do it this way."

The boy stared at the magus like he had just grown another head.

"Morons?"

"Yes, you know. The fellows who work with rocks and mud and such."

"Do you be meaning masons? Who the bloody hells is 'they' anyways? 'They' not be doing it this way because 'they' be thinking a mage will come and find it 'cute'."

"I know that!" Plinius face was a reddened beet. "All I be saying- all I am saying is it looks nice!"

"You need to stop staring at everything like you be a bumpkin in the city for the first time," said the boy quietly, sternly, but not unkindly. "It is very suspicious for someone seemingly your age not to know what the bloody hells a bar is. If these fine gentlemen find out who you are…" He trailed off.

Plinius nodded slowly, getting his gist. A quick look around the room at the unsavoury characters making up its clientele was evidence enough for Plinius that a magus would find no friends here.

"We do be safe now," Boy continued, leaning in, and speaking low, "As long as we be keeping quiet. This is where I was instructed to be bringing you. Now we just need wait."

Plinius nodded, not feeling reassured.

"Fine by me," belched Pots.

"What is that room?" Plinius asked, changing the subject.

Boy sighed. "It be a games room."

"Ah," Plinius replied, as if that explained anything to him. "Games. Like Minions of Dublain? Or Twilight Empire? Euchre?"

The boy looked like he had bitten into something rotten. "No, Plinius. I be having no idea about any of the words you just be saying. Games, eh? Pub games. Darts? Billiards? Horseshoes?"

Plinius nodded in understanding, not understanding the words Boy had said.

A bell clanged as the exit to the stairwell leading back up to the street opened and half a dozen dwarves entered the room. The mid-day sunlight snuck in at the opportunity, the patrons grumbling for them to close the door at their earliest possible convenience. The dwarves sauntered up to the bar, dust trailing off their clothes like ripples in a wake. They were all dressed in black-stained clothes of varying states of disrepair, thick black beards trailing in varying lengths from their collarbones to their waists, every one of them bulging with muscles. *They all look identical. I could not tell them apart if I tried.* Each one nodded their head towards Pots as they noticed him, who returned it in turn.

"Morning gents," drawled the man behind the bar.

"Mornin' Samanicus," answered one of the dwarves, as all half dozen or so of them hopped up onto the stools surrounding the bar. "A round o' ales for me boys, eh?"

"Comin' right up."

The bartender was a man of gigantic proportions. *One of his parents was probably a goliath. Maybe a giant.* His large belly strained the hemp rope holding up his breeches, a green chemise plastered across his body so tightly that Plinius wondered how in the bloody hells he got into it in the first place. Plinius found it difficult to discern where the man's wild beard of bushy brown hair ended, and where his thick woollen vest began. A comically small beret perched on his head like a cherry on a sundae completed his ensemble. He moved with deliberate, calculated movements reminiscent of a chameleon, a man of quiet calm and stoic demeanour.

Pots waved his hand frantically as the barkeep turned at a glacial pace towards the barrels stacked and tapped along the wall at the centre of the bar. Holding up the mug, Pots upturned it and shook it. Flecks of foam splattered on the table as an aghast Plinius hurriedly scooted his chair away from the mess being made. "Another mug of ale, if you please, barkeep!"

"Grmph," replied the barkeep, turning his back to them.

Pots vibrated his bottom lip, smacking it repeatedly against his upper lip, making a mee-mee-mee sound while the rest of his face looked bewildered. "Uh," he whispered. "Is he getting me another ale or not?"

"Put his ale on me tab, Sam," said the dwarf that had spoken when they had entered. Turning towards Pots, the dwarf doffed the leather skullcap he wore in greeting. "Pleasure t' make yer acquaintance, coz." He then said something in dwarvish that Plinius could not understand. *What are you talking about? I can speak dwarvish. He introduced himself by his clan-name and prime achievement.*

Pots smiled and returned words in kind. Plinius looked between them with a paranoid look. "What are you saying, Pots?"

Now Pot's saying his clan-name! I've always known dwarvish- this is incorrect. Tales, I'm disappointed in you. Don't you have fact checkers out there.

I'm just reading what's written.

Pots turned to Plinius and smiled. "Just sayin' hullo is all, ser," he said. He turned back towards the dwarves, this time speaking in common. "Well met, coz. What bring ye here this fine mornin'?"

The dwarf pulled his skullcap back down on his head as the barkeep started handing out full mugs of the thick cloudy ale. "Ah, th' docks are a fuckin' disaster today, on account o' whatevah happened up in the Runs. Looks like a damn volcano blew its top! Cannae get any work done when the Horts are crawling all o'er the waterfront, beatin' on e'rybody that gets in thar way. Judgin' by how pissed off some o' them lictors looks and thar fucking smoke eruption, it looks like someone kicked o'er their anthill somethin' fierce!" The dwarves cheered and laughed heartily, clinking their mugs together in celebration. The rest of the patrons joined in, as well as the bartender, lifting a cup.

"Fuck the Horts," he toasted.

He was met with a resounding cheer from the rest of the clientele. Even Pots and Boy clinked their mugs.

"Fuck the magi!"

Plinius was frozen in shock, completely taken aback.

How vulgar. I would have much rather preferred for this book to remain acceptable for all ages.

Wait, up until now, you have thought this story was appropriate for all ages?

Of course. Why would I not? Sure, there has been some light cursing and cartoonish violence, but this is, I do not doubt, a seminal historically and culturally relevant document. Like the Bible, or Harry Potter.

The Bible? Harry Potter? Are those books?

Books? Well, yes, but more like cultural milestones! Oh, they were big in their time.

I will take your word for it.

Naturally, as you should.

Plinius realized belatedly that he was the only one in the bar not to raise his glass in cheer. It was in that moment he realized that every single person in the tavern would gladly rip him in two if they knew who he truly was. Maybe even Boy. *Magi do not belong on the Lowhill. Common do not belong on the Highhill. Not a rule per se, but a pretty good guideline for not being beaten to death.*

The talkative dwarf hopped down from his stool and walked over to their table, taking the lone empty seat between Pots and the boy. "Jokin' aside me boys, the Horts are riled up somethin' fierce t'day. Me and th' boys nearly had our heads busted in down at the dock by some of them wand-kissers."

"You be a wise man, getting off the street," the boy said. "All lictors be bastards. Even the good ones. No reason to be out and about today."

The dwarf nodded his head. "That's Cronus' truth me boy. Story is that they be searching for some mage gone off the deep end. People say the robe killed a whole bunch o' other robes on the Street of Sighs and set fire to some poor bastard's house, then killed a whole crowd o' Terrans at the Runnings."

Plinius squeaked out a strangled cry, followed by a loud yelp after he was swiftly kicked under the table.

"That be what we hear as well," Boy concurred, drawing the dwarf's attention back towards him. "We also heard the mage be lurking around the Silver Docks."

"Ah," said the dwarf. "Probably lookin' fer passage to Vokgorod- Not that I or any dwarf would dream of doin' that personally! Goin' to the north makes sense for a mage though."

The boy and Pots both nodded. Plinius remained confused.

"In any event," the dwarf continued, raising his glass, "It gave me and the boys here a good 'scuse to knock of fer the day and set up cave in here. To the Horts- thanks fer the day off ye pricks!" A round of laughter and clinked glasses followed. This time Plinius managed to fake joining in, taking a meagre sip, and hating every drop of it.

"So!" The dwarf drained his mug in a single gulp. "Sam! Another round for me and me new friends here!" The dwarf beamed. "Sorry, I dinnae introduce meself- th' name is Jyroki Sootwhiskers."

He stood up on the rungs of his stool and leaned over the table, offering a hand to each one of them in turn. Boy and Pots gladly shook his hand. Pots introduced himself as such, plus another few words in dwarvish Plinius did not understand. *He gave his family patronymic.* When the dwarf reached out towards Plinius' mysterious guide, Boy grasped the dwarf's arm and said, "Nice to meet you, I'm just a stranger from Dunemere passing through," as if reading it from a scroll, completely different from his usual strange way of speaking.

Those within earshot went suspiciously quiet, Plinius noticed. Jyroki gave the boy an appraising look and nodded his head slowly while stroking his bushy beard, looking intently at Pots and Plinius in turn. The silence of earlier was replaced with a silence more sinister. Plinius' gaze floundered around, not able to make eye contact with the rest of the patrons who were now making a supreme effort of ignoring their table.

"Strangers are welcome, rest and be well," the bartender said, seemingly joining the conversation out of nowhere. The boy tilted his head towards the silent bartender in acknowledgement. Plinius felt completely at a loss to what was transpiring. *This is passing strange. Maybe they're speaking in code?*

Jyroki sat there in thoughtful appraisal before snapping out of it and offering a hand to Plinius. "Jyroki Sootwhiskers! Pleasure to meet ya!"

Plinius slowly extended his arm and Jyroki grasped the offered hand with his own, shaking it vigorously to Plinius' chagrin. Plinius disengaged from the handshake as quickly as he could, drawing his hand back into his sleeve while rubbing his wrist. *Ah, look. I at least had the presence of mind to hide my tattoo and shake with the opposite hand.* The dwarf was staring at him expectantly. *This feels awkward.*

Plinius winced as the boy gave him another swift kick to the shin. "Pleasure to meet you, Jyroki," he croaked, his mind scrambling, "My name is, ah, Anatoli."

Boy rubbed the bridge of his nose between two fingers while letting out a low nearly inaudible groan. The dwarf did not notice, merely nodding. "Anatoli, you say?" His eyes narrowed. "That be a Tsarusskan name." The dwarf made the words sound like a threat. *What a curious reaction. I wonder why?* Plinius realized his error immediately. *Blessed Concord, you make me sound like an idiot sometimes.*

"Oh, ah, yes," stammered the grandmagus. Plinius blinked. "Yes, it is."

Chairs scraped as hard looks flashed their way.

"So ye be a Tsarusski, eh?"

"Blessed Concord! No!"

Some of the younger dwarves started to titter. "Blessed Concord!" one of them mimicked in a trembling old man voice. Everyone laughed at that. "Grandpa!"

Jyroki was the only dwarf not laughing. Even Pots was giggling uncertainly, not wanting to be left out of the joke. Jyroki chewed the inside of his lip as he stared intently at Plinius. "So what ye be then, eh?"

"I was, ah, born in Terrastra."

"Is that so?" He looked at Boy, who nodded slightly. "Well, pleased to meet ya, Anatoli," he said genuinely.

Plinius took a moment to find his voice. "Ah, yes, a pleasure," he murmured. He felt slightly nauseous. The mood in the room instantly lightened a bit as the other dwarves went back to a raucous conversation in their language.

Jyroki leaned into the table, Boy and Pots leaning forwards at the same time. Plinius remained seated back in his chair. The dwarf looked around the room theatrically before he pushed in even closer, forming a partially closed circle with Plinius' two compatriots.

"True talk now me boys, yar clearly not with the Horts, eh?" hushed Jyroki, his voice not travelling beyond the table, "so, any word 'bout what's actually happening? Tradebasin to the docks is good an' riled. All sorts a' rumours flyin' 'bout. Is it a purge?"

Plinius was lost. *Purge?*

"No, no, nothing like that," said Boy, shaking his head. "Rumour through the Runs is some rogue mage was breaking the Concord. Lictors are coming down hard now, and you know what that means."

"Shit rolls downhill," Pots said absently, drumming his fingers on the tabletop.

"Exactly," agreed Jyroki. "Concord violation? Wha' a fuckin' joke. Thar's the pot callin' the kettle black. Whatever' the real reason be for the Horts lookin' fer this fella, best not be a dwarf on th' streets today. Or really anyone not looking like a robe. Ha! No offense, gentlemen."

"None be taken, friend," the boy replied genially. "No magi here. Just honest to Cronus commoners." Plinius nodded belatedly in agreement, electing that silence was probably the best course of action.

"Yet," corrected Jyroki. "No magi here yet. It's only a matt'r o' time before the Magistracy's lickspittle dipshits make their way into the commons. Th' entire Hall's been emptied out thar sayin' today; thar must really wan' this renegade bad if thar so brazenly marching through the streets. And what do the old militiamen do? Hmmm? Terrastra's finest? Thar stand by and watch the Horts do what they will! No finger t' be lifted! What in the name of the Concord are they doin?"

The bartender interrupted to Pots delight with four mugs of ale unceremoniously dropped on the table, spilling their contents slightly. "Where the hell is that wench?" he asked rhetorically.

"Thank ye fer the ale, Sam," said Jyroki thankfully. "Let me pay fer me new frien's here. How much do I owe ya?"

"Four ales comes up to thirty lyons," grunted the barkeep.

"Thirty silver! Cronus' fat cock Sam! That's almost double what it was last time," complained the dwarf sourly. He emptied some silver as well as a few gold skellions into the palm of his hand from a leather pouch.

"Price has gone up for me; price goes up for you," said Sam as a matter of fact. "It could be worse- even getting my damn hands on some barrels of ale is a fucking chore. I had a shipment of Thessalonia bitter from Cervidium held up at the Tradegate for two damn days! The Magistracy have their heads up their asses- they keep changing the damn rules for imports and it's wreaking fucking havoc down in the Exchange. You're lucky I have friends in low places." He said the last part with a knowing nod towards the boy, who dipped his head once in reply. *Who in the hells is Boy?*

"It's fucking robbery it is," grumbled Jyroki. "Dunno gimme that look Sam-boy-o, I aint sayin' it 'bout you. The fucking Empire is to blame. It's a conspiracy I tell ya, to fuck over Terrastra." That elicited a few laughs from the other tavern goers. Plinius did not understand why they were laughing, but nervously joined in anyways.

"Cronus' sweaty balls, Jyroki," laughed one of the men sitting over near the door, "You see the Empire in every shadow. Next thing you'll be blaming the Empire for the fall rains." More laughter, but this time Plinius joined in having understood the joke. *Ha! I get it too! It's a pain in the behind to control the weather.*

"Aint surprise me a bit if they do," said Jyroki, dead serious. "The magi are all bastards, aye, but the Magocrats are the worst of all those fucking robes. That fucking Emperor of theirs is a right bastard. The worse of the whole lot of 'em. Ever been to Aliston? I have. They treat him like a fucking god there, as if Cronus' hand was up his ass like a puppet. The whole city is like one o' those damn churches here but multiplied by a thousand. Look a' what they've done to the other independent states- this is how they do it! Start off small, so n'body objects, then slowly take a bit mar, take a bit mar."

"Like boiling a frog," murmured Plinius unintentionally.

"'xactly!" said Jyroki, pointing a hairy callused finger at Plinius. "Slow and steady like, eh? O' course ye all know this though." He tapped the same finger against his nose. Boy merely smiled in response.

"I see what you're saying, Jyroki," rumbled the bartender. "It does seem pretty obvious if you think about it."

"Aye, and ye best believe the robes up in their fancy white palace know it too." Fancy white palace? What does he- oh! He's talking about the Lyceum!

"You think so?" asked one of the other dwarves.

"Of course! Why d' ye think the Magocrats put their hall right up next to them? T' keep an eye on them o' course. Old Heuronicus Cato ain't no dummy."

"Pointy-headed rat," quipped Pots, in a broken cadence which suggested he was repeating something he had heard but did not quite understand. It still set the tavern-goers off into a tumult of laughter, and Plinius assumed this was some running joke among the hoi poli. Pots was beaming at his joke's reception, but he became disappointed when he saw Plinius' confused expression.

"Who is Heuronicus?" asked Plinius.

Everyone in the bar turned to face him. The expressions on their faces ranged from confusion to incredulity. Some thought they were just missing the joke and tittered uncertainly. A few became instantly suspicious, mostly the one's that had overhead him introduce himself with a Tsarusskan name.

The bartender coughed into his elbow. Samanicus, Jyroki and Boy exchanged glances.

"How 'bout a game o' billiards boy-os?" Jyroki said suddenly, standing up abruptly. He walked around the table and placed a hand on Plinius' arm, gently pulling him up out of his seat. Dwarves are surprisingly strong- there's a reason Tsarusska chose them. *I remember how powerful and firm his grip was despite being so gentle.*

"Now see here!" began Plinius in protest until the Boy placed his hand on his arm. Plinius heart skipped a beat at the human contact. I hated being touched. The thought of hands holding me tightly…

"I be thinking a game will do us good! Come Anatoli, I will play ye first."

Plinius' looked like a landed fish as his mouth worked up and down wordlessly. They lifted him up and out of his seat, herding him with some haste down the hallway to the backroom. The quiet din of the main barroom resumed as they reached the back.

"Now what is the meaning of this!" Plinius demanded as he leaned against a large oak table with a recessed green surface. A single glossy white ball sat forlornly near a corner. Six pockets evenly spaced stood guard along the perimeter of the table.

I love billiards! It's a math game- geometry. Angles and force. Physics.

Physics? Do you mean Psychics?

Pardon me?

Psychics. Clairvoyance.

I most certainly am not referring to that! Although I suppose you could adjust certain prognostication spells to anticipate the vector beyond simple- nevermind that! I remember playing billiards… I played billiards that time when… EDGE TAKE ME! Damn this amnesia. What a tired trope.

Trope? Plinius; you're not making much sense at the moment.

I'm just having trouble getting things straight. I apologize for my outburst Tales. Please forgive me.

It's ok Pliny, there's nothing to forgive. I get it, I do. It will get better, I promise.

Yes. Yes, of course. Sorry again.

"Wha' hole did ye dig this fella outta?" asked Jyroki wonderingly. "He sticks out like a vein of basalt and every time he opens his mouth, he has me guessin' what year it be. He speaks like me grandda fer Cronus sakes!"

Boy walked around the table, liberating multi-coloured balls out of the pockets, rolling them towards one side. "Aye, that be about right. I appreciate your discretion, friend."

Jyroki waved his hand. "Dunno mention it, brother," said the dwarf humbly. He pulled aside his beard and pushed back his soot-stained tabard. A dull bronze broach pinned to his undershirt barely glinted in the dim light. It was three separate concentric circles, a cross with equidistant arms ending in points centred atop the circles. *Ha! Hahaha. I sure as gremlin shit remember what that is. Edge take us. Are you sure this is what happened? What a damn joke.*

Boy flourished his hand and as if by magic an identical broach appeared in his hand. "Brother," he said. "Me be glad at this serendipitous turn of events. We were sent here by-"

"Anatoli?" supplied Jyroki. Plinius' tried to maintain a façade of ignorance at the mention of his friend, but only managed the least convincing look imaginable. *I'm a terrible liar.* Jyroki chuckled, his suspicions confirmed immediately. "Aye, me thought as much. Maybe pick a better alias next time, mage."

"Now see here! It's magus, not mage, and I would-" Plinius stopped abruptly as Boy sighed. Plinius' went red. "Something to add, Boy?"

"It be a terrible choice in a fake name, Plinius," chuckled Boy.

"Oh, is it? I suppose 'Boy' is better? Cracking great name there, you little gremlin shit." Both the dwarf and the boy chuckled heartily.

"Aye, ye be a funny robe, eh?" Jyroki said gleefully.

"I am not funny!" Plinius said stomping his foot. This set them laughing even harder. "What would you consider an acceptable alias then, Boy?" hissed Plinius through his clenched teeth.

"Oh… I be thinking," he said, his chest shaking, smiling wide, "Maybe Jyroki." The two Wayfarers leaned on each other, laughing.

Plinius' confusion set them laughing even harder.

"Wait," he asked, "Jyroki is not your real name?"

The dwarf tried to answer but managed to sputter a couple words between cackles. He settled for shaking his head.

Plinius tried to hurt them through imagination, which proved to be ineffectual. *It would be so easy to squash them. All of them.*

That's not you, Pliny.

Is it not? Am I not a grandmagus? The moral of this story is clearly one that seeks to prove that I am an utter jackass, a damn joke. I must have been a terrible man if this literary scorn and humiliation is my legacy.

Quite the contrary, Pliny. Remember- we're only in the first steps of this story. We have a way to go my friend.

Remember? Ha. Don't you start mocking me too.

Sorry Pliny. I didn't mean it that way.

Sigh… I know Tales. I know. Sorry. Please carry on.

"So, what are ye doin' with his kind?" Jyroki asked Boy in a tone that implied a great deal of what would transpire next would be decided by his answer.

The boy pulled out a black triangle from underneath the table, placing the balls inside. "You break," he said as he reorganized the now full triangle into a pattern so obtuse Plinius could not see the purpose. "He is wanted on the hill. Kaeso's orders."

"Kaeso? Who is that?" asked Plinius.

"Kaeso? No shitting? Then what th' fuck are ye doin' down here at Murks?"

"What is a Murks?" asked Plinius.

Boy shrugged his shoulders. "Just be following orders. The sooner the captain be getting here to take him off my hands, the happier I be."

"Who is the captain!?" cried Plinius.

The dwarf whistled, his eyes faraway, looking through the stone and rock to the east. "Fuck off? The top brass himself?" The dwarf looked the magus up and down, his eyes betraying what he clearly thought of the magus. "Wha' the bloody hells makes ye so special, robe?" Jyroki walked over to the wall, choosing a long, tapered stick out of several choices leaning on a wall mounted rack. He continued talking, more to himself than anything. "A fuckin' mage summoned up to the Lowhill. That there is a unique situation I must say." He looked at Plinius. "I swear robe, yar lucky this fella be who he is." He motioned the tapered stick at Boy as he pulled a raised platform on rollers from underneath the table. "Or else I'd be breakin' ye instead."

Jyroki hopped up onto the riser. He leaned forward and started sliding the stick along his outstretched hand. With a sharp crack the dwarf struck the tip of the stick against the white ball. It went streaking like a white blur across the table towards the other balls. With a loud bang the balls scattered across the surface, caroming off the sides and each other in a chaotic ballet. Jyroki and Boy were talking to him, something about being circumspect and holding fast while they waited. Plinius barely heard them as he watched Jyroki line up a shot on the table and sink another ball. A minute of watching the game and Plinius thought he had the gist of it. *Naturally it came to me. This game was made for me.*

"Mage! Magus! Plinius!" Boy waved his hand in front of his face. "Are you paying attention?"

"Oh, yes, yes, no magic let's keep quiet," Plinius answered, not taking his eyes off the table. "Can I play? May I take a shot?"

Jyroki laughed. "Why not, robe," He threw the cue at the magus, who managed to hold on to it after juggling it awkwardly in his hands. "Yar gonna wan'a aim fer the balls wit' the stripes there. Good luck."

Plinius tongue peeked out the side of his mouth as he bent over the table uncertainly, trying his best to mimic the dwarf's previous attempts. He tried lining up and aiming his shot, but his attention was more concerned with getting the stance right. He went to strike the ball and missed wildly, losing his balance, and falling face first on to the tabletop, giving his cheek a little rugburn. The dwarf and the boy began to laugh uproariously as Plinius hmphed.

"Maybe this ain't your game, mage," chortled the dwarf.

"Let me go again," said Plinius, thinking that he had figured out how his stance should be set.

"Oh, by the Edge, please do so," Jyroki said smugly, "I'll nevah deny a robe the chance t' fall flat on thar face."

"Plinius," said Boy, walking around the table to join him, "You be slightly off balance if you be keeping your stance like that." Boy adjusted Plinius feet with his own. Instantly Plinius could perceive the advantage of standing the way Boy had instructed. "Oh! Yes, I see. Thank you, my boy," thanked Plinius sincerely.

"Boy," he said shaking his head. "Mage, how old do you think I be?"

"Mmmm," Plinius said, now unsure. *How quickly did commons mature? It's not the same aging as magi, at least at some point.* He studied Boy intently this time. His skin was unblemished, but he had very little hair. Copticians were renowned for their youthful appearances. Plinius tried to remember what it was like to be a child, a teenager, a younger man. That was so very, very long ago. "Eight?" he guessed.

Jyroki started crying he was laughing so hard, asking Boy between breaths where he had dug Plinius up from. Boy laughed and winked at him. "Way off, my friend."

"Younger?" Boy let out a surprised, boisterous laugh.

"Cronus be good, Plinius. Do you not be knowing the difference between a man and a child?"

"How old are ye, mage?" asked Jyroki sincerely.

"How rude," said Plinius, "But seeing as how you are my honoured hosts, I will tell you I am not a day less than a hundred years old."

Both Jyroki and Boy were stunned. *Commoners know about magus agelessness, of course. But I don't think they truly believe it.*

Before Plinius could hazard another guess at Boy's age, Pots came waddling back with a tray of new ales, placing them on a table as gently as a mother laying her baby down for a nap.

"Ah, thank ye, Pots! Mighty kind of ye to get the round."

"What?" asked Pots blinkingly. "Oh! Yah, these beers are for all o' us alright, thar why I got so many. Ha!" He turned to Boy sheepishly. "You owe Sam 30 silver."

"Uh-huh," said Boy, shaking his head with a suffering smile. "I will be right back."

Plinius turned his attention to Jyroki, who was helping himself to one of the full mugs. "So, I aim for the striped ones? And what happens when I sink one?"

"You keep taking shots, mage," said Jyroki, taking a gulp of ale. "Keep going until ye miss. Sink that there black ball last in a called pocket to win th' game. Good luck." The sarcasm of the disingenuous last comment was not lost on Plinius.

He squinted and lined up his shot. Biting the inside of his cheek, he inhaled slowly and pulled the cue back. He visualized the trajectory of the ball, the point of impact and the resulting motion of the spheres. He saw not just where the first ball would go, but the resulting impacts and spiralling certainties of the other balls stemming from the initial impact. It felt very close to accessing the River, but not a drop of magic was drawn upon. *It would be embarrassing if I needed to. It's just some common game.*

"Black ball, side pocket? Like that?"

Jyroki rolled his eyes. "Aye, mage. But ye do that when ye've sunk yer other balls.

Plinius struck with the cue. The green ball he had aimed for went plonk in an open pocket. The cue ball curved forward and away to a cluster of balls near the far end of the table. Jyroki watched with growing disbelief. The ball made contact. Plonk.

Plonk.

Plonk. Plonk. Plonk.

The eight ball, after deflecting and bouncing off the table sides half a dozen times, rolled into side pocket.

"So I win?" asked Plinius genuinely.

"Edge take me!" exclaimed the dwarf, just as Boy rejoined them in the backroom. "How in the bloody hells did ye just do that?"

"Do what?" asked Boy, arching an eyebrow while walking back in.

"The bloody bastard just sunk five balls and bloody called the eight on the same shot! Off one strike! It was fucking amazing!" exclaimed Jyroki.

"Is that so?" replied Boy.

"Duh, it was just the grandmagus using magic," said Pots matter-of-factly.

Jyroki shook his head. "Nae, good coz, he didn' do no spells. We would've known." *Now that's interesting. I think we've established they're common as dirt at this point. So, they must have a charm to detect magic on them.*

"Then how the heck did ya do it, ser?" asked Pots.

"Quite simple. Using Euclidean geometry, I anticipated the geodesic flow of the little white ball and, applying an ergodic theory to the theoretical movement of the resulting impacts, enabled me in being able to anticipate the movements…" he trailed off as his words seemed to be physically hurting Pots. Jyroki and Boy looked equally lost.

"Uh, actually it's quite simple, my good Pots," said Plinius, "It's just about having a good stance."

For the first time today, Plinius joined in laughter that felt like he was in on the joke instead of being the subject of it. For the next half an hour the magus forgot about why he was in the basement of a common hovel and enjoyed the company of people for the first time in nearly a century. The dwarves and Boy were constantly dumbfounded by the preternatural skill the grandmagus exhibited across the billiards table, even more so by the fact that a magus was good at something other than, and in absence of, magic.

They continued with their merriment this way until Plinius froze mid-shot upon seeing the expression on Jyroki's face. The front common room had gone unnaturally silent. Pulling open his shirt, the Wayfarer broach shone with a faint red ethereal light. Boy hurried determinedly towards the mouth of the hallway, sharing a look with Jyroki as the dwarf abruptly dropped the stick he was holding, flopping it down onto the billiard table unceremoniously. Plinius was slightly confused at their behaviour, assuming he had made a mistake in the game. It was not until he heard a familiar voice in the main room that understanding came to him like a hammer to the face.

"In the name of the Emperor, this establishment is under interdiction by command of the Iron Cohort."

The reaction to this announcement was evident by the hostile, pregnant silence that permeated the bar. Plinius immediately ran over to the corner where the games room wall met the corridor to the main room. It was hard to miss the towering, implacable figure of the centurion dominating the room. His steel-clad helm, a galea with side-to-side feathers, brushed the basement ceiling with barely enough headroom to accommodate his dominating and towering stature.

Four lictors stood behind him, as well as the blue magus, his robes slightly singed and covered in soot. The magus was entranced- whites of his eyes showing, a hand hovering over a crystal orb floating above his outstretched hand. *He's scrying. Probably detect magic.* Plinius recognized the lithe and cold Venem as well as the bruised and bitter Weasel hovering behind the gigantic centurion. A sweet coppery scent filled the air, vanishing as if it never was when the pupils returned to the magus' eyes.

"Nothing," said the magus, "I sense nothing in here. She may have lied, Ox'vacar." The crystal ball hovering above his hand continued to do so, a foggy light crackling within the crystal.

Ox'vacar grunted at the magus, his eyes hooded as he surveyed the dingy room. The pommel of his sword peeked over his left shoulder; a blue cape draped down his back. The patrons sitting at the table closet to the exit slowly tried to stand up and make a quiet exit. Without turning around the centurion spoke in a voice like the rumble of an avalanche. "Sit down. No one leaves."

Someone sniggered, and the four other lictors unclasped the axes from their belts.

"What's the meaning of this," growled Samanicus, "You have no authority here, 'Hort. Go get the militia if ya have a problem."

Ox'vacar walked towards the bar, each step a clanking jumble of plate and chain. He loomed over Samanicus by a good two feet, and the bartender was not a small man to begin with. "In accordance with the compromise," the centurion intoned, "As an agent of the 1st Legion, centurion of the Iron Cohort, in the name of the Emperor, we so exercise our right to enforce compliance of the Concord within the independent city-state of Terrastra." The faces on the patrons made very clear how enamoured they were with the centurion's decree.

"Ain't no Concord violation here, 'Hort," replied Samanicus as if he were talking about the weather, "Just honest workers keeping off the streets so you fine folk can do your job."

"We shall see," promised Ox'vacar, "Lictors. Find the magus."

Plinius began to panic. "Edge take us! We're trapped!"

Boy looked around, nodding his head in agreement. "It do be seeming so, magus. We have maybe a minute before they get back here."

"What!" said Plinius aghast, "That's not what you're supposed to say! You're supposed to say, 'no be worrying, Plinius, here be the secret exit!"

Jyroki took up post at the hallway entrance, peeking around the corner to watch as the lictors began to spread out, interrogating each table. Pots picked up one of their ales and started chugging while their attention was elsewhere.

Plinius grabbed Boy by his shoulders, shaking him frantically. "What are you talking about!? You should be telling me not to worry! You have a job! Do your job!"

Boy seemed completely non-plussed despite the manhandling by the magus. He gently took Plinius arms into his hands, lowering them. "Plinius," Boy said, "I need you to be taking a breath. I know my job. You need not be worrying, for of course I have a plan."

"Oh, thank Cronus and the Blessed Concord," panted Plinius in relief. "What do we do?"

"Get under the billiards table."

Plinius felt like throwing up. He looked at the large open space underneath the table as Boy pulled out the risers and shoved them in the far corner as quickly and quietly as possible. It is quite roomy. "Hide under the table? That's your plan?"

"That be it," confirmed Boy. He guided Plinius over towards it.

"Have you gone absolutely mad? You want me to hide under that table, which is open completely to view. That's your plan?"

"No," corrected Boy, crawling under. Pots followed quickly. "Not just you. Pots and myself as well. No telling what they saw back at the Cockatrice. Now come on and be getting under here."

Plinius started tittering involuntarily. "This is insanity. Enough of this foolishness, I have a scroll here that will-" He stopped midsentence as Boy reached forward and placed a hand on his. His hands were so warm; I was so surprised.

"Plinius," said Boy earnestly, "You need to trust me. I told you I have a job, and I be intending to do it. Please, Plinius. Trust me."

"You need to trust me!" hissed Plinius, "You keep saying trust you, trust you. How can I trust you when you don't trust me!?"

Boy looked as if he was going to argue, when a queer realization lit up his face.

"Ohotepe."

Plinius blinked. "Excuse me? Ohotepe?"

Ohotepe… that's a Coptic name.

"My name, Plinius. My name be Ohotepe. I be telling you, because I be trusting you," he grabbed the grandmagus' hand, "Now please, please, be getting under the table!"

Plinius hesitated, looking towards the main-room and back at Boy. Ohotepe. After a moment he nodded his head. Jyroki began to motion for him to hurry as Plinius went scuttling under the table. The dwarf picked up a cue. Pots crammed in beneath the hunched over magus like a bunny sheltering under a bush.

"Now Jyroki! Now!" urged Ohotepe, squished into a foetal position so they could all fit.

The dwarf grabbed three balls and placed them quickly in three specific pockets, followed by him jamming the black triangle rack into an open slot on the side of the table. As soon as the rack was set, an invisible energy washed down over the three companions under the table, as if they were being drenched beneath a cool mountain waterfall. Plinius gasped at the unexpected wash of magic over them. His panic reared back up immediately.

"This table is enchanted!? But the magus out there! We just alerted them to our presence!"

Ohotepe waved his worries away. "We be safe here, magus. The cloaking enchantment on the table is shielded from scrying."

Plinius' mouth dropped as far as it could. "A masking spell!?" he whispered astonishingly, "But that's 9th circle magic! I haven't even mastered the River that much!"

"Shhh!" whispered Ohotepe urgently.

The lictors Venem and Weasel came sauntering into the backroom, projecting authority like street-kid bullies. They split up, Weasel glancing around the room as Venem walked towards Jyroki leaning up against the billiard table.

"Dwarf," said Venem, "What are you doing back here?"

Jyroki did not reply at first, choosing instead to spit at the lictors feet. Venem did not react, but Weasel let out a cackling laugh that set Plinius' hair on end.

"The lady asked you a question, bitty," sneered Weasel, "I suggest you answer her if that pipsqueak brain of yours knows what's good for you." The rodent-like lictor was standing alongside the table now, his legs close enough for the magus to reach out and touch. Plinius was desperately trying to not relieve his bladder.

"Ain't it obvious, Horts?" asked Jyroki, his words dripping in sarcasm, "I'm waitin' here for ye Emperor to show up. We 'ave a date to play some billiards before I bugger him up his arse."

Venem did not laugh. She looked merely thoughtful, biting her lip, with her head tilted to the side. She lifted her axe slowly, before bringing it down into the table filled with half empty mugs. The crashing of glass, splintering of wood and splashing of beer exploded outwards from what was moments before a perfectly acceptable table. Weasel cackled delightfully at the destruction.

"Very funny, stump," drawled Venem, no hint of humour in her voice, "I wonder though, why so many mugs of beer for one dwarf?"

Jyroki shrugged, looking bored. "I be a thirsty dwarf, Hort. Is that a crime nowadays?"

"I'm sure your guilty of enough crimes, bitty," chortled Weasel.

Venem hefted her axe in her hand, the wicked smile of the crescent blade reflecting the dim fire from the braziers. Taking another glance around the room, she cocked her head back towards the common room.

"Go join your friends, dwarf."

Jyroki picked up a chipped half mug that had miraculously held on to its contents despite Venem's best effort. "Aye, ma'am," said Jyroki after taking a big swig.

"Filthy pieces of shit," spat Weasel.

"Mmhmm," hummed Venem, watching Jyroki walking back towards the bar. "Do not under-estimate the dwarves, Wetzel. There's a reason there's still so many of those disgusting creatures when all the rest of them have been wiped from the face of Mir. Even worse if you think about up in Tsarusska."

"Whatever," said Weasel sourly, kicking the table leg, causing the hidden fugitives to silently wince in tandem. "There's no one back here. That bitch was lying."

Venem did not respond; she merely turned and walked back towards the common room.

"Fucking bitch, you'll get yours," muttered Weasel when he was sure she was out of earshot. He slowly began to follow. Picking up an abandoned mug of ale, he turned to hide it from the front of the room and downed it in a single gulp. Wiping his mouth with his sleeve he threw the mug over his shoulder and with a large shattering crash the glass ricochet off the dirt floor, a large sliver of it signing a great signature across Pots' cheek in red ink. Boy's hand shot up and quickly muffled the dwarf's cry of pain before it could escape his trembling lips. Tears welled up in Pots' eyes as blood began to trickle down over Ohotepe's hand.

"No one in the backroom, centurion," reported Venem to Ox'Vacar. "I fear the woman lied to us. He's not here."

"See?" said Samanicus in a tired voice, "Nothing amiss here. No reason for you to be hanging around."

Ox'Vacar stood as still as moonlit shadows. The sustained silence stretched throughout the basement of the bar. Chairs creaked uneasily and the sustained tension smothered any conversation as increasingly questioning glances passed between the patrons. Finally, like a crack of thunder to signal the coming storm, the centurion spoke.

"Lictors Venem and Wetzel- please escort the magus outside and wait for us."

The blue-robed magus looked up at the centurion in surprise. "Centurion, I think it would be best-"

"Irrelevant. I am commanding officer here, magus. With all due respect, adhere to the chain of command and please vacate to outside the premises."

The magus started to protest, but a guiding hand from Venem steered him away from the Centurion and towards the exit. Weasel cackled as he walked past Jyroki, purposefully smashing an elbow carelessly against the back of his head. "Have fun!" he sniggered. The centurion turned his head almost imperceptibly towards the lictor, a guttural growl reverberating through the steel shell surrounding him. Weasel coughed nervously and beat a hasty exit out of the basement.

"What is your name?"

It took Samanicus a moment to realize the centurion was addressing him. Placing the rag in his hand down on the bar, he crossed his arms across his expansive chest.

"What does that matter?" replied the bartender defiantly.

The centurion stood silently. "Fair point," the centurion allowed, "Your name is irrelevant. Are you the proprietor of this establishment?"

Plinius could not see the bartender's face, but the uncertainty in his voice was unmistakable. "Prepitur?" he asked, his tongue fumbling the word, "I don't understand."

"Ignorant. I am asking if you are the operator of this business?"

"Yes…" the bartender said warily with hooded eyes.

"And what circle have you achieved?"

"Pardon me?"

Plinius could hear Ohotepe take a sharp inhale of breath. *Uh-oh. I don't see it yet- but he does. Perceptive one, this Ohotepe. This will not end well.*

"Answer the question," demanded Ox'vacar, his words sounding like grinding rocks in a tumbler.

"Are you asking if I am a magus?" a few scattered laughs dared to flit across the room. Ox'vacar did not join in.

"Affirmative," the centurion confirmed, "Answer immediately."

"No, I'm no fucking mage," sneered Samanicus, sealing his fate.

The centurion began to speak, reciting words in a manner that bespoke to the hundreds of times he had said them before, slight variations with the same meaning. It was a prayer of violence to a cruel god.

"By the authority vested in me as an agent of the Eternal Magocratic Empire, in accordance with the Terrastran compromise, I charge you with defiance of the Concord in regard to law five. No common is to operate any landed business-"

"Hey now!" protested Samanicus, raising his arms up in a pose reminiscent of surrender, "I just run this place- the owner is-"

"-without explicit approval of the-"

"Are you listening to me!?" Samanicus was now leaning towards the centurion over the bar while some of the patrons started shifting very uneasily in their seats, "I'm telling you were on the up and up! I just run this place-"

"-local Magocratic governing body. I find you in contravention-"

"Just shut up and listen to me you fucking 'Hort! I'm telling you that we're a legitimate-"

"Of the Blessed Concord. The verdict has been passed, and the sentence shall be carried out immediately. In the-"

The bar burst into a frenzy of activity. The table patrons began to fall over each other in their desperate attempt to escape the basement, chagrined as they found their way blocked by the two remaining lictors. The soldiers brandished their axes, a promise of violence for anyone who came near. Jyroki and the dwarves unhurriedly stepped up from their table, unslinging hammers and axes from their belts and forming a defensive circle. Samanicus ran directly away from the centurion, the intimidating warrior unslinging the sword from his back as he continued his speech.

"-name of the Emperor, by the River so sworn, I declare all within this establishment anathema and direct threats to Mir-"

Samanicus vaulted the back of the bar, running past the dwarves into the backroom. Running up to the rack holding the cues, he spared a quick glance to the three invisible men beneath the table. "Whatever happens, stay still and stay quiet!" he commanded earnestly as he tore the rack off the wall with both hands. Reaching into a hole that had been hiding behind the billiard cues, Samanicus retrieved a papyrus scroll that had been hidden in a small hole in the wall.

Samanicus ran back towards the main room, slowing down in the hallway before entering the room proper with his arm held high. "CENTURION!" he bellowed, everyone in the room turning towards him. Even Ox'Vacar paused, whether out of deference or intimidation Plinius could not tell.

"Centurion!" he repeated, "Do you know what this is?" He held up the scroll, unfurling before him in his upraised hand.

"Irrelevant. Submit, anathema, to the law."

"It is a scroll of fireball!" The faces of many of the patrons went white at this pronouncement, Plinius included. *A commoner holding a scroll that powerful is grounds for arrest as it is. A commoner holding a scroll forged with a simplification modifier? Executed on sight. I wonder where in the bloody hells he got it from.* "Get the bloody hells out of here right now, or I swear to Cronus I will immolate every last one of us!"

"He can't cast that in here!" hissed Plinius.

"Samanicus is a Terran. He know what he be doing," grimaced Ohotepe.

A low and unsettling sound began to undulate in the depths of the centurion's armour. It was a sound of despair, a syncopating and dirge-like bassline that offered nothing but callousness and cruelty. The forlorn sound cut everyone who heard it, an icy knife kissing the napes of their necks. *Blessed Concord… he's laughing! That's his laughter!* The scroll trembled in Samanicus' hand.

Ox'Vacar lifted his arm, the sword held out in his hand before him, stretching well out over the bar. After his laughter died down, he spoke his judgement in a cold and unyielding voice, reminiscent of the iron which gave his Cohort its name.

"In accordance with the Blessed Concord, I pass judgement in the name of the compromise and the Eternal Emperor. By the River so sworn, I sentence you all to death."

"Wait!" screamed Samanicus, holding the scroll before him. Time froze for an instant. The men under the billiards table held their breath in concert.

"I'm not joking!" threatened the bartender, sweat staining his shirt, "I'll cast this spell right here, right now, if you don't. Get. The. FUCK. OUT!"

Ox'vacar's arm did not move an inch, the sword suspended as if in stasis.

"Irrelevant."

What would happen next would be the second worst thing that Plinius would witness that day. *Blessed Concord… maybe we should skip this part…*

The centurion erupted into a flurry of movement that was hard to follow, especially from Plinius' vantage point. If anyone with a firsthand view had survived the ensuing slaughter, they would have attested to the supernatural and unrelenting fury of the centurion as he set about his bloody work.

In the first five seconds after the centurion had passed judgement, Samanicus had barely recited half of the scroll before Ox'Vacar had cut a swathe through the patrons that stood between them. He spun his great claymore as effortlessly as the girls from earlier had twirled their skipping rope, a tempestuous whirlwind in his outstretched hand. Three different patrons lost three different body parts as they futilely rushed towards the exit. He strode confidently and measuredly towards Samanicus, his blade flashing left and right at any resistance or submission he encountered in before him, a few of the patrons dying on their knees begging for their lives.

The two lictors barring the exit were less successful- one of them managed to catch a knife-wielding woman in the throat with his axe, sending a fountain of arterial spray across the ceiling in a splattering crimson rainbow.

The woman's partner let out a blood-curdling cry of anguish at the sight of her death. He pounced forwards at the lictor with a face contorted into a demented, bestial snarl, knocking them both down to the floor as the soldier's axe went spinning off into a far corner. The man knelt on the struggling lictors chest, sprawling in front of the exit. If the man had the presence of mind to flee at that moment, he could have stood and walked out the door-he would have lived to see another day. Instead, he elected to stab downwards in a flurry of emotional release and bloodthirsty revenge, screaming his dead lover's name as his dagger violated the neck of the lictor over and over again. He enjoyed his vengeance for a dozen stabs before the other lictor cleaved the man from collarbone to heart with one fell swoop.

This proved to be his undoing. The lictor shouted in primal triumph as he slew the killer of his fellow soldier. The scream of victory turned to frustration as he desperately tried to free his axe, but the metal had bit deep into the ribcage of the dead man. The viscera of such a violent end made the lictors grip on the weapon's shaft slippery and fickle. The last thing he did was curse his own weapon lodged into the prison of bone as the group of dwarves swept around the opposite side of the bar from the centurion and descended upon him with half a dozen hatchets. Plinius was shocked as they released the pent-up rage built up over years of abuse, the dwarfs screaming triumphantly as they gave into their worse impulses. *I think I'm going to be sick watching this.* They hacked and smashed into the imperial agent for much longer than they needed to, relishing in his utter destruction, and in doing so sealed their fate as well.

Ten seconds after passing judgement, Jyroki took two bounding leaps. Once on top of the bar, the second jump with his axe held high as he sailed towards the centurion in a display of athletics Plinius would have thought impossible in a person so small. Ox'vacar, arrogant in his assumed martial superiority, barely raised his sword arm in time to deflect the descending blow. Jyroki's axe slid down the hastily raised blade with an ear-piercing screech, skipping off the guard at the hilt and bouncing upwards with enough momentum to smash the centurion's helmet upwards, popping it off with a crack like a corked bottle and pulling the black scarf with it.

The face that glowered down at Jyroki was human enough to seem familiar, but distorted in ways that told the truth of his nature. If the centurion's height was not enough to indicate the inhumanity beneath the armour, his grim visage left no room for doubt. Mottled vitiligo skin in patches of white and grey made a patchwork of the giant's face, mismatched eyes of two different hues radiating malice towards anything his gaze fell upon. His entire head was a ruin of scars, old burn marks and roughly done piercings carving swathes of irregularly healed flesh from his brow to his neck. He is the ugliest and most pitiable creature I have ever seen.

If the terrifying countenance of the goliath had given the fiery dwarf cause to pause, even in the slightest, Plinius would never get the chance to ask Jyroki.

With a blood-curdling war cry, Jyroki engaged the centurion. His axe rolled and hacked like a possessed spirit, furious blows raining down in relentless strokes. Ox'Vacar roared in delight as he traded blows with Jyroki, an all-out frantic duel that challenged the giant in a way that he had missed since being posted in Terrastra. Despite the gross difference between the size of the two combatants, Jyroki and Ox'Vacar fought each other over the course of the next few seconds in a frenzied and unrelenting dance of anger and unrestrained hate. The fight might have stretched for minutes, hours even, if not for Samanicus' completing his invocation of the fireball scroll.

Fifteen seconds after Murk's had descended into a chaotic nightmare, both Jyroki and Ox'Vacar raised their weapons, fully committing to reckless attacks, when the scroll in the bartender's hand crumbled into stardust, a shimmering golden light encircling his forearm before flashing into a brilliance that illuminated every corner of the basement. With an ear-popping whoosh a molten ball of flaming death exploded outwards from Samanicus' hand, the pure force of the spell backwashing into the unfortunate bartender. *An unwarded common casting a fireball. Insanity.* His forearm disintegrated instantly, the remaining charred stump of his arm thrashing for a brief instant before the heat melted the flesh into rivulets of tallow, the charred bone of his forearm flaking before turning into swirling ash. His leather vest ignited in spontaneous combustion before the rest of his body followed suit, engulfing him in magical flame. His ear rending scream harmonized with the wailing crescendo from the other patrons as the fireball impacted the far wall.

At least they never felt a thing.

Jyroki's companions, some still plunging away into the bleeding corpse of the mutilated lictor, vanished in a flash of light, fire, smoke, and dust. The building shook with violent tremors as the roof of the bar became enveloped in licking flames traveling across their entire length. Smoke and dust enveloped the basement, the grocer above and the street out front as the outer wall exploded outwards, fieldstones soaring like fleeing birds up into the sky across the area up top, the bystander's unfortunate enough to find themselves passing by at that moment were pummelled into bags of broken bones and bruised flesh. The magus, Venem and Weasel were spared a grisly end purely by luck- Weasel having cajoled them into walking a block up the street to an ice-fruit vendor.

The explosion stunned Jyroki just long enough for him to lose his grip on his axe, and the centurion pounced on the advantage. His open palm, clad in a gauntleted glove, shot out and grasped the dwarf by the neck. Jyroki's legs kicked out wildly as they soared off the floor, rising higher with Ox'Vacar's outstretched arm. With a terrifying cracked glass smile, the centurion dropped his sword to the ground with a clatter. His now free hand pulled back before driving a clenched fist into the chest of the dwarf. A sickening squelch preceded Jyroki's involuntarily gasp as his ribs cracked and impaled his lungs, the air escaping in a bloody splutter from the single meteoric punch. The centurion did not stop there- with a smile bordering on manic he dug his fingers into the dwarf's shattered chest, yanking forward in one fluid motion, the dwarf's back cracking like a hammered stone as the giant warrior pulled the dwarf into two, separating his head and spine from the rest of his body. Jyroki's lifeless body was tossed aside without a second thought from the centurion. Plinius clenched his eyes shut and choked down the ale in his stomach, a sour feeling threatening to force its way up.

Compared to the people trapped down in Murk's, those on the street proved to be the fortunate ones. The heat and flame from the spell turned the rest of the room into a charnel house. The patrons who had managed to survive until that point finally had their luck run out, the powerful spell sparing no one from a burning death. *Edge take me and Gods above…* The bar ignited into flame, the bottles along the middle wall exploding under the extreme temperature. A blizzard of glass shrapnel embedded itself in any willing receptacle it could find, ending more than a few lives in a merciful instant. The three men hiding under the enchanted table pressed together, attempting to shield their exposed flesh from the debilitating heat back-drafting into the games room. *Thank Cronus that it was just a normal fireball scroll, unlike that firewall one from the Runs.*

The flames died down and the smoke cleared through the now gaping exit in the façade of the building. Plinius gasped as he looked towards the now smouldering remnants of the bar. Standing in shimmering armour throbbing with red and orange residual heat, Ox'Vacar remained seemingly unscathed by the devastation wrought around him. As if completing a chore, the centurion calmly reached down to retrieve his weapon, sliding his monstrous blood-splattered sword onto his back.

"Hullo? Anyone alive down there?" yelled the reedy voice of Weasel down from street level.

"Marcus and Gaius are dead, lictor," said Ox'Vacar as he strode across the rubble towards the front of the now destroyed bar. Sacks of potatoes collapsed into the basement from the grocer above, most of them burning, and Ox'Vacar batted away the ones near him effortlessly. With one powerful leap he jumped up out of sight and into the street. Even from this far away, his powerful voice was clearly audible. "As are the anathemas. No sign of the renegade mage. I am unscathed. Send for the militia to clean up this mess- I would like a word with that barmaid."

It was a few minutes before any of the hiding men dared to breath. The scent of violently upheaved soil and charred lumber filled the air, a cloying and musty smell overpowering with its strength. Bells and terrified yells echoed down from street level. The boy crawled out from under the table on the far side, far out of view from the hallway and front room.

"Come, come now!" implored Boy, "A stroke of luck! The wall has come loose back here- we can sneak out and be away before the militia comes."

Plinius and Pots were both shook, trembling as they crawled out from underneath the table. The grandmagus looked at Boy, not even trying to hide his fear or confusion now. He looked towards the front, his gaze lingering on the remains of Jyroki. Plinius, having finally lost the battle of wills with his stomach, vomited on the billiard table.

"Jyroki-" he began.

"Magus, mourn later," said Boy, surprising Plinius with his cold pragmatism, "We need to be gone, and now."

"But we were supposed to stay here! Anatoli is coming here!"

"With this many lictors around, there be no way he comes anywhere close to here!"

"But that's his job!" cried Plinius.

"Jobs be changing, Plinius."

"What in the bloody hells do we do now!?"

Boy bit his lower lip. "We can't be staying here; that's for sure. Time for the plan to change, I think. I have an idea- follow me!"

Plinius followed.

Chapter Seven

Traders & Tailors

Plinius coughed violently and rubbed his eyes, the ground kicked up from a passing team of stomping, annoyed horses, plastering his face with dust and making his eyes sting. Boy had led them to the edge of the lower market. Stretching out for a few kilometres before them was the bustling heart of trade in Terrastra. It was far more horrifying than Plinius could have even imagined.

"So… so many people," muttered Plinius to himself, wrapping his robe tighter around him as if would make him look less conspicuous.

"Be it not wonderful?" asked Ohotepe in a way that Plinius took as meaning he did not really care to hear the magus' thoughts on the matter. *That's rude, people sought me out for my opinions all the time when I was at the Lyceum. Many of my magisters had proclaimed they had never met a more opinionated magus!* Boy led their small group into the mass of people crowding the market, heading past lines of parked wagons along the interior into a riotous tempest of colourful tents erected along the main street.

"It's too flat here. It's… unnatural," whined Plinius. *I prefer this to the Runs.*

A seemingly unending stream of eager merchants steadily made their way in from the far southern gate with wagons laden with all manner of goods. As they were let in by the Magistracy customs officials, they turned right immediately and rolled forward in a great counter- clockwise circle around the entirety of the low market. As each merchant reached their destination, their carts and wagons would split off and carry on- once finished, they would proceed back the same way until reaching the inner caravansary. There they could rent stalls, warehouses, or a designated camping spot on bare hard-packed dirt to store their chattels for their stay in Terrastra.

Ohotepe chattered in a hushed but excited tone, commenting on the endless parade of caravans, wagons and simple single horse drawn carts. He told Plinius that they came from nearby farms, factories, ranches, and wineries, supplying Terrastra with the means to keep its teeming citizenry fed. They came by way of the Imperial highway from neighbouring Avalon, laden with weapons and tools from its golem run manufactories. They came from the shadowy islands of mysterious Mazburundi, laden with exotic spices and reagents picked from around the lairs of degenerate monsters. Ohotepe proudly pointed at a large wagon whose canvas was a ballooned patchwork of a dozen different materials, if Ohotepe could be believed it was some adventurous merchant who had made the trip to Terrastra from the far southern jungles of Kanga. Ohotepe winked at the grandmagus as he said without a doubt it was brimming with strange and colourful skins from beasts not seen this far north in decades.

"How could you possibly know that?" sniffed Plinius.

"Oh, you know, I be talking to people."

Plinius noted that he enjoyed being down here in the dirt, with its choking haze and chaos. He felt a twinge of pity for him.

"I know all this stuff anyway. Do not forget, I have lived in Terrastra a great deal longer than you."

"That be so, mage?" replied Ohotepe, unfazed by the magus' patronizing tone. *I do sound like a bit of a prat.*

"You do not need to go on," muttered Plinius haughtily. The truth was he did not know the half of it- Plinius had never given much thought at to where the things he enjoyed had come from. He knew of these places in an academic, detached fashion. The only time he truly cared was when he complained of shortages that made getting his hands on necessary material impossible. *The incompetence of the customs house! Worthless, utterly devoid of any sense.* Regardless of Plinius' arrogant dismissal, the Coptician ignored him and continued his commentary.

"Those lightly guarded caravans- you see, over there?"

Plinius turned to look.

"Don't be staring! They be coming in along the Emperor's Highway from the heart of the continent, bringing magical artifacts from the capital in Aliston," Ohotepe whispered conspiratorially, despite the clamorous noise making even a conversational tone nearly impossible to hear.

"I know that."

"Do you? Did you know that Aliston be having the greatest spell-forges in all of Mir?"

"Blessed Concord… yes, I know that. I was born there you know."

The previously adroit Ohotepe missed a step, taking both Plinius and Pots by surprise. He quickly regained his footing and pressed on as if nothing happened. He looked at Plinius eagerly. "You be from Aliston, magus? Truly?"

"Grandmagus," corrected Plinius, "And yes, I was born in Aliston. I moved away a long time ago though- I am sure it has changed much since I left."

"Why did ye move, Pliny?" Pots asked with genuine curiosity.

"Plinius," corrected Plinius. 'To study at the Lyceum, of course. I was awarded a full scholarship at age thirteen! Youngest pueri in nearly four centuries." A thought entered his head and spilt out of his mouth before he could stop it. "Why did you two come to Terrastra?"

Pots beamed. "Born and raised!"

"I escaped from slavery," answered Ohotepe matter-of-factly, not a hint of emotion in his response, "Woke up halfway up the peninsula and then be walking down here."

Plinius face went red. "Oh," was all he could say in reply. *Awkward.*

"How do you know so much about the caravans?" asked Plinius, desperate to steer the conversation back to calmer waters.

Ohotepe laughed, and Plinius relaxed.

"Those guards be so bored along that route; they will gladly tell you their life story for a flask of rum to brighten their day."

Plinius sneered. "I cannot imagine a caravan guard has much of interest to say."

"Spoken like a true wonder boy from the Lyceum," replied Ohotepe in a jolly way that belied the insult. Plinius noticed Pots nod his head in slight agreement.

"What is that supposed to mean?"

Ohotepe shrugged. "You be the wonder boy; you tell me."

Plinius could feel warmth rising back into his face. *Impudent man. I hope I teach him some respect!* He opened his mouth to do just that when Ohotepe abruptly darted into a nearby tent. Pots and then Plinius stumbled to a stop and quickly turned and followed.

His eyes took a moment to adjust to the dim interior in contrast to the glaring sun. The tent smelt of saffron and something familiar. *Mandrake! I haven't smelt that in years! Since that time in Kanta. Wait- I have been to Kanta, haven't I?* It was surprisingly cool inside the tent despite the warm spring sun shining outside. The interior was a riot of colour- long ropes festooned along the tent boasted dozens upon dozens of jackets and coats, robes and trousers, skirts and tunics. A pedestal with a silver lanx brimming with grapes upon it stood prominently next to a high stool occupied by a flamboyantly dressed man. His hair was bunched into a tight white top knot, his dark ebony skin bare but for puffy silk trousers of alternating cherry and grey vertical stripes. He smiled widely as Ohotepe reached out his hand. The shopkeeper- *he looks like a clown-* popped a grape into his mouth and clasped his now empty hand with Ohotepe. "Teeps! Me boy how good it is to see you!"

Ohotepe glanced embarrassingly at Plinius, before turning back to the shopkeeper.

"Same being for me Qubo, you old rascal!"

The handshake turned into a hug as Boy-

He said Teeps! Now that rings a bell! I know that name! I know it!

Do you?

Oh, most assuredly. Like Anatoli and Pots- the name Teeps… that was Ohotepe's nickname… it carries weight. Strength? In my heart. What a queer name. Definitely

Coptic in origin, or perhaps from one of the splinter tribes in the Aurum volcanic archipelagic. He said he was a slave but then again… he could have lived here his whole life and not been out of place. Hard to discern with Terrastra's cosmopolitan demographics. I am interested in hearing more about this fellow. Do some exposition.

Do some exposition?

Yes, you know, explain some stuff. Go into detail… tell don't show.

I don't think it works like that. It doesn't work like that.

Jesus Christ who's writing this story?

Jesus who?

Who? Nevermind- tell me more about Teeps!

We'll get there.

Blessed Concord… fine, whatever, very well. Carry on.

Ohotepe laughed a deep belly shaking laugh that seemed incongruous coming from one so young. Plinius played with his sleeve awkwardly while Pots wandered off slowly, mesmerized by the panoply of brightly coloured garments, fingering through the clothes.

"Ser! Dwarf!" called out the shopkeeper. "Please, whatever you wish to try on, go right ahead. Any friend of 'Tepe is a friend of Qubo Zhang. Please, don't hesitate to ask for any assistance!" Qubo beamed at Ohotepe. "What brings you here today my boy? Undoubtedly a new shirt- look at the affront to Cronus you are wearing! Edge take me before I would sell that rag to anyone! It's not fit for a gremlin."

Ohotepe laughed. "Sure, you would, you old pirate. When's the last time you said no to anything that would make you some money? You'd sell it to your own mother."

"Ok, ok- I probably would," laughed the shopkeeper, "I'd definitely sell it to that friend of ours. Where is that rogue Anatoli? That's close enough, eh?" Both men laughed at the joke, irking Plinius.

Plinius squinted at the shopkeeper once he got past his jealousy and actually heard his words. *I was not jealous! Jealous of what!?* "Anatoli? Did you say Anatoli? You know Anatoli? Where is he?"

The shopkeeper's gaze wandered over to Plinius, as if noticing him like someone notices a fly in their soup. "How rude of me. Welcome to my shop, Master Magus."

"Grandmagus, thank you." *Oh, this Zhang fellow did not like that.*

Qubo smiled a wide teeth-bearing grin that never reached his eyes. "Apologies, *Grand*-magus."

The way he said the last words made Plinius feel rather off-put. *Off-put? That's putting it mildly.* Turning his eyes back to the Coptician he asked, "What brings you here today with such odd company, Teeps?"

Ohotepe looked back at Plinius for a pregnant moment before answering. "I be looking for a special coat. One of which the poets of old have wrote."

Plinius looked at him, bewildered. *What a strange time to indulge in poetry.*

Qubo's jaw clenched. He let out a strangled moan from the pit of his throat. Quickly brushing past Plinius to the front of the tent, he took a quick look outside. He pulled on a hempen rope dangling next to the opening and a heavy canvas sheet abruptly fell across the opening. Reaching a hand into his pocket, the shopkeeper made a great flourish with a showering of what looked like sand across the threshold. The ongoing clamour and commotion from outside became instantly muted, as if the sound was being spoken underwater, a vibrating gurgling that dampened every sound from the chaotic market. Turning around Plinius was taken aback at the abrupt change in the shopkeeper's demeanour. Where before Qubo had been the epitome of merchant-client geniality, at least to Pots and Ohotepe, there now stood before him a man of unmistakable menace.

"Are you mad, boy?"

Ohotepe met the shopkeeper's stare, his face completely at ease. "Boy? Be remembering who you speak to, Qubo. You be asking if I am mad? I could be asking the same of you; if this be your reaction."

"Yes, I'm asking if you're mad! Damn the consequences to the Edge! It's a simple question!"

Ohotepe waved at Qubo dismissively. "You know the rules Qubo. I be not having the time for your attitude."

"Attitude? Attitude!" Qubo was clenching his teeth so tightly Plinius thought he could hear them grinding into powder. "On today of all days you drop in and make this demand of me? Are you stupid or a fool? Or both?"

Ohotepe rolled his eyes, clearly unimpressed by the insult and ignoring the bait as calmly as possible. *I would have lost it already.* "Give me a break, Qubo. Stop with the dramatics."

Qubo flung a hand back towards the entrance of the tent, nearly hitting Plinius in the face. "Do you have any idea the basilisk's nest that fool has kicked up today? If I were you, I would be laying low until tomorrow, not marching through the heart of the market with a thousand Imperial eyes searching for you!"

"Those eyes are precisely why I am here. Our rendezvous with our contact was... interrupted. We need to get to the *father's house*, and right away. And there being no quicker, or safer, way than through here."

"Where is Anatoli! Have you spoken to him?" Plinius asked again.

Qubo paced around the tent, one hand worrying at his top knot. "By Cronus' fat cock! Fuck me! You are asking more than I can give- if you are caught, I am caught. No one told me to expect this! Well, expect some things, maybe this qualifies, but fuck! If this is what you want, you know I am burnt here? Do you know how much I am going to lose? I've worked hard to set all this up, to build my connections- that all goes away if we do this! You know that right?"

Ohotepe was as implacable as a glacier, his face frozen in a tableau of determinism. "This is exactly what we worked towards, Qubo. To use it in time of need, to burn it down when that need arises." Ohotepe folded his arms across his chest. Plinius was confused. Qubo's shoulders rose and fell as he tried to control his breathing. "None of this be yours to keep, remember."

Qubo stared down Ohotepe, his jaw clenching. "Easy for you to say. Not all of us enjoy sleeping in alleys, bilges or under hedges."

"I's enjoy sleeping in alleys," interjected Pots offhandedly as he rubbed his fingers across a silken mauve blouse.

Ohotepe never broke his gaze from the shopkeeper. "The time to harvest the fruits of your labour is now Qubo. Complaining won't change anything. Remember who commands you. Remember what you owe. Remember the oath you swore."

Qubo let out a frustrated yelp. "Well, it would seem complaining is all I'm going to have left! You think I don't know you're right Teeps? I know I have no choice. The least you can do is let me fucking complain." Qubo's shoulders slumped, popping one of the grapes into his mouth and chewing forlornly. Plinius was beginning to feel pity for the fellow when the shop-keep rounded on him, his mouth spitting foam in anger. "You! You fuck stupid bastard mage! This is all your fault!"

Plinius was shocked into silence. *What the bloody hells did I do?* It took him a heartbeat to find his voice.

"Now see here! I have not the foggiest idea what you are speaking of. Coats and connections and harvesting? You all sound mad! I will not be talked to-"

Plinius trailed off as he realized his tirade was being completely ignored. Ohotepe had not moved a bit. His gaze was fixed on the indignant shopkeeper. He stood with his arms crossed, his face a mask of emotionless command that Plinius had not thought him capable of. Qubo stared right back, tears of frustration sneaking out of the corners of his eyes. Pots had stopped perusing and had elected to slowly back into the clothes along one of the long display racks, his upper torso hidden by skirts and long-tailed jackets. His filthy shorts and bare feet egregiously stuck out below his hiding spot. Plinius stomped his foot in frustration.

"Tell your mage to shut his mouth, Edge take him," seethed Qubo.

"Qubo, relax," said Ohotepe in an even tone.

"What in the bloody hells is going on here!" cried Plinius, "I demand answers!"

"Shut up mage!" The venom in Qubo's voice made Plinius shirk back reflexively. It had been nearly a century since Plinius had felt the sting of a harsh rebuke. *I must say it's rather unenjoyable.* Qubo jabbed a calloused and crooked finger towards the magus. "Does this look like the Northhill? Know your place and shut your mouth! You've already done enough."

"Done enough?" Plinius scoffed, "Ser, are you deaf? Or dense? As I have said, I have no idea who you are, and I most certainly have never aggrieved you in any way."

The man laughed as if this was the funniest thing he had ever heard, a hard-edged guffaw so over the top Plinius suspected it was mocking in nature. *No shit. "Haven't done anything!?!* You have ruined me!" he accused.

"*I* have ruined *you!?*" Plinius was so taken aback he worked his mouth up and down furiously, trying to find words in retort but so unaccustomed to argument he flailed around like a beached kraken. "I- I do not even know who in the Blessed Concord you are!"

Qubo's face screwed up in disgust and derision. "In the Blessed Concord? Fuck you and your mage oaths. No, shut up! It doesn't matter. And when has familiarity ever been required for magi to fuck someone's life up?" Qubo spat back.

"There's a bit o' true," coughed a paisley tunic from one of the racks, sounding suspiciously like a certain hoi-poli dwarf.

"S-Shut up!" stuttered Plinius at the jacket for a moment before rounding back towards the shopkeeper. "Shut your mouth! I am a magus of the eighth circle! A grandmagus scrivener! I will not be talked to that way by- by-" He trailed off, trying to keep his anger in check.

Qubo puffed out his chest, taking a step towards Plinius with a dangerous gleam in his eye. "What's that, mage? Talked to by what? What are you going to say?"

Ohotepe rubbed his eyes. "Please you two, be keeping it down, lower your voices. We are on the same side here-"

"Same side?!" screamed Qubo, tugging his hair violently while rounding on the Coptician, "Do you even *hear* yourself? He is the enemy!"

"*ENEMY!?*" Plinius exploded, "That is the most scurrilous accusation I have ever had levelled against me! I am a Terran citizen- shut up!" Plinius stomped his foot as the tailor started barking his mocking laugh at him.

"Terran? You Imperial-"

"Imperial! I never-"

"Yes, Imperial! All you mages are the same-"

"Stop it! Stop calling me mage! I find your manner rude and offensive, ser. You are just a-"

"Let me guess, mage," interrupted Qubo, "What were you going to say? Anathema?" the shopkeeper spat the word. "A filthy subhuman? Was that what you were going to say?"

Plinius gasped. "What! No! Never!"

"Aha! Admit it! Say it, you magi piece of-"

"I wasn't going to say it! Blessed Concord-"

"Bleeseed cooncoord," mimicked Qubo in a reedy voice.

"Gentlemen, please, be-"

"Heeheehee," giggled a black fuzzy-hooded coat.

"Be quiet Pots!" snapped Plinius.

"Better be quiet, dwarf," sneered Qubo, "Wouldn't want to offend the mage, would we? He might turn us into a frog!"

"Mmm, nope," disagreed the coat.

"Plinius! Qubo!"

"What is your problem, ser? What, specifically, have I ever done to warrant such hostility?"

"My problem? Are you that dense? You're the most wanted fucking person in Terrastra! You're in my fucking shop! You think that would be enough but no, you also have to insult me."

"Insult you? When did I insult you!? I haven't at all! You insulted me!"

"You were going to insult me-"

"I wasn't!"

"Then what were you going to say? Hmmm? What were you going to call me? You were going to say I was just a…"

"Just a-" repeated Plinius, trying to get a word in over Qubo's forceful over-talk.

"Just a commoner? Just a simp?"

"I would never!"

"Admit it. You were going to call me a simp," the shopkeeper rounded back on Ohotepe, "You see? You see? We are *nothing* to them!"

"That's not true!" protested Plinius.

Ohotepe frowned at Qubo. "He did not be calling anyone a simp, Qubo. On the contrary, he be showing me these past few hours he not be like other magi." A warmth bloomed in Plinius' chest as Ohotepe came to his defence.

"I would not! You could ask Anatoli! I have nothing against commoners! This is Terrastra for Cronus' sake!"

"All magi are bastards," seethed Qubo. "Then just a what, mage? If not a simp, then what."

"M-magus…"

"Just what?"

"Just a tailor!" Plinius blurted, his brain spouting the first word that felt non-disparaging. "I was going to say you're just a tailor!" *I'm sure that what's I was going to say all along. I am not a mean person. I would never call a commoner a simp. I've known plenty of smart commoners, as I have mentioned.*

The shopkeeper's mouth dropped open, unprepared for Plinius answer. Both magus and shopkeeper turned towards Ohotepe as he started laughing in a deep baritone rumble that escalated until he was nearly doubled over. A fine evening robe of Mazburundi dyed silk began to laugh weakly as well, desperate for the atmosphere to stop being so volatile and more than ready and eager to follow the young man's lead. The shopkeeper's eyes lingered on Plinius for a moment longer before switching back towards the Coptician as he threw up his hands. Plinius was shaking and felt the overwhelming urge to pee.

"Edge take you!" swore Plinius, "What in Cronus' name is so funny!?"

"A tailor!" Ohotepe wiped a tear from his eye. "Oh, Plinius, you be funny, that be true. A tailor- Qubo Zhang! The thought be equal parts sad and terrifying! I am beginning to like you, scrivener!"

Plinius bristled. "Funny be I- Fuck! Funny *am* I, you little…"

"Oh, yes," interrupted Ohotepe, "Indeed."

"Listen here, I have had enough of this!" Plinius scrunched the scratchy and uncomfortable commoner clothes with his hands, both arms shaking as he wrung them in frustration. "Would someone please tell me what we are doing? My life is at stake, and here you are laughing your head off! I demand to be taken to Anatoli now! I don't find this at all amusing!"

"*Your* life is at stake?" Qubo walked over to the stool and slouched down on top of it. He absently plucked a grape and chewed on it noisily. "All of our lives are at stake you pompous, arrogant fool!"

"Pompous? Arrogant?" Plinius straightened up, his jaw clenched. *Such disrespect.* "As I have said, I have never met you in my life, ser. I take umbrage with your slanderous tongue, and demand satisfaction."

"Demand satisfaction?" sputtered Qubo, completely agog. "Did you just challenge me to a duel? When in the bloody hells do you think this is, mage?"

Plinius squinted his eyes at the commoner shop-keep, attempting to emote malice as best he could. "Please enlighten me, *Kantan*," he spat, "Where are we?"

"We're knee deep in gremlin shit, you fuck dunce! Thanks to your utter stupidity!"

Plinius threw his hands up. "My stupidity? MY STUPIDITY?! From where I am standing, I seem to be the only one around here with any wits!" He rounded on Ohotepe, an accusatory finger jabbing towards him like a militant spear. "Where is Anatoli, Ohotepe?" He rounded on the shopkeeper, "Where is Anatoli, tailor? You clearly know him, but to you I am but a stranger. What in the bloody hells do you think you know about me? How dare you judge me! Edge take you!"

Qubo fixed him with a disgusted look. "Oh, I don't understand magi, is that it, mage? I don't know magi, because I'm just a simple common, eh?" He slid off the stool and started walking in an embellished stagger around his tent, his eyes crossed and spittle dripping from his corner lips. "Oh geez, master, I just a dumb common, what do I know 'bout big impor'nt matters. Duuuuuur!" He snapped out of his childish impression. "I don't know *grand*magus, how about dealing illicit scrolls to Tsarusska? Playing at necromancer to line your own pockets? Selling maps of the Empire to their sworn enemy?"

Plinius felt his heart sink further and further with the shopkeeper's words.

It fell right into his stomach and the room felt a little colder with each word the irate man spoke, until Plinius found himself having difficulty breathing and shivering. He glanced sideways towards the merchandise, but all he could see was two dirty trunks standing stock still behind a blue chamise. Ohotepe grimaced and threw the shopkeeper a dirty look. Qubo scoffed.

"What? We all know why he was chosen. His dirty little secrets."

"You be knowing that is only part of the reason, Qubo."

"I didn't know," murmured Pots, his face poking out from between two petticoats.

"That's… not… how did you…" Plinius mouth worked open and closed. Abruptly he sat down on the ground and placed his head in his hands. "I was so careful. No one knew!"

Qubo barked a humourless laugh. "Everyone knew, you old fool. Well, anyone who would know about such things. There's no such thing as secrets in Terrastra where death magic is concerned. Quite frankly that fact alone would make me toss you out of here in an instant and let the damned lictors have you. But no! No one ever asks Qubo Zhang for his opinion on the matter. Now that I've met you, I'm beginning to think this was all a huge mistake."

"Mistake or no," Ohotepe said slowly, "It is too late to back out now." The fight seemed to go out of the shopkeeper. He nodded his head resignedly.

"A mistake!?" Plinius could feel hysteria creeping into his voice. "What in the bloody hells is going on? Who the bloody hells are you people?"

Silence settled inside the tent. A loud voice arguing over the cost of raw iron filtered in through the canvas then receded away into the muffled background. For a moment all four men sat with their thoughts, the only sound in the tent being Plinius' laboured breathing.

Plinius looked up at Ohotepe and pointed at Qubo. "He said I was chosen. Chosen for what? What does that mean?"

Ohotepe returned Plinius gaze. What Plinius saw in those eyes frightened him for a reason he could not fathom. "It be meaning that a certain shopkeeper needs to learn to keep his mouth shut. The reasons for today's events… that is not for me to be saying. Not here, not now. Nor could I be giving you the full picture even if I could," The man walked over and placed a hand on Plinius shoulder. "It be my job to be bringing you to meet with those who can be giving you the answers you be deserving. It be my job because I know it needs to be done- not because I was told to do it. I ask you- do you trust your friend Anatoli?"

Plinius swallowed. "Yes, I suppose so," he replied, not entirely lying. "More than anyone else, I imagine. Where is he?"

"We will see him soon. At the conclave."

"The conclave?" asked Plinius, confused. "What conclave? A conclave for what?"

"A special meeting has been called of..." Ohotepe twirled his fingers, trying to think of the right word, "interested parties. Parties that would see you not come to harm."

"Like Anatoli?"

"Yes. I- *we* will get you to him. You can be trusting me, as he trusts me." He inclined his had to Qubo. "And be trusting him as well, for he is also under the thumb of good Anatoli as well." He looked at the shopkeeper expectantly.

"Yes, yes," Qubo sighed. He shuffled over to the table and gently picked up a grape, staring at it wistfully for a moment before popping it into his mouth. "We all must honour fealty to our king, don't we? I am sorry for the outburst. Very inconsiderate of me. I just wasn't expecting for my life to be utterly fucking destroyed today."

"That makes two of us," agreed Plinius glumly. Qubo did not appreciate the correlation.

"Um, excuse me fella's," Pots piped in as he slowly creeped out from behind his shielding row of garments, making no eye contact as he shuffled towards the canvas flap. His trembling hands gripped tightly around the straps of his bag. "It's getting' preeeetty late, I's reckon I's a just gonna get going, it was a pleasure meeting ya all- but I's has a lot of work to take care of, yer know, so I's will... be going."

"Not so fast, dwarf." Qubo stepped quickly towards the dwarf who let out a frightened yelp.

"Stand down, Qubo," the command in Ohotepe's voice once again surprised Plinius.

Who in the bloody hells are these people? Ohotepe seems to give the orders to this loudmouth. How pathetic. Then again, if Anatoli trusted them, I supposed I did too. I can't believe I haven't blasted that annoying shopkeeper yet.

Plinius, that isn't you. You wouldn't 'blast' him.

Oh, I don't mean literally. I would never use my magic to harm someone.

Is that so?

Why are you asking me? I reckon you would know better than I at this point. The quality of my character, I mean. You say we are friends; have been for a long time. You have memories of me that I am denied. So, when I say I would never use my magic to harm someone, and you reply with 'Is that so?', it makes me question exactly who I am. Can you understand that?

Better than you remember.

Exactly my point.

Ohotepe walked over to Pots and kneeled, so they were eye level. "I am afraid the time for you to be leaving has come and gone, Mr. Pots," he said, not unkindly. "You be hearing too much."

"Sorry buddy," interrupted Qubo off handedly, swallowing his grape, and not sounding sorry at all.

"I be having no choice but insisting you come with us. Do not be worrying- I be assuring you be getting what is owed to you."

Pots rubbed his beard with his mottled-stained hands and Plinius thought he might start to cry. "Very well then," Pots replied, sounding completely unenthusiastic. "My Da always said to nevah leave things half done; I reckon that goes for adventures as well."

"That be the spirit!" Ohotepe clapped the dwarf on the back. "That is exactly what this is! An adventure!"

"A quest," murmured Plinius.

Ohotepe looked at Plinius, smiling even wider. "It be a quest! That be the spirit, Pliny!"

Plinius and Qubo groaned audibly at the same time, which was promptly followed by them exchanging dirty looks.

"So… what exactly is the quest then?"

"All in good time- *never a straight answer out of commoners-* first we need to get through the market to Wayfarer's Road. That be the tricky part."

Wayfarer's Road? That's the main raise on Lowhill. What's so tricky about that? Plinius could guess where they were heading but kept his mouth shut, letting his protests die on his lips.

"What's so tricky about walking to a road?" asked Pots, perplexed. Plinius imagined the map of the city sprawled out before him, a perfect copy of the one that used to hang behind his desk at the bookshop. His hand twitched, and the scent of the River filled Plinius' nostrils. The lower market was the largest 'district', for lack of a better word, in the city. Wayfarer's Road was the main thoroughfare up the smallest of the high hills. From where he guessed they were, based off where they had come from…

"The publicans," said Plinius, realization dawning.

Qubo arched an eyebrow. Ohotepe nodded. "Just so, master magus. Hence why we are here to be availing Mr. Zhang of his services.

Now, Qubo, how about you be getting us those coats?" Ohotepe appraised the dwarf. "I hope you be having some in small. You two- be listening good. This is what we be going to do."

Chapter Eight

Maps & Magocracy

"This collar itches like crazy, how can those cretins stand it?"

"By Cronus' balls, would you shut up already?" implored Qubo for what seemed the hundredth time.

Ohotepe and Plinius were dressed head to toe in the garb of the Terrastran militia. *Oh, the indignity of it all. I'm eminently thankful none of my old magisters can see me.* It made Plinius incredibly uncomfortable for a variety of reasons. Firstly, impersonating a member of the militia was a crime punishable by death. Not just from the Empire's overreach, which was growing further and further by the hour, but since the founding of the city by decree of the Lyceum Council itself. Plinius had no real qualms with breaking the Empire's rules but flaunting the laws of Terrastra gave him a queasy feeling. Qubo's sardonic response to that objection had been the magus was already on death-watch for crimes far worse so there was no sense in troubling himself about it. Plinius had begrudgingly admitted the arrogant shopkeeper had a point.

The second reason was of a more personal nature that he kept to himself. Dressing up like a common soldier wounded his pride immeasurably. *See! I am a bloody magus of the bloody eighth circle! Look at the low they've brought me to.* Although he didn't voice this objection, he was convinced all three of his companions were fully aware of and relishing every minute of his discomfort. *They do seem to have varying levels of disdain for me. It is rather strange.* For the thousandth time that day Plinius wistfully imagined his bookstore, intact and whole.

The third and final reason was the uniform was incredibly uncomfortable, period. A starchy, dirty, and matted woollen undershirt with a turtleneck collar, a chainmail hauberk and coif, thick leather gloves missing a few fingers, second hand boots and a fraying cloak of striped blue and red were decidedly outside of Plinius usual wardrobe. *I remember I had never worn armour in my life until then. How do people do that all day? How do they even fight in it?* For the millionth time in his life, Plinius thanked merciful Cronus and the Blessed Concord he had been born a magus. He knew the plan made sense- Ohotepe had explained it well.

Oh, gremlin shit another flash-

Ohotepe had laid out the plan on the dirt floor of Qubo Zhang's shop while the shopkeeper rummaged through chests. *I think I'm going to be sick. Don't worry about me; I'm just going to ride this out.*

"Now, this square be the low market, with the Exchange in the middle. You be seeing?" He used a small dagger he had procured from some hidden place on his body to carve furrows in the dirt. Where Ohotepe could have possibly hidden it, Plinius could not figure out for the life of him. "With the southern Exitgate here," he marked a big X on the perimeter of the circle, "and the Tradegate here. And we are here."

"Where's the Crowgate?" asked Pots.

"Be not mattering."

As Ohotepe made a small square near the western edge of the circle, Plinius began to cluck his teeth, snapping his tongue along the roof of his mouth. It took Plinius a moment to notice everyone had stopped and were looking at him.

"Ah," Plinius' cheeks warmed. "Sorry."

Ohotepe pursed his lips.

"Why are you looking at me like that?"

"What is it, Plinius?" asked Ohotepe, "Out with it, now is not the time to be holding back your thoughts."

"Ah. It is nothing… well, it's just, it's not very accurate, is it?"

Something in Qubo's eyes made him uneasy. "I'm sure you could do *much* better."

"Well, maybe I can!" bristled Plinius, "but it would require the use of the River."

Ohotepe looked uncertain. "How warded is this tent?" the Coptician asked the Kantan.

Qubo frowned. "Warded enough. As long as it's below 7th circle, any spell should be sufficiently masked from detection." *A 7th circle scryward? Impressive, that does NOT come cheap.*

Ohotepe mulled this over, then nodded to Plinius.

"Excellent. Do we have parchment here?"

Qubo laughed. "Why the bloody hell would I have parchment?"

Plinius sucked air in through his teeth. "Hmmm… Oh, I know! May I see the dagger, please?" asked Plinius politely.

Ohotepe nodded, tossing the dagger upwards into the air, catching the blade effortlessly between his fingers and proffering the hilt. Something in the Coptician's eyes said he knew more than he was letting on. "Let us be seeing what you can do then, Plinius."

Grabbing the dagger, Plinius used his sleeve to wipe away the map.

Kneeling in the dirt, he reached into the magical bag on his hip and pulled out the jet-black quill. He smiled sadly as he cradled it. Taking out some string, Plinius wrapped around the quill and the blade of the dagger so that they were securely attached to each other, both of their points aligning. The others, even Qubo, looked on with curiosity. *Every commoner loves to see how the sausage is made.* He concentrated, his eyes getting a faraway look. The others could feel a tingling on their skins, a rush of energy into the air that gave them goosebumps. His hand twitched.

Muttering under his breath, he surrendered himself to the River.

The dagger/quill took on a life of its own as his astral self was born aloft by the River. Terrastra appeared below him, from this perspective as if it was a city built for mice. He ignored the smoke pouring from the west side of the city. He quickly began etching lines and shapes on the dirt in front of him. His hand worked without conscious thought- like a musician or a painter, the hand listened to the memory and did not as what Plinius told it to do but just did it of its own accord. It was as natural as a breeze pushing leaves or water spilling over a cliff. First the Exchange in the centre, then the wall, then the gates- like what Ohotepe had drawn but with precise turns and lengths that Plinius just knew to be correct. In the span of half a minute the wagon wheel shape of the twelve main Lowmarket roads and nearly double that amount in side streets took shape on the dirt floor. The tents and stalls, the thoroughfares and docking pens, the auctioneer stands and the public fountains, all marked out with supernatural precision. Even the public bath and the lesser fornicaes with their silt trenches running back towards The Runs. All this and more Plinius sketched out at the same time it had taken Ohotepe to draw his crude approximation. With a final long exhalation, Plinius eyes regained focus and the shop came back into view, the view of Terrastra dissolving back into the River. With five quick slashes he gouged five identical furrows around the map, with a final point stabbed into the earth directly adjacent to a long thick spiral line that could not be anything but the Wayfarers Road. Plinius looked down at the map and nodded in satisfaction.

"What the bloody hells was that?"

Plinius snapped his eyes up. Qubo had his arms wrapped up in a bundle of various clothes half pulled out of a chest, his task forgotten as his wide eyes fixed upon Plinius. Ohotepe studied the map, no awe or wonder on his face. *Pure business that one.* Pots let out a low whistle before breaking out into a huge grin, the first one on the dwarf's face since Qubo aired the grandmagus' dirty secrets. "Edge take ye, Plinius! How'd ya learn how t' do that? It were magic, weren't it?"

"Well, yes and no," answered Plinius sheepishly. He had not had an audience when casting his unique spell for many years. He unwrapped the quill from the dagger and stroked it lovingly before returning it to his bag. "I just have an excellent memory, you see. I see something once, and, well, it's up there," he tapped the side of his head with two fingers, "That memory is a springboard, a base reagent that I can use to reproduce drawings even beyond what I can immediately, physically, see. I can reproduce it with near accuracy using a few modified incantations that my mentor and I had devised. But the key is something completely normal; because of my memory." *An excellent memory? Isn't this rich. Why can't I remember shit?*

"Is this something all scriveners can do?" questioned Qubo.

"No, not at all! In fact, not a one can do this. In truth, the spell is closer to the school of ritualism than it is scrivening," Plinius answered. "As far as I am aware, I am the only magus among all magi who can do this. It was my mentor's belief that it was a lucky combination of my natural talents and chosen studies. We call it chorogramancy."

"Cho-rug-a-man-cheese." Pots repeated slowly, clearly annunciating each syllable, the incorrect ones doubly so.

Plinius patted him patronizingly on his shoulder. "Close enough."

Qubo leaned over the map, clearly impressed, "And you would say this is accurate? At least to what you remember from a map you've seen?" Qubo asked sceptically.

"That's the best part!" Plinius smiled excitedly, his pointed finger darting at the shopkeeper. He noticed Ohotepe looking at him intently with a curious look that seemed like satisfaction and paused, before the Coptician nodded encouragingly, and he continued. "As long as I'm somewhat aware of my surroundings- like from an old map, or if I could get a good look from a particular vantage point- then I can use a certain spell I devised to, well, how do I explain…" he searched for the words. "It's like far-seeing, but not? You know scrying? Good- it's somewhat like that." *I'm really dumbing it down here. It's not based off scrying at all. A completely different spell base and unique somatic gestures, most amazingly no semantic component required at all! Brilliant, isn't it? This spell was my thesis; it earned me my grey robe.* "I see but at the same time I don't see. It's an impression I can sense of the place that lets my hands reproduce it. Completely automatic and of the River's accord. Does that make sense?"

The shopkeeper snorted. "Not a Cronus-damn bit," spat Qubo, turning away and busying himself with the clothes. Plinius dug his fingernails into his palm.

"Far-seein'?" Asked Pots, his tongue sticking out of his mouth as his mind worked. "I thought that was against the Concord?"

"Like he cares about breaking the law," quipped Qubo.

Plinius frowned, not deigning to reply to the surly shopkeeper. "No, not at all, Pots. Far-seeing is used routinely for weather prediction, scouting, infrastructure planning, animal herding and such. Obviously used in research where surveillance is paramount. All of that is well within the remit of the Circles. The Blessed Concord bans us from using it to look west over the ocean."

"Bleeseed concooord," mumbled Qubo.

"Only *west?*" Pots said the second word with a mixture of awe and dread. Plinius noticed Qubo and Ohotepe shiver at the utterance of the word as well.

"Yes, only west," Plinius nodded solemnly, leaning in a bit closer, unable to help himself. He looked Pots deep in the eye whispering ominously.

"The Edge."

Ohotepe made a ward with his fingers. *That's the somatic motion for dream warding. Not at all curious that you would see such things aped by commoners- they have been appropriating our culture since the dawn of time.* Pots eyes grew even wider at the word Edge, his breath escaping in a frightened wheeze like a deflating bellows. Plinius was sure he even saw Qubo lean in a bit closer at its mention.

"So, you know of the Edge?" asked Plinius conspiratorially.

"Of course we know," interrupted Qubo. "Everyone knows the Edge."

"Ah yes, but do you know of its nature? Do you know its true name?"

"True name?" Qubo looked dubious.

"The Edge is the Edge, ser," answered Pots.

"The Stygiaqueore," supplied Ohotepe quietly.

Plinius looked at Ohotepe in surprise.

Ah, I do look surprised. I'm assuming I was too distracted in the Tradebasin warrens to notice his use of the word earlier.

Boy- I mean, Ohotepe- used the word earlier?

That he did. You do not recall? I expressed surprise earlier. Wait- are you not paying attention when I offer my insight? Tales, that is most disheartening.

I pay attention! I just did not remember.

"How did you know that?"

Ohotepe shrugged nonchalantly. "I be picking up the word here or there."

"Well," Plinius began slowly, reappraising the Coptician for what seemed like the hundredth time today, "Yes, exactly. The Stygiaqueore. From the ancient tongue. It means the endless sea. The end of the world. The abyss. The void. The end of the horizon, Mir, and all things. As it were."

"The Edge is a punishment and a promise that all things end and only through the magi can we forestall that end," recited Pots proudly.

Plinius looked aghast. "Where in the bloody hells did you hear that doggerel?" he asked incredulously.

"Church," he answered, shrugging, momentarily excited at the mention of dogs.

"Church? The Stygiaqueore isn't a punishment! Nor is it a promise. It just is! Always has been! It's a natural phenomenon- the edge of Mir. The end of the River. Where else do you think Mir Firma would end and the Heavens begin? Really, Pots, your ignorance here is most dispiriting."

"His ignorance?" exploded Qubo, "Who in the bloody hells do you think taught him that? It was your kind! And if it's so natural, why does it make magi go mad?"

It was Plinius' turn to shrug. "The closer one scries to the Edge, the greater the danger grows. That is the prevailing theory the last time I read up on the current discourse regarding Stygiology-"

"Stygiology?" asked Ohotepe. *He seems sincerely interested. An inquiring mind. I approve.*

"The study of the great abyss. It's not a very… popular field of study, as one might imagine."

"Why's that ser?" asked Pots.

"Something about the Edge addles the brain. No one knows why- the fools brave or stupid enough to attempt scrying always wind up in no position to let us know what they saw. Some think it's natural, some think it's Cronus' divine will… I don't know if we'll ever know. That's the inherent danger. Every time it has been attempted it renders the magus a gibbering idiot."

"As opposed to the usual idiots they naturally are," retorted Qubo, holding up and inspecting a blue and red cloak. "Teeps, I seriously hope you are not going to trust this bastard."

"Believe it or not, tailor," Plinius relaxed at the sound of Ohotepe's stifled chuckle over the word tailor, "This is about the most accurate current map of the lower market you will ever see. *This* is what a grandmagus is capable of!"

Qubo snorted, spitting on the ground.

"Cannae ya do this trick with other things ya remember?" interjected Pots, his brow furrowed in thought. "Like faces or letters?"

Plinius turned and smiled at the dwarf. "Very astute, Pots! Indeed, I can. It's what makes me such a successful scrivener. I need only see an incantation once, regardless of the script, and I can reproduce it in full. Sometimes in even better quality than the original! It really depends on the medium I'm working with," he gestured at the map at their feet, "with parchment and ink, I could show you the location of every merchant stall. With the right ingredients- reagents of nature and such- I could draw the ruts in the roads, the flowers blooming in sheltered corners. I could even draw you each drying puddle from last week's rain!"

Wait, wait, wait. You're telling me that 'past' me has an eidetic memory? And here I am trying to remember the names of people I've apparently known for years?

It's your excellent memory that has encouraged us into thinking this will work. We are sure we can get your memory back- and it does seem to be working.

You just have an answer for everything, don't you? Yet answers that deflect and obfuscate. I take away less than I brought in most of our conversation.

I'm sorry you feel that way.
Save your false apology.

Qubo snorted again, mumbling something under his breath. Plinius once again elected to ignore him.

"What about people?" Ohotepe said hopefully. "Could you be showing us if there are any lictors in the lower market?"

Plinius shook his head. "Sadly no. As I said, it is not quite far-seeing. People, animals- anything moving, really- are beyond the scope of my talents. Well, I have other spells that could show us all the humans, or elves, or dwarves in the market. Nothing so specific as 'lictors' I'm afraid. I have the advantage of being very prompt and quick with my chorogramancy over a true far-seeing spell. That spell is taxing in nature- it's quite interesting! One needs to gather seven mages of at least fifth level and then-"

Ohotepe interrupted the magus and pointed at the final furrows made. "Excuse me magus; I would be guessing that these marks are the locations of the publican's tax outposts. The dagger being the main office?"

Plinius nodded. "Very good! Exactly so."

"This is being most excellent," Ohotepe nodded in approval, patting the grandmagus on the back. Plinius shot Qubo a smug grin and was dismayed to find the shopkeeper with his back turned to him. "Anatoli has sung your praises; but seeing it in person is another thing entirely."

Plinius's grin fell from his face. "Anatoli told you about this?"

"Pay that no mind; we trust each other, remember?"

Plinius chewed his lip. "Mmmm."

Ohotepe ignored his noncommittal answer. His eyes scanned the map ever so slowly.

"We will be steering far clear of the gates- given the ongoing search the likelihood of lictors being stationed at them in force is all but certain. That means the outer concourse and streets two through six are out of the question."

"The outer concourse would be too packed anyways, notwithstanding the fact it would take us well out of our way," said Qubo, not bothering to look up from the pile of clothes he was sorting.

"Just so. Still, a less direct route might be better."

"Why is that?" asked Plinius. "Should not speed be of the essence? I really have no interest in running into that centurion brute again."

"No, friend magus. See? These two publican posts patrol between each other constantly, harassing merchants from here," he pointed at the northernmost spoke next to Wayfarers Way, then swept his finger down to the southwest, "to here at Seventh Street where it be turning into Harald's Way."

"Why dinnae we just stick to the sideways between the' Spokes?"

suggested Pots, eager to contribute.

"Spokes?" asked Plinius.

"What the commoners be calling the streets that be running perpendicular to the Exchange," answered Ohotepe, "Too crowded with the type of people who will be raising the alarm if Grandmagus Scrivener is recognized." Ohotepe shook his head at the thought. "We be having a better plan, one to keep us as ordinary as possible with the least amount of risk."

Studying the map Plinius could only come to one conclusion. His uneasiness grew exponentially. "You mean for us to traverse across the Exchange?"

"Just so!" Ohotepe clapped silently, impressed at the magus' inference.

"That's mad!"

Ohotepe nodded. "Indeed, it would be, in most situations."

Plinius shook his head. "I'll be spotted for sure! It's arguably the busiest place in the whole city! It'll be crawling with lictors!"

"Wait a dang second," Pots piped in. "Ye said th' sideways would be too crowded! The Exchange 'as a sight more people."

"You be correct," Ohotepe agreed, "but there are two different types of crowded."

"The people along the sideways," jumped in Qubo, dropping a mound of carefully selected clothes on the ground which he promptly started stomping on repeatedly, grinding them into the dirt floor with his heel, "are talkers, gawkers, guards & hawkers. Some of these people live all their lives walking between the spokes. They know a thousand people by name and tens of thousands by sight. Remember the dock fire a few years back? How quickly it moved up to The Runs? Good- that is exactly how gossip spreads in the Wheel. Information travels faster than a voidcrow down here. And there's nothing the people love down here more than something out of the ordinary that'll break up the monotony of common living."

"I imagine you are coming to a point?" said Plinius tersely. *I wish this fool would get to it.*

"Hold on to your pointy hat, mage," spit Qubo, "I'm getting there. Now, the Exchange, we might run into easily five times the amount of people we would if we went through the spokes. It's the type of people that make all the difference. Do you get it?"

Qubo paused and looked at them expectantly. Ohotepe was looking back at him with a grin, clearly enjoying the explanation. Pots nodded his head as if he understood but Plinius doubted it. Plinius' impatience got the better of him. "Just out with it for Cronus' sake!"

The patronizing smile Qubo gave him made Plinius want to punch someone for the first time in his life. *How do you make a proper hitting fist? Which is the correct fist to use?*

"The people in the Exchange are *busy*. They're making bids at auction, or carting bulk goods down to Harald's Way, or were mad enough to try and take a shortcut between the spokes and are consequently running later than a dwarf to a Tsarusskan birthday. The point is they're far too busy to stop and smell the gremlin shit. With a little bit of blending in, no one will ever know we were there."

"So, you be seeing? A good plan, no?" said Ohotepe, clearly asking for Plinius' thoughts.

"Sounds good t' me!" agreed Pots.

"One obvious problem," stated Plinius condescendingly. He snatched the dagger from the dirt and waggled it towards Ohotepe. "This route will take us right past the main office! I thought the whole plan was to circumvent the publicans!"

"On the contrary," replied Qubo, looming over Plinius in a sickly-sweet voice relishing his big moment to put down the magus, "I'm going to say hello to my good friends from the Imperial Publican Bureau, like I have a million times before. And you will be walking right beside me." Qubo held up the uniform he had been doing his best to kick to death.

Plinius let out a groan as he moved his thumb around his clenched fist.

Pots wheezed as he tried to adjust the bundle on his back.

They were making decent time towards the interior of the lower market. A large cloud of disturbed dust kicked up in front of them, a hazy beacon drawing them towards the Exchange. Once they had gone over the plan half a dozen times, mostly for Pots benefit, they headed out from the shop. Qubo had lingered at the entranceway, taking a long look back inside before promptly turning with an air of finality about him. He did not look back again. Plinius thought he saw a little moisture in Qubo's eyes and was going to snidely remark on it before he remembered his bookstore. He kept his thoughts to himself.

They made their way down the spoke nearest to Qubo's tent, south-easterly towards the Exchange, making their way through a daunting press of foot and cart traffic. This part of the lower market was mostly stalls and temporary tents erected by merchants from outside the walls, in the city for a day of frantic trading before heading out at dawn the next day back to their homesteads and ranches. Competition for business was fierce as most merchants wanted to clear out their stock before sundown- all to get a better spot in the caravansary ahead of the end of day rush. There was a constant battle in the low market to jockey for a prized bivouac near the Last Gate in the south- the Imperial customs officials were notoriously less lenient as the day wore on, so ensuring a quick exit from the city by virtue of where you camped was a goal shared by any merchant familiar with Terrastra.

Consequently, most merchants tried their hardest to stand out from the crowd with all manner of attention-grabbing strategies. This area of the market was a riot of colour and noise and smells. Banners of blue and red spun wool advertising Terrastran stock pandered to the patriotic. Meat pies that wafted savoury scents of cooked pork and musky spices sat atop common-made brick ovens, catching the hungry and gluttonous alike despite the cost being much higher than what Plinius thought fair. A large heavyset man worked a music box from an open threadbare tent, a dancing monkey in a tiny wizard robe bounding from one foot to another much to the delight and mirth of commoners walking by. Plinius found it less funny than Qubo who stopped and threw the man a piece of silver, but he could not deny it worked as many people stopped to peruse the cheap trinkets he had on display.

The man nodded at Plinius as they walked away. "Terrastran strong!" he said, holding his fist over his heart. Plinius stared at him dumbfounded for a moment until he remembered what he was wearing.

"Ahem, yes, Terrastran strong," Plinius stuttered out, quickly returning the gesture.

Qubo leaned over and whispered in Plinius ear, "You're in the militia, magus. For the love of Cronus act like one."

Plinius ignored Qubo but took the advice. *It's not hard to play the part. Just look like a dumb brute.* Plinius studied Ohotepe and how he was carrying on. The Coptician walked with the unhurried but self-assured rolling swagger of a militiaman, carrying a certain air of casual authority. Plinius straightened his back and tried to walk with more confidence. *Ohotepe is more interesting by the minute. If I didn't know better, this was a completely different person. His talent at impersonation and mimicry is amazing.*

"Dinnae see why I's 'ave to be th' porter," Pots grumbled.

"We've been over this, dwarf," said Qubo, exasperation evident through the clenched teeth behind a fake smile as he waved to someone across the way. "We didn't have a uniform that fit you."

"Ye could have adjusted it. Yer a tailor ain't ya?"

Qubo clenched his fists. "For Cronus' sake, I am not a bloody tailor. How can you not get that through your thick skull?"

"Ye look like a tailor." Pots pouted.

"Yes, and you look like my porter. Now please shut up and proceed to 'port'." Pots was laden down with twined and burlap wrapped parcels of fine cloth and apparel. Stacked one on top of each other, the burden was nearly twice the height of the dwarf himself. He carried it effortlessly if not a bit clumsily. Qubo had him remove his soiled clothes back at his shop and replaced it with the simple flax-spun tunic and wool pants of a common Terran day labourer. Pots had protested vehemently about losing his clothes and insisted that he bring them along in one of the bundles. This was deemed to be too much of a risk as the smell itself would draw too much attention. Plinius had offered to clean them, but Ohotepe was very quick to shut that idea down, saying it was a frivolous use. *A magus who can't use his magic. Like a dragon who can't breathe fire. A beautiful thing diminished.*

"Maybe I could have been the merchant, and you could have been the pack mule," Pots muttered, clearly unwilling to let it go.

Qubo rounded on the dwarf, lowering his voice. "Listen here you piss-addled dolt! The whole plan hinges on the publican's familiarity with me! Not to mention a dwarf merchant would undoubtedly be singled out for harassment by the Imperials. How do you not understand this?"

"I reckon I'd make a good merchant," Pots insisted, adopting a high pitched, grating voice that sounded just enough like Qubo. "'Ello good sers, may I interest ya in some dandy hats?"

Plinius did not even try to stifle his laughter. Qubo looked at him with annoyance, then back at the dwarf. "I do not sound like that."

"I-dunno-sound-like-that," Pots mimicked, his accent even worse than before. This time Plinius could not stifle his laughter.

"Attention, friends," Ohotepe muttered just audible for the three of them. "Look lively Qubo."

A short man with a fat face in finely threaded robes of what looked like Xeijpangian silk was approaching. *Those robes must cost a fortune. No less than a dozen skellions at the least.* A shock of grey hair wrapped around his temples in a tonsure while the top of his head was completely devoid of hair and the colour of an angry, ripe tomato. Dangling from his neck was an ostentatious gold chain that glittered in the midday sun, a large iron pendant emblazoned with the symbol of a gaping and toothless mouth swallowing an hourglass, resting against the top of a bulging belly. In one hand he carried a cloth covered basket which smelled of fresh baked bread, while the other hand was outstretched as the man beelined towards Qubo.

"Qubo Zhang! What a pleasure running into you today!"

Qubo smiled gregariously and clasped the man's outstretched palm into his own. "Deacon Albus! Indeed, a pleasure! Cronus' grace to you!"

The deacon bowed his head slightly. "And also, to you, my friend." The deacon glanced at Plinius and Ohotepe, his eyes passing over Pots for a moment with disinterest before returning to Qubo. "Quite the retinue you have in tow! What brings you this far down the spoke today?"

Qubo waved a lazy hand back towards Pots. "Business, what else? I am heading up to the guildhall to fulfil an order. You know their type- I thought it best to enlist the aid of some of Terrastra's finest to protect my interests."

Albus nodded wisely, his chins wobbling. "Mmm yes, Terrastran's finest. I hope you did not pay too much- you should have consulted with me, my friend! I could have helped. I have friends you know- one lictor are worth five of these… locals."

"No doubt!" agreed Qubo. "But then I would be in your debt."

"We are all in debt to the Allfather, my son," intoned Albus pompously,

"'Let all debts be mine, as I am the collector of all debts. Fear not when the debt comes due, for in the night hour I shall satisfy all debts; know that those who break faith with the blessed will be cast out from the light. This is the promise of the Emperor. By the Emperor so sworn."

"By the Emperor so sworn," repeated everyone but Plinius, who was too shocked to speak.

"The Magocracy is here as a friend! You can place your trust in the Empire, friend Qubo. You would know this if you came to service more regularly!"

"My apologies, Deacon," Qubo looked contrite, "Surely you do not doubt my faith in Cronus or our glorious Emperor?"

"Of course not! Of course not, my dear child!" Albus patted Qubo on the shoulder, "I know you are a true friend. In the coming times, we will all need to lean on each other, eh? One faith, one people, one Empire, eternal may He reign."

"Eternal may he reign," repeated the three Terrans, followed quickly by Plinius half a syllable behind. *Eternal, may he reign? Who reign? Are they talking about the Emperor?* The deacon blinked his eyes at him for a moment before turning back to Qubo with a frown.

"Truly, though, a man in such good grace as yourself should be accompanied by the faithful. Next time come to me, and I will see you have an escort fit for one of the Emperor's most blessed children."

Qubo bowed his head reverently. "You are of course as correct as you are generously kind, good Deacon. You know the guild though. I thought it better to adhere to local flavour so as not to ruffle their feathers."

"Pah!" The deacon scoffed, spitting a ball of phlegm into the dirt that narrowly missed Pots foot. "Those fools will get what is coming to them soon enough." The deacon leaned in close to Qubo. "Have you heard the news? Apparently some Terran scum from Midhill has fled the Emperor's justice. Not just any Terran- a magus nonetheless! That's what caused that ungodly column of smoke rising from the middle of the city. A magus! Who has ever heard of such a thing? One of the acolytes from the shrine told me that he heard it from a centurion that he was consorting with daemons, committing all manner of carnal acts that profane the light of Cronus." The deacon tittered indulgently, "Even now the entire force of lictors in the city are breaking skulls and kicking in doors. Turning out all the vile anathema from their unclean dens to find the man. Can you believe it?"

Qubo nodded slowly, a large frown on his forlorn face. "I fear I must believe it, if it is coming from one as holy and trustworthy as you, Deacon. I must confess, though, I find your news almost impossible to believe! A magus? Why would one such as he turn from the light of the Emperor? Are not all magi part of the Magocracy?"

Plinius was hoping his face was staying neutral. *All part of the Magocracy? I think not! Commoners think we're all the same, all of us in cahoots. They certainly love to generalize us. They know so little.*

The deacon nodded in agreement. "Far be it from me to comment on politics amongst the blessed magi, but I understand what you mean. How could one of Cronus' chosen turn from the light? It does happen, unfortunately. Magi are just as susceptible to the allure of anathemic practices as men. Go visit Vokgorod if you need proof. I have it from my sources at the Hall that there are still hold-outs among the Terrans. They refuse to accept their place in the Magocracy. They break faith with the Blessed. They are a prideful and stubborn people."

"Too true, too true."

"Worry not, brother Zhang," the Deacon said reassuringly, winking. "This lot will be brought to heel soon enough. Just you wait and see. The Emperor will not be denied. Cronus wills it."

Qubo arched an eyebrow. "Is that so? What have you heard?"

"Oh, just more rumours you know. Let's just say change is coming quicker than these anathema loving freaks and this sorry excuse for a city realizes." The deacon laughed.

Plinius could see the shopkeepers' shoulders tense for a moment. By the time the deacon had finished laughing, Qubo had regained his disguise. "I look forward to the day, Deacon. Thank you for the chat- I must be off. Business to attend to and all that."

"Of course, of course," the deacon replied amiably. "Go in the light of Cronus, my son." The deacon's jowls glistened with sweat as he turned his face sunwards, holding out a hand bedecked with rings of silver and gold, faceted gems adorning them like a berry bush in full flower.

"And also with you, deacon," murmured Ohotepe as he leaned over and kissed the top of his sweaty hand. *Gross.*

When they had walked far enough to be out of earshot, Qubo fell back alongside Ohotepe. "What in the bloody hell was that fat old fraud talking about?"

"Focus, Qubo." Ohotepe replied, keeping his eyes forward. "Pay the words of that viper no mind. Be focusing on the task at hand."

Qubo was insistent. "Teeps- don't. Just don't. I know you know something. What did he mean by a change coming soon?"

Ohotepe kept walking, his lips sealed. With a grunt of dissatisfied frustration, Qubo strode ahead of him, leaning heavily into the persona of arrogant merchant.

The rest of their walk down the spoke was uneventful except for Pots stumbling in a wheel rut and almost dropping the entire load. Qubo lambasted the dwarf audibly and forcefully for a minute as he sorted himself out, much to the delight of a few human onlookers and a hooded stare from a dwarf merchant. *That's the second time today Pots has taken abuse, even if Qubo is only playing a part.*

You mean third time.

Third time? No, you are mistaken.

I don't think I am.

When was the third then? The pueri asshole in the midmarket, and now with this insufferable fool. What third time?

The alleys?

The alleys? Behind my house?

Yes!

What of them?

You asked when the third time was.

Truly? I didn't even notice when we were there. Who was abusing him?

Are you being serious right now?

What?

It was you!

EXCUSE ME?

You threatened Pots! With the thaumaturgy!

I most assuredly did not.

You tried to terrify him! You accused him of being an agent of the Empire!

Preposterous. I'll show you.

No! Plinius wait-

Chapter Two
Plinius & Pots

Anatoli slapped Plinius on the back encouragingly, as the magus strode heroically into the alley, hiking his bags on to his shoulder, an unshakeable aura of determinism about him as he answered his call to adventure. He leaned against a stack of wooden crates, rocking slightly as they accepted his weight. Plinius rounded on him just in time to hear Anatoli whisper "Remember- the market! Be quiet as a mouse, *da?*"

He took a step forward, clasping his friend's arm in his own. "The market. I won't let you down, Anatoli."

See, here we are. You'll see for yourself.

Plinius… this… you can't do this…

What are you talking about?

This… isn't… how it's supposed to work…

Oh shush. Are you in pain?

No… it's just… nauseous…

I'm sure no worse than what I've been experiencing, I assure you.

Please Plinius, let's just return to where we were-

I think not! You accused me of unbecoming behaviour. You'll see the truth of it shortly.

He found himself facing a brick wall. Plinius couldn't help but admire the craftmanship of his bolthole- no seam or crack betrayed the slightest hint that the back of his shop was anything but a normal wall of red brick. He had a fleeting thought to cast the spell of opening to march back in and join Anatoli in facing the lictors head-on. He faltered as he lifted his hand up, a slight distaste creeping up his throat. *Anatoli was counting on me to follow the plan. I could not let him down.* With a quick shake of his head, he turned to survey his new surroundings. That was when the smell hit him.

His nostrils puckered up in revolt as a foul smell found access through his mouth. The smell was more of a living thing, coating his tongue and travelling up backwards through his throat. His body instantly rebelled, gagging and convulsing until he managed to control his reflexes and get himself under control.

Wait a minute. That's not what happened.

What are you talking about? That's what happened.

I don't think so. Hand was here!

Hand? Don't be preposterous.

He was! He cupped your nose to mask the smell.

I don't think so. Anatoli said no magic! You think I'd be foolish enough to cast-

ARE YOU SERIOUS!? YOU DIDN'T LISTEN TO A WORD HE SAID! WHO STOPPED YOU FROM CASTING MAGIC? IT WAS-

Shut up Tales! Here it is-

"G'day!"

Plinius remained as still as a frozen pond, his inherent survival skills kicking in. His eyes darted methodically up and down the alley, giving everything that might be a threat a thorough ocular pat-down. No one was in sight. Looking up he saw a large crow perched on the edge of the roof. The bird cocked its head and stared at him with one beady eye.

"Begone, foul symbol of a corrupt Empire," commanded Plinius.

As the crow flew off, desperately fleeing the wrath of the magus, an awe-struck dwarf stepped out from behind a pile of stinking, crusty rags.

"By the Blessed Concord! That was amazing, grandmagus!" exclaimed the dwa-

This is not what happened!

Sure, it is. Can't you see the words? It's written right there.

Plinius!

Tales!

Edge take me… fine, whatever. Plinius, you can't hijack the story like this. It's counterproductive. Can we please return to where we left off?

First admit that I did not abuse Pots. I won't move on without it.

You can't be serious…

Admit it!

Fine, fine! If it lets us move on, I admit it! You're not like other magi, you're one of the good ones… does that make you happy? Cronus' balls…

Thank you. Was that so hard?

Plinius was slightly aghast at Qubo's treatment of Pots and the acceptance from the surrounding public. Not a single soul stopped to intervene on behalf of the dwarf. Plinius stared in barely restrained horror at Qubo, even knowing this was just for show, he found himself still wondering if the large man was truly laying into Pots. *Qubo is an amazing actor.* If the purpose of such an ugly scene was to blend in and belay any suspicion, it was to Plinius' supreme disappointment that it proved so effective. *When did that become acceptable in Terrastra? That's not the city I remember.*

The last word anyone would use to describe Plinius would be social. *That's fair I suppose. I'm more of a quality over quantity man when it comes to relationships.* Despite that he felt he still had an adequate grasp on what passed for proper behaviour in civilized society. He knew for certain that the idea of publicly mocking a non-human on the streets of Terrastra, purely for the asinine reason of being different, would have been unheard of a few years ago. *By the 15th century the pogroms were a thing of the distant past. Modern civilization had risen above such barbaric practices- Terrastra was- is- an enlightened nation! Sure, I'll admit I've berated dwarves before. But no more than I would berate a human! Everyone can be stupid, regardless of race, and I have no time to suffer that from anyone.*

Plinius jumped back in shock, roused by his reverie as a passer-by threw a half-eaten tomato at the dwarf as he stooped to pick up one of the fallen packages. The crowd around him laughed uproariously as tomato seeds and juice leaked down Pots' face. Ohotepe stepped forward, his spear pointing towards the culprit.

"Enough of that!" barked Ohotepe in a harsh voice, his far southern accent completely vanishing. Plinius could never have imagined him capable of making his voice sound so, for lack of a better word, normal.

"Leave the dwarf alone! He is under our protection."

The man who threw the tomato sneered. "Just 'avin' some fun, suh-ser." Plinius' nose reeled at the stink of alcohol from even a few feet away. "E's just a bitty ya know, it don't hurt him none."

Ohotepe planted the butt of his spear in the dirt, looming over the drunkard and glowering down at him menacingly. The man wobbled as he tried to maintain his dignity, which he promptly abandoned as he plopped backwards onto his ass. "He is my master's servant, and he is on my master's business. Move along!"

The man sat indolently in the dirt, staring up at Ohotepe with a slack jawed. He rubbed snot from his nose with the back of his hand, snorting loudly before spitting in the dirt towards the dwarf. All he managed to accomplish was an impotent dribble of spittle frothing down onto his chin and chest. Somehow the man managed to stumble upright, staring in an impudent manner at Ohotepe for a moment before sticking out his tongue and shambling away. "Stupid milita… -hic! - lictors would'a let me have my fun!"

Ohotepe stared at the man's back as he disappeared into the traffic heading upspoke. *He looks disgusted.* Turning, he helped Pots with the remaining bundles. Pots waved him off, but the Coptician would not be deterred. The final package back in place, Ohotepe squeezed then patted the young dwarf's shoulder. "We be wasting too much time here- let us be quick now."

The sun was halfway past its zenith when they finally reached the Exchange. Plinius was awed at the immensity and vast commotion of what was happening around them. It was one thing to see the size of it on a map, another entirely to have it before you. The only frame of reference Plinius had for it was the midmarket. It was very much like the market, yet completely unlike it in a hundred different ways. A sea of people and beasts churned and crashed across the flat plain of the Exchange for kilometres, a hazy cloud of brown dust kicked up to mingle with the pervasive smoke from a legion of dung-fires, cook-spits, bread-kilns, and farrier-forges. Plinius' eyes watered and his ears throbbed as a thousand voices shouted to be heard above each other, a choral pandemonium of people hurrying every which way, clasping hands, shaking fists, pounding backs, and hordes of people picking up goods and dropping them off, only for them to be picked up by other hands and dropped somewhere else. He strained to make sense of it all. It was like a colossal hydra- every merchant that emptied his carts and stuffed his pockets was quickly followed by two more merchants eager to take their place. Vendors with chest high mobile barrel-wagons on two wheels offered brined pickles and salted meat to the merchants unable to leave their post for repast. *In a world where you can't go to food, food will come to you.* Voidcrows zinged overhead this way and that, relaying time sensitive information from brokerages on the Northhill to their representatives in the auction pits far below. Herds of branded cattle, giant pack-sloths, woolly and not so woolly sheep, cartloads of chickens, bobbing terrostriches and adorable pygmy mammoths were whipped by men on horseback from pen to pen as money exchanged hands between breeders and homesteaders, ranchers, and abattoirs.

The Exchange was like the midmarket, but only if someone had taken it, broken it into its disparate parts, reassembled and grafted them upon each other into something entirely monstrous, a bloated and gluttonous beast of coin and commerce. Plinius wiped his forehead with a trembling hand. *This is the most horrifying thing I have ever witnessed. Or did witness. This is kind of confusing, tense-wise.*

"Ahhhhh," exhaled Qubo, breaking into a wide smile. "Isn't it glorious?"

"Where does everyone tinkle?" asked Pots concerningly.

"Let us not dawdle," Ohotepe urged. "Straight that way, as the crow flies," he pointed towards the Wayfarers Road, rising like a coiled cobra among the whitewashed buildings around the Lowhill. It twisted around the hill until it disappeared behind the eastern edger. Where the road met the low market sat a newer building. The brutalist Magocratic aesthetics was a stark contrast to the more eclectic architecture of Terrastra. Thick walls of spell wrought stone bared teeth of black iron-rod windows. The building looked as if it did not belong. It was devoid of artistry, merely adorned with red and black banners proclaiming their allegiance to the Magistracy and the Empire. Plinius, despite growing up there, had never been a big fan of Imperial architecture. He much preferred the fluted buttresses and clay tile roofs of elegant Terrastran design.

"Here we be going, gentlemen. Keep your wits about you." Ohotepe warned as he waded into the Exchange.

They plunged onwards into the chaos, and Plinius found himself subconsciously gripping his spear tighter as his gaze shifted quickly at the faces hurrying past. *Little good that stick would do keeping me safe.* When Ohotepe had handed him the weapon to fill out his disguise, Plinius had protested on the principle that he would not be able to use it as he did not know the first thing about wielding a weapon. Qubo had chimed in saying that if we were in a situation where Plinius had to use the spear they might as well all slit their own throats.

Pushing through the crowds, Ohotepe yelled to make way. Plinius judged that it was only partially effective. Half the people – *mostly the non-humans it would seem* – would quickly make way for an entourage with two Terrastran militia. The other half, especially those with clear allegiances to the Magocratic Empire, would at best begrudgingly make the minimal amount of room to let them through. At worst they would openly defy the order. That is until Ohotepe fixed them with a glare that encouraged their compliance. *He does not carry himself like the child I mistook him for.*

"Ohotepe?" asked Plinius, a thought popping into his head.

Ohotepe tilted his head, not taking his eyes off from the crowd in front of them. A richly dressed city merchant was berating a stout and plainly attired farmer. The farmer stood next to a donkey-drawn cart laden with some of the sickliest looking vegetables Plinius had ever seen. Limp bundles of carrots and sad looking turnips peeked out from underneath an oilskin cloth. The farmer was barefoot and uniformly brown- he was so crusted with dirt; his true hair colour was almost impossible to discern. The man had clearly come a long way from outside the city and seemed completely past the point of caring about civility. The merchant screamed at him about the price of the vegetables he was there to sell and had drawn a group that shared his sentiment.

"What's am I to do?" The farmer held his hands up and shrugged his shoulders. "I don't set no tax rates; I just sell at what the Empire sets the market to don't I? It's their tariffs and taxes raising the price. You have a problem with it? Take it up with the Emperor! I don't give a basilisk's ass."

"It be robbery is what it is!" said one of the merchants wearing an apron fringed in the green leaved pattern of the grocer's guild. Running a hand through his thin hair he cried "how am I supposed to make a profit when the price has doubled since last month? People won't pay for this!"

"They'll pay if they're hungry enough I reckon," shrugged the farmer, "Take it or starve."

That last sentence did not sit well with the crowd. Plinius did not see who threw the first punch, but in short order two dozen people were rolling around in the dirt, the cart of sad vegetables toppled and being ransacked by people of all ages. A grey-haired old lady shuffled past them as fast as she could go, an armful of yellow celery clutched tightly to her chest. People were running in every direction as the farmer curled into a ball under a hail of stomping feet. Ohotepe quickly ushered them away from the commotion, ignoring the pleas of help and cries of anger directed towards them. The brawl faded into the cacophony of the Exchange as they marched quickly away.

"Hmmm?" Ohotepe said, nodding his head at Plinius. "Did you say something?"

"Oh! No, it was nothing. Ah, I was just wondering. Where are you from?"

"Oh, it looks like the crowd is thinnin' out, that's good," remarked Pots absently.

Ohotepe frowned, his eyes never stopping with their constant scanning. "Why, from Terrastra, fellow militia," he said it in a voice that was not his own, the words hollow and automatic, as if they were very far from what was currently on his mind. "Just like you. Doing the best we can." His demeanour made it clear he was uninterested in further discussion, his focus entirely on the Exchange around him. Plinius nodded in return sheepishly.

"Oh. Sorry."

Ohotepe sighed, softening for a moment. "No, don't apologize. I apologize. Nothing to be sorry about." He smiled warmly at Plinius.

Plinius wiped sweat from his brow. *No shade anywhere in the Exchange.* "Sorry. I am just nervous is all, I've never been- I mean this is just… you know, so my mind begins wandering. Sometimes my mouth just plops open, and I spit out whatever is on my mind before I even know what I'm saying. I think about the stupidest stuff. Not that I think you're stupid!" *Blessed Concord, I'm babbling.* "I don't think you're stupid. Not that I was thinking about you. You just strike me as interesting is all, and-"

Something in his companion's demeanour changed and Plinius abruptly stopped talking. Ohotepe's eyes flashed, his voice turned to hard steel. "This be not good."

Plinius mouth worked like a floundered fish at Ohotepe's sudden anger. "I-I'm sorry- I didn't mean to offend."

"Oh shit," Qubo whispered, "We're screwed."

They had walked out into the centre of the wide-open plaza, the very centre of the Exchange. People were slowly backing away, calmly but deliberately retreating from the centre, a hum of concern driving a rising panic. Erupting from the middle of the plaza with a ground shaking tremble, directly in their path, a pustulating boil was slowly growing from the ground beneath the Exchange. Dirt tumbled like a geyser as it pushed up from the dirt, creating an ever-expanding earthen mound. It quickly levelled out at a height of roughly three metres above grade before expanding outwards. A crackle of energy whipped across the surface, flashes of light banging off like firecrackers. With a keening electric scream from the mound itself, a long scaffold of twisted iron rose like a profane monument, half a dozen hempen cords slithering up through the air, knotting themselves then dangling like writhing snakes from the crossbar. The mound and the scaffold raised up until it could be easily seen across the entire Exchange.

Qubo rounded on Plinius. "Why the hell wasn't this on your fabulous map, magus?"

"Because it obviously wasn't there when I made it! Look!" Plinius pointed and his companions followed his gaze back towards the scaffold.

Even now a half dozen magi in the black leather and chain hauberk hoods of the Empire's aedifactioneers chanted away, working their magics, each of them wading in the River. They twisted earth and wood through sheer manipulation of reality, skills learned then nurtured over decades of intense study, into the shapes they desired. A crowd was quickly swelling in size, the initial panic giving way to curiosity, the commoners intrigued by this powerful display of magic. A long ramp rose connecting the mound to the ground, pointing directly back towards the heart of Terrastra. Carts and stalls in the way of their work were reduced to splinters of wood with a casual disregard. The protestations from the merchants owning those carts and stalls were habitually ignored. Hefty planks of timber half a dozen metres long flew upwards from a stack nearby, as easy as a man flicking matchsticks, and assembled themselves into a framework of a tower. As the edifice took shape the natural brown and beige hue of the wood faded and become black and glossy like pitch.

Two other magi nearby rose their arms in tandem and a swirling mass of iron and copper ingots twisted out of a nearby cart and swirled like a tornado towards the foreboding tower. A sizzling sound grew louder as the metal melted into a floating ball of molten alloy before pancaking out into a large disc. It rotated slowly in the air as it rapidly cooled, floating backwards until it fused with the upmost part of the tower. With an air-shattering clang the imprint of the Gladia Virgum indented into the disc, the crossed sword & staff of the Empire a blazon challenge to every Terran witnessing this display of might and magic. A faint fire glowed from within its recesses, like the deep embers of a forge. In the span of a breath the structure was finished, a terrifying edifice of Magocratic Imperial posturing that had instantly become the highest point within the entire Exchange.

Kaaa-Roooom. Kaaa-ROOOOM. KAAA-ROOOOOOM.

An angry choir of drums rose in clanging cries across the city, echoing between the hills, the outer wall, and the natural escarpment. The sound rolled across the choppy waves beneath the Sapphires, between the stained walls of the Runs, and out across Drake Bay. The drums invaded every corner of the city, from the bustling docks to the towers of the Lyceum. It rattled bottles and pans in the alleys. It roiled along the black smoke still pouring from the raging fires on Midhill. *I don't understand how the magi haven't put that out yet. I find it hard to believe there are no elementalists available to combat it.* People began to slow across the city, lagging in their business as they held their breath at the heralding of the drums. The pendulum swung once again, and numerous people in the heart of the Exchange began to move outwards in every direction, wincing and cowering each time the drums sounded. Others stood rooted in spot, torn between the thought of fleeing, and leaving their goods behind, or remaining to bear witness.

Kaaa-Roooom. Kaaa-ROOOOM. KAAA-ROOOOOOM.

"Teeps, what is this?" Qubo asked anxiously.

Ohotepe craned his neck, extending upwards onto the tips of his toes, trying to see what was happening.

The stream of people leaving the plaza began to turn into a rushing tide, more people flowing past Plinius, making their way south and east in hopes of finding an escape. His natural height gave him an unobstructed view over most of the heads in the crowd. "Something is coming towards here from the city centre!"

"We MUST move. Now!" Ohotepe pushed Plinius by the shoulder and grabbed a hold of Pots collar and urged them towards the northeast, forcefully urging them onwards. Plinius was more than happy to oblige, as their current course put the mound between them and whatever was coming.

Kaaa-Roooom. Kaaa-ROOOOM. KAAA-ROOOOOOM.

The flood of people pushing their way towards the spokes came crashing back abruptly. Over the thrashing sea of humanity Plinius could see shining crescent shapes like sails on a horizon, glittering steel halberds pushing back towards the mound, blockading off all escape from the Exchange. His anxiety flared as he quickly glanced around and saw Ohotepe being pushed away from him as the crush of people slowly surged backwards towards the mound. Of Qubo there was no sign at all, and he could barely make out the top of Pots baggage a stone's throw away to the north.

Kaaa-Roooom. Kaaa-ROOOOM. KAAA-ROOOOOOM.

Entering from the City Road, an entire cohort of lictors pushed their way into the already crammed mass of people now bottled tightly in the Exchange. The crowd had no option but to make way, the lockstep movement of the disciplined soldiers with their overlapping tower shields intimidating enough to do the job without violence. Walking in formation six abreast and twenty deep, the outermost lictors on the left and right peeled off and raised their shields while drawing their gladius', yelling at the people to get back and make way. With brutal efficiency they established a kilometre long cordon through to the foot of the mound at the heart of the Exchange. The remaining lictors circled the mound, weapons held at the ready, a solid wall of steel and arms separating the centre from the trapped crowd.

Kaaa-Roooom. Kaaa-ROOOOM. KAAA-ROOOOOOM.

A platform of solid steel floating a metre off the ground made its way into the plaza. Ribbons of orange smoke roiled beneath it like the tentacles of a jellyfish, leaving a sheen of wet umber slime on the ground in its wake. Atop the platform a retinue of Imperial soldiers stood imperiously, stoic and forward facing at attention. Two large drums of stretched hide as big as oxen were mounted on the front corners. Both drums announced their arrival in the same thundering cadence as two imposing goliaths, stripped to the waist with their chiselled mass of muscles on full display, beat on them with mallets the height of a man. Standing between them was an acolyte of the third circle in her yellow robes. Her arms were outstretched before them; she was the source of the platform's locomotion. Orange smoky wisps of spilling watery light emanated from her palms down into the steel, her eyes wide open and dilated so large barely any white could be seen.

Gasps began to rise from the crowd, mutterings of discontent and fear. The arch magistrate, Heuronicus Cato, stood in the centre of the platform atop a raised dais. His silver hair was pinned back into a long ponytail, the tautness of his hair exposing his slanted forehead. His face was all bones and sharp angles, tight lips, and squinty eyes. *So, this is the man everyone fears? He looks rather ghoulish.* Those eyes looked upon the common crowd with barely contained contempt, like an exterminator eyeing a rodent in a trap. His robes were austere but for a single golden broach fashioned in the shape of the Gladia Virgum, inset with a glowing ruby pinned on his collar- the mark of the Emperor, denoting his status as arch magister.

Plinius had never met the man- not even him specifically, but a magister of any stripe. The archmagister for a region anywhere in the Magocracy was usually the highest-ranking local magus, appointed by the Aurum Circle and the Imperial bureaucracy to oversee all business both magical and mundane. Terrastra was the exception to this- given the Lyceum and the city-state's ostensible autonomy, the arch magister here was of the fifth circle and consequently was in a circle well below nearly a thousand other magi currently residing in the city. Being in such a position, it was hard for any archmagister in Terrastra to be taken too seriously by his betters, knowing that his position was not earned but granted by a whole other set of his betters. Still, he was the ultimate authority for the Empire in Terrastra, he sat on the Lyceum Council by dint of the compromise accord and zealously sought to dig the

Emperor's claws into the city with all opportunities that presented themselves. Suffice it to say, Heuronicus Cato was widely mocked and despised by both Terran magus and common alike. *A rank amateur is what he was. Yet I look at him, and I feel a strange feeling. Pity? Fear? Disgust? Maybe all of them? Passing strange to feel such emotion for someone I've never met.*

Kaaa-Roooom. Kaaa-ROOOOM. KAAA-ROOOOOOM.

If the drums were meant to cow the crowd, they were having minimal effect. Protests and insults bloomed up from pockets well out of reach of the lictors halberds. A lithe elvish man next to Plinius shouted "Murderers!"

As the platform inched closer, the knot of lictors standing at attention behind Cato broke their tight formation and spread out along the platform, revealing what they had been guarding. Five people stood on the platform, dishevelled clothes stained with fresh blood, each one hooded in black sackcloth. Chains of solid steel bound their wrists and ankles to the platform. One of the prisoner's shoulders heaved up and down, sobbing. Another, either a dwarf or child given the size, collapsed to one knee. He or she only stood up when one of the lictors turned and beat them with the butt of his halberd. Plinius choked back a gasp as he recognized the lictor as the one who he had seen in the Tradebasin a few hours before, and then once again in the basement tavern. Sure enough, as he scanned the rest of the platform, he saw the other lictors Weasel and Venem standing guard. Weasel looked especially excited; his face split in a wide grin despite the fresh bruise across his cheek.

Kaaa-Roooom. Kaaa-ROOOOM. KAAA-ROOOOOOM.

As the platform reached the mound, one edge began to dip like butter melting in the sun, freezing into the shape of a ramp. The controller magus moved her arms in a gesture as if she was laying a baby in a cradle. The orange smoke dissipated, and the platform settled on the ground with a resounding thud, like a nail on a coffin. The goliath drummers gently laid down their mallets, then began a slow roll with their fists on the drums. The archmagister, always one for spectacle, floated upwards towards the tower, carried up on a beam of light that emanated from him. Plinius was irked when he heard a few gasps of awe. *What a cheap trick. Lightbeams, really? Since when has that ever been required to invoke levitation? Totally unnecessary. Any magi in the second circle or higher could see right through it.*

As the archmagister took his place on top of the tower, the chains that bound the prisoners separated from the platform. Not in a mechanical fashion- they were literally part of the platform, and then they were not. The Centurion stepped up behind the prisoners, causing them to cringe in terror as he roared like a lion.

"MOVE!"

His lictors began to prod the prisoners forward up to the scaffold. Plinius felt a growing sense of apprehension clawing up from the pit of his stomach. His eyes darted back and forth from the hooded wretches to the dangling cords. The lictors guided the prisoners, lining them up, one poor soul for each waiting cord. Five magi in yellow robes joined them on the scaffold, taking up sentry a metre behind each prisoner.

The drums stopped.

A gull cawed from somewhere far away. The wind whistled, pushing a lock of hair into Plinius' eye. The muttering in the crowd died down, and distant indistinct voices could be heard carrying from somewhere deep in the city; a woman's laughter that felt sacrilegious in the relative silence. Every eye in sight fixed with dread fascination on the tower. Heuronicus Cato stepped up, moving his hands and lips as he invoked an incantation. He was momentarily cast in shadow as a cloud streaming inland from the vast western ocean passed in front of the sun.

"PEOPLE OF TERRASTRA!"

The archmagister's voice, magnified by the spell just cast, echoed across the Exchange and back again, off the city walls, off the homes and shoppes, off all three hills, as well as the cliffs that encircled them all. The entire city was his amphitheatre, and he relished in it. A startled flock of swallows alighted from their roost on the publican office at the sound, wheeling around and fleeing the Exchange in artful flight. Plinius watched them until they disappeared around to the far side of the Lowhill. Heuronicus paused, and Plinius could tell he was relishing in the attention he commanded in this moment.

"It is with great sadness I come here today." Another pause. "The great people of Terrastra have welcomed the Emperor's subjects as brothers, as sisters, as cousins in common cause to bring light to a savage world. The great William Lyon, rest his soul, saw the wisdom in binding the magi of Terrastra to the magi of the Empire. He welcomed us as family. For this the Emperor would always hold a special place in his eternal heart for our friends of Terrastra. Eternal, may he reign!"

A response was returned by the soldiers of the Iron Cohort, automatic and rote. A half-hearted cheer limped out of the crowd and promptly died.

Heuronicus' face hardened and his voice cracked like ice. "Yet not all people of Terrastra have the best intentions. Some deny the light of the Emperor, some scorn the fellowship freely offered in good faith. Some turn their back on harmony. Turn their back on the Concord. Turn their back on love! They damn themselves with the machinations of their black hearts. Cronus weeps!

When I was chosen by the Emperor to come to Terrastra, I prostrated myself before the Throne of The Tenth Circle and swore to him that I would never forsake the solemn charge invested in me by his grace. To not only become the friend of all true Terrans. To not only become a brother in arms. To not only become a gentle hand to guide us mutually into a better future. All these things and more have I sworn to become.

I also swore to become the iron fist of justice, the shield that protects the truth, the spell in the night to keep at bay all that may bring this great city to ruin!"

This time the applause from the assembled lictors and centurions masked the mutterings of discontent from the crowd. The elf next to Plinius openly spat on the ground.

"In making these sacred oaths I have bound myself in service to you, citizens of Terrastra. Just as you have been bound to me. We have brought you trade, and science, and art, and strength. In return all we have asked for is your friendship." Heuronicus dropped his head as if the weight of his responsibility had humbled him. Raising his eyes, he scanned the crowd. "Yet some have taken advantage of our good will. Some have abused and denied our friendship. Some," he flung an accusatory finger down to the prisoners below, "have chosen the path of heresy!"

Murmurs in the crowd spread like ripples in a pond as Heuronicus nodded his head. "Yes. Yes, it is true, shocking as it is. The five terrorists before you have sought to destroy all that we have worked so hard to build. They are villains with the blackest of hearts. They have consorted with our enemies. They have turned their cloaks from Terrastra and the Emperor. They have usurped and twisted the very essence of magic to their foul ends. And for this they must be punished!

For as long as I serve, I will not let these undesirables infest our good city and threaten the true people of Terrastra!"

Plinius was surprised as voices of agreement rose from the crowd. He glanced sideways at the elf. All his focus was on the archmagister, the sun gleaming off his pure white eyes, still and quiet as a moonlit pond. Plinius expected a frown, or some sort of outburst, but the elf remained tight lipped and still, until in a smooth motion he swept his hood up over his prominent ears. He noticed Plinius' staring and raised an eyebrow questioningly. *This elf looks familiar. Do I know him?*

"Yes?" asked the elf.

"Ah, excuse me, ser," Plinius said, looking away then looking back. "True Terrans? Whatever does he mean?"

A humourless laugh escaped the elf's lips. "He means like you, magus. Like you, but not like me. I find it incredibly surprising that you do not know this?" The elf did not look surprised.

Plinius gave the elf an incredulous look. "Magus? Me? Ha! No, no. I am but a simple… brick. Man. Brickman. You are, ah, mistaken."

The elf shrugged. "You positively reek of the River, magus."

"You must be, ah smelling? Smelling them?" Plinius asked lamely, pointing at the assembled magi.

"Smelling them? Not quite. Though I do find them offensive," The elf chuckled. "I know magi when I see one, ser. It always pays to be careful when you're a knife-ears."

Plinius was taken aback by the elf's casual use of the slur. "Yes. Yes, of course," he said guiltily, trying not to think of his parents. *My parents?* The Empire is known for its brutality in those regards. But this is Terrastra!"

The elf shook his head sadly. "Look around you, magus. Does this look like Terrastra to you? The Sea Wizard has abandoned us, and the Lyon is dead," he gestured up towards the frightened prisoners, then the cohort of lictors ringing the Exchange, "The Empire crushes us between its grip as we speak. How can you be so blind to what has been going on?"

That was when, by happenstance or fate, Plinius looked up.

Plinius froze, his and the elf's eyes gazing into each other. He felt like he was falling. *Gellar. His name.* Gellar's eyes bore into his mind; or did his mind fall into them? *I never could remember.* An entire age stretched out before him in those eyes. Bubbles of time and space danced like seedlings on summer air across an endless void, connected by the flowing majesty of the River. It shown in all its glory and Plinius felt humbled. *Never had I seen it from this perspective.* Plinius' could not feel the single tear drop from his left eye, but he saw the mirrored tear falling from Gellar's eye in perfect unison. He saw the River as he had never seen it before- a cosmic cloth spreading across infinite. He saw towers brushing against the stars. A pack of beasts of metal and smoke barrelling through a field, fire belching from its mouth as men in strange looking attire followed behind. Halls of stone and glass, immense beyond reason, adorned with pictures that moved and talked. Three large pyramids, a shade of black so devouring that it consumed the lightning that flashed around them. Plinius had no control- these images flashed by his face as if he was watching an illusion show or a horse race. People in bizarre uniforms, running from wailing horns deafening in their triumph. A city on an icy shore, crumbling ruins, empty of life. A pack of dogs, walking and howling like men beneath a forgotten moon. And Lights. Everywhere. So, so many lights.

Plinius gasped as the elf grabbed his hand, snapping him back to reality. His face was a blazon of intensity. "Who are you?"

Plinius' brought his hand up to his mouth. His lips moved but no sound was forthcoming. The elf cupped Plinius' cheek, rubbing his thumb below the eye. He withdrew it and Plinius was surprised to see his hand come away wet. *When was the last time I had cried?*

The elf looked Plinius up and down. "I see you, grandmagus. Our meeting was no accident. Stay with me, no matter what happens."

Plinius nodded, compliant as a scolded child.

The drums began a staccato roll, drawing their attention back to the platform.

Archmagister Heuronicus had finished his speech. He lifted his arms and crossed them across his chest. The right palm lay flat while the left palm made a circle. "Let it be known throughout all Mir that the Empire demands justice! Centurion Ox'Vacar!"

Plinius felt exposed as the hulking goliath stepped forward. All he had to do was look this way, and Plinius was certain he would be discovered. A freshly stitched cut swelled up below the centurion's left eye, a fine addition to the man's already battle-weathered face. The centurion turned smartly and returned the symbol of the Imperial Magocracy, the sword and staff salute of the Gladia Virgum. "I serve, your excellency!"

"Please, announce the charges levied against these criminals of Terrastra. You, there! Remove the first hood."

The goliaths began beating their fists anew, continuing the slow, low rumbling from before.

Weasel walked up behind the first prisoner- the small one that had stumbled. With a savage yank he ripped the sackcloth hood from the prisoner's head, revealing the small man to be a dwarf. He squinted in the daylight as he reflexively tried to raise his arm to shield his eyes. Instead, the chains snapped taut, and the dwarf lost his balance, falling forward onto his face. Weasel swore as boos and jeers were thrown from the crowd.

"Get up bitty!"

"I's is hurt! Please!"

"Get up you filthy bitty. Get up!" A swift kick into the ribs and then Weasel was dragging the dwarf up by his hair. "Stand!" Blood gushed down the dwarf's face from a large gash above the eye, pooling into his beard and making it glisten in the sunlight. A small child a stone's throw from Plinius began to weep, turning his head into his mother's skirt.

"HAFLIR SMITH!" The Centurions voice needed no magic to be heard across the plaza. "YOU HAVE BEEN CHARGED WITH THE CRIME OF AIDING AND ABETTING A KNOWN FUGITIVE OF THE EMPIRE. HOW DO YE PLEAD TO THE CHARGE?"

The dwarf blubbered through his beard. "I- I am innocent! I was just running errands for-"

"SILENCE!" roared Ox'Vacar, his face losing its stoicism and contorting into a rictus of pure hate. The dwarf staggered back as if he had been physically slapped by the centurion. "THE TRAITOR PLEADS INNONCENCE. LICTOR, NEXT TRAITOR."

Weasel reached up to pull the hood from the man standing next to the dwarf. Long hair the colour of sunset spilled out. *That isn't a man at all! Cronus! I can't believe it!* A shocked gasp and fierce whispering rippled through the crowd. A muted, wounded cry escaped Gellar's lips as he clutched Plinius' hand. The elven female Plinius had seen earlier in the Tradebasin gazed imperiously out at the crowd, a face of serene defiance and disdain that made Plinius feel both pride and shame in equal measure at once.

"ELF FEMALE! YOU HAVE BEEN CHARGED WITH THE CRIME OF AIDING AND ABETTING A KNOWN FUGITIVE OF THE EMPIRE. HOW DO YE PLEAD TO THE CHARGE?"?"

The elf maiden turned to look at the centurion, then looked up at the archmagister with her sombre eyes. "There will be no justice here!" She barely had to raise her voice, but no one had trouble hearing her. "Not for me. Not for him. Not for any of us."

"SILENCE!" Ox'Vacar took a step towards the elf. "THE TRAITOR PLEADS-"

She turned to the crowd. "TERRANS! THE EMPIRE IS KILLING US! SIL'DORIN IS A BLIGHTED WASTELAND DOTTED WITH DEATHCAMPS! WE-"

The centurion was on her before Plinius even realized he had moved. With a mailed fist he crushed her stomach, sending her doubling over and instantly retching onto the mound. "THE TRAITOR PLEADS INNOCENCE," he wrapped a cloth gag around her mouth even as she was spitting out the vomit. "LICTOR!"

Weasel reached up with both hands and slowly rolled the hood up off from the third prisoner's head. The sobbing shoulders man was dirty and ill-kempt with an uneven splotchy beard and shaggy hair. His eyes darted back and forth growing wide as he took in his surroundings. Someone in the crowd yelled a vulgar insult involving the man and a gremlin to a smattering of laughter. The man looked up and a low wailing escaped his mouth at sight of the rope. A large wet spot spread down his trousers. Centurion Ox'Vacar stood straight, towering almost to the top of the scaffold.

"KESTUS PTOLEMY! YOU HAVE BEEN CHARGED WITH THE CRIME OF FAILURE TO REPORT SEDITIOUS ACTIVITY TO THE MAGISTRACY. HOW DO YE PLEAD TO THE CHARGE?"

"In-in-innocent."

"THE ACCUSED PLEADS INNOCENT."

Ox'Vacar himself walked over to the fourth prisoner. Cautiously raising his hand, the goliath held it for a moment before he snapped forward like a striking cockatrice. With one clean motion he took the hood from the prisoner's head and quickly backed away. The crowd gasped, their voices first dying in their throats before turning to venomous hostility.

Oh my, that man is demonkin! Bonafide anathema. How curious. Horns like a ram's sprouted from the top of the prisoner's head, curled backwards like cornucopias at the side of his head. They were mottled brown, beige and red in a pattern reminiscent of the back of a turtle. The demonkin's olive skin had a tinge of green. Fine, overly large clothes that looked like they had been well-travelled in hung from his bony frame. His hair was a fresh drift of snow curling around his horns and down past his shoulders. Plinius thought he looked bored.

"Let's get on with this please," he yawned.

"THE ANATHEMIC IS ACCUSED OF VIOLATING THE CONCORD- TO WIT, THE SUMMONING OF DAEMONS, PRACTICING DAEMONOLOGY, BARGAINING WITH DAEMONS, THE PRACTICE OF FORBIDDEN MAGIC, AND FAILURE TO SURRENDER TO THE IRON COHORT UPON ARRIVAL IN THE EMPIRE. WHAT SAY YE TO THESE CHARGES?"

The demonkin fell to his knees dramatically. He cried in an anguished falsetto. "Please! I throw myself at the mercy of your sexy, sexy Emperor! I am a victim of circumstance! I am a sex addict; I couldn't help myself! I'll pleasure each person here if you let me go! I can do amazing things with-"

This time Ox'Vacar merely nodded his head at Weasel. The lictor raised his boot and kicked it forward with all his weight behind it. At the last second the demonkin rocked on his knee, swaying his body to the side as if he was going to fall. Weasel, trying to turn his hips to keep on target, misjudged terribly and brought his foot down wide of the mark. The demonkin laughed maniacally as he twisted his arm around the lictor at the ankle. Throwing all his weight into it, the demonkin rolled into the lictors leg. The leg audibly snapped as his shin cracked through the skin, filling the lictors boot instantly with gushing blood. Weasel let out a pitiful wail as the demonkin used his legs to kick the injured lictor prone.

On the first stride towards the prostate prisoner, Ox'Vacar drew the massive great sword from his back. The blade was dark, drinking in the light like an abyssal trench, a river of darker rippling raindrops along the steel, blues and blacks not so much catching the sunlight as consuming it. On the second stride he lifted his sword high in the air, more than five metres at least. Heuronicus atop his tower could have reached out and touched the tip if he had so cared to. On the third stride the centurion was upon him, the sword slicing downwards with the full strength of a goliath behind it.

The sword bit into the demonkin's snowdrift hair and carried down, down, down. It reached his pelvis before stopping, and with his boot pressed against the one side of the now split man. Ox'Vacar drew the blade from the gore, flinging a rainbow of blood out into the crowd. "ASSAULTING AN OFFICIAL OF THE EMPIRE. THE SENTENCE IS DEATH."

Plinius' stomach roiled as many in the crowd burst into raucous applause and cheering for the brutal execution. Not so much for the gruesome scene of imperial justice, but more for the utter acceptance and sense of righteousness that exuded from most of the crowd.

That is not the Terrastra I remember. When did this become acceptable? Why is so much familiar yet so much alien? Plinius found himself tightly gripping the elf's hand back.

"Well done, Centurion Ox'Vacar," said Heuronicus, leaning forward on the rail of the tower. "Justice has been served swiftly and honourably. Have your man seen to the Hall of Staffs for treatment before continuing."

Ox'Vacar motioned for Venem to help Weasel up, drenched in blood. "Take him back to the Hall. Await my return."

Venem saluted the centurion with the Gladia Virgum, then turned and did the same to the archmagister. Hoisting Weasel up she walked over to the magus who had been piloting the platform, now resting against its side. A minute later Venem and Weasel were soaring atop a large saucer shaped disk a few metres off the ground, making their way back to the Hall faster than a galloping horse. This too drew a smattering of applause from some of the commoners who had never seen a floating disc before. *Amateurish and inelegant. Look how basic the disc is. No divan? No caf service? No personal flourishes or adjustments at all. Pathetic.*

"We may resume when ready, Archmagister," reported Ox'Vacar with no apparent enthusiasm.

"Very good, Centurion," Heuronicus' fingers drummed along the railing of the tower. "Please, remove the hood from the heretic."

Ox'Vacar sheathed his sword, blood stained and all, as he turned towards the final prisoner. He removed the hood.

Plinius looked up in astonishment at an all too familiar face.

"PLINIUS SCRIVENER! YOU ARE CHARGED BY THE EMPIRE FOR THE FOLLOWING CRIMES!"

The elf looked at Plinius in shock, then up at the prisoner, then back again.

It was his face. His eyes. His nose. His mouth. Down to the crows' feet and the scar underneath his right ear. *He's dressed in clothes I wouldn't be caught dead in. Very poor looking.* Other than that, he was completely identical to Plinius.

"ASSAULT. ARSON. MURDER. HERESY. TREASON. UNLAWFUL PRACTICE OF FORBIDDEN MAGICS IN VIOLATION OF THE CONCORD. PRACTICE OF NECROMANCY IN VIOLATION OF THE CONCORD. DEFILEMENT OF THE FLESH. ILLICIT SCRIVENING. CONSORTING WITH THE TSARUSSKAN DOMINION IN CONTRAVENTION OF THE ACCORD. THE TRADE OF FLESH TO THE TSARUSSK DOMINION IN CONTRAVENTION OF THE ACCORD. WHAT SAY YE TO THESE CHARGES?

Every ear in the exchange strained to hear the prisoner with a repulsive and morbid curiosity. It was a queer feeling for Plinius to hear his own voice spoken back at him.

"I regret NOTHING!" Doppelganger Plinius stood tall, a look of defiance and bravery that the real Plinius did not recognize on his face. *Sure I do. Remember, in the alley? I was brave then.*

"I admit to every charge!" bellowed his double defiantly, "DEATH TO THE EMPEROR! HE IS NOT A GOD! FREE TERRASTRA!

TERRASTRA STRONG!"

Plinius found himself one with the crowd as they let out a collective gasp. A woman shouted "Heresy!", followed by an Imperial publican yelling "Traitor" from near the mound. From further back, Plinius thought he heard some muffled cries of anger.

The centurion motioned towards the drummers, and the goliaths began the low rumbling roll again. The archmagister raised himself up to his full height and made the sign of the Gladia Virgum.

"I, Archmagister Heuronicus Cato, acting on behalf of the Blessed Emperor of the Magocracy, and in my duly appointed capacity as His representative to the Lyceum Council of Terrastra, in the name of the Blessed Concord, I do hereby find you all guilty of the crimes of which you stand accused. This decision is immutable and final. The sentence is death by enchantment assisted asphyxiation. The sentence is to be carried out immediately. Graduati!" *Wait, did he say death? This is an execution!? Not in Terrastra! This couldn't have happened!*

The four yellow clad graduati standing behind the remaining prisoners stepped forward at the archmagister's call. A growing murmur of discontent began to proliferate through the crowd in contrast to the cries in favour of the execution. A nearby man was yelling at the Archmagister, cursing him with every vulgar word in the book. A couple of common men, possibly imperial loyalists, began to push the speaker, and a minor skirmish broke out as their friends and some zealous bystanders wrestled each other to the ground. The lictors around the mound did not move an inch to intervene to put a stop to it.

Heuronicus Cato leaned forward. Gripping the railing of the tower, Plinius could imagine him as a gaunt and sallow gargoyle. His lips and cheeks were twisted with sick pleasure, and the archmagister shouted in his amplified voice, "In the Emperor's name - execute the prisoners!"

On cue the yellow graduati lifted their arms, twisting their wrists in a macabre choreography. Half of the assembled crowd hushed as the air crackled with energy, the River sweeping t across the Exchange. The other half grew louder in their damnation. A woman's voice rang out clear by some fluke of acoustics, demanding that the execution be stopped in the name of Cronus. The four cords glowed with a yellow light, burning with spectral prismatic fires. The dangling ends were lifted by the invisible hand of the magi's spells until they were poised in front of the prisoners' faces, swaying back and forth like wary vipers. They hung there for what seemed like an eternity.

This is monstrous! Plinius heartbeat thumped against his chest along with the rumbling drums. His palms were sweating as fear squeezed his guts.

"This is not happening. This is not happening," muttered Plinius.

Not in Terrastra. This is NOT Terrastra.

The drums stopped.

The ropes reared upwards; then attacked.

Shooting forward the magically animated cords pressed against the mouths of each prisoner as they strained against their chains. The dwarf screamed and was instantly silenced as the cord entered his now open mouth, dislocating his jaw as it violently forced its way further in. The dishevelled man's arm hung limply from its socket as he desperately tried to break free with animalistic terror, his wrists raw and bleeding from the doomed effort. The Plinius lookalike did not fight at all, merely closing his eyes and opening his mouth. The elf maiden held out the longest, using the best of her limited mobility to dodge the enchanted cord in an ultimately futile gesture. The last cord hung lifelessly above the equally lifeless corpse of the defiant demonkin.

One by one the ropes forced their way past pursed lips and clenched teeth, growing in length as they moved under the watchful concentration of the yellow magi. The coarse strands of twined hemp forced past tongues and tonsils, worming their way further down their throats into the bowels of each prisoner. Tears of blood and salt streamed from their eyes as the coarse material scraped against the inside of their throats. Bellies began to expand in grotesque bulges as the ropes began to inflate their stomachs.

Someone in the crowd vomited audibly. Many openly wept.

The dwarf collapsed first. His eyes were rolled back up into his head as his body convulsed, blood streaming from the tight slits between the corner of his mouth and the rope.

Plinius could not tear his eyes away. He wanted to turn away. *I want to turn away.* He yearned to turn away. Yet he did not look away as the dwarf died. An overwhelming compassion washed over him, a hidden empathy that had slumbered for a century. It drowned him. A painful dirge, a soul-crushing wail emanating from his throat, twisted the compassion. In the deepest, untapped corner of Plinius' being, his wrath stirred. The hairs on his arms began to stand on end. A crackling of energy began to swell around him. The elf released his grip on his arm with a cry of shock. The smell of burnt skin and ashes began to permeate from the grandmagus.

I don't think I like this.

Plinius' day flashed before him as the circles on his arm lit of their own volition.

I definitely don't like this.

A wide berth began to grow around Plinius as people sensed the growing power roiling off of the grandmagus.

A grandmagus losing control.

Only the elf stayed at his side. He was whispering something urgently into his ear, but it was too late for any calming words.

I could not, would not hear it.

The River cascaded into him, torrents of power that would obliterate any lesser magus.

Not just lesser magi.

Plinius felt calm for a single moment.

Not calm. Singularity.

He unleashed the rage of a true wizard.

No words, no gestures, no reagents.

Just pure thought and willpower.

The River turned black.

Cronus weeps.

He blinked, and the ropes were gone. All four senior mages were flung back and sent sprawling across the mound, their spell broken and snapping back on them like a whip. The force of the immediate disjunction liquefied every bone, muscle, and organ in their body. When gravity took hold and brought them back down to Mir, the force of the impact burst open, splattering their innards across the platform like water balloons full of liquid meat and bone paste. The entire Exchange was shocked into silence.

He blinked again.

The chains disappeared from around the prisoners' wrists. It was too late for the dwarf and the demonkin. The shaggy man and the elf maiden were still alive, coughing and retching uncontrollably, their lungs suddenly able to greedily suck in breathes down through their shredded throats. *Look at the fake me! Isn't that strange?* The fake Plinius stood there serenely, as if nothing was happening, as if everything was normal and he was merely on a street corner waiting for a coach.

Archmagister Cato was incensed. Spittle flying from his mouth he apoplectically screamed, his voice thundering across the Exchange. "What is the meaning of this!" His face scanned the crowd, looking for the source of the counter-magic. "Who dares interfere with the Emperor's justice? The Emperor will not be denied! This Terran scum will die- I demand it! Lictors! Strangle them with your bare hands if you must!"

The lictors stood around for a moment, equally shocked as the crowd at the sudden and brutal effects of the counter magic. The only one to retain his focus, Ox'Vacar stalked towards the Plinius imposter, his hands reaching up to his throat.

Then a lone voice cut through the din. "DEATH TO THE EMPEROR!"

The crowd- the lictors- even the Archmagister froze.

"TREASON!" screamed Heuronicus, pointing an accusatory finger at people in the crowd, "TREASON! FIND THAT MAN!"

It took a moment before Plinius realized it had been Gellar, the elf next to him, who had shouted. He glanced at Plinius; his hands cupped around his mouth. He turned and shouted again.

"FREE TERRASTRA!

Another voice rang out from the far side of the mound.

"FOR THE SEA WIZARD!"

Others began to join, a rising crescendo of righteous grievance.

"FOR THE LYON!"

"DEFEND TERRASTRA! KILL THE IMPERIALS!"

The crowd turned.

"FREE TERRASTRA!"

"DEATH TO THE EMPEROR!"

"DEATH TO TRAITORS!"

"HERESY!"

"FREE TERRASTRA!"

The shouting quickly transformed into an amalgamated and inarticulate roar of vicious fury unleashed from a thousand screaming Terran voices, a thousand Terrans roused from their complacency, in a hundred different Terran languages they all demanded the same thing.

Vengeance.

The first stone went tumbling through the air, clanging off the bronze disc of the Gladia Virgum. Rocks, stones, and bottles began to multiply, arcing through the air before striking down like thunderbolts hurled from the heavens. The imposter Plinius was struck in the shoulder, sending him spinning off balance to the ground. Ox'Vacar turned his back to let his armour take the brunt of the assault before a jagged piece of glass found a fleshy spot exposed between two plate joints. The centurion grunted in annoyance. The prisoners in their open and indefensible position were catching the worst of it, except for the elf maiden who adroitly dodged or absorbed any rock thrown her way. A large piece of slag metal caught the shaggy man in the face, crushing his orbital socket and leaving him a sobbing crimson ruin.

The crowd heaved forward against the shields of the lictors. Half were fighting desperately to flee while, but the momentum of the other half proved greater as the crowd surged towards the mound. The centurions above the fray bellowed orders to their lictors, demanding they form up tightly and retain discipline.

"ENOUGH!"

Heuronicus held out his hand as he screamed eldritch words of latent power. A bar of blue energy shot down from the tower, breaking apart every few centimetres into multiple strands until there were hundreds of individual dart-like needles of energy. They arced through the air, each one whistling like a kettle as they flew outwards and proceeded to meet the incoming missiles mid-flight. Each line found a rock unerringly. Like a flock of birds in a murmuration, each piece of the spell contacted with a projectile simultaneously. At a speed faster than the eye could see the spell superheated and detonated each projectile, the implosions blowing backwards and showering the crowd with flechette of rock, glass, and metal.

Please Tales, can we skip this? I remember…

The ensuing shrapnel eviscerated anyone within one metre of the platform, killed in an instant as a million little molten hailstones cut through them, pulverizing them into ragged sheets of hole-riddled flesh. The lictors arrayed between the mob and the front of the mound fared little better. For some of them, their helms protected them from instant death. For others, they mercifully proved to be no protection at all.

Most people standing past that initial line fared a little better. An Indus man wearing the traditional headwrap of his people and standing roughly three meters from the mound screamed as a stone no bigger than a thumbnail obliterated his nose, leaving behind a gaping crater. A noble woman who was regretting her choice to go slumming that day bled to death as she was trampled underfoot, her ankle a shattered ruin. One of the drummers was hit by not one but two thimble-sized pieces. He never walked again for the rest of his very short life.

The magi on the mound saved themselves by dint of their reactive magic, throwing up shields of purple and blue arcane magic to deflect the danger. Ox'Vacar grabbed a hold of one of his lictors and used the poor man as a shield. The elven maiden's luck finally ran out as she was cut down by a metal fragment ricocheting off the centurion and into her brain.

Tradesmen, merchants, nobles. The elderly, the young. Commoners one and all were struck down indiscriminately by the power of cruel magic. Injuries ranging from welts to jagged wounds were inflicted on anyone unlucky enough to be standing in the wrong place, while those next to them suffered nary a scratch. Still, thousands would be leaving the Exchange that day with all manner of fresh scars.

Plinius found he couldn't breathe as painful cries filled his ears. He watched with muted emotion as if from a great distance, the River shielding him from feeling the insanity threatening to take hold of him. People crawled over and amongst human remains wrecked beyond recognition, just as many of the injured begging for death as there were people begging for aid. A child clutched onto the arm- *Cronus no! Stop!* Plinius had never seen such utter devastation in his life. He found himself completely at a loss in the ensuing chaos-

No, no.

Excuse me?

'I found myself utterly lost'? Perhaps a little at the time, but to say I was utterly lost is a bit of a stretch. It's insulting. I'll admit, so far, I have maybe come off as kind of a babe in the woods in some respects. But I wasn't completely helpless, not totally ignorant of the world. I'm beginning to think you just don't have the full picture.

Well, I'm sorry Plinius, I'm just going by the story I have here. I'm not here to insult you. If you disagree with the words, well, feel free to correct them as needed.

Exactly what I'm doing, ser. Dame? Did you even mention your gender? Not that it matters much, other than giving me some clue as to your identity.

Plinius. I see what you're trying to do. Is now the time? You're stalling.

No, I am not. Sorry to digress, but I want this story to be as accurate as possible. Oh, Tales! I have an idea! This might provide some clarity.

Tales?

Tales, are you there?

Oh. Oh, *Cronus.* Yes, I'm here. *Edge take me…* what did you just do to *me*?

I just provided some missing information. A remembrance that floated up in my consciousness.

Just… just like that? I can't even describe how I feel. The knowledge, the memory? It wasn't there. Now it's in my head, as if it always was. Does that make sense?

I guess so? Not quite sure how I did it to tell you the truth. It just felt… natural? I'm learning as I go here, too. How about you add in the part I just gave you?

Ok, Plinius, I will. An interlude as it were. We need to return though. The next part is important.

It is horrible.

Still. An interlude then? Before the horror?

An interlude! Yes, excellent. We can hold off on what comes next. I think I would like that. Thank you, Tales. Please, let us 'interlude', as it were.

Alright Plinius. Where to begin?

Chapter Six

Golems & Games

Plinius once had quite a collection of books pertaining to the art of war. *All ashes now. Sigh.* War was the closest thing to a hobby one could consider Plinius of ever having.

At the age of five, he had started fantasizing about battles in his head. This stemmed from his custodian and governess introducing him to the old stories of the Magocracy at bedtime. The young master Plinius would lay in his downy bed, the fire crackling merrily in the hearth, the cold wind howling outside. He would be rapt as they regaled him with tales of glorious victories.

His first love was the Ninety-Nine Parables of Sorcerer Sun Wu Changqing, the eminent and foremost treatise on large scale warfare ever written. He would grow wide-eyed over the desperate engagements for naval supremacy in the Marelocus during the Concord War. He would beg again and again for the well-loved adventurous history of Marcus Gaul, the greatest general the Empire had ever known. These were just a few stories amongst countless others that Plinius had at first been read, and then eventually read personally, and then re-read again and again with a self-sustained passion only the very young can harness. Logistics. Combined arms. Mobile infantry. Calvary. Tactics and strategy. As with most things in youth, this proved to grow boring over time. Instead of turning to other interests, young Plinius had instead come up with a novel idea to grow his beloved hobby.

At the age of six, Plinius' uncle had given him a small knife as a gift. He was unsure as to what possible use he could have for it until he was shown the art of whittling. This quickly proved disastrous- Plinius did not pick up the knife for another attempt until his thumb had fully healed. The second attempt was a resounding success- a small pine soldier he named Marcus, with fine (if rudimentary) details on the face and hands. His custodian, at first, didn't believe he could have created something so advanced at such a young age. Plinius had promptly been set to writing out '*I will not utter falsehoods*' repeatedly until Plinius finally convinced his governess after much badgering to observe him in the creation of a second one. The young man proudly showcased his skills, showing that the trick was that he just needed to concentrate, to really focus, on what he wanted out of the wood. Then it was easy as having the kitchen make you a pie. *I miss pies.*

After completing a dozen or so tiny simulacrums of the famous warriors he had read of in his books, Plinius instantly set them to battle. He whittled away hours from his days, as his infantry of oak elvish partisans sought to take the ridge of his bed from the glorious cedar brigade. His parents noticed their son's growing obsession around this time, drawn to his room by war cries and childish laughter. He expanded day by day-

Wait, what? No! Go back to my parents!

That was it, Plinius. Sorry.

Edge take me! Ok, ok, keep reading. I'm sure they'll be back.

Sometimes a new unit, or a new piece of field equipment. The Battle of Camelot. The Elven Insurgency. Merlin's Stand. A hundred miniature battles drawn from his childhood stories were waged across the nursery floor to the delight of his parents and chagrin of his nursemaids- the latter due to feet stepping on a mislaid pikeman in the dark of night. His parents encouraged him, overjoyed to see their boy so happy. Some of Plinius' favourite memories were of when his parents would visit him in the nursery and join him in his games.

Describe it! Describe them!

I can't Plinius. It doesn't say anything about that.

Maybe you missed something, maybe you skipped a page.

I think you know as well as I do that I haven't.

I know that do I? This is such gremlin shit. What the hell do I know? I'm like a drunk man stumbling for a light switch in the dark here!

I don't even know what that is supposed to mean.

It means I don't even know who the fuck I am!

That is not true.

Yes, it is!

You have provided a lot of insight so far. Think of all the things that are coming back. This is working. Bloody hells, the only reason we're here in this flashback is because you provided the memory!

Hahaha, memory! You dare speak to me about memories? I can't even picture my own parents! Damn story says I have such great memories that I can't recall, and you obviously know more than you're letting on. Meanwhile here I am clueless like some common moron. What the fuck even am I? Did you fuck up a spell and trap me in a book? Did I? Am I dead? Is this the hells? FUCK!

Plinius. I am beginning to sound like a parrot I have said this so often. You need to be patient. I'm sure it will come back in time.

Oh gods… again with the patience. I think I have been very patient up to now.

You have.

So?

So what?

So fucking give me some god damn answers!

Plinius… just be… just wait awhile-

FUCK!

I get it. You're frustrated. Calm down-

Don't tell me to calm down!

Plinius-

Jesus Christ! Why do I even fucking bother talking. Just... just keep going with the story.

At the age of seven Plinius was on his third knife and had enough wooden figures to mount expeditionary forces and bring the grim spectre of his wars to the expansive gardens on the estate grounds. Detachments of archers stalked alongside Marcus Gaul through the lily pads, on their way to eradicate the fearsome orcish tribes of the rosebush fortress. The bird feeder became the Eternal Hall, and the nearby great willow the Heart of the Forest. The Stand of Jascinthinius, The Last Elf King, raged between the two- *I always liked playing as Jascinthinius, even though I had to lose.* On any given afternoon, as soon as his custodian had signalled the end of his lessons for the day, you would find Plinius marshalling his forces in the shade of one of the garden sycamores.

Time went by, and the capriciousness of youth turned Plinius for a time towards other pursuits. Dressage was always acceptable fun. The cycle carried on, and these other pastimes eventually grew boring as well. He attempted to return to the games he had so enjoyed, yet he thought of himself as so much older now, and the little soldiers seemed so dull and childish. He found the mechanics of the game tedious as well, moving each individual unit, and what had once been a delightful pastime turned into more drudgery than it was worth. And so, back in a chest they went, away for a time in the forgotten corner of a random closet. Plinius vainly tried to find some other interest that could rival his once beloved soldiers. One by one in turn those hobbies *-I just remembered my improv phase, Cronus weeps-* proved frivolous and were likewise discarded. For a short time Plinius despaired at ever being truly happy again. *Things always seem so dire when you're young.*

Then one rainy day, as Plinius lay in his bed flipping through the pages of Half-Life: The Shortcomings of Halflings and The Scouring, he felt the spark of a new idea.

That day was when items began to go missing from the kitchen.

At the age of eight, Plinius emerged from his bedroom flush with triumph. He was eager to show off his results to his parents. *I can remember thinking how proud they were going to be.* Young Plinius marched down the halls past gasping servants, onto the grand staircase, right into the main ballroom where his parents were currently hosting the 1394 meeting of the Aurum Circle.

I've read the minutes of the Aurum Circle general meeting from last year- I assure you that The Ontario Room Invasion is still talked about to this day.

Really? You've read the minutes? When? How?
What do you mean how?
Never mind. Forget it. Let's focus on this story.
Whatever. You're the one who interrupted.

Plinius stood before the assemblage and asked, voice trembling with pride, what they thought of his new and improved army. He had been so eager for his parents to see what he had done. Their faces were not what he expected. His fathers complete shock and his mother's apprehension. *Are you sure about that? This is coming back to me…*

Standing at attention behind him ten rows back, a cohort of small silver soldiers shifted uneasily from one foot to another, mostly due to imperfections with their legs.

Cut me some slack, I was a child. Look at them! Four hundred and eighty automatons, tiny golems created by my hand, their tiny little lives plucked like fish from the River. The Silver Cohort. Not that I knew what I was doing then. Pure natural talent. I'm not bragging- it's just a fact.

Each soldier carried a fork or a spoon. Two rather large ones wielded butter knives. Clanking malformed horses pulled a couple of the toy cannons brought back from one of his father's business trips to the capital.

Wait! I remember!
Plinius, stop, what are you- OH CRONUS-

A lady with dark skin draped in fur yelled "Mon Dieu!" as the masterpiece stalked in, letting out a pitiful cry.

Pliny! Stop! I can't see- oh Cronus! Trunk! Help-

Shambling forward on wings made of knives, the dog-sized amalgam of animated cutlery came to sloppy attention next to the boy. It's gravy boat head dipped at the end of a sinuous neck unable to stay steady as its serpentine body flopped and clanked against the hardwood floors.

Oh, Blessed Concord! How could I have forgotten Theomeofury? 'The Gravy Dragon', my father used to tease. I can almost hear his voice… my oh my, see how terrible Theo was at first? I wonder what ever happened to him.

PLINY-

CHAPTER XII

THE ONTARIO ROOM

I can remember laughing with glee, savouring the stunned expressions as I surveyed the magi who stood still like statuary. The clicking and clanking of my army of automatons was the only sound. I started to grow a little uneasy until a hearty laugh broke the tension. Walking up to me, a kindly magus bedecked in golden robes tousled my hair. The magus was bald and pudgy, clean shaven rosy cheeks like a chipmunk, bushy arched eyebrows, and a ruddy nose. He whistled in wonderment as he surveyed my creations. I'll never forget what Alister whispered.

"Well done, kid. I'll be keeping my eye on you."

Oh, Cronus be merciful! Where am I? I can... I can see it! Pliny, what have ye-

Can you imagine what that was like? What that kind of public praise from one such as him does to an already gifted child's self-perception? Recognition is a powerful drug to start chasing at such a young age.

It was the only time I can remember my parents letting me stay up at one of their circle meetings. You must understand, back then children were meant to be seen, a polite and entertaining diversion perpetuated by cultural tradition, and then put away until they had matured. That night staying up was not only my first peak into Imperial politics, but it was also the first time I got to see my mother and father in an unscheduled setting.

I can see them there! Do you?

Plinius, please, stop. Can you read this? Do you- Oh Cronus- Gellar, Trunks... you need to-

Like vague smudges, like smeared paint. Can you see them clearly? Is it just me who's denied? I wish I could remember them... I don't understand why I'm having such trouble seeing them... it's coming back in flashes. Something so important should be easily remembered, shouldn't it? Other things though… I remember so clearly…

I particularly remember Alister of course- how do you forget arguably the most powerful man in the world? He didn't leave my side the rest of the night, making me feel at ease with his easy laughter and playful spirit. I was absolutely mobbed with questions from the magi in the room. Almost everyone- especially the delegation from Baltica- used the chance to fete me and by doing so fly a bit closer to the sun. Try as they might, the Emperor's full attention was on me that night. Two of the archmagi were in attendance as well- well, three, including my mother- Morgana and Abe. Morgana with her black hair, her relentless questions and disbelief. So haughty and beautiful. Abe with his stern gaze. He was terrifying until he smiled; then the warmth broke like sun through a storm cloud. He was an amazing man, his keen strategic mind and willingness to answer an eight-year-old boy's barrage of questions endearing him to me instantly. The Emperor, Le Fay and the Astral Shogun. Three of the greatest magi who had ever lived, pulled out of the history books, and letting me eat as many candied fruits and drink as much ginger ale as I wanted to. Ha! I remember having to pee terribly. I'm glad that I learned at a young age that people are just people, even if they have books written about them.

This is such a great memory for me. Everyone was so happy and-

Wait!

Wait.

I told… I told Alister that I had to 'freshen up'. That was true, I really did have to relieve myself. But walking to the garderobe I saw them standing on the balcony… they… they were arguing.

"I will not let you bring him into this, John!" threatened his mother, her hands on her hips.

"For the love of God Almighty, Circe- he needs to know! He has the right to know!"

The archmagus shook her fists and screamed. "Of all nights! Of all nights for this to happen! It's bad enough my sister is here, but that *MALÁKAS* Alister? Zeus almighty, John. Who next? What are we going to do?"

Plinius, where are you?

Tales, is that my father? Yes, yes it was. I'm sure. Tales, do you see it? It's… they're just out of focus…

Plinius? Where did you go? This isn't our story, Pliny, we need to get back to-

"We're going to do exactly what we were told to do," John said grim-faced, pulling a small palm-sized runechit from a pouch on his waist. He crushed it in his weathered hand. Purple and black mist swirled up to his shoulder, coalescing as a voidcrow. It obediently dipped its head towards John's mouth as he began to whisper his message to it.

Circe was trembling.

"GAMÓTO! Why did we even come here, John, if not to save the ones we love?"

"God damn it!" swore John after fumbling the words to his message, "Crow, forget that last part."

The crow bobbed its head mechanically, waiting with all the patience in the universe as John turned to his wife.

"If we can't save one..." she began, but John cut her off in frustration.

"It was never about saving anyone! We came because we were running away, you know that as well as I do,"

Circe stepped back as if slapped. "How fucking dare you."

John sighed. "I didn't mean it that way. I mean, I didn't-"

"How fucking dare you. I have never run from something in my life."

"Hun, I'm sorry-"

"We decided to come here as a family. A family decision, John. Our family. Our decision. Alister and his damned speech had nothing to do with it. And if it did," she spat acidly, "If I'm remembering correctly, it was you who wanted to run. Or have you forgotten the kidnapping?"

Plinius!

"You're mad," said John in a soothing voice, "I get it. But this is what we promised him we would do. When the time came."

I held my breath as the silence between them grew, afraid to breathe.

"I won't let him have him. I won't, John. If he tries... well, fuck him. And fuck Lyon, fuck Alister, and fuck you too!"

John waved his arms up and down in alarm.

"For God's sake, Circe, keep your voice down! Please, people are going to wonder where you are- Go back to the party."

"John," she spat, stabbing a pointed finger at the great glass window of the Ontario Ballroom, "Don't you dare lump *me* in with that paranoid MALÁKAS! EVER. AGAIN. DON'T YOU DARE!"

I can hear the sadness behind the anger.
I need to see them.
Just a little closer.

Circe was crying, pulling away from her husband. John sighed and let loose the voidcrow.

Plinius, where are you!?

I can almost see their faces.

Mother…

Oh, Cronus! I'm back! Oh, thank you Cronus! Thank you, thank you!

What did I say about leaving me here alone?

Plinius! You're here!

What? Of course I am. I can't be where I'm not, and not like to be where I can't be. So where else would I be? You're the one who disappeared to talk to your bloody associates again!

What?

Ugh, nothing. You just stopped with the story.

We were just in- you took us to- it was like-

Are you drunk?

What!? No! Don't you remember-

I find I'm having a great deal of difficulty remembering things, but you know that, and I know that, and I find it rather uncouth that you keep bringing it up. We don't need to go over this ground again. Please, just continue with the story.

Yes… ah, where were we? You were going on about Alister?

Alister? Alister who?

You don't remember?

It would seem I'm not the only one with difficulty remembering things. Or are you just an idiot? What's your name again?

I'm… Talespinner, remember? Tales.

Yes… Tales… my old chum Tales. You are reading my story, the biography of the great Plinius Scrivener and his many adventures! We were just going over my childhood when you rudely vanished.

Uh, is that so? Sorry Plinius. Shall I continue with the story?

Ah, I guess? Yes. Please continue.

Thank you.

At the age of nine Plinius had perfected his simulacrum. No longer the static wooden toys, no longer the janky collection of stolen silverware with their twine-bounded joints. *I can see how funny it is now. The innocence of youth, yes? I never questioned where my materials were coming from. I had always assumed my parents were providing the metals for me. Ah, the sweet naivety of youth.* The miniature infantry and calvary, then beasts and monsters of all types, then terrain upon which they could wage their eternal wars. All these improvements to his skill came in quick succession, his art improving with every new creation. Each 'mini', as he came to call them, that marched out of their moulds on their own volition was like a child to him. *Child is a bit much. More like… cherished pets.* His passion for warfare was rekindled in an instant as he went from painstakingly setting up tableaus of famous battles to commanding the forces in them. His childhood dreams became reality as he commanded Marcus Gaul and his Wayfinders against the

He learned much in that time- trial and error, going from having entire cohorts wiped out to turning famous defeats to his favour. Always reading, always commanding with whatever hours he could steal from his studies.

It was Plinius first taste of success. His first exposure to what he could accomplish if he set his mind to a task. He would never stop chasing that feeling. *I never have. I need to be the best.*

When he had turned ten, his hobby had grown again as his talents increased at an exponential rate. He learned transfiguration in a week so he could give the minis detail far beyond what any common knife could produce. It was then they went marching out of the uncanny valley, perfect miniature men, magi, and anathema in every little physical detail. His skill in golemry proved far, far beyond what any child his age should possess- his parents watched on with increasing wonder as he trot out his little wonders for them, eager for their approval. If they had been watching his process, they would have been even more in awe.

With no formal training, Plinius began to tinker with the River as he infused it into his creations. He could picture what he wanted, and the River would respond as naturally as breathing. What took some magi decades to master, Plinius could intuit in an afternoon. *I just… got it. I could see… how it wanted it to be.*

It was not long before his little metal soldiers possessed the discipline and intellect to carry out a string of orders, whether advanced pincer movements, enfilading, and covert manoeuvres into his sisters' bedrooms to frighten them. *I have sisters!?* He began to invite others to compete against them, providing spare armies to whatever of the house staff he could find to order into a game, relishing in the chance of victory against a live opponent. He went quickly from losing games on account of his own childish blunders, to losing to his betters because of lack of skill, to eventually beating them soundly through the intense study and application of centuries of military scholarship. One day the Warmagus came to him in his study, his father in tow with an invitation to the command school at the Bellumarcis in Aliston, delivered in person. *My father smiled and laughed when I turned him down.*

Soon after that the kindly man began to visit. *I remember the deference my father and mother paid him- how he frightened me at first.* He was a tall man, spindly with ill fitted robes and a long grey beard. His eyes were kindly, warm and without a hint of arrogance. He swore like a pirate, which is something any child on the cusp of puberty cannot help but idolize. Sometimes another man would accompany him- a smaller, serious man with bald head and large blazing ginger mutton chop sideburns framing his jowly face. He was always immaculately dressed in queer, stiff outfits, form fitting jackets with collared shirts and very long pantaloons. *My father greeted them like old friends. He explained they had come to watch me, having heard of my creations. I asked them numerous times to play my games with me- they always deferred.* They had just come to watch him work, much to young Plinius' bewilderment they had no interest in the game at all.

The serious man would take notes, the kindly man would ask questions. *Why did I use this reagent instead of this one? Why did I adjust the time on the curing from five minutes to ten minutes? How did I account for the anima degradation resulting from using limited materials? I remember feeling… arrogant, when answering.*

Then, one day, on the last time Plinius would see him for a long while, the kindly man asked Plinius what he imagined his life was going to be like when he was older.

"I want to be the greatest mage who ever lived," answered Plinius with complete certainty, "greater than Alistair Crowley himself!"

The kindly man had laughed at that. "Magus, son," he said with a wink.

Funny, I had forgotten that…

The kindly man had tousled Plinius hair, much to his annoyance. *Even then I hated being treated anything less than an equal.* They then made Plinius sit in the foyer while the two men talked at length with his mother and father. His mother had argued loudly at first, then quietly, then not at all.

On his eleventh birthday, Plinius was on his way to Terrastra and the Lyceum. One of the youngest students ever to be taken into the circle. All stemming from a boy's fascination with miniature soldiers. *I was excited for a grand adventure. The grandest adventure… until… wait. I… am… so confused? Hold on a minute-*

When he had turned one hundred, war was something academic. Golemry was a practice more suited to factory mages in Aliston. Tools to master. They were diversions to enjoy sparingly if they managed not to interfere with Plinius' studies, which they invariably did. But he never lost his interest. By the time Plinius had lived a century, his interest was tactics and strategy. Strengths to be tested and weaknesses to be exploited, logistics to be supported and opportunities to be seized upon. It was numbers on pages, dots on maps. It was a symphony of movement and order applied by force of will on emerging chaos. It was-

I wonder how my life would have turned out if I had taken up the Warmagus' invitation. My skills of warfare had waned over the years as my studies had taken the lion's share of my attention. I do not doubt that if I had applied myself sufficiently to any discipline, I would have invariably succeeded. Will and Time. That is all these things boil down to, if you possess the natural ability to-

Plinius! Ahem.

Sorry- sorry. Did I interrupt again? Just... the memories… I feel like I am stepping out of a cave. Where had these memories of that time gone? Those thoughts of what if and the roads not travelled…

Plinius. Please focus. I need you to listen, I can't have you commandeering the narrative. We can't have a repeat.

A repeat? A repeat of what?

Ah, I mean repeated interruptions. It, ah, ruins the flow of the story.

I apologize, it was quite boorish of me to interrupt.

No need to apologize. I enjoy having you here. This interlude, this memory, was… enlightening. Stay and listen and please add when you think I might be erring in the telling, but let the book do its work. Ok? That's important. Can you do that?

Naturally, I'm not an obstinate child. Please don't patronize me.

No one said you were a child. All I'm asking is that you don't… take control. It is *imperative* that I don't lose my connection. For both of us. It might be your story, but this is OUR story to get through, if you get what I mean. We need to do this together. Just relax and listen, ok?

I see your point, I think. We must abide by the rules after all. The River will guide us. I must admit I am quite enjoying the telling, overall. You live up to your name, Talespinner. This… next part will be tough. Best we forge ahead and get it over with.

I know. I am glad we can agree. Let's get through this- together.

Chapter Nine

The Archmagister & The Grandmagus

I do not like this memory.

Things were happening so fast that Plinius could feel his anxiety threatening to choke the breath from him as his heart pounded on his ribcage. He fought the raging emotions within, desperate to maintain control, refusing to let go of the River. He looked around in a daze, wondering where he had misplaced his spear.

Gellar clung tightly to Plinius' hand as he pushed forward through the crowd. Pandemonium had erupted in the Exchange with the wholesale massacre wrought by the archmagister's spell. As lictors pushed towards the centre, the crowd crashed into them like stormy waves on a break wall, desperately attempting to reach the high ground. A man's scream was abruptly cut off as a wave of lictors bowled him over, crushing him underfoot. Plinius nearly stepped on a lictor crying for help, a dangling mass of shredded flesh and smoking red metal all that remained of his right arm. Any semblance of order the lictors had tried to enforce that day had imploded with Cato's rashness and callousness. A taste of acrid copper hung in the air, mixing with the putrid stench of shit and a sweet, cooked meat smell. A large ringing clang of steel on steel accompanied by inhuman screams of rage caused Plinius to whip his head around.

A group of Terrans charged into the lictor's broken lines with butchers' cleavers, breaching the Iron Cohorts defence on the southern side of the mound, rushing towards the prisoners. Ox'Vacar, wielding his massive great sword in two hands, cut three of them down with one wide sweeping slash. The sword cut through like a whisper through wind, slicing two of them in half and coming to a rest in the centre of the last man's chest. The remaining butchers bellowed "TERRASTRA FREE!" as they set upon the centurion with their knives, hacking at the goliath in a flurry of blows from eight different hands. It was nowhere near enough. Weathering a few ineffectual dents on his plate armour, Ox-Vacar then regained his composure. Releasing his two-handed grip, with his great sword in one hand he brought the pommel down on one of the attackers as if he was hammering a nail, bludgeoning in the man's head as easily as breaking an egg. His free hand shot out and grabbed the neck of a woman dressed in a milkmaid's apron. Her eyes widened in terror. A quick twist of his hand and the woman's head limped backwards at an obtuse angle. He used her corpse as in improvised weapon, hurling the body into a group of fighters a few metres away, knocking them to their feet where his fellow lictors quickly finished them off. The remaining Terrans were not deterred, a credit to either bravery or stupidity, as they tried to circle and surround the hulking, murderous daemon. They approached the centurion from all four points of the compass. Ox'Vacar snarled at them, a tiger's face, white teeth prominent on his blood drenched face, a calico coat of red along with the goliath's natural vitiligo. He held his great sword aloft in his right hand while he stood waiting for the attack with his left hand cocked back in a fist.

With a wordless cry, the Terrans tried to rush the centurion. With his open hand Ox'Vacar jabbed a mailed fist into the first man's nose, obliterating it in a spray of blood and cartilage. Simultaneously he brought his sword down in a diagonal slash that lopped another man's head off with an effortlessly clean swipe. More lictors rushed up to join him and the fight was quickly decided, a healthy pocket of space widening around the imposing figure of the blood-drenched goliath warrior. He roared orders at them, and they rushed to join their comrades repelling the incensed mob at the ramp. The Terrans were slowly pushing the Imperials back with their overwhelming numbers. *A crowd and rage. Always a potent combination.*

Bells began to clang, first at the publican houses and then picking up across the city. Plinius could see numerous columns of thick black smoke rising from the tents along the spoke leading back towards Qubo's shop. The terrified scream of 'fire!' followed by numerous wailing sirens could be heard over the tumult.

Plinius was at a complete loss at what to do.

Heuronicus sent firebolt after firebolt down into the crowd, flinging conjured fiery projectiles from his fingertips as fast as his mouth could keep up with the required gesture. Plinius watched in horror as the archmagistrate immolated a crowd of Terrans attempting to flee the Exchange, their screams only a few among thousands, a drop in the ocean. Waves of chaos and violence heaved all around him.

"We need to get out of here- quick!" Gellar urged as they crouched behind an upturned cart, blocking their view of the bloody work around the mound.

"Yes," Plinius agreed hollowly, his blood pounding in his ears. He did not need to peek around the cart- he could see the River as clear as day through the obstacle. It was a swirling whirlpool, a tornado of multi-hued magic veins pulsing around the archmagister's tower. Hundreds of Terrans rushed past them, armed with combinations of bravery, patriotism, anger, vengeance, justice, and whatever they could lay their hands on that might serve as a suitable weapon. A burly dwarf with a coal-scuttle helmet and a dented furnace door for a breastplate dived into a mass of lictors with a bellowing battle cry, swinging a hammer in each hand as he laid into the still reeling

Imperials. Plinius watched as he knocked out a half dozen lictors before a lance of crackling flame passed through his chest, killing him instantly as well as the lictor behind him.

A woman and a small child decided at that moment to run from their hiding place beneath a nearby wagon. Plinius watched as another firebolt came raining down on them, setting them alight as the magistrate cackled like a deranged lunatic. Time slowed to a crawl. The last thing the child ever saw was the eyes of a grandmagus.

It wasn't sadness or fright I saw in that child's eyes. It was hate. It was as if she knew what I was, despite the stupid disguise Ohotepe had made me wear. It was Hate; a bitter poisonous anger, so perverse and so wrong in the eyes of one so young. Why? How? How could a child, barely off her mother's breast, know a hate so deep?

I don't know, Plinius.

I think you do. Hate is not born in a person, Tales. You need to be educated in hate before you can accept it into your heart. It is learned. It is an education taught to the weak by the powerful. It is a lesson dispensed by the hand of a harsh and uncaring master, as much through pure indifference as it is through their violent discipline- maybe more so, as indifference is much easier. It is much easier to lock yourself away from the world, to keep your eyes fixed upwards, to ignore the daily suffering of those below you. Whose only crime was to be born different.

I saw the truth, then, in that moment. The truth I had been denying all day; the truth of what Mir had become while I hid away like a coward.

Why did you hide, Pliny?

I hid because I could. It sounds so… banal, doesn't it? I hid because it was easy. The commoners… they don't have the privilege to choose which world they live in. Mir is all they get. And what had Mir become? Two worlds. Two worlds; one for magi, one for commoners. I am ashamed, Tales; I admit it.

Ashamed? Why?

For only realizing the truth far later than I can ever forgive myself for.

What truth?

The truth I saw in the eyes of that child as they turned to ash.

The Terrans nearby screamed in furious anger as the two unfortunate bystanders were turned to black dust blowing in the wind. The fighting became frenetic as they set upon the lictors guarding the mound with renewed rage. It was only when his throat started to burn that he realized the most anguished scream was coming from him.

A harsh master.

"We're pinned down here," the elf said through gritted teeth, Plinius dimly aware of Gellar's words. "We can't risk running out while that mad bastard is flinging death from up there."

Plinius had not moved his eyes from the spot where the mark of black ash still danced along the ground. His teeth were clenched so hard the muscles in his jaw started to hurt. His nostrils flared, filled by the stench of death. The screams and cries for help faded away, a ringing in his ears growing louder.

"Plinius, did you hear me? We need another option here," Gellar sounded practical and calm, as if they were working on a theorem in the Lyceum, "We can't stay here, the lictors will rebuff this soon enough, and then they will have us."

Plinius reached into the bag dangling at his hip. He did not need to look through each scroll that sat in there- the River worked through him, telling him instinctively as he touched the wax seals on each one what spells they held. It took him but a moment to find what he was looking for.

He pulled out a rolled parchment. Plinius had scribed this spell for a buyer that was due in a fortnight- a buyer that would be most chagrined to discover the burnt-out wreck of the scrivener's bookstore. The wax seal was embossed with a twisted dragon, its wings outstretched in waves of crimson wax. As he snapped the seal in two between his thumbs, the smell of sulphur and charcoal masked every other smell. Both sides of the riot slowed in their battle as the smell spread quickly across the Exchange, confused faces with upturned lips at the foul smell. Rolling out the scroll with shaking hands, he began to read.

His eyes flashed as the runes on the scroll began to burn with a blue flame. The scroll itself did not burn- the runes disappeared one by one as flame spread along the filigreed lines drawn along the border. The flames reached Plinius fingertips. His hands began to glow, absorbing the magic stored within the scroll until he could feel the power of it filling him up, supplementing the power with his already tenuous hold on the River. Plinius crackled with barely contained magic, like a cup sloshing liquid over the edge. The elf had backed up as far as he could while staying behind the protective barrier of the overturned cart, his eyes wide with apprehension as his hand covered his nose at the overpowering smell. A young and bloodied lictor duelling with a middle-aged hammer wielding blacksmith nearby faltered in his stance as they both felt the surge of magic crackling through the air. Their hair standing on end, corposant energies bounded across their weapons. Any metal caught within the sphere of the spells expanding influence began to suffer the same condition.

As the last of the scroll's azure fire flowed into Plinius, the scroll dissolved into what looked like sand at first. Writhing maggots fell through his fingers, plopping on the ground at his feet. In place of the scroll was a small, perfectly round orb of matte black mist, purple lightning illuminating it from somewhere within. He looked at the elf. "Get ready to run," he warned Gellar in a hollow whisper.

Standing up and stepping out from behind the cart, Plinius raised his hands up towards the tower. Heuronicus had one hand pressed up against his forehead to shield his eyes from the glaring sun, searching the crowd below for the source of power he had most assuredly felt. His face was not one of concern but of anticipation. *Undoubtedly the fool thought one of his Imperial brothers had arrived to help quell the riot.* His eyes locked onto Plinius, his smile faltering in confusion as he glanced down at the body of the fake Plinius in surprised recognition.

Plinius intoned a single word in a language long forgotten.

The power of the River, once bound in the scroll, amplified by his own excessive drawing from the cosmic magical force, coalesced into his hands. Obedient to his thoughts, at his bidding a prismatic beam of blinding solid light erupted from his hands. His arms panned in an arc across the mound from the tower to the ramp in a quick back and forth sweep, as if they were branches pulled back taut and then released. Wherever the beam contacted the tower, the wooden support struts shrivelled and rotted away as if a century of entropy had passed by in an instant. Screams from the lictors unlucky enough to be caught in the beam's path strangled out dry whispers as their skin turned to thin wrinkled parchment, their internal organs atrophying into dry husks as their emaciated corpses collapsed into piles of now rust-eaten armour. The tower, now supported only by decayed sticks of powdery pock-marked lumber, slowly lurched off balance towards the gallows. A loud noise like river ice cracking during a spring thaw rumbled across the Exchange, barely masking Heuronicus' scream as the tower beneath his feet fell away. Making impact with the gallows, wood groaned and then screamed as the magi-created tower exploded in a shower of debris. A deafening crash shook the ground as the embossed disc of the Gladia Virgum came loose and went bounding across the mound like a children's hoop, bludgeoning over half a dozen men in its deadly path. With one spell Plinius had most assuredly killed the magistrate along with nearly two dozen lictors. *I had never killed anyone before that day. And now I had killed over three dozen people in a quarter of an hour.*

Plinius swayed on his feet. He burped. *Oh. No, let's, uh, skip ahead.* The River vanished instantly as Plinius lost his concentration.

"I'm going to be sick," burped Plinius, his one hand pulling at his collar. *We really don't need to watch this.*

Then the contents of his stomach came forcefully up. Gellar put a steadying hand on his back as he doubled over and heaved, a rainbow splatter of barely digested matter decorating the ground. *Really? Is this level of detail necessary?* His stomach empty, Plinius was dimly aware that he had begun hyperventilating. Try as he might, his eyes refused to stop turning towards the carnage he had visited upon the Imperials. Half a man, his mummy-like face forever locked into a terrified scream, stared accusingly at Plinius from a few metres away.

The Terrans still in the fight did not give up the fortuitous opening

Plinius' magic had literally cut through the enemy for them. They rushed up the now undefended side of the mound, screaming dozens of battle cries, some for Terrastra, some for Merlin, some for the Lyon, some for death, some for life, some for justice and some for vengeance. Some for nothing at all. The entire city could hear them, as they raised their weapons high, their feet carried along by the pushing crowds, a rising tide of angry revolt that had been simmering the entire time Plinius had retreated from the world. The war-cries jumbled into a bestial roar of inarticulate gibberish, yet not one of the Imperials misunderstood its message. A high tide of common steel crested as the commoners swung their weapons overhead. Cleavers and daggers, kitchen knives and blacksmith hammers, iron bars and wooden clubs, farming implements and spears and even the odd sword rose and fell in one concerted movement. They crashed upon the lictors that had been devastated by Plinius' attack, the charge breaking upon them and pushing through like a devastating storm surge brought in by a fall tempest. A bloodthirsty cheer rose from the Exchange as they swarmed through the lictor lines and formed a beachhead on the high ground.

Plinius could see the centurion easily amid the melee, methodically hacking at the men and women who came within reach as they pushed deeper behind his lines. Anyone who had the misfortune of coming within reach never had time to regret it. The lucky commoners who ran well wide of him engaged into the far rank of lictors. Those lictors had so far been maintaining their defensive line on the lip of the mound, standing strong against sporadic attacks from the northern part of the crowd. Dozens fell instantly, surprised faces as spears erupted through their chests and hammers bludgeoned the backs of their skulls as the commoners fell on their flank from behind. The northern crowd, emboldened by this turn of events, attacked the northern line en masse.

Panic began to spread along the lictors as the battle turned against their favour. A few threw down their weapons, throwing their hands up in surrender. The crowd, frenzied and mad, succumbed to the raging spirit of the riot. Refusing their surrender, they elected instead to take a page out of the Imperial's book and began an immediate and frantic execution. The crowd roared in satisfaction as a small boy lifted the severed head of a lictor, still wearing its galea with a blue plume of feather.

This is horrible. I never desired to use the River to hurt people. Something so beautiful, something so vicious. All depends on the person wielding it.

Ox'Vacar was desperately trying to reform his defences, his orders booming across the plaza from his goliath-strong lungs. The bells were echoing through the hills. Black smoke smothered the sky as the western ocean wind pushed smoke inland. Ash began to fall like thick flaky snow and visibility began to diminish as a grainy haze filled the air. *I'm starting to grow quite fatigued from the constant fire and smoke.*

The elf grabbed Plinius' free hand.

"Run!"

The crowd had thinned considerably as they ran away from the mound, yet still thousands remained trapped as lictors poured into the Exchange down every spoke. Pockets of fighting erupted wherever Terrans met with Imperials, the Emperor's lapdogs attempting to restore order in as brutal a fashion as they could muster. Plinius and the elf gave wide berth to a crowd of men mercilessly beating a lictor curled up into a foetal position, his still body accepting the rain of blows without so much as a twitch, as if they were punching a sack of flour. The smoke and ash was ubiquitous, masking the Exchange with constantly shifting and choking walls of soot, like a labyrinth formed by the wind. Plinius hoped he knew where he was going, moving in what he thought was a direct route to Wayfarers Road.

Rushing out of the smoke came a lictor drenched in blood, madness, and fear. One side of her face was swollen shut, making her look like a lop-sided cyclops. She rose the sword clutched in her hand as she charged towards them. Plinius flinched backwards in shock but luckily the elf was faster. A dagger flew from the elf's hand, embedding itself in the lictors open eye as her sword went flying out of her now lifeless hands. Her sprawling body grated against the ground awkwardly before coming to an undignified stop at their feet. The elf quickly reached down and with a squelch retrieved his dagger.

They began to run again. Angry sounds of battle and the agonizing, bitter cries of dying men and women bounced around the choking smoke like lamenting phantoms. Plinius eyes itched fiercely, his sweaty tears stinging his eyes worse than the smoke. His breath was ragged, his feet were lead, his heart felt like a volcano straining to erupt. "I- I need to rest. Please-"

"No- not until we get out of here," said Gellar, no hint of worry in his voice. "We should be close to Wayfarers Road."

Plinius cried out in dismay as his foot caught and sent him sprawling. His knee came down awkwardly onto a rock. His breath caught as a sharp jolt of pain knifed up his leg. He tried to pull himself up with the help of the elf. He let out a gasp of pain as he tried to put weight on it.

"I can't walk! I think I may have broken a bone!" Plinius cried.

"We can't stay here!" The elf implored the magus, taking in their surroundings. A terrified merchant, his shirt singed and his arms overflowing with goods went running past them, not stopping, or even seeming to notice they were there.

"Give *me* a minute- I have something- I just need to find it." Plinius began to root through his scroll bag.

"Please hurry Plinius, we are too exposed here."

Another man, armed with a long scythe, came charging up to them but stopped short at the sight of the Terrastran uniform. His eyes were wild and jumpy, blood seeping from numerous cuts across his arms. He screamed

"TERRASTRA!" as he plunged back into the smoke, disappearing into the obscuring grey cloud.

"Here it is!" He clutched a small scroll with the symbol of a heart pressed into green wax. "This shall only take a moment," he promised through gritted teeth. He cracked the seal and began intoning.

"Hurry!" urged the elf. As Plinius began to absorb the magic from within the scroll, his concentration nearly faltered as he saw the elf's gaze look up and past his head. Plinius noticed the elf's jaw tighten.

"Lay down your weapons, get on your stomachs!" a husky voice commanded from somewhere behind them. "In the name of the Emperor!"

Four lictors stalked warily towards them, four mis-matched spears pointing at the scrivener and the elf. Each of them was bruised and bloody; they reeked of desperation and fear. The one leading from the front repeated his request in a shaky voice, doing his best to sound like he was in control.

"I can't stop now, elf," whispered Plinius through gritted, grinding teeth, "I need to concentrate!"

"My friend is hurt," the elf said. "Please, help us get to-"

"I won't say it again!" He commanded shakily. The end of his spear wavered unsteadily in their direction. "Get down!"

Plinius did not dare move, unwilling to risk losing his concentration on the spell, sweat pooling in the nape of his thin, bony neck. Spreading tendrils of brown and green energy grew from his hands, looking like vines of ivy. This was the only scroll of salubrity he had. *I couldn't stop, not once begun. Ending the spell prematurely would have left me worse off. Wasting it would have left me stranded there.*

"Lictor, ser, please-"

"Cronus' cock, look at 'is ears!" One of the lictors, trembling like a bubbling kettle, pointed at the elf.

"It's a fucking long-ear! Fucking bastard! Kill him!"

Plinius held his knee in his hands, a different warmth spreading out into his leg. He willed it to go faster, but his wishes went unanswered.

The elf stood up, daggers flashing into both his hands. His right foot slid forward as he shifted his weight to his back foot. He maintained steady eye contact with the lead lictor while still acutely tracking the flanking soldiers in his periphery. Gellar was as still as fresh snow, his face a mask of pure calm. The lictors found his demeanour more unsettling than the weapons he brandished.

The lictors fanned out, spears bristling towards them as they completed the circle, surrounding the elf and the magus.

Plinius could feel his knee and leg mend themselves as the River did its work, but it was not quick enough. One of the lictors yelled "Now!" and they rushed forwards. There was nothing Plinius could do. Locked in the spell, he watched as their death closed in around them. *Come on Gellar!*

The elf managed to fell one of the lictors with one of his daggers, the precision of his aim preternatural, before the Imperial managed to take more than two steps. Another thin stiletto appeared in his hand before the first one had even reached its mark. The three others pressed forward. Plinius closed his eyes, resigned to what was coming. *Such a fatalist.*

A loud, unique war-cry startled Plinius' eyes wide-open. *A Kantan witch-cry of challenge. The undulating, back and forth trilling is unmistakable.* A blur hurtled out from the smoke, contacting the jaw of a lictor with a flying fist. The lictor's eyes rolled up into his head as his jaw cracked too far to the left. The other two stuttered to a stop in their charge and turned their focus to meet this new attacker, but by then it was already too late. The attacker slid towards them like he was on ice, sweeping his outstretched leg before him and knocking both much larger men down. Springing from his kneeling position up into the air he delivered a swift kick to the nose of the first lictor attempting to get up, a spray of blood exploding outwards. Without losing his momentum he turned midair and came down with both feet onto the head of the remaining Imperial. All this transpired before the first Imperial's body had hit the ground.

By the time Plinius was getting up, Ohotepe was wiping the dust from his knees with a big grin. "Pliny! It being good to be finding you, whole and healthy."

"Ohotepe!" Relief washed over Plinius as the spell finished. *I never thought I'd be happy to see Boy again. Ohotepe, I mean. Teeps. And he fought like a bewitched savannah priest! He is a veritable Swiss-army knife.*

A what?

A utility knife. Useful thing, you know? Great gift for a young boy who wants to whittle.

But what is a swiss-army?

It's the type of knife, dumby. It's its name.

Well, I get that, but where does the name come from?

Where? Uh… that I can't remember. Or maybe I just don't know? I would have to ask my uncle, he's the one who gave it to me.

"Who being this?" Ohotepe asked with a nod to the elf. It was said genially enough, but Plinius knew there was a concealed threat under his words.

"Yes!" Plinius nodded. "He is a friend! This- ah- elf. Has been helping me." Plinius felt dumb. *His name is Gellar. We know this already.*

The elf, retrieving his dagger, held out a hand for Ohotepe. "Thank you for the timely assistance, ser. My name is Gellar. You must be the Coptician? I am attempting to escort Plinius to the Wayfarers Guild, but it would seem the lictors intend to stop us."

"The Wayfarers Guild?" Ohotepe frowned. "Why would you be going there?"

The elf met Ohotepe's frown with a slightly abashed grin. "My apologies- when we first met, Plinius and I, he accidentally impressed upon me."

Ohotepe's stance shifted ever so slightly as his face hardened. "What do you know?"

The elf shrugged. "I only saw what Plinius saw, ser. It was a brief impression, nothing more, but today's events were so stark in his mind it was impossible to hold them back. They were quite insistent. Our friend the magus here has had quite a day so far."

"Just his memories, you be saying," mused Ohotepe, "So you know as much as he?"

"Well, that is not entirely true," admitted Gellar, "Our friend here is woefully ill-informed of the modern world. He is practically a baby out here. I see by your face you are wondering how much I have inferred given my glimpse into our friend's memories. The answer is- quite a lot. I saw and knew, where he could not see the connections." *Well, he's not wrong. I was a babe in the woods.*

Ohotepe rubbed his forehead. "This be most unfortunate, for us and you. You know secrets you should not. That does not be leaving *me* with many choices."

The elf shrugged again. "You need not fear *me*, ser. Fuck the Emperor, and fuck the Horts, and fuck the entire Magocracy."

Ohotepe scrutinized Gellar for a long moment. "That being what someone would say, trying to save himself." Ohotepe bit his lip and glanced around. Looking down at Plinius, Ohotepe asked "We do not have time for this. Can this man be trusted?"

"Trusted?" Plinius repeated dumbly. The implications of what answer he gave dawned on Plinius. "The elf- Gellar, sorry- saved my life. And, well, helped incite the riot to begin with. I think we should bring him with us."

Ohotepe nodded at Plinius. "Good enough for me. Quickly now, do not be falling behind. Qubo and Pots are waiting for us up ahead."

With Ohotepe's guidance they made quick time to the northern part of the Exchange. The smoke began to thin, pushed southwards as the trade winds coming off the bay shifted with the setting sun. The sound of fighting and death receded as well, replaced by the shouts of frightened people and the incessant clanging of bells. The publican house was now in view, a sizable crowd pressing in on a small barricade that had been hastily improvised with makeshift material to lend it a bit more strength. A half dozen publicans in the gold and green of the Imperial tax office stood nervously at the small but crowded opening of the barricade, each of them shouting to be heard as people desperate to escape the Exchange argued to be let through.

Ohotepe led them up to the front, pushing past merchants and ignoring their protests. *The Terrastran Guard uniforms came in handy after all. If we hadn't had them, I'm sure the good people of Terrastra would have beaten us to death for queue jumping.* As they approached the gate, a small figure broke out of the crowd and crashed into Plinius with a strong embrace.

"Plinius, ser! Oh, how happy I's be ta be seein' ya, boy-o! I knew you'd get through that there madness ok, I told Qubo as much, he didna believe but I did fer sure!" Some of the people nearby gave them queer looks at the sight of a dishevelled dwarf hugging a Terran guard.

Plinius awkwardly disentangled himself from Pots fierce iron grip. "Ah, yes, well, thank you Pots, it was close there for a moment, but it seems we all made it out ok." Plinius' hands shook uncontrollably.

"There be time to talk later, we need to be moving," urged Ohotepe, pushing them forward.

Qubo was gesticulating wildly to a frazzled looking publican as they got near the barricade. "I need to be up on that hill, damn your emergency orders Eolaus!"

The publican, Eolaus, was exasperated. His pinched face seemed on the verge of tears. "Qubo, I don't know what to tell you! The standing orders are to not let anyone out of the Exchange until this mess is sorted out! This comes right from the Hall!"

Qubo threw his hands up in the air. "I thought we had an understanding, Eolaus. If you think the Hall of Staffs would be upset with letting myself and my employees through, think about how irate they would be if they were privy to our-"

The publican scowled. He looked around furtively, scratching the back of his neck. "Cronus damn it! This will be my ass on a hot kettle, I'm sure of it."

Qubo squeezed the publican's shoulder firmly. "No one will ever know, Eolaus. Who did you let through? Some of our brave boys, rushing to defend the church of Cronus uphill. Nothing strange about that. Let us not ruin a good thing, eh?"

The publican wavered for a moment, then broke. "Fine. Fine! You five-get through now before I change my mind. Go!"

"You are a wonderful human being, Eolaus," said Qubo thankfully, motioning for the rest of them to pass through the barricade. One of the other publicans looked to protest but was quickly silenced by the irate Eolaus. As Ohotepe passed the barricade angry mutterings and cries of 'unfair' could be heard from the crowd. In short order a press of people and thrown rocks assaulted the barricade, the publicans forgetting all about Plinius and his companions as they tried to push back the mob. One of them took a punch on the chin for the effort, and additional publicans came rushing out of the tollhouse to reinforce them as a brawl broke out.

"Quickly, let us be quickly now," Ohotepe urged again, moving quickly up the Wayfarers Road.

Qubo fell in step beside Plinius. "Well magus, we did it. I thought for sure you would have got yourself killed down there in all the excitement. What a day for surprises, eh?"

"Excitement?" asked Plinius, not even trying to hide his disgust.

"What? You didn't find that exciting?" Qubo smiled predatorily. "It's kickin' off good now, boy-o."

"People are *dying*," replied Plinius, repulsed by the Kantan's tone.

"Terrans die every day. Today, Imperials are dying," answered Qubo, as if that explained everything.

"Indeed," growled Plinius. A thought popped into Plinius head, and he looked at Qubo. "The fire- back along the spokes- was that you?"

Qubo beamed. "Slow acting alchemical solution back in the tent. The timing was meant for a simple distraction to pull some attention away from the northern roads, but it all came together kind of nicely, didn't it?"

"But your whole shop! For someone who made such a big fuss about having to leave, how could you do that?"

"Better *me* to kill my baby than some magus bastard doing it. Just look behind you if you doubt what your kind is capable of."

Plinius was doing his best not to think of the horrors being perpetrated down at the Exchange. *The horror I committed.* Looking back over his shoulder, they had a decent view of the market and the city beyond now that they had climbed a good distance up the Lowhill. The clouds of smoke crouched over the western end of the city like a wolf feasting on a corpse, great gouts of flame three stories high snapping in the wind as it spread. The mound where the tower had stood was still being fought over, yet a flashing pocket of steel gave evidence that lictors were holding their ground.

Qubo followed his gaze and sighed. "It's only a matter of time- the rest of the Legion will be pouring into the city and putting down the riot. It served its purpose though- we're practically home free."

Plinius stared at him, completely disgusted with the man. "How many people died down there? How many so that we could be 'home free'?" He said the last words with as much acid as he could muster.

Qubo shrugged. "You're hung up on the dying, I get it. It's not pleasant. But people die every day, magus. Every day, in every part of the Empire, people are crushed under the boots of Imperial tyranny. At least the Terrans down there died on their feet and not on their knees."

"That hardly seems like justification for such… such… death." Plinius thought of the mother and child, quickly trying to banish the image from his mind as he could feel his legs start to go limp. This left room for the thought of Heuronicus plummeting to his death, and then of the disintegrating lictors. It was different from the former image to be sure, but Plinius was unsurprised to find he could not stomach it any less. *Death is death. Well, unless you're in Tsarusska.*

"I'm not trying to justify it, magus," Qubo replied tersely, "Justification is far above my pay grade. But if you think it wasn't worth it for those people down there, not worth their lives just to spit in the Empire's eye and know you hurt them back, ask them what they think." Qubo hocked a thumb towards Pots and Gellar.

Plinius chewed on that for a moment. "I disagree. A life lost is a life wasted. What does it matter? It is pointless. You said so yourself the Empire will win. How could that," he pointed a finger down at the riot, still roiling and thrashing like a frenzy of sharks across the Exchange, "be for anyone's benefit?"

Qubo looked at Plinius' long and hard. "I suppose we will find out, magus. Those people died to get you here. Let's hope you're worth it." He picked up his pace and joined with Ohotepe.

For the second time today Plinius looked down from on high at lower Terrastra, this time from the opposite end of the city. The sickness in his belly threatened to claw up his throat again. *What was I feeling then? Pity, disgust? Not the disdain from before. That mother and child. The madness of the archmagistrate, the brutality of Ox'Vacar. My own brutality. All these horrors in a day. It leaves a person feeling hollow. A single day, Tales! How many other atrocities had been carried out, had happened while I cared only about myself? About my research? I turned a blind eye to it all, hiding away in my bookstore.*

Plinius quickened his step as Pots fell back to keep stride with him. Pots did not say a word. The Exchange disappeared behind some houses as the winding street of Wayfarer's Road climbed in a spiral around the Lowhill. Plinius felt a relief so strong to be away from the sight of it that he began to weep. Screams of death and despair still managed to nip at his heels. His weeping turned to unabashed sobbing as the image of a mother and her child replayed over and over in his mind.

Chapter Ten

Friends & Wayfarers

It was during the hollow hours of darkest night when they came and dragged Plinius and his new friends out of their cell. Not that he knew the time at that time. *I didn't know our cell doubled as a broom closet at the time, either.*

He, Pots, and Gellar had been unceremoniously dumped in there shortly before sundown. They had ascended the Lowhill in great time, the roads being nearly deserted save for the odd citizen furtively moving quickly from house to house, shadow to shadow, terrified mice hiding away, praying that the madness consuming the city would pass them by. Behind high whitewashed stonewalls a church-bell clanged noisily as they passed by, its large oaken doors sealed tightly as the bell clanged steadily in its belfry. Halfway up the hill they stepped out onto a wide square that afforded a panoramic view of the city to the south and west. Plinius had felt a tear come to his eye upon looking down at his beloved Terrastra. *Oh, my poor bookstore!*

The rioting had spread from the Exchange to join with madness consuming the Tradebasin, rampaging its way along the docks until meeting stiff resistance among the lower villas, spas, and boutique shoppes of Northhill. The sun had sunk low in the west, casting a bloody golden light that turned the water of Drake Bay and the great ocean beyond it into coloured glass. Plinius wondered if the thin clouds peeking above the horizon came from the great mists of the Edge. The wind had begun to settle, and a colony of smoke columns thrashed skywards like greedy tentacles across the city, grotesque invaders among the natural beauty of the city. The south gate could be seen as well- the shimmering of a metallic snake emerging from the shadow of the southern wall. Marching soldiers had begun an invasion of the commoner market, a spinning web of steel expanding out into Terrastra. *Like spilt ink spreading on a page.* An amplified voice boomed across the city, the rumbling thunder words of a god, drowning out the errant screams echoing up from below.

"In the name of the Emperor, by order of the Aurum Circle, by the power of the Magocratic Empire, martial law is now in effect in the city of Terrastra. Lay down your weapons and proceed to the nearest Imperial outpost for processing. You will not be harmed. The Empire is here to help. You have nothing to fear. Empire Eternal!"

"By Cronus' cock," exclaimed Qubo. "They're finally doing it. You were right, Teeps. The Empire is making its move on Terrastra."

"Or at least tryin' to," whispered Pots.

Gellar nodded. "There are many who will never accept Imperial rule in Terrastra. They will have to kill them all to make it so."

Plinius was shocked speechless. *What of the Concord?*

"What about the Concord!?" exclaimed Plinius.

Qubo snorted a laugh. "*Bleeesed Concooord!* The Concord!? That old rag? What of it?"

"What of it?" gaped Plinius, "It guarantees Terrastra's independence!"

"Edge take me," laughed Qubo, "Maybe three hundred years ago! The Concord hasn't mattered for as long as I've been alive."

Plinius was shocked silent. Even if what Qubo said was true, he could not believe the Empire would so flagrantly flout the bedrock of order on Mir on the flimsiest of pretexts. Terrastra was *the* free city. Plinius shook with anger. *The Emperor I remember would never have condoned this! What the bloody hells happened?*

Ohotepe clapped his hands. "Quickly now! No time for sight-seeing. Let us be going. Almost there!"

In another hour they had approached the zenith of the Lowerhill. Plinius' legs and feet burned with the exertion, yet despite his many pleas Ohotepe refused to allow them a rest. *I probably walked more that day than I had in the past fifty years.* Having only the Midhill to compare it with, the top of the Lowerhill seemed desolate and mundane in comparison. The plaza was unadorned of any aesthetic improvement, not a tree nor a bench to be seen. Plinius wheezed as he walked to the only visible seat in view, a simple unadorned rockcrete fountain the size of a large table occupying the centre of the square. *I remember that fountain! The most curious thing, it was formed by some alchemical method devised by a common. No magic involved at all.* The water was, for lack of a better word, old. Brackish, overgrown with weeds and lousy with dancing bugs gave the impression that it had been that way for quite some time. Plinius tutted and dipped a finger into it. With a few whispered words the water in the fountain turned from a thick brownish green to a shimmering pool of clear and pure water. Pots ran forward and buried his face fully into it, gulping greedily.

A large stone wall nearly five meters high stretched the entire length of the square. What had in a time long past been a marshalling yard and then a bustling market, now spent its days as a sleepy dead-end street with numerous ramshackle homes crowding against the wall in every direction. The large drum tower of the Wayfarers Guild loomed up behind the wall, it's blue and red pennant flapping and snapping in the wind. A large green and red rooster pecked in the dirt nearby, blissfully unaware of the mayhem transpiring beyond his demesne and completely unconcerned with their arrival.

Ohotepe approached a gate wide enough to allow the passage of a full wagon team and knocked four times on a postern door. Plinius noticed that the door was of newer wood- the large gate itself was cracked and rotting in some places. Ohotepe waited for what seemed like an inordinate amount of time before he followed up with a quick staccato knock like a drummer's roll. Plinius held his breath, expecting something to happen. *At the very least for the door to open.* What he did not expect was a knife being placed to his throat as two dozen men and women materialized from seemingly nowhere around them, swords, spears, and loaded crossbows drawn on them. Plinius shifted his eyes and looked at Qubo, holding a knife to his throat and smiling his insufferably wicked smile.

"Let's hope you were worth it, mage."

They had sacks thrown over their heads. In the darkness of the hood images flashed before his eyes. The River coursing through him, frothing and crashing and angry. The heat from his hands, fuelled by his anger, turning into angry torches. The look on the archmagi-ster's face as he crashed to the earth. The looks of horror on the lictors faces as whole swathes of their bodies decayed to nothing-ness in front of their eyes. The pure destruction he wrought. He could see their faces, looking at him, accusing him. He shuddered and blinked away tears.

A loud creaking sound and a smack on his shin let Plinius know he had crossed the threshold into the Wayfarers Guild. It did not take long for Plinius to completely lose his way, any attempt at simple spells to see beyond the hood failing instantly. *The hoods are threaded sewn with scale of ripanulite. Clever.* He strained with his other senses to make an image in his mind. Footsteps echoing through a large hall. Right turn, down a flight of stairs, left turn, left turn, up a short flight of stairs, down another, a long hallway, down yet another flight. It seemed to him that whatever route they had taken was designed to obfuscate exactly where in the guildhall they had been taken. Wherever they were, Plinius was pretty sure they were deep within the hill itself. After at least half an hour of tromping around blindly, the sacks had been pulled off and Plinius blinked in the dimness of the windowless room. Ohotepe gently pushed him further into the room as two cloth masked men did the same for Gellar and Pots.

"Be not worrying, my friend," Ohotepe said reassuringly with a sheepish smile, patting him on the chest, "I will be back for you, and soon all will make sense. You just need to trust me."

"Ohotepe-" the door shut firmly in his face and Plinius was left with the elf and dwarf to ponder their fate.

Turning around in the oppressive total darkness of the small room, Plinius swore as he bumped his hip into what was either a mop and bucket or Pots. He raised his hand and clicked his tongue against the roof of his mouth the same time he snapped his finger.

Nothing happened.

"Gremlin shit!" swore Plinius, "The room is warded. I can't access the

River in here. We're stuck in this blackness!"

A striking sound clicked once, then twice, then a third time. The tiny flash of light was enough for Plinius to make out Pots face for a split second, his tongue extruding from his mouth as he crouched over something on the ground. Another half of a dozen strikes, and a small pile of wood and tinder alit in the centre of the room, a meagre and pathetic campfire that produced little smoke and more than enough light. A tiny wisp like a candle flame danced along the pile of fuel like a moth, dancing shadows illuminating their cell.

"Well done," Plinius said to Pots, sincerely impressed. Pots looked quite satisfied with his accomplishment where the magus' had failed.

No more than two metres squared, four walls of damp grey fieldstone enclosed a smooth stone floor speckled with dirt and cobwebs. A small copper drain in the middle of the floor gurgled sporadically and indignantly at the disruption to its quiet little space. *It's just a drain. Don't personify.* A mop spilling out of a foul-smelling wooden bucket sat forlornly in the corner. No window, no light except for Pot's meagre fire. With a sigh, Plinius sat down with his legs crossed, his back against the wall. Gellar followed suit. Pots flipped over the bucket and sat down on its upturned bottom. He smiled as a viscous black ooze leaked between his toes towards the drain.

Plinius sat on the floor in silence for a long time. *I refused to be the first to speak. Swore an oath to myself. No more words until I got to see Anatoli. Believe it or not, but I could be very stubborn when I wanted to be.* Gellar sat next to him, his legs crossed, and eyes closed as his breathing slowed until the scrivener began to question if he was still alive. *It was the first time I had seen an elvish trance. If I hadn't been so out of sorts, I would have been unfailingly curious.* After an hour, Pots stood up and wandered around the room, tapping on bricks and stones with the mop's wooden handle.

"Dwarf," murmured Gellar after ten minutes of this, not opening his eyes. "What in the sweet name of Selune are you doing?"

Pots jumped as the elf's voice broke the code of silence that two-thirds of them had been maintaining. "Oh! Well, ye know, I's just searchin' is all."

Plinius hoped Gellar would leave it at that. His hopes were dashed when the elf inquired further.

"For what, pray tell?"

Pots scuffed the floor with the toe of his boot, his face turning a little flush. "Well… y'know. Secret doors."

Plinius surprised even himself as a sharp laugh escaped his lips. "Secret doors? Really, Pots? Really?"

Pots face screwed up. "Well, yup. Dinnae know where we be?"

"Given the smell," Gellar muttered, "I would hazard a guess that we're in some manner of latrine."

"It's probably just Pots," said Plinius, tut-tutting at his own joke. When no one else laughed, he scowled. "Where are we, Pots? Well by my observation we are in a bloody room with a stinky bucket, a mop, and no idea what the hell is going to happen to us."

"Well, thar's half the truth, true enough," Pots conceded, now down on his knees and digging his fingers into any loose mortar between the fieldstones. His voice dropped to a conspiratorial whisper. "We're in th' *Wayfarers Guild!*"

Plinius could not have rolled his eyes harder. "Cronus' mercy, Pots. What the hell does that have to do with you accosting the walls?"

Pots looked indignant. "I wasn' a coasting anything. I was searchin' fer secret passages."

Plinius hmphed, "Whatever."

"Alls I's is saying is everyone knows th' Wayfarers are secret types. Have fingers in e'ery pie and a foot in e'ery caper that goes down in Terrastra," his voice had dropped back down to a whisper. "Da used t' tell stories 'bout them when he were tuckin' us in. Stories 'bout Marco of the Long March, and the Robbin' Hood. They's got their agents in e'ery city from here to Nozomi. They pull the strings in th' city, if not the whol' of Mir, don' ye doubt if fer a second, boyo."

Plinius sat in silence for a moment before breaking out in uproarious laughter. Pots scowled and went back to tapping on the walls. Even Gellar smirked slightly before regaining his composure.

"Oh Pots, you are too much." Plinius wiped his eyes with his sleeve. "Do you truly believe a bunch of commoners- sorry, a guild, has that kind of power? That the Magocracy would not absolutely crush any sort of common threat to their authority?"

"No offense now, Plinius," Pots wagged an accusatory finger at the scrivener, "But yer mighty Magocracy isn' as all powerful as you reckon' it to be."

Plinius waved his hand dismissively, forgetting completely about his oath of silence. *I just chose to end it.* "Oh, I do not disagree with you on that point, not even slightly." Plinius stood up and stretched his legs, feeling the ache in his arches and shaking the pins and needles out of his soles. "The Magocracy is *not* all powerful. I will be the first to tell you so. What is happening down in the city is proof enough of that, I would say."

"Easy for you to say, Plinius," Gellar stood and likewise stretched. "I wonder if you would say the same if you were in my shoes."

I was very naïve back then.

Plinius bristled at the comment. "Now then, what is that supposed to mean?"

Gellar looked at Plinius, and it unsettled him a great deal to be under the gaze of those piercing eyes. *It always did.* "You are a magus, Plinius. A *grandmagus.* I impressed on you- and I saw flashes of your life. Your very privileged, very quiet life. Do you think any person on Mir who isn't a magi could ever even dream about living a life like yours?"

Plinius shook his head. "That may be so but believe it or not I am completely capable of empathy," his eyes glanced towards Pots, who was now desperately pressing bricks in the corner, "I understand all too well what the Magocracy is capable of. More so than most."

Gellar tsked. "Believe me, magus, not more than myself or your dwarven friend here."

"Oh! My apologies, friend elf," Pots walked over and held out a hand. "Nevah forget yer manners, Da says, and 'ere I's go fogettin' mine. I's be Pots, it's what th' people call me!"

"A pleasure, Pots," replied the elf cordially, having picked up on Pots name hours ago. He grasped his hand firmly. "My elven name will be known in death, but my Imperial name is Gellar La Fontaine. You may call me Gellar, friend."

Plinius sat back down in a humph. "I *do* get it!" he said, not willing to let the argument go. "The Concord Wars, the Consolidation, the purges. I am all too aware of the atrocities committed by the magi. Not just the Empire. All magi.

Why do you think I chose to live in Terrastra? Why do you think I turned my back on…" Plinius groped for the right words as he pushed the truth down as far as it could, "the Emperor, the Legion, all that nonsense?" Plinius waved his hand around the room as if he was encompassing the entire city, "What's going on out there couldn't be happening if the Magocracy was all powerful. The Empire had the advantage at first, naturally, because magic is a powerful force. Maybe the most powerful force in the universe, but like wind and water and fire it's only powerful if harnessed by the right hands. And despite all it's power, it will never be more powerful than a person's desire to be free."

Gellar was non-plussed. "That might be so, magus, but tell that to the drones in Tsarusska," he pointed at Pots, who looked very uncomfortable to be mentioned in the same sentence as the northern kingdom, "or to the other elves in the Sapphire Ghettos, or the deathcamps in the wasteland that was Sil'dorin. Those of us that are left. Don't doubt for even a second that they will use today as an excuse to eradicate more of my brethren. Do not be surprised if us elves, and dwarves, and *simps* do not celebrate in your principled stand."

Plinius floundered, desperate to get out of this conversation of his own making. *Run away, Plinius, run away from the hard truths. As always. Can we please move this along?*

"We are off the original topic," Plinius decreed, "We were talking about Pots ridiculous delusions about the Wayfarers."

"Very well," Gellar agreed graciously, "I have no wish to antagonize you,

Plinius. I have a feeling that division amongst us three will only be detrimental in our current situation. Please, illuminate our stout friend and disabuse him of his Wayfarer fantasies. But try to do it nicely."

Pots rounded on Gellar. "They are not fantasies!"

"Oh? How many secret doors have you found?" asked Plinius.

Pots grumbled and turned back to knocking on stones.

"The Wayfarer's guild is a morose ghost," began Plinius, "a relic, centuries past the time when they had a purpose and a calling."

Plinius adopted an imperious tone, usually reserved for exclusive use by professors and know-it-alls. "They were once revered across Mir as the women and men at the forefront of exploration and human expansion- the trailblazers and mavericks that trampled over every horizon, expanding the influence of what would later become the Magocratic Empire. Did you know that the Wayfarer's were the first ever guild to be granted a charter? It's true- this was back when Al- the Emperor personally presented the charters to the guild councils. How is that, eh? The first guild charter granted was for a commoner guild, and by the magus who would be Emperor no less! Back before the Concord, they were integral to the growth of the kingdom of Aliston. They served as guides and guards for magi and men alike. They were heroes and villains, they were knights and thieves, they were tomb-robbers, and diplomats, and merchants, and negotiators. Even some magi would join over the years, though this was frowned upon by the Circles. They were known across all of Mir for their intrepid spirit and amazing discoveries."

"Every child knows this," Pots whined.

"Do not interrupt," Plinius admonished gently, like a schoolteacher to a dullard child. *That's an unfair characterisation.* The patronizing tone flew right over Pots head. *I'm not patronizing!*

"The Robbin Hood and tireless Marco, as you said, but also Iolo of Aliston, Preston Jacobi and the Hidden Kingdom, the Thirty-Three sojourns of Stannislaus Stevonivich the Steel Bear, Alnuathor'ael the Wise (an appreciative nod from Gellar accompanied that addition)- all of them legends in their own time! At the Wayfarers height, just as the Empire was coming into its own, well, then I would say that maybe they had political power to rival the magi. They were absolutely adored by the masses, and that sentiment has, although diluted and diminished, largely survived to the modern era. People take great comfort in the familiar, and the Wayfarers are familiar across all of Mir. So, you see, their power was not in spells, and mostly definitely not in constructing secret doors, but in the hearts and minds of a continent enamoured with their endeavours. If not in actual strength of arms than most definitely in the court of popular opinion amongst the people of Mir.

But all things must end. Kanta, Tsarusska, Xeijpang, and the Empire standing large above them all- they cover the breadth of Mir from the rocky, barren shoals of Gentia in the south to the frozen wastes of the White Death in the north. There is no place left to discover. There is no great unknown left for the Wayfarers to trailblaze into.

And so, they have become a sad collection of phantoms, sitting in this sad dusty hall, telling sad stories of times well before they were born, when they had meaning and purpose. There are NO secret passages, NO hidden halls of power. Just a sad group of people looking for relevancy in a world that no longer needs them. It is also rumoured that they steal children and eat them, but no evidence has ever proven such."

Pots had stopped tapping on stones. He sat down in the corner and curled up, quiet and indrawn. Plinius chewed his lip, a strange feeling washing over him. *I couldn't even recognize shame when I felt it then. What a prig I was. I didn't mean to deflate him so much. I should have apologized.* Plinius shook his head in irritation and crouched down against the wall. Gellar patted his knee, which at first annoyed the scrivener but he quickly realized it for what it was. He smiled weakly at the elf.

The hours passed, but with no way to tell the time the trio had no concept of how long they had been hidden away in their dank cell. The small bucket in the corner proved to be their only source of natural relief, and after much protesting the scrivener managed to convince the other two to face away while he did his business. Plinius wiled the time away etching on a nearby stone with the small piece of flint Pots had used for the fire. He scrivened on the wall despite being unable to access the River behind the wards. *Why the hell is a broom closet in the sub-basement of a commoner guild warded anyways?*

It was right at that point where Plinius thought he would go mad from the sheer boredom of the situation that the clomping of footsteps approached. Pots and Plinius stood abruptly, backing up against the far wall from the door. Gellar remained sitting, completely at peace. The footsteps grew louder until they stopped suddenly. A couple of large clanks from sliding bolts and the door to the most protected broom closest in existence opened.

"Pliny! *Moy drug*!"

Plinius nearly collapsed in relief. "Anatoli! You are a sight for sore eyes!" The rogue walked into the room and met the scrivener in a fierce embrace. They held it for a moment, Anatoli pounding the thin mage roughly on the back. Plinius pulled back and smacked the rogue gently on the cheek. "You're hurt!"

"What, this?" Anatoli pointed to a fresh bandage around his forearm, little veins of red seeping through the linen. "*Nyet*, it is no big deal, just a little cut I picked up on my way here earlier."

Plinius tsked, taking his eyes off the bandage to look at Anatoli, pounding a fist on his shoulder. "It is very good to see you. I have had quite a trying day; you would not believe half of it."

"*Da*, it is good to see you my friend," Anatoli beamed, holding him out at arm's length, "I hear you ran into a spot of trouble making it here. My apologies, I should have been there. It shouldn't have been happened this way. Shouldn't have been such a trial. Next time, you will listen to your *drug* when he says it is time to go, eh?"

Plinius waved a hand in entirely insincere dismissal. "It was no trouble at all, I had my friends here to show me the way."

Anatoli turned to the elf and the dwarf. "You must be Pots and Gellar! I cannot thank you enough for the service you have done my friend Pliny!"

"Pliny?" Pots asked, arching an eyebrow at the mage.

Pliny! Yes… that's what they called me! You knew that thought, didn't you Tales?

I think it was mentioned a few times through the story. You might… have missed it.

Oh, remember now! Pliny, that's what my mother and father called me! And everyone else who mattered.

Plinius ignored the dwarf. "What is happening, Anatoli? I've been so desperate to see you," words began to spill from his mouth, "and I think you owe me some, excuse me, fucking answers! Where is Ohotepe? What has happened to the bookstore? Where were you? Why didn't you meet us at Murk's? What is happening in the city? How did you manage to get away? Where is-"

"Easy, easy, *moy drug*," Anatoli held his hands up, palms forward. "Answers are coming soon. I can tell you this much- the Empire has sent the entire 1st Legion into Terrastra. Thankfully we are better prepared than they ever could have realized. We are resisting, but it is only a matter of time before the city falls. We had hoped for more time, but-"

"We? Who is we?" asked Plinius.

Anatoli clasped the magus' shoulders. "Come with me and find out. It is time you knew what has happened, what is happening, and what will happen going forward." Despite the warmth of the words, Plinius grew more apprehensive at his friends promise.

Gellar and Pots stood, attempting to follow Anatoli and Plinius out. Anatoli hesitated, holding up his hand. "I am sorry, my friends. Only Pliny. You must remain here."

Plinius looked at Gellar and Pots. Gellar seemed to take this without any undue emotion, but he could see the disappointment on Pots face.

"No."

Anatoli's face could not look more surprised, his lips pursed beneath his moustache. "Excuse me?"

"No." Plinius repeated. It had been enough for one day. Dumped out of his bookstore. Dragged across town by strange commoners. Harassed by lictors. Almost burnt to death. Introduced to drinking ale. Dressed up as a common guard. Hunted, and tested. His feet hurt. His body hurt. He looked down at his hands, and flashes of flame and death filled his eyes and ears. He had been abused, disabused, ordered, attacked, kicked, thrown, shoved, hidden away, run like a dog, kidnapped, and just overall, Plinius had concluded, generally treated quite poorly. "They are my friends. I would never have made it this far without them. They are coming with *me*, or I'm staying here with them."

Pots could not have looked more astonished. Gellar looked like he was browsing vegetables.

Anatoli stared at Plinius for a long time, long enough to make him feel a little nervous.

"Very well, Pliny," Anatoli conceded, and then continued in grim seriousness. "They can come with, but I will not have their fates on my conscience. If they choose to come, they will come with eyes wide open."

He turned to the elf and the dwarf. "Let me be clear- if you come with us now, there is no turning back. You are committing to something blindly, but you will be committing to it all the same. There will be no returning to the lives you have lived up until now. The way forward will be dangerous. It will be long. It will be hard. I know this is asking a lot, but it is what it is, and any true Terrans such as yourselves deserves to know beforehand."

Plinius blanched. "What the hell are you talking about? I haven't committed to anything!"

Anatoli ignore him, staring intently at Gellar and Pots. "Well?"

The two looked at each other, then at Plinius, then at Anatoli.

"I's in," Pots said. "At this point my pots and cleanin' stuffs are burnt husks along the Midhill. Don' see what' I's gots ta lose, and ol' Pliny here, well I's reckon I's should keep an eye on 'em. Trouble prone this boy-o. Plus, Da always said 'Yung Pots, ye best grab adventure by the tail when it comes walkin' by, cause nuthin' great ever came about by not goin' fo'ward.'"

Gellar nodded. "I am intrigued. Whatever you have to offer must be better than returning to the ghetto or being strung up by the lictors. You say it is dangerous? I do not fear death, for at least then I will know my name."

Anatoli nodded in turn. "So be it. Follow me."

There were no hoods this time.

An escort of four identically masked men armed with short, slightly rusty spears fell in behind them as Anatoli led the way down hallways of cracked, mossy, sweating, wet stone. Plinius assumed the guards were there for him. Before today he would have taken umbrage at the affrontery that they could even remotely think it possible for a commoner to guard a grandmagus. Given Heuronicus' actions earlier in the Exchange he supposed he could understand their security around him, even though it would be completely ineffectual if Plinius decided to push the matter.

Walking through the dusty halls of the Wayfarers guild convinced Pots more of their fall from grace than any speechifying could accomplish. The walls were littered with off-coloured spots where pictures had once hung, only to be unceremoniously torn down and sold for a meagre sum long ago. Empty planters and dusty bookshelves bereft of anything but spiderwebs. Only every third sconce along the way was lit, casting a depressing gloom in each hallway they traversed. A smell of musty forgotten rot permeated from behind closed doors that had remained shut since anyone now living there could remember. Dark stains dripped from sagging plaster ceilings. *I imagine they wore the hoods more out of a sense of shame than any desired mystique.*

They did not walk for long. Unlike earlier they took no flights of stairs- rather they marched down a long hallway until they stood before a door of oak banded in iron with no discernible handle or means of opening it. Plinius could instantly sense the innate magic infused within it. This struck him as particularly interesting. The Wayfarers had always been known as a common guild- they most assuredly procured the use of magic, but Plinius would be surprised to find magi among the membership. *First the broom closet, and now this anomaly. Maybe a magus went in for some slumming? Fifth circles loved to tease the simp guilds with their patronage. Sorry, common guilds. A big joke at their expense.* To find such an artifice of magic deep within the bowels of Lowhill was curious to say the least.

Even more surprising was when Anatoli approached the door and rested his hand against it. He recited a few words under his breath and the door illuminated in an azure light. Runes lit up one by one along its arch and an ethereal handle spilled out from the centre, coalescing into a doorknob of intangible glass. He looked at Plinius with a sheepish smile. The door swung forwards slightly, as if some invisible force was attached to the rogue's hand. *Invisible force? It was magic, Tales!* With the slightest effort, he pulled the door open.

As they stepped into the room, Pots felt slightly vindicated. In sharp contrast to what they had just seen, this room was opulent in its decadence. The room was a large ballroom, larger even than the Ontario room back at his parent's estate. Tapestries of elvish, orcish, and dwarfish design hung from the left wall. A long mahogany bar stretched along the right wall, stools with plush ivy-coloured cushions occupied by the roughly two dozen masked Wayfarers from earlier. They all turned, watching their motley group shuffle in. Glass bottles of rare vintages, from ancient spirits long forgotten alongside the newest innovations from the Ausland Archipelago. The bottles lined mirrored display shelves hung along the wall on the right side of the room. Most shocking was a goliath bartender polishing mugs behind the bar, a white collared shirt with black suspenders giving him a very professional look. *That was the first time I had seen a goliath unchained from an Imperial master.* His grim visage was still very much in character, however.

The far wall across the length of the room took Plinius breath away. A bas-relief mural of exquisite detail adorned the entire space, a work of art so amazingly rendered in stone and paint that Plinius was simultaneously inspired and humbled. Illustrating all of Mirysh history, Merlin dominated the centre of the mural. The Sea Wizard looked identical to his fountain in the midmarket, which wasn't strange, as common belief held that Merlin had stopped aging centuries ago, the first magus to discover the secret of prolonged life. *That alone would have sealed his legacy. Can you imagine dying at fifty years of age?*

The founder of Terrastra was surrounded by the rest of the Thirteen Magi of the Aurum Council. *Curious, so many familiar faces, there's Abe, Morgan... but I can't put names to a lot of the faces. Why can't I remember? I know those people, bloody hells two of them are my parents! I'm sure of it!* Spreading out from the original council, images of the Concord Wars, the Consolidation, even the Tsarusskan Domination and the Sack of the Eternal Hall were depicted in detail that took Plinius' breath away. *Back to the magi! Why can't I remember them, Tales?* It took a great deal of will for Plinius to pull away from the artistry and focus on the moment. Sitting at the

ANSWER ME!

Plinius. We talked about this. You're interrupting the flow of the story.

I'm… I'm just… having a very hard time right now. That mural…

Yes. We anticipated this happening. It's ok.

We? Again with the we. Who's We? Anticipated what?

Please Plinius, do you trust *me*?

Trust you? Tales, I don't even know you! How can I trust someone who I can't see? Who is purposefully evasive?

Then trust yourself. Just enjoy the story. It will come back to you, just be patient.

Say patient again. I swear to god I will-

I don't know what else to tell you! I'm just doing what you-

OH NO YOU DON'T! GET BACK HERE TALES! GET BACK HERE NOW!

Pliny I'm sorry! I was just, I can't-

You're just doing what? What!?

I'm trying to help you!

I don't like this! What is the point of this? You know what? I think I've had enough. I'm done. What the bloody hell is actually going on here? Why can't I remember? Where the hell are you? I refuse to be party to this for a second longer. Not until I get some answers.

It will all become clear, I swear. You just need to be patient.

PATIENT PATIENT PATIENT!
I'm feeling decidedly impatient at the moment!

Plinius please calm down! Focus on the moment! Focus on the words, where we are at in the story, use it to anchor you! Let your mind exist in the moment! Your memories will come back. I promise.

Be warned, Tales. My patience is wearing very thin.

Tales?

Tales?

Plinius?

Look who's back! Oh, how wonderful!

Is that sarcasm?

You can't tell, Mr. Patience? Mr. Disappearing-act? Mr. Know It All?

Well, it's hard to discern sarcasm in print.

Fuck you.

Woah! Language please.

Fuck. You.

You keep treating me like that, and I won't give you the good news.

Plinius?

Good news?

Yes! Good news!

I remain sceptical.

I have conversed with our associates, and we have decided that you have earned some answers.

I have earned some answers, have I? Have I been a good boy, Tales? How magnanimous of you!

Ok, that's sarcasm.

Oh, is it?

Are you done?

Fine. So, you'll answer some questions, eh? Finally?

Let's say… three questions for now. We can't diverge from the story for long, this has already gone much further at this point than we anticipated and we're running out of room.

Running out of room!? What the fuck does that mean!?

Just in this first book, Pliny. We have others to continue the story into, don't worry. As many as it takes.

Oh yes, why worry about this situation? Nothing alarming going on here! EDGE TAKE ME ARE YOU SERIOUS!?!?

Ok, ok, Plinius, calm down for Cronus' sake. I told you it will be fine. What do I have to do to get you to start trusting me? Haven't I proven myself up to this point? That I have your best interests at heart?

Can you understand that trust is kind of hard in my position?

Yes. All I'm asking for is a little bit of faith. I appreciate your you have granted *me* to this point. To reward that faith, I fought our associates' tooth and nail to allow some illumination on your current situation. Doesn't that deserve a modicum of trust in return? You don't see it, Pliny, but currently I am your staunchest advocate. I'm the one rooting for you. It is cruel, but somewhat necessary, to keep you in the dark for the time being. I wish I could make you understand that by the end you'll know it was done for the best reasons. Please, Plinius, ask your questions. Take this for the olive branch that it is, so that we can continue and achieve what *we* set out to do. Please. I promise, that at the end of all of this you will understand.

You promise a lot, Tales.

My name is not Tales. Plinius, it's-

No!

Excuse me?

No! Stop!

Pardon?

You're just repeating yourself.

What the bloody hells are you talking about?

Don't tell me your name! You said it would come in time! Patience; remember?

Are you serious? *Now* you want mystery? After almost a whole book of badgering *me* for illumination?

Illumination? That's a big word. Don't overextend yourselves.

Really? Cronus, I sometimes forget what a petty asshole you were.

You didn't know that already?

Fuck you Pliny. I didn't think this would be easy, but honestly, I didn't expect you to be so… Plinius, about it.

What can I say? You know I love a mystery. Don't give up the plot in the first book!

Blessed Concord. You are unbelievable.

Tales?

Sorry, Plinius. I keep going away, although I said I would try not to. I just needed a second. I lost my temper. I'm sorry.

Oh. Well, I am sorry as well, Tales. I know I haven't been the most congenial partner in this. I hope you can understand why though.

I can. Trust me, I get it more than you know.

How about moving forward, we try a little harder, eh? Partners. Deal?

Deal.

Most excellent. So... what is your name?

No, no- you were right. Now is not the time. Any question but that.

And you promise that your answers will be completely truthful?

I never promise anything I can't follow through on.

I respect that.

Yes. I know you do.

Very well then. Who are your associates?

They are all friends of yours.

Vague.

I like to maintain mystery.

Har-har. Fine, be that way. It is... comforting, to know friends are close. Am I... dead?

Cronus, Pliny, no!

Well, that's a relief. The old 'he was in heaven or hell or Valhalla or a dream' trope is so overused. Remember LOST? What a letdown.

Lost? Who's lost?

Never mind, just an errant thought, a memory...

I'll take your word for that. One more question, Plinius, then back to the story.

Yes, mother.

Plinius?

I' m thinking. It needs to be a good one.

Fair enough. Please don't take too long.

Ok, I've got it.

Let's hear it.

Are you one of the characters that has appeared in this story so far?

Good question.

Tales?

Yes. Yes, I am.

Oh, this is so delicious! My gut tells me that you're Pots, but I doubt he can write, so maybe not.

I'm pleased you're entertained.

Was that sarcasm?

Oh, you can't tell? Sorry Pliny, you got your three answers already.

Haha! Touche. Please, my mysterious friend, let us carry on.

The scent of sandalwood and sweet cinnamon hung in the air, supplying a nice counterpoint to the reeking tension. A large table intricately finished with carved runes along the edge sat in the middle of the room set for a dozen occupants was occupied by ten, two varnished cedar chairs upholstered in violet sable remaining empty. Anatoli led them directly towards the vacant seats.

Plinius was not a person accustomed to feeling disadvantaged. His life and passions set him above most people, his knowledge and mastery of magic putting him a league apart. *You make me sound like an asshole.* It was a strange sensation, walking into the unknown, a knot of tight apprehension in his gut. Ohotepe, leaning against the wall just inside the door, stopped Pots and Gellar and encouraged them to follow him. They walked to the side of the room and took seats at the bar, Pots waving off a helping hand from Ohotepe as he scrambled up on one of the stools. The Goliath began pouring out amber liquid from a green glass bottle into three glass tumblers, sliding each to one of Plinius' companions with a finger the size of a cucumber.

Plinius followed closely behind Anatoli, timorously approaching the table, noticing that all eyes were fixed on him. *After a whole day trying to stay invisible.* For the first time in his life, he felt completely out of his depth. *I truly hate surprises.* It was not because of who was around the table, as almost all of them were unknown to him at first glance. *The man at the head of the table is very familiar… on the tip of my tongue.* He imagined he could hear their thoughts, inspecting him – *judging?* – yes, judging him as he stepped up to the foot of the table. Whatever reason he had been brought here for, the grandmagus knew he was about to find out.

"Plinius Scrivener." It was not a question but a statement, given by the man at the head of the table, directly opposite of the empty seat that Anatoli now directed him to stand besides at the closer end of the table. His voice had a unique accent, his vowels sounding very high, spoken from the back of his mouth, a primitive Terrastran accent. "Born November 9th, 1385, in Aliston, Avalon province, seat of the Emperor and capital of the Magocratic Empire. Graduate of the Lyceum, earning his grey on April 30th, 1403. Grandmagus of the 8th Circle, Grandmaster Scrivener. Until this morning, proprietor of an unnamed and unadorned 'bookstore' in the Middle District. Accused criminal. Accused heretic. Traitor to the Empire. Executed for his crimes on June 25th, 1499."

Plinius stared at the man. *Why can't I place him? Bloody hells, I know I know him!* "Most of that is true I suppose. Except for the dead part, obviously. And I do contest the application of traitor. I am no citizen of the Empire. And my bookstore did have a name! I just never got around to putting up the sign."

The man at the head of the table did not respond at first. He was a bulldog of a man. Boxy, staunch, and dour with eyes aware and active. He looked like a man apart from the rest. His cheeks hung down around his mouth in a perpetual frown. His head was bereft of hair, but his eyes had shadows and his chin bore the stubble of a man who had been up too early and stayed up too late. His pale skin betrayed the fact that he had not seen the sun in far too long. His clothing was of a queer style that Plinius found quaint yet oddly familiar, a jacket and matching pants of a fuzzy material in an argyle pattern. His collared shirt hung loose around his meaty neck. A ribbon of some glossy black fabric looped around his neck like a noose, the tail end flaring out and resting halfway down his chest. Plinius was certain that this was the man in charge of the meeting, as the rest of the table turned towards him, attentive and deferential.

"Whether you are a traitor or not is precisely what we are here to determine, Plinius Scrivener."

A man to the Bulldog's right rapped once on the table, arresting the magus' attention. "Were you not raised in Aliston? Are you not personally acquainted with the Aurum Circle? Are you not personally acquainted with the Emperor himself?"

Plinius' took a deep breath, his mind imagining himself as a rabbit merrily bounding through a meadow, blissfully unaware of the steel jaws lying in the tall grass. His gaze drifted over the table. A few of the men and women proved equally interesting. A woman dressed in a flamboyant brocade of purple silk that complimented her crème coloured, curly tresses, her hair spilling from under an overlarge black hat. The flamboyancy of her clothes contrasted with the serious sternness of her face. She picked her teeth with a squat steel dagger as she eyed Plinius coolly.

Six soldiers seated on the right side of the table wore the blue and red uniforms of militiamen. The oldest looked to be near fifty given his thinning grain hair, the stars on his uniform and scars on his face meaning he could be no other than Commander Eriksen, senior officer, and commander of the Terrastran militia. The other five were ranging in age from twenty to forty, each one no lower in rank than 2nd lieutenant. The scrivener was a little surprised to see them here given the current state of the city. All their faces might have been carved from granite, their military training making each of their faces taciturn like a row of emotionless busts.

The one smiling face belonged to the man sitting on the Bulldog's left. He wore simple high-collared black robes, an inky black from neck to toe with the only ornamentation being a silver broach fashioned in the likeness of the Lyceum. A shock of curly red hair tumbling like a heap of yarn and fair face devoid of wrinkles belied the man's age. *Archmagi Orillia Orthinticus! Dean and head of the Lyceum council! I remember him, Tales! It… had been about forty years or so since I'd seen him last. He hasn't aged a day.* He greeted Plinius with a slight dip and twist of his head, his kindly eyes giving the scrivener a boost of confidence.

The eyes of the man to the left, the one who had questioned Plinius' loyalties, were still firmly affixed on the magus. Given the current and insistent drumming of his fingers on the table, Plinius deduced he was a highly strung common. Plinius guessed him to be on the quieter side of middle-age, his face bristling with a thick salt and pepper beard, his short black hair shot through with white streaks like falling stars. Thick black eyebrows gave his face a hooded look. He sat to the right of the Bulldog, leaning over to whisper something into his ear. He wore simple leathers embossed with the symbol of his guild- the blue and gold compass of the Wayfarers. His eyes arched as if to ask *'Well? Any day now?'*

Plinius cleared his throat. "Yes. Well. Yes indeed, I grew up in Aliston in my earliest years. But I left for the Lyceum when I was eleven- Archmagi Orthinticus there can attest to that. I rose to the azure veneficus by age fourteen and donned the grey on my eighteenth birthday. Youngest person to earn the title of magus ever recorded. I then chose to remain in Terrastra for personal reasons, earning my grey within the year, and settling into my own residence shortly after. And so, for the past ninety-three years I have considered myself a Terran. I eat Terrastran food, I drink Terrastran water, I pay Terrastran taxes and give to Terrastran causes. Everyone I have had dealing with know me to be a true Terran!"

"'E is!" agreed Pots loudly.

"Yes, he is," chimed in Gellar.

"He be a true Terran. By the River, I be swearing," said Ohotepe.

Plinius felt a hundred feet tall.

"Quiet!" barked the Bulldog.

"Your friends character references will be taken under advisement. Everyone you deal with, you say?" The Wayfarer man scratched his beard. "You're dealing with me now, and *I* question your allegiances. From what I have been told, you have barely left your home in the past sixty years. That doesn't sound a lick like a Terran to me. Sounds kind of like what an Empire spy would do."

Plinius bristled internally, taking an intense dislike to the man's attitude. *I don't like him either.* Plinius sighed, making a show of being intently focused on wiping some imaginary dust from his shoulder. 'Is this what passes for manners on the Lowhill? Accusations from unknown accusers?"

The Wayfarer shot up in his seat, fists clenched as he leaned forward on the table. 'We will ask the questions here mage!"

"Magus," replied Plinius calmly.

"This is Citizen Kaeso Exonicus," snorted the Bulldog as the Wayfarer shot him an exasperated look, "Master of the Wayfarers Guild and one of the only men I know with the balls to talk to a grandmagus that way." This elicited a choked laugh from Orillia and an angry frown from Kaeso.

"Please, Grandmagus," the man continued, "bear with this indignity but a moment longer. Answer *me* with the truth, and you have nothing to fear. Are you an honourable, true, son of Terrastra?" All eyes looked at him expectantly.

Plinius breathed shallowly, urging his choler back to calm. "I was born in Aliston, as I said. I was raised as magi, as you all probably damn well know. I answer true, on my soul, may Merlin take me, I have never done anything to endanger Terrastra or Terrastran ideals or Terran lives. I have always paid my taxes; I have always donated to charitable causes. I have always supplied aid when needed and done fair business with anyone who came into my shop. I am true, I am neutral, like my home is- I am Terrastra. Is this not the Jewel of the West? Is it not supposed to be the home to all, a home for knowledge? Damn politics and all the rest. Like the Concord states. Now what could be more Terran than that, hmmm?" Plinius stared defiantly at the Wayfarer.

"Still," replied Kaeso, pulling out a paper from a loose stack in front of him, "In the past twenty years you have left your home only half a dozen times. It is curious behaviour, wouldn't you agree?"

"You tell me, common. Who better to speak on curious behaviour."

"Answer the question, mage."

"Magus."

"Are you refusing to answer?"

Plinius petulantly stomped his foot, his mouth sputtering as he collected his thoughts. "What a ridiculous assertation. Bah!" Plinius laughed with a dismissive flick of his wrist. "Poppycock. I may get, ah, focused a little too much on my work, but I am not a hermit! Six times only? I don't believe you."

"Our sources say it *is* true, and frankly given what else I've heard of you, I am inclined to believe my sources over *you*, mage," the last word laden with disgust, he glanced down at the paper in his hand, "Our records are most thorough. Shall I? May 12th, 1496, target (Inkpot) left home to walk next door. Yelled at tenants about noise level. Returned home."

Plinius looked unsteadily towards Anatoli, who steadfastly refused to meet his eyes. He looked back to the Wayfarer, the man's lip turned up at the corners in a satisfied smirk.

"What is this? You were spying on me!" he accused.

"October 30th, 1492," continued Kaeso, "Agent Bazarevich observes Inkpot running outside in a hurry. He catches up to a frozen fruit merchant passing by. Purchases two dozen fruit treats. Inkpot returns to residence. Merchant detained and put to question."

"What? Ah, now wait a minute…"

"December 8th, 1489-"

"Enough!"

The man frowned at the magus and let go of the page, letting it waft down onto the table. "Suit yourself. Any of that ring a bell, mage? I trust that was enough for you to accept the veracity of my claim?"

"Fine- fine! I admit it, I'm a recluse! Congratulations on uncovering my insidious plan to be left the hells alone! I am a grandmagus! I have important research. What does it matter anyways? Why the interest in me? I am a busy, upright citizen, and I do not deserve to be spied on by the likes of you!"

"You're one of the magi, *mage*," spit the Wayfarer, stressing the slur, "Even worse, you are a mage with unknown allegiances," said Kaeso, his hand resting on the stack of papers. "Your kind are all worthy of my scrutiny. At least with the Imperials I know where they stand. So, yes. You are correct."

Kaeso stood in his chair. "Let me summarize so far. A boy comes to the Lyceum, earns the rank of grandmagus, and then mysteriously goes underground in the last independent city on Mir. The last independent city that just so happens to be preparing for war with this grandmagus' home-"

"Terrastra is my home!" protested Plinius.

"-and now, of all days, this grandmagus has decided to re-enter the game."

"I did not decide to do a Cronus damned thing! This was all-"

"You definitely made a decision when you murdered the archmagister!"

Plinius felt bile rise in his throat. "That- that was- I didn't-"

"A nice piece you took off the board! You reckless fool!" yelled the Wayfarer.

"A piece of the board?" exploded Plinius. "What about this is a game to you?" he demanded.

"A game I've been in a sight longer than you, mage. It's the great game. The one for all the pickles in the jar."

"Is that so!?" Plinius felt like he was treading water. He rounded on Anatoli. "What do you have to say, *friend?*" Plinius pointed an accusatory finger at Anatoli. "Is this what our friendship was? A task set for you by this buffoon? To spy on me?"

Anatoli gave his friend a sheepish grin that fell from his face immediately and shrugged his shoulders. "At first, *da,* I was sent to keep tabs on you. I practically lived outside your house for a few years. That changed when we finally met. The friendship is real, Pliny." *He's telling the truth- I know it.*

"How long has this been going on?" Plinius asked rhetorically.

"Since you left the Lyceum," Anatoli answered, "The Wayfarer's have kept an eye on you for generations. On Merlin's orders before he disappeared. They roped me in by calling in some old debts,"

'Ha!" laughed Pots, startling Plinius. "Da knew it! Fingers in pies, boy-os!'

"Pots, be quiet, please," said Plinius, louder than he wanted to. His shoulders sagged, the fight going out of him. "Why though? Why me?"

The Bulldog spoke and all attention focused on him like a siren from myth. "What are your thoughts on today's events so far, Grandmagus?" *Look, even old Orillia is looking at this man with reverence. Who is he?*

"My thoughts?" Plinius laughed "My thoughts? Well, I think the so-called events are a load of gremlin shit. My home is gone. The Imperial bastards burnt it to the ground." Plinius rubbed his eyes- *Blessed Concord, I'm tearing up-* and looked up to Anatoli for support. Anatoli would not look at him, offering no comfort. "A lifetime of work all but destroyed. I've been chased around the city like a cri-criminal! I mu- I murd- I-" Plinius hands were shaking, and his throat felt like he was choking.

A hand squeezed his shoulder, a drinking glass appearing before him. He looked up and smiled appreciatively before taking a big gulp of water.

"Be taking your time, Plinius," said Ohotepe reassuringly.

"Thank you, Boy- I mean, sorry, Ohotepe." Plinius squeezed his hand in thanks.

The Bulldog was less sympathetic, pressing as Ohotepe returned to the bar. "Answer, Grandmagus. Now is not the time to have a tied tongue. Specifically, what do you think of the Empire's involvement in today's events?"

Anger. "I'm angry is what I am! Maybe I have been a recluse, but I can't believe how out of hand everything is! Since when does the Empire dare show its face in Terrastra? Who let the Empire get their claws into her? They spit on the Concord and what? I came here to get away from- from all that! And yet here they are!"

The Bulldog ignored his question. "So you renounce any allegiance to the Empire?"

Plinius huffed and threw his hands up in exasperation. "What is that supposed to mean? Do I serve the Aurum Circle? No! Do I serve the Lyceum Council? No! I am my own magus, and if I am being honest with you, I quite frankly just want to be left alone." He bit off the last words with as much emphasis as he could muster.

Silence hung in the air as they regarded him. Orillia leaned towards the Bulldog and whispered in his ear. Eriksen gave a curt nod towards Kaeso, who sighed. "He'll do," he said addressing the table.

"Really? You have no objections, Kaeso?" Orillia asked.

"Plenty of objections about this whole damn thing. But what choice do we have?"

Old me looks as lost as I feel.

The Bulldog nodded in turn. "Grandmagus; please, have a seat," he pointed at the opposite end of the table, "Ohotepe, bring our new friends over as well."

Sliding slowly into the chair, Plinius allowed himself a small moment to enjoy the comfort of the soft padding. Plinius pleasurably purred. *Now that's some alliteration. Good job!* It was a welcome change after the hard floor of their cell. Anatoli sat down in the chair next to him, smiling encouragingly at the magus.

The Bulldog stood. He leaned forward, searching the inside of his jacket for a moment before pulling out a short square pipe. He tapped it on the table, leaving a small scattering of ash swirling around. Looking at everyone in turn, he fixed his gaze on Plinius.

"Alright, listen up. I am sure the grandmagus, as well as his companions, have many questions. These will be answered in time. For now, please listen. Once we have explained our purpose, we shall be glad to answer all the questions you may have.

First, I will have you three swear an oath. Except for those present, you will never speak to anyone else of what is discussed here. You will carry what you hear here to the death. Swear on Cronus, the Edge, or whoever you hold most sacred.

Much is happening; time is short. We need to make this quick so let's dispense with any formality. No minutes will be taken. What is said here never leaves the lips of those who hear it. We are here to finalize the plan now that the final piece has been safely delivered. For the plan's success to be assured, the oath of silence is paramount. I know we all but three," his finger quickly darted at Plinius, Gellar and Pots, "have already so sworn. I hope this necessity emphasizes the point and reminds you of the dangerous game we are playing."

He had barely ceased speaking before Pots shouted and Gellar answered, "We so swear."

Plinius looked at them. Gellar was as stoic as ever, giving Plinius a single shrugged shoulder, as if he was here purely because he had nothing better to do. Pots was nearly bursting with excitement. He noticed Ohotepe staring intently at him. He held up his hand, making a circle with his thumb and fourth finger. *The sign for trust. Coptician hunters use them for silent communication in the gorges of their home.* Plinius glanced at Anatoli, who sat there smiling his best roguish grin. Plinius turned back to the Bulldog, sitting and puffing away, waiting expectantly for his answer. *He's so familiar! Any hints?*

"What if I refuse to swear the oath?"

Commander Eriksen and Wayfinder Kaeso replied at the same time.

"You will die."

Plinius thought about it for a mere moment longer. "Hmm, death or the unknown. Fine. I so swear."

The Bulldog shook his head. "Not good enough, Grandmagus. From you, I demand the true oath. Now."

Plinius's companions, the militiamen and a few of the others looked confused. *How does he know the true oath? Is this man a magus? He would have to be grey or black. Not dressed like any magus I have ever seen. A very powerful magus I would think.* Plinius gave the man an appraising look, seeing him in truth for the first time. He nodded his head slowly, his doubts easing.

He reached out with his being, opening it up and letting magic flow in until he was submerged in the River. He reached up and drew a finger from neck to nave, and where the tip of his thumb touched the shirt burnt away, the now open shirt falling aside. His chest bared, his eyes shining like brilliant gold as he swore his oath, the words reverberating like rolling thunder.

"I swear the oath, and in turn you are to *me* the blessed. Woe unto Those who Break Faith with the Blessed. By The River So Sworn."

The River burned within him, the words of his oath flaring to life across his chest as the words appeared, burning into his skin. Plinius ground his teeth, refusing to break his concentration as the spell continued. Beads of sweat stung his eyes. As the word 'sworn' finished with a flourish of singed skin the pain vanished. Plinius' senses returned to normal as the Bulldog gave a satisfied nod of his head. The smell of burnt hair filled his nose, wafting from the irritated pink flesh and black words- one single long cursive scar reading 'By The River So Sworn' across his pale chest. Plinius could hear Anatoli give off a very quiet sigh of relief.

"Very good," said the Bulldog sitting down and looking at Anatoli. "That satisfies me, and therefore satisfies everyone else here. You are one of us now, irrevocably. Captain? If you will, please begin. Tell our friend the Grandmagus how we have come to be here."

Anatoli stood up. He ignored Plinius mouthing the word 'captain' with an inquisitively arched eyebrow. The rogue began to slowly make a circuit around the table, speaking directly to Plinius the entire time.

"*Moy drug,* this morning you scoffed when I told you of the Empire's infiltration of Terrastra. After what you have been through today, maybe you will not be so disbelieving this time."

Anatoli stopped by the mural, pointing up theatrically at the Gladia Virgum.

"The Empire is coming, Plinius. Not just for Terrastra, but for all of Mir. The Emperor's ambitions were made clear when we received the minutes of a clandestine Aurum Circle meeting from the Fall of 1492. Our intelligence tells us this meeting was held on the eastern shore of the Marelocus at the Emperor's winter palace. Archmagus, if you would please play back the relevant part."

Archmagus Orillia leaned over, depositing a small, polished orb of cloudy, pink crystal that floated a few centimetres above the centre of the table. *A spheracord; a genius artifact. Created by- wait! Wait a minute!* He lightly tapped the top of the object and the spheracord stirred. *I think I've got it!* Swirling ribbons of twinkling mist began to curl in orbit around its centre. *One second... one second...* He made a series of quick flicking motions with his fingers.

I went up and got a closer look. It's him.

Keep it to yourself! No spoilers!
Spoilers? Spoilers for who? It's just you and me here.
Well, someone might find this, later.
What? Who?
I'm just saying! Don't spoil it, just in case.
Fine, fine.

What sounded like the chittering of high-pitched squirrels began emanating from the sphere. Orillia changed the somatic movements of his fingers to an open palmed swipe. Bodiless voices rang out from within, a high-pitched squeaking completely incomprehensible. The wizened old magus slowed the sounds down as he waved his hand until it sounded ethereal and muted, like listening to someone whispering under water. Orillia flicked his hand a few more times. Voices materialized out of the sound from the spheracord. To Plinius' ears it was as if the speakers were arguing in the room with them.

"And what about Terrastra?" asked a raspy feminine voice to people unseen.

"If the campaign against those witches in Kanta is to be commenced by the end of the century, I tell you that now is the time to strike! The city has lost its last defender." A large bang like a fist pounding on a table rapped indignantly. "It is abundantly clear that now is the time to strike," the voice repeated, carrying a hard edge like forged steel.

A scholarly voice piped in, nasally and genial. "I disagree with Archmagi Kelley." Someone could be heard snorting. "We can use soft power to tend the orchard. We will twist the city into something more amenable to our goals. Only then will it be ready for harvest. The financial models Simon and I have concocted will bring the city to its knees. The trade erosion will drive up inflation, the common filth that infests the city will grow increasingly volatile, and we will have an advantage in an assault. Not to mention that this course of action could possibly forestall a lengthy siege. *Mon Dieu,* in a best-case scenario we could even get the scum to fight our battle for us. Their economic science is barely above a classical model, and our Malthusian tactics will create an atmosphere ripe for exploitation, especially now that the colonial bumpkin is gone. No one from the old times remains there to steer the ship, only mediocre Mirborn imitations. We must squeeze the fruit before savouring the juice. It could save thousands of lives."

"Spoken like the cautious *frosch* that you are, even after all these years, *Herr* Flamel."

"You mistake my patient strategy for cautious blundering once again, Kelley."

A light, airy voice chimed in. "Your patient strategy does look suspiciously like cowardice."

"*Fous le camps et crève*, Violet."

"What the fuck was that? Simon, what did he say to me?"

"You do not want to know, Ms. Fortune."

A moment of strained silence. Then a kindly voice full of warmth joined the conversation. Plinius would recognize that voice anywhere.

"I prefer my fruit ripe," a throaty voice said. *I would never forget that voice. The Old Crow himself.*

"But I also want it for breakfast and not for dinner. Nick, how long will it take for this plan of yours to adequately infect and destabilize their trade routes?"

A pause. "Forgive me, Emperor. The abundance of variables decreases the accuracy of any estimated timeline. If we go too fast, if they catch wind of our intentions, then they may renege on the compromise, and we are back to square one. We need to be careful; we need to be slow so we can deflect any suspicion. Like boiling a frog. I would estimate the best-case scenario at… seven years."

The playback became staticky, multiple overlapping voices creating a cacophony that only let a few words get through. "-----ludicrous-- esus--return and----Edge take you---infiltrate-----SILENCE!"

Silence.

"Nick has the right of it," the Emperor continued, "minimal bloodshed. Never forget why we are here. Never forget what we witnessed, and what we swore to each other. The situation in Terrastra has bought *us* time, not them. The old fool is gone, gone and dead chasing his stupid dreams. Now the young fool is dead. That reminds me- it is time we made room on the Circle to replace them. The greatest of Mirborn magi we can find. Perhaps Orillia if we can pull him away from his books. I think it is safe to say that the old man and his kitten are gone for good. That is, unless old Raspy can get his hands on them."

Chuckling.

"*Monsieur* Flamel; instigate your plan at the earliest launch window we can manage. I want weekly reports. Kelley, Scotty, Deedee- expand the 2nd and 3rd Legions out past the western shore of the Marelocus. Deploy the 3rd and 4th fleets along the main trade route in rotating patrol... and have it push out as far as the Strait of Heracles until further notice. It is far past time we let the rest of Mir know that the Marelocus is ours. Reinforce and replenish the watchtowers on the Imperial highway, and let's widen the highway while we're at it. We will show them the rewards that the Empire offers. We will revisit the numbers in session per annum, and I'm sure we will see results from Nicky's little dip in economic fuckery." More chuckles. "Minimal bloodshed, correct?"

"Ah, yes… but…"

"Out with it."

"Naturally, Alister, some will die in the famine and riots."

Quiet.

"Fine. Can't make an omelette without breaking some eggs. Good, good. It is decided."

"By the River so Sworn!"

The mist in the spheracord faded out as the chorus of voices echoed out on the word sworn. It went dark and dropped to the table, rolling to the edge until the Bulldog put out a hand to stop it. Plinius opened his mouth to deny it, deny that the Emperor would commit to this course of action. *The man I knew… he would never. That voice was never anything but kind to me. The others… it's fuzzy, but I think I remember…* Anatoli raised a hand to cut him off.

"*Da*, Pliny, it is true," Anatoli said, a tinge of regret in his voice, "The veracity of the spheracord is absolute. The one who attained it, well, I trust him as much as I trust you.

Regardless, Archmagus Flamel's plan has worked flawlessly. By the time we received the spheracord, their infiltration of the economy was too far along to halt. The Lyceum Council met and decided that one way or another- with Merlin missing and the overwhelming strength of the Empire- Terrastra would fall. So we did the only thing we could do."

Plinius whistled, the truth dawning on him. "You helped the plan along, didn't you?"

Anatoli smiled a devilish grin.

"Exactly so," answered the Bulldog, "Or at least, we made it seem like we were playing into Flamel's hand. Remember, too, that at a time of war, nearly everyone is under great strain. Does not matter the type of war, does not matter which side. The truth, as it is said, is a double-edged sword.

Still, the writing was on the wall. The Empire was coming for Terrastra. No matter what we did, it would just delay the inevitable. Perhaps not at the end of the seven years, but most assuredly one way or another. And today we have seen the first domino fall.

Another way would have to be found to save Terrastra. We needed a miracle. As if by luck, fate or God's providence, a new discovery had given us hope. Orillia?"

Archmagi Orillia stood. "Plinius, my dear boy, much has changed since you last walked the halls of our Lyceum. The Lyceum has taken great strides in our fieldwork by fostering positive relationships with our neighbours on Mir. There is no inch of Mir that can't be accessed and researched by our scholars, from the islands of the Auru to the boreal forests of Tsarusska." Plinius was quite impressed- he believed Orillia implicitly, and so what he said was undeniably true. *Lyceum scholars in Tsarusska. Cronus' balls.*

"I can see you have deduced the import of such a statement. Indeed- our glimmer of hope has come to us through Tsarusska. In 1497 a scholarly detachment of Terran magi were sent north to investigate the rumours of a possible pre-historic tribe of orcs that had survived the purges. The Tsar and Tsarkova thought the idea ridiculous but assented to the field team due to... ah... certain favours we had performed for them.

"Setting out from Terrastra, they made way to a small northern village called Svengdok. Last report from the team was of them following a lead beyond the Tsarcovy tundra into the White Death. The team was thought lost; truth be told, we had quite washed our hands of it. Imagine my surprise when they pulled into Drake Bay three months ago, with a tale even more surprising." Orillia sat back down and nodded to Commander Eriksen.

The commander did not stand, merely turning in his seat to face Plinius. "The ship they came in on was a Tsarusski junk trader- naturally it was impounded for inspection and its crew detained immediately. Captain Mooreland was the first commanding officer to step on board." He nodded to the militiaman closest to Plinius.

A blond woman with short, cropped hair, a crooked nose and a wicked scar across her cheek stood. "Upon securing the vessel, I boarded the junk with my fellow officers," she indicated the other militiamen sitting at the table. "Who we found aboard were first mistaken for Tsarcovy seal hunters. Although their garb and, ahem, general hygiene led us to believe they were Tsarusskan in origin-"

"I resent that," interrupted Anatoli.

"Shut up Anatoli," said the Bulldog, the glimmer of a smile twitching on his upper lip.

"Yes, ser," said Anatoli.

Mooreland stuttered, her face red. "Ah, my apologies, ser. Where was I? Oh- their use of common English and insistence on seeing Archmagus Orillia immediately gave us pause. They were babbling about... things... and I was not about to be the captain that let Tsarusski spies into Terrastra. So, I demanded proof. Sometimes I wish I had just-"

"That is enough, Captain," growled Eriksen.

"Yes, ser," she said obediently, sitting down promptly.

Anatoli stood again. "The proof Captain Mooreland brought to us is what has convened this conclave. Please, if you would, Kaeso?"

The salt and pepper Wayfarer nodded. From his pocket he procured a piece of parchment- *No, no, it was tanned seal leather. I remember that-* sorry, tanned leather, that he held a hand over and muttered a few words. The lights in the hall dimmed and a reproduction of what was inscribed on the leather projected off to the side, blown up in scale to fill most of the height of the room.

"It's a map," said Plinius, instantly intrigued.

Plinius studied the map for no more than a second before his jaw dropped. He looked around the room, where everyone but Pots, Gellar, the

Bulldog, and Ohotepe were gazing at the map intently with stoic faces. Pots was confused, Gellar frowned as he rubbed one of his long ears between his fingers, the Bulldog was staring at Plinius, while Ohotepe gave a satisfied nod confirming what Plinius had deduced instantly. "The magus do see it."

The right side of the map was of the northern territories of Tsarusska. It showed in the lower half the flat expanse of the Tsarcovy Tundra, a small village labelled in orcish on the frozen shores of what must be the Benzinovy Sea. It read *človeška jama*, directly translated to "Man Cave", which in Orcish could mean town, village, city, anywhere men and women congregated in a stationary place. In the middle of the map was the Edge of the World, the boundary between Mir and the eternal void beyond, the expanse of nothing set down at the dawn of the Concord as forbidden to all people, both magi and commoner. The White Death, the impassable land of snow, churning ice, and eternal night stretched across the top part of the map, further and further, past the Edge of the World, all the way to the western part of the map. There the map ended; a jagged outline of coastland marked in scrawled Orcish dežela obilja.

Land of Plenty.

Plinius swallowed hard. "A path west." It was not a question.

Anatoli nodded. "A way west," he echoed.

"This is our hope," the Bulldog rose from his seat. "If there is a land beyond- a land beyond the reach of the Empire- a land where we might retreat and buy time, gain some tactical advantage against the Empire- then what do we have to lose?" He nodded towards the militia commander.

Eriksen spoke up. "Plans have been drawn up and resources secured for an expedition. I will personally command this expedition. We will enter Tsarusska at the Cape Wall under the guise of merchants, utilizing the Wayfarer spies there to enter without suspicion. We will then head to Nekrovogorod and secure passage to Svengdok on board the *Daring Dorothy*, the ship of Captain Bira, which is currently furloughed in dock there."

The flamboyant woman who had up until now remained silent and looking slightly bored tipped her hat to Plinius. "Charmed," she said, "Furloughed? More like impounded on bullshit charges."

"Once there," said the Bulldog, ignoring the captain's complaint, "The expedition will proceed overland, hopefully contacting the orcish tribes that drew this map. From there… West."

It went quiet around the table. Plinius could not look away from the projection, stroking his chin thoughtfully. Plinius looked at them all in turn, then faced the Bulldog.

"Proceed overland?"

"Correct."

"Into the White Death?" *It wasn't a question.*

The Bulldog nodded his head solemnly.

"And across the Edge?"

"Yes."

"Are you out of your bloody mind?"

"Plinius…" began Anatoli.

"No, Anatoli!" Plinius slammed a hand down on the table. "This is the worst kind of madness. It is called the White Death for a reason! Nothing of intelligence lives up there! There is nothing up there but endless ice and snow- anyone walking into that better have their affairs in order."

"We have prepared enough provisions," said Kaeso, pulling another sheet out from the pile. "Rations and materiel for a prolonged expedition into the north. The map proves that *something* lives up there. I'm surprised a magus isn't curious to know the truth of the matter."

"Ha!" snorted Plinius. "How do we know the expedition didn't just fabricate this map to save themselves the embarrassment of coming back empty handed? Huh? Tell me that!"

"The researchers were questioned, and questioned again," answered Orillia, "This is no fabrication- of that I am certain. But your point is valid."

"Fine, fine. Let us presume the map is real. But what of the implication of what we are doing? This whole idea is in direct contravention of the Concord! There's a good reason why going West was forbidden."

"No one knows why the West was forbidden," answered the Bulldog, "Only Merlin and Alister were in the room when that provision was added. I believe it was something the Emperor saw in one of his visions. Something he fears. Something that scares the Emperor. Something that could be used against him."

"That is quite the leap in logic," scoffed Plinius.

"As for breaking the Concord- the Empire has already begun ignoring its laws to suit their purpose. What good is the Concord if the largest nation in Mir has decided it is above it? That it has grown so powerful that it feels emboldened to ignore that which bound us in peace? To flaunt their broken oath when it is found convenient. A regime that commits atrocity after atrocity in the name of protecting its own, and anyone who can't touch the River must be either controlled or eliminated? If the old Crow will break the Concord to serve his mad desire for power, well, I will break the Concord to save Terrastra."

"The Edge!" Plinius held up a finger. "The Edge remains. You say the only way there and back is across the top of the world?"

"It would seem so," answered Kaeso.

Plinius threw up his hands. "Then there it is! What good is a Land of Plenty, with no way to bring anything back? Ore? Jewels? Gold? This mystery weapon that will save the day? Carrying it across untold kilometres of jagged ice and snow? Do you know what manner of savage beasts live in the White Death? Herds of sharguins. Packs of winged carnivores the size of carriages!

Wyrms that burst through the ice the moment you realize the ground is shaking! What of worth in the bloody hells are you expecting to find? What could *possibly* be worth such an insane, suicidal risk?"

"Hopefully," Orillia said, "You find someone sorely missed."

It took Plinius a second to realize who they were referring to. "Cronus' cock. He' dead! He couldn't still be alive. The Edge killed him, everyone knows that."

The Bulldog nodded. "That is the generally agreed upon sentiment, eh? At least in the Empire. The Empire likes to jump to conclusions for its problems because it's easier to assume the problem is gone than coming up with actual solutions," everyone around the table but Plinius nodded.

"Merlin is pronounced dead because that version of the truth is what benefits the Emperor. I for one will never believe Merlin is gone until I see his lifeless body. That wily old bastard has more lives than a cat. He was the best of us."

Anatoli chimed in, "Plinius. The map shows there is land beyond the Edge. Maybe there are more people out there- maybe there *is* a way across the Edge!" He grinned in excitement, but behind his eyes Plinius could see something else. T*he glory, the fame*, *the madness.* "The quest! The adventure of a lifetime!"

"Elves."

Plinius turned around, seeing Gellar leaning against the bar. His eyes shined with hope. "What was that?"

"Elves," the elf repeated, "If there are lands to the West, then maybe my people not only survive but flourish. Somewhere."

Kaeso leaned forward in his seat, elbows on the table. "The Wayfarers have sat idle for too long. This is what we were made for. If anyone can make the crossing, we can. If there is anyone out there, we will find them."

The Bulldog leaned back, taking a puff of his pipe before he took it out and jabbed towards to the magus. "So, I say again, what do we have to lose?"

Plinius laughed derisively. "Your lives for one. Right there in the Concord. Number ten, if you forgot. To go West is death."

"If we do nothing," Anatoli said softly, kindly, "We are all dead anyways."

"In death we learn our true name," prayed Gellar.

Plinius shot Anatoli a dirty look but had no answer to him. "Well, if that is all, I wish you all the luck in this doomed venture. To think- betting the future of Terrastra on a- on a scrap of dead animal scratched on by some commoner savages. Ha. HA! I swear to keep this secret, and all that. I have my own business to attend to. I wish you luck."

Plinius made to stand up, but Anatoli's firm hand pushed him back into the seat. The scrivener gasped at the audacity, feeling the need to regain some sort of self-respect.

"Now, here! I will not be manhandled. I am-"

"You are integral, *moy drug*, is what you are," Anatoli crouched so that they were eye level, "Please, listen to him." *Ha! Just listen Plinius, just wait Plinius, you must wait Plinius, be patient Plinius. My how some things never change.*

The Bulldog spoke up. "Believe it or not, Plinius, but I will not send men and women to their deaths based on ephemeral rumours and scant evidence. My mentors taught me better than that. We have used all tools at our disposal to verify the information presented on this map, yet I too am still not fully convinced."

Understanding dawned again. "All methods? No, you did not." Plinius eyes narrowed, "Or did you? It would be madness even to try!"

"It is true," the Bulldog said. "We scried it out as far as we could-"

"Blesse Concord, you did have someone scry it! Knowing what the result is! Cronus take us all, you *are* insane!" Plinius shot up in his chair. "This… this will mean war! This will- you *have* broken the Concord! This is anathema!"

"Do not be dense, grandmagus," growled the Bulldog. "*We are* at war. To reiterate, the Concord has already been broken with the Empire subsuming into fascism and slavering over manifest destiny. Whether you want to accept it or not, that fact is indisputable. Scry it we did, but like all scrying, it ended abruptly at the Edge and with the immediate death of the scryer. Her sacrifice was not in vain, however. Orillia managed to impress on the scryer before she burst into flames. Orillia?"

Without a word and not looking up from the table, the archmagus muttered a few words. The image of the map was replaced with another.

The image was blurry at the edges, but the middle was in sharp detail. The endless white fields of broken ice spread out to the horizon in sharp contrast to the black and turbulent sky. On the left was the unmistakable abyss of the Edge, torrents of water pouring out from underneath the ice, cascading off into the infinite void. A lightning bolt, frozen in time, slashed down the centre of the image. Silhouettes of three black triangles on the horizon were illuminated by the lightning, a bridge of ice stretching out before them beyond the Edge.

Plinius swallowed to calm himself, finding no words.

"Still," said the Bulldog softly, "I want further proof. The River works mysteriously- there's no way to know if this impress is true or just some illusion of the Edge."

Therefore, they brought me. Of course. It all makes sense.

"You know of my gift," he said, the hurt plain on his face. Anatoli opened his mouth but closed it before saying anything.

The quill. He was so insistent.

The Bulldog nodded. "Chorogramancy. You are quite the remarkable magus, Grandmagus Scrivener."

Plinius pinched his nose and rubbed gently, his eyes screwed shut in concentration. *I wanted to leave. I wanted to go home. I wanted to forget about everything I had learned that day- isn't that ironic? There truly is nothing worse than being trapped and helpless, at the mercy of others. Not a great feeling.* With a resigned expression he feebly motioned towards his friend.

"What you ask is impossible."

"No, Grandmagus Plinius," spoke Orillia, "I do not believe that is so."

"It will kill me!"

"It would if you scried," nodded his old teacher, "But I remember the details of your unique spell. It is no scry. Anatoli tells me you have the quill still. I am certain it will work."

Plinius slouched in the chair. *I thought he was my friend.*

"Parchment, please," he breathed out.

One of the aides on the far wall sprang forward and deposited the parchment along with a pot of ink and a quill. He scoffed as he batted the quill to the floor.

"Where is my bag?"

It took a moment for the bag to be retrieved from wherever it had been stored. Reaching inside, Plinius extracted the black quill. It felt heavy in his hand as the swaying feathers gave his arms goosebumps.

Plinius looked up at the Bulldog leaning eagerly over the table, then he glanced up at Anatoli who was nodding encouragingly. "If this kills me, Anatoli, I will come back and haunt you."

With a sigh, he closed his eyes and put quill-tip to parchment.

He whispered a few words in an arcane language of his own devising. A tap, flourish and tap again of the quill. A change of pressure and the room dropped a few degrees in temperature. A cold wind conjured from the expanse between worlds sent anything loose and light scattering across the room. Whirling dervishes of paper danced around, everyone scrambling as cups overturned and bottles smashed off the floor. The chorogramancy took hold.

His eyes opened, sightless but seeing past the room, further and further, flying upwards and northwards like a bird, sailing on the currents of the River. He knew his hand was moving now, faster, and faster, his consciousness retreating from steering the ship while his subconscious, his soul, the magic in his very being took command.

The magic flowed north along the River. His perspective shifted as his spirit rose higher and higher, until the three hills of Terrastra were so far below they lost all detail, resembling a trio of upturned shiny thimbles. Tiny pinpricks of light from glow globes were visible in the long shadows cast by the dying day. His spirit involuntarily turned his back on Terrastra, facing Drake Bay and the great expanse of the Atlantic Ocean beyond as the sun began to dip below the curving horizon. Even at this height the Edge remained beyond sight. Turning towards the north his ethereal consciousness began accelerating at tremendous speed. After a few moments the landscape below was slipping past as rapidly as a mountain river current. He could not feel the rush of the wind or the force of the speed, but his mind was dimly aware of a nauseous feeling developing in his stomach.

He travelled over the Death's Head peninsula, the land covered in old forests that from up here looked like carpets. The land jutted north from the continent like a beckoning skeletal finger. The forests abruptly ended as he passed over the towering mountains of the Isthmus Peaks, above them for only a moment before he was passing over sodden bluish-yellow mud lands that stretched for leagues south of the Cape Wall. The wall itself passed under in a blink; an imposing barricade shrouded in mist and the gloom of the rapidly falling night. The difference between the lands bordering the wall was striking even at this height. Where to the south verdancy and life grew with ever green wild abandon, the northern landscape was a black wavy starkness divided into thousands of squares between chalky white lines of stone. Shiny dots like marching ants travelled in orderly precision along the paths. Plinius had but a single moment to ponder what he was seeing until it was gone, and he was above dark grey waves of turbulent water. He looked behind him, the quickly receding shoreline of the peninsula shining bright like a false dawn.

A city of fair size spawled along the shore to the east, but unlike the soft glow globes of Terrastra the city of Capovogorod was crowned with a light that challenged the sun in intensity. Plinius could make out a huge skeletal structure of white bone rising along a river that emptied into the forbidding and restless Benzinovy Sea. It looked like a ribcage or a turtle shell squatting in a bed of glowing green fog, banishing the stars above with columns of pulsing poisonous light emanating upwards like pillars into the sky. Even after the dome disappeared, the shafts of light were visible for a few seconds after. When the columns disappeared behind him, all magi-made light was gone, and the world was plunged into a cloudy blackness. When those clouds ended abruptly, Plinius gasped at the beauty as the heavens exploded into glory above him.

The nearly full moon hung heavy and high in the sky nestled in a blanket of black velvet, attended upon by millions of stars. Luna's reflected light lit up the crests of dark blue waves far below like ghostly fingernails. The ocean stretched as far as his eyes could see in all directions, the only change in scenery coming from little orange blips of light in the distance, sailing ships winking above the horizon far to the east. This too proved only fleeting, as larger and larger icebergs began to dominate the sea below, bobbing like apples among the water, until the entire expanse was a sheet of never ending white. In the reflected light of the full moon, the icebergs looked like skulls, empty eyes and mouths of broken icy teeth bobbing in the vast northern ocean. It went on and on, an endless desolation of never-ending snow and ice. The White Death. He turned westward now, further, and further west again. He was moving so fast now all detail turned to a blur of streaking colours lost in the whiteness of the most inhospitable land Plinius had ever seen. *Terrible and beautiful.*

He did not feel the presence until it was too late. *Wait, what?*

The horizon began to disappear, at first not comprehending what he was seeing, Plinius urged himself onwards. A dark scar of yawning, gaping nothing stretched from north to south, the ocean ending abruptly in a jagged line that separated the ocean from a vast void of emptiness beyond. He could feel his hand- his real hand- begin to twitch.

Plinius gazed the void, and the void looked back.

As his hand began to furiously scratch and swoop and mark on the parchment of its own accord, his vision went black as his perspective was encompassed by the Edge. That was when he felt it come. It began as a pressure, as if someone was massaging his scalp with their fingers. It sent shivers down his spine, and he flung his senses out in all directions, finding nothing there. The pressure turned into probing jabs of pain across his head. It pulsed with an intelligent rhythm that frightened Plinius to his core. It pushed in and flooded every corner of his mind like the tide. Something had come, attracted by his magic, following the river right to him. *The Aurum said never to scry West. To go West is death.* Something alien, something that sensed his magic the moment he pulled the river close to the Edge. *Tales, I don't like this. Please skip ahead.*

The presence was a leviathan, a dragon noticing a mouse crawling across its foot. *I can feel it. Can you? Maybe you should stop this part, Tales.* Closer it came. Closer still. He could feel a franticness to the spell now, a fearful hurrying coming from the River itself. Back under the Wayfarers guild, thousands of kilometres away from his spectral form, Plinius cried out in terror. The River was in pain. It spiralled out, attempting to flee from the alien presence as it loomed closer. *This is a bad idea. Tales, we need to move past this!*

A presence of unfathomable agency pressed against Plinius' mind. For the briefest moment he resisted before the entity swatted away his defenses as if they were cobwebs, a violent and absolute violation that sent him reeling. He could feel, dimly aware as if trying to look down from a great height, that back in Terrastra he had hot tears running down his face in rivulets. His fingers were aching. His legs were spasming. He was groaning, a low pained gurgling from some pit deep inside him. His hand was flying around the parchment at a pace that shattered his wrist, a continuous grinding crunch as the now loose flesh and muscle of his hand flew around the parchment, guided by the River itself. He could not tell if he still held the quill. Now he was shouting. *Oh, Cronus it can see me!* His tears pooled on his upper lip and spilled like waterfalls over his lips. The taste of blood filled his mouth. Plinius' could feel his identity pushed away, shrinking into a dark corner of his mind as the monstrous eldritch presence entered his inner mind. All too easily, his mental defences and wards were nothing but walls of paper being blasted away in a hailstorm of psychic fire and ice.

A demonic scream of anguish ripped through his psyche. *Too much.* It was then that the presence sensed that not all was as it seemed. It was not alone. *This is too much. Tales you need to stop.* It sensed the interlopers in its midst. *The eyes, oh Cronus, those eyes! LOOK AT THOSE EYES! IT'S TOO MUCH! TALES, PLEASE! STOP!*

But Tales could not stop reading the book. The narrative was being corrupted, twisted by the presence that now fought to dominate their carefully cast ritual. He read these words; his attention arrested to them as if two great hands had trapped his head in place, callused fingers roughly peeling back his eyelids. These words appeared before him on this page. He desperately tried to speak to Plinius, to make sure he was there *I am here! Tales I can-* the presence quieted the loud one, the one he could see more clearly. The presence looked for Tales but could not find him at first. The presence had been lonely for so long, the only one left. And now it sensed two like him. He would not give up the search easily.

I SEE YOU.

Tales was struck dumb, his eyes burning with pain, begging to just blink but unable to, staring in horror at the words before him. Plinius tried to wrest control of the page, to force his *-Tales! What is-* but the presence was too strong. The Watcher would have to be content with doing just that. Plinius felt a strange wave of vertigo taking hold, as if they were madly tumbling through open air, plummeting into a field of stars. Plinius wanted the screaming to stop. He did not realize that he was the one doing it. Back in Terrastra, his hand made three final marks before he passed out, a violating voice like orchestral horns blaring into his mind. The sound became so overwhelming that all colour fled from the world, and a great shadow loomed over him, ripping holes in the sky as he bled from bleeding stars. Plinius could feel it's power, its overwhelming power, and knew there was nothing he could do to resist.

Tales tried to warn Plinius, tried to sever the spell that bound them. As he touched the book in front of him, the River reacted. All he had ever been, all that he was, all he ever could be, was swallowed into the River as it's prismatic light turned black, enveloping the room in darkness. Magi and commoner screamed as things hidden beyond the veil of reality pawed at their legs. The entity shook in anger, and the universe shook with it. Ceiling tiles plummeted to the ground in the Wayfarer's hall as the room tremored, an unlucky wayfarer killed outright in the collapse, as the words hammered down on the page a world away. Time and space twisted. Tales and the others performing the ritual panicked as the book on the altar before them began to emanate a negative column of light upwards through the skylight of the temple. Plinius Scrivener rose like a ghost from the pages, his face a serene mask of calm. He exploded into a million trailing points of light, screaming as the River turned against him, rending him asunder.

NO!

COME WEST.

WATCHER, SPINNER, READER.

COME WEST.

INTO THE WEST.

FIND ME.

Hello?

Hello?

Plinius?

Yes?

Are you ok?

Of course, Tales. Why wouldn't I be?

Ah, sorry. I just lost my place there for a second. Um, what do you remember last?

I had just turned monumentally stupid and decided to try and use my chorogramancy to map the Edge in what I can only assume was either a suicide attempt or me just trying to impress my old teacher. I saw something… strange. Pyramids? Then I passed out. I'm assuming the scrying killed me and this is the afterlife.

No… no, it didn't kill you. We're still here. The spell held, but I… nevermind. Truly though, are you ok? You don't feel… different?

I'm perfectly fine. Are you ok?

Yes. Do you mind if I talk to our friends for a second.

Go ahead. Thank you for asking for once.

Hollow Man, Hollow Man…

Plinius? What was that?

Hmmm?

Were you… singing?

How could I do that in print?

Uh, yes, of course. Plinius?

Yes, Tales?

Are you sure you're good?

Blessed Concord, Tales. I'm fine! What are you, my nanny?

Ha, no. If you're good, I'm good. Shall we continue?

Please do!

Plinius collapsed across the table. The conclave rushed in a panic, calling for salubrists as they quickly dismissed the illusion of the northern map. The Bulldog crossed over and eagerly snatched up the map Plinius had been drawing.

"He's breathing, thank Cronus," sighed Anatoli in relief. *Not dead! After 'scrying' the Edge! Not really but you know what I mean. No magi had ever done that before!*

It was quite the accomplishment, Plinius.

Thank you, I know.

A long, thick black line stretched up the middle of the parchment until it met a jagged perpendicular line. The outline of a shore extended downwards from the Edge on both the left and the right, one leading east to Mir and one leading west for just a few centimetres before trailing off. Directly above the long, thick black line, where the land stretched over where no land should have been, were the three final marks Plinius had made before succumbing to the *spell*.

Three black pyramids.

Eriksen looked at the Bulldog expectantly. "William? Well?"

He sighed, rubbing his chin with his hand, looking down at Plinius. "Well, Orillia, he didn't die. As you predicted."

"I thought it a close thing, there, for a moment," admitted Plinius' old teacher, "But his… nature ended up protecting him in the end. That bodes well for what is to come, doesn't it? I still wish we didn't have to lie to him, though."

"I know; I do not like it either," agreed archmagus William Lyon, pupil of Merlin and Archregent of Terrastra, "I think it highly doubtful that his parents will ever forgive me for this. Have your people within the Magistracy prepare the wagons, and don't forget to neutralize them after. They must leave before our ruse is discovered. God save us all."

Chapter Eleven

The Lyon & The Scrivener

Plinius awoke to the sound of rain.

A woollen blanket scratched against his skin uncomfortably. His head felt like it had been pecked in by an owlbear, scooped out and promptly shit in by said owlbear. This was made worse by the jostling and bouncing of what he assumed was the coach he was laid up in. His eyes seemed very against the idea of opening, only managing to do so a fraction after a supreme application of will on Plinius' part. He groaned as he pushed himself up on his elbows, closing his eyes again and swearing furiously after he smacked his head off a low beam.

"Wha' the bloody hells?" he slurred, rubbing his forehead while wincing in pain.

"Easy, Plinius, easy," a soothing voice said, "Lay down, take your time."

Plinius slowly opened his eyes. A grey and meagre light slipped in from a small filthy glass window nearby framed with thick burgundy curtains. The wagon was small- a makeshift door of crudely hammered planks across from him, a small woollen cot he laid on, and bundles of sacks piled up alongside strapped barrels and crates. It smelt of vinegar and damp wood, the scent burning Plinius' nostrils. Sitting cross-legged on one of the barrels was William Lyon. Instead of the clothes he had worn at the conclave, he had the simple black robe of an archmagi on. It finally dawned on Plinius.

"No."

"Yes?" William replied, arching an eyebrow.

The black robe seemed too tight on the broad chested man. Gone was the stern man from the night before, in his place a ruddy faced magus with the cheeks of one who laughs often and loud. It was if a coin had flipped, and the sunny side of the man had arisen upon dawning the robe. Strange as his clothes were at the conclave, they had a certain sense of seriousness to them that had reinforced the man's force of presence. That force of presence was still here but the pendulum had swung the other way. Where before he was solid iron, now he was shining gold. *That hideous suit? Projecting power? Who the hell is writing this, anyways?* Plinius spared not a thought for the aesthetics or the man's aura, only the symbolism of the black robe itself. *The suit was ugly. Just admit it.* An Archmagi. A wizard of the 9th circle. One of the Aurum, the Everlasting, The Guardians of the River and the Shields of Mir. *The wearers of terrible evening wear. Admit it. Admit it. Admit it.* Plinius was both awed in his presence as well as completely confused. *Admit it. Admit it. Admit it. Admit it Admit it Admit it AdmititAdmititAdmitit-*

Cronus' balls, fine! It was hideous.

"I can't believe I didn't recognize you right away. This can't be… you're dead!"

William Lyon, Archmagi of Terrastra, smiled. "I wondered how long it would take you to remember. Don't beat yourself up, it's been a long time since we saw each other last, and I looked younger then. I also kept you at the far end of the room at the conclave for a reason. I needed to make sure before I revealed myself. Also I suppose you weren't used to seeing me dressed in such a way as at the Conclave, eh? Not many official paintings of me in my old wartime suits," he chuckled. *Remembering doesn't come easy some days, does it?*

Plinius slowly shook his head side to side. "I was sorry to hear of your passing."

William laughed deeply, brightening the room. "Not quite. To quote a favourite author of mine, the reports of my death were greatly exaggerated. That is what we wanted the Emperor to believe, and Crowley was never very good at seeing through subterfuge as well as he was at perpetrating it. In allowing the Empire to believe they had another advantage over Terrastra, we helped accelerate their timetable and overcommit to their garrisons along the Imperial Highway. Even now our friends in Kanta are raiding Imperial outposts along the River of Set. Drones from Tsarusska are rattling their bones over in the High Pass, forcing the Empire to turn their attention towards there on the chance the Tsar is making another incursion into the Sword Vale. Even old Seimei is driving hordes of manticores out of the Yellow Layan Mountains into the lower Magocratic provinces, causing havoc among the sharecroppers. I am quite sad to say that poor Crowley is facing a variety of crises at the moment, just when he has committed so much towards Terrastra. What I wouldn't give to be a fly on the wall in the Aurum Hall right now." William chortled the self-satisfied laugh of someone luxuriating in a big win.

Plinius chewed on that for a moment. "They thought Terrastra much weaker than it is. The Witchlady of Kanta, Tsarusska, Xeijpang… they force him to split his forces. The 1st Legion will be facing Terrastra alone, the other nations forestalling the advancement of any new legions into Terrastran land for the time being. At least until the rest of the Empire is secure."

"Exactly right. Thank god for old Flamel, eh? That recording went a long way to convincing the other nations. You were always quick on the uptake, Plinius."

"Was it Flamel who made the recording?"

William waved a hand dismissively. "Never mind that son. You need to focus on what is ahead, eh?"

Plinius gave him an empty laugh in response. "Focus on what's ahead you say? When my home is being destroyed and occupied by Crowley's goons? I'm assuming the city has fallen then. Is that why you're here?"

"Do not jump to conclusion, son. I am here incorporeal," William answered. Plinius chided himself silently for not noticing sooner. *I chalk it up to the dimness of the wagon and the splitting headache.* William Lyon's figure was not opaque- a slight switch in focus and the eyes could see through him to the crates beyond. "No, I will not leave Terrastra at this time of uncertainty and jeopardy. As you said, the Iron Cohort has overextended itself. The Terrastran militia is much stronger and disciplined than we have led them to believe. Even now they are beating the lictors back across The Runs. The Hall of Staffs has been surrounded and all Imperial bureaucrats taken into custody. Our lists of Imperial sympathizers have been systemically rounded up and detained. We have enough stockpiles of food, scrolls and artifacts to rebuff a siege for at least ten years by our estimation. I hope that is more than enough time for our hope to be realized."

Plinius gingerly pulled himself up to a sitting position, wincing. "Hope? Hard to feel it when I feel this terrible. Where am I? How long was I out?"

"You are in a coach, part of the caravan heading north from Terrastra. You have been on the road for two days now. I placed a charm on you to alert me when you awoke."

Plinius eyes widened. "Two days! A coach? So that means…"

"Yes," William said, slightly remorsefully, "Your spell worked. With the impress and your map it proved, as far as I am concerned, the veracity of the orcish map. You are currently heading up the Atlantic coast to the Cape Wall. I do apologize for taking away your agency in the decision, but I hope in time you will understand it was vital. Pliny, you are more important to this expedition than anyone."

Plinius bristled, not even listening. "Please, call me Plinius. I could have been on my way to Kanta by now. Abe would shelter me in Nozomi if I asked, I'm sure of it. This plan of yours is asinine. It is suicide."

"It is the wish of a tired man for some salvation."

"And do you know the thing about wishes?"

"Please tell me, Plinius."

"They. Never. Come. True." Plinius crossed his arms, as if that settled the manner. *He is being a dick.*

"And your plan, then, grandmagus?" asked William in a tone Plinius did not appreciate. "Surely you cannot return to Terrastra."

"And why not? You say yourself the Iron Cohort is being beaten back. I can help!"

"Yes, you *can* help," agreed William, "By going West. That is where Terrastra- where *Mir* needs you."

"I will not break the Concord! I will not!" protested Plinius, wincing at his own loud voice. "I need to return to Terrastra where it's-"

"Safe?" interrupted William.

Plinius punched the coach, doing less damage to the wall than to his fist. "Yes! Safe!" His scraped knuckles rubbed away tears. "I was safe! I was comfortable. I just want my bookstore back…"

"Do you not get it, Plinius? You are the brightest, most skilled, most studious magus I have ever met. You may even rival Merlin someday. And I refuse to believe that you cannot see the truth of the matter. The Empire will not be stopped, it cannot be stopped. Crowley will not stop until he controls all of Mir. All we can do is buy time. Time for you to go West and perhaps, by the grace of God, find the key to salvation. Only then will Alister be stopped."

They sat in silence as Plinius tried to gather his thoughts and master his anger. *Life is unfair. I'll get over it.* The rain had increased in intensity, beating against the creaking boards of the coach as it bounced and jangled along the roadway, lurching as a wheel dropped into a rut.

"So, all of this was by design then? First the Empire's plan, and then your own plan to counter. I feel like a piece in Minions of Dublain."

"Good game, but I prefer chess. Plans within plans my boy," agreed William, folding his arms across his chest, "I would wish for it that you do not see yourself a pawn in this. In truth I view you as the most valuable piece on the board."

"William," began Plinius uncertainly, "Why me?"

"Why you what?" William asked.

"Why did you choose me for this? Of all people- I- I- I am no adventurer. I'm not made out for this kind of thing!"

"Well, I'll answer you with my own question. Why not you?"

"A thousand reasons!" Plinius exclaimed. "I am no hero! I am not Anatoli! I am not Ohotepe! I am a recluse- bloody hells and Cronus' balls, I've barely left my home in the past eighty years! You know that! I am an academic, a hermit, a bookworm, a- a- a scrivener!"

The Lyon shook his head wonderingly.

"From what I've been told, you can add advocate for the weak, runs runner, life-saver, and warmagus to those titles. Pool shark as well if it's to be believed."

Plinius stared at the archmagus dumbfounded.

William sighed. "I am going to chalk this up to fatigue from your ordeal. I expect more from you Plinius- I was not just pumping your tires when I told you how brilliant I think you are. No, grandmagus, I speak and deal in facts and that is all. You have one of the sharpest minds I've ever known. If you cannot see your own value to this endeavour, then maybe I *have* misjudged you."

He held up one finger. "But as I also said, I can appreciate the fact that you have been through a great ordeal already. One that I hope has steeled you for the greater ordeals to come. Currently though you need to rest. So, I will make this quick and spell it out for you.

You are a scrivener, yes, but you do yourself a disservice. Orillia tells me you are by a large margin the greatest scrivener who has ever lived."

"I don't know about that." *Oh, what false modesty. I surely was.*

"No time for false modesty. That alone would qualify you for an expedition such as this. When you also consider your chorogramancy- that is a singular skill unique in all of Mir. One that makes an insane amount of sense for where you are venturing and the boon it will provide to ensuring the missions success."

Can't argue with that reasoning. I was great.

He held up a second finger. "The Emperor is unaware of you. That gives us a tactical advantage. We needed at least a grandmagus to accompany this expedition given its implication and sending any 8th circle magi would rouse his suspicions. We cannot be sure we apprehended all his spies in the city."

"The Emperor is unaware of me?" Plinius pointed his finger at William. "You have erred, Archmagus Lyon."

"Plinius-"

"I am well known to Alister. I have known him since I was a boy!"

"Plinius-"

"My parents-"

My parents!

"Plinius!" shouted the archmagus, "Are you aware you have been considered dead for over fifty years!?"

My… my parents think I'm dead?

Plinius fish-mouthed silently for a moment. "Dead?"

"Yes, Plinius, dead," William repeated, "You disappeared off the face of Mir. Your parents were distraught. They had a state funeral for you in Aliston- if I recall correctly, it was the last time I visited the capital. The Emperor himself gave the eulogy. There is a rather splendid monument dedicated to you in the Hortus Publicis."

Plinius could not believe his ears. "Wh-wha-why? Why didn't you tell Mum and Father that I still lived?"

The Lyon chuckled again. *William always had such a friendly laugh. It's what made him such a good politician. Couldn't be mad at that laugh.* "Truth be told, until Anatoli mentioned you at a conclave a few months back when we were drawing up a list of potential candidates for this mission, I thought you dead as well. I was absolutely astonished when Anatoli announced your name. To think you were under my nose the whole time! Merlin would have a good laugh at the thought. Hence a lot of the secrecy of bringing you in. We- no, I- needed to make sure it was you. And if it was you, to not let Alister know.

And if he did know, to make him jump to another conclusion. Hence the impostor at the Exchange execution. I also needed to make sure where your head was at."

William held up a third finger. "Third and most important. I needed to send someone that not only I could trust, but someone that Merlin will trust. I find myself questioning the loyalties of magi I have known for decades. My friend, my master, the last magus I truly trusted heart and soul, has been gone for nearly a century. I have no idea how he might have changed in that time. One thing I am willing to bet on is that he will not have changed his opinion of you."

Plinius screwed up his face. "Opinion about me? What in Cronus' name are you talking about?"

"Merlin respects you a great deal, Plinius. Always has."

"Merlin? Respect me? With all due *respect*, I'm not sure where you get your information, archmagus. The greatest magus of all time, respecting me? Poor joke. I have never even met the Sea Wizard."

"Oh, you haven't?" Even as an apparition there was no mistaking a glint of wry amusement in the archmagus' eye. "If that is true, then I suppose we have not met either, eh?"

Plinius screwed his mouth up into a look of confusion. "What? No… not at all. I think I would remember meeting…" he trailed off, his voice going quieter as he squinted at the archmagus. The eyes, the shake of his jowls, the nose…

"You shaved your mutton chops."

William laughed out loud, a big bellowing laugh that set his belly shaking. Plinius could not help but smile as well. "Oh God, the mutton chops. Shaved those ridiculous things off decades ago. One of the worst things about being one of the magi, eh? You have all these years to make fashion *faux pas*."

"What is a *faux pas*? No, never mind. I can deduce it means hideously strange attire like you wore yestereve. You look different enough," said Plinius accusingly, "Then again, it has been what? Nearly a century?"

William nodded. "About that time, give or take a year."

"And the other man was…" Plinius eyes widened. He felt dumb.

Oh Plinius, how embarrassing.

"Merlin himself," William nodded. "Do no fret about not recognizing him. You were young, and that infernal man changes his face like an actor changes costume. We have always taken a keen interest in you, Plinius. Not just old Merlin and I, but the Emperor as well, and the whole damn circle. Even Leveaux. Hell, even Ol' Raspy and God only knows what that madman is up to. When you died, a lot of archmagus' plans were thrown awry, I will tell you that much. You were… a hope. We all looked at you and felt emboldened in our own vision of Mir. A sense of… righteousness, I suppose." He laughed again. "Despite all that, no matter what I will always think of you as the brilliant boy with the incredible army of tiny golems."

More silence as Plinius tried to order his thoughts. "My mother and father… the Emperor… I still don't understand how they could be committed to this course of action. That their desired version of Mir is one where the Concord is in tatters, and they reign supreme across all of Mir. That… that's not the people I remember."

That seemed to deflate William a bit. "You know the history of Mir better than most, Plinius. The genocide. The indoctrination. Atrocity, after atrocity, after atrocity. Expand, conquer, subjugate, eliminate, repeat. The Empire likes to pretend that kind of vile methodology is the sole dominion of Tsarusska, and that pretention is enforced under the staff and sword of the Gladia Virgum.

We know better. Crowley has always been driven by one unbending principle- protect magi. No cost is too great. The fear of magi losing the power they have accumulated over history, the fear of being vulnerable to another living soul consumes him. There is no one he will not crush, no thing he will not destroy, no line he will not cross to make sure the Magocracy reigns forever. Emperor Eternal and all that nonsense. The Church of Cronus has become his mouthpiece, and the slow process of deification is being rolled out to the populace. The Aurum Circle is in lockstep with him. That includes your parents."

My parents were monsters?

A sick feeling constricted his heart. "They must be reasoned with. They must be made to see there's a better way."

"On that we agree." William looked at Plinius pointedly. "And there is one man in all of Mir, in all of creation, that the Circles will listen to. Only one man that Alister fears more than the phantoms in his paranoid mind."

Archmagus William Lyon sat looking at Grandmagus Plinius Scrivener for a long time. The much younger magus stared out the window, watching through the dirt a muddy looking world go by, lost in his thoughts.

Plinius finally nodded, looking the archmagus in the eye. "So be it then. Westwards."

William smiled. "Bring him home, Plinius Scrivener. Bring my friend home. I'm counting on you. We all are."

And with that his form evaporated and was gone.

Plinius emerged from the wagon the next time it lurched to a halt, wincing in the midday sun. *Holy gremlin shit it's bright out here.*

The rain had blessedly stopped, and the fresh scent of wet wild grass was so full Plinius nearly swooned. *I don't swoon! Everything smells… so clean. Fresh? Natural.* Their caravan was made up of three vehicles. Only his wagon was a coach- the other two were large trader's wagons with waxed oilcloth tarpaulins covering their cargo. The driver of his coach gave him a curt nod, and the scrivener recognized him as one of the militiamen from the conclave. He was dressed in common and unadorned leather and chain armour, a man similarly attired but wielding a crossbow sitting in the seat next to him. The loaded weapon tracked lazily across the grandmagus' path as he walked by. Driving the second wagon, the female militiamen-

Captain Mooreland.

Captain Mooreland. The elven pirate sat next to her. He raised a hand in greetings. Neither gave him a hint of acknowledgement. He quickened his step, seeing a commotion at the front wagon and setting off to see what was amiss. He stepped gingerly, his feet squelching in the ground.

They were on a narrow dirt road beaten muddy from pounding rain, the lead wagon trying to crest a low hillock. Long green grass grew alongside yellow flowers on both shoulders. The rain had let up slightly for now, but the day was blustery with fast clouds streaming in from over the ocean. Gulls cawed as they rode the western wind along the shore. Plinius pulled his robe tight around him as large, dark blue clouds prowled along the northern horizon. A few crows wheeled above them before giving a harsh cry and beating their way east. Sweat began to stain his armpits as the tried to attune to the vastness of it all. *Living in a four-room house for a century does tend to give you a little case of agoraphobia.* He tried to take a deep breath to calm himself but choked on the unfamiliar aromas of wide-open Mir. The smell of rain on the wind, the smell of wood and sand, rot and life-

And horseshit. Nothing like a caravan to teach you about the varied bouquet of horseshit.

A large birch and pine forest encompassed the lands to the east, with no sight of Terrastra to the south, just more rolling hills. He tried to resist at first, but his gaze was pulled inexorably west. The Ocean was no more than a kilometre away, a vast grey ribbon stretching out both northwards and southwards. All the way north, beyond his sight, to the White Death. But not turning east. North and west again. The thought made his head swim and his stomach queasy.

"Plinius!" Anatoli stood smiling on the driver's perch, reins dangling from his left hand as he waved with his right. "It is good to see you up and about! Please, join me up here while these *sobach'i ublyudki* get us unstuck."

Plinius walked up to Ohotepe, Pots, Gellar, Qubo and some other Wayfarers as they laid down planks to catch a wheel stuck in a particular deep squelch of mud. Eriksen hovered over them astride a black and brown horse, shouting at the mud-covered labourers what he undoubtedly considered encouragement. Ohotepe noticed him first, smiling as he ran up to him, clapping him on the back. Pots went in for a hug that Plinius hastily deflected due to the soiled state of the dwarf's tunic. Qubo scowled at him, wrenching a large plank out from under the wagon. Gellar nodded. Plinius smiled widely, a little surprised with himself, as he realized he was relieved to see them. *Not*

Qubo.

Plinius attempted to pull himself up on the wagon. His hand slipped on the slick handhold, and he fell back on his rearend, splashing himself with mud much to the mirth of Qubo and the Wayfarers. His face reddened at the feminine laughs coming from the second wagon. Eriksen scowled at the magus.

Qubo loomed over him. His voice became airy and with mock sincerity talked down at Plinius. "Oh no! Dost thou need a hand, Grandmagus?" The laughs grew louder.

Plinius eyed the man darkly. One good thing about being asleep for two days was he could feel himself brimming with magic potential. He could tell the River had missed him. *I remember my Father used to call it recharging the batteries, whatever that meant.* Plinius stood up slowly, the laughter still rolling in the air. A simple thought accompanied by a flick of his hand and the mud slid off him like butter on a hot skillet. He recited a phrase while twisting his fingers in a pattern he had memorized in what seemed like a lifetime ago. With no fanfare he gently rose into the air and floated on to the perch, sitting down with a smug grin. The laughter had quickly died, although Ohotepe, Gellar and Pots were still smiling. "No help necessary, tailor."

Qubo scowled and some of the militia muttered. Qubo looked as if to say something else when Commander Eriksen interceded. "What in the bloody hells is the hold up? Zhang, stop fucking around and let's get this wagon moving. Now!"

Qubo's eyes simmered as his lips grew taut. Turning back, he slammed a plank down under the wheel. "Help me push it in, damn it!"

"I could have this wagon out with a spell…" offered Plinius.

Anatoli tsked. "We are going to be keeping a low profile, Plinius. Perhaps save the magic for more dire moments, eh? Stunts like will not win you any friends."

Plinius nodded. "Oh yes, Anatoli. Of course, you're right."

"Excuse me? What did you just say?"

"Oh, bugger off, you rogue. Don't think I have forgiven you."

"Forgiven me? Whatever are you referring to?" At a shout from Ohotepe, he snapped the reigns and the team of horses stepped forward, popping the stuck wheel onto the plank. The rest of the caravan scrambled to get back on their respective wagons and horses, and quickly they were underway northwards along the coast once more.

"Oh, let us see… spying on me for the Lyceum, dropping in uninvited, kicking me out of my house. Your little underlings have proven to be just as boorish and discourteous as you- well, Ohotepe seems decent in a rough sort of way- and they have almost got me killed. Have you ever tried ale? They made me try it- horrid stuff. And now here I am on a suicidal quest to find a most likely dead magus no one has seen in a hundred years in a land no civilized person has ever been to let alone believes in. All in all, I am beginning to reconsider our friendship."

Anatoli looked wounded. "My dear Pliny, all I have done and more has been because of our friendship, not despite it! Remember, it was I who came to warn you of the lictors."

Plinius chewed his lip as he watched some cows graze in a nearby field. "A part of me still cannot believe what happened. I was so careful- WE were so careful. I wish I knew how they found out."

"Oh, that's a mystery easily solved," Anatoli said offhandedly, "I told them."

"Oh!" he blinked, still parsing Anatoli's words.

Plinius rounded on the Tsarusskan.

"YOU WHAT!?"

Anatoli seemed non-plussed. "What? You do the crime you better be prepared to do the time. Every criminal knows this. And now you do too. Criminal."

"That's not funny, you son of a hag! You gremlin shit! You! You! You Rogue!"

"You needed to leave, Scrivener, one way or another. It was just a little push out the door is all. If it wasn't me, it would have been someone else. You should know, dealing with Tsarusskans never ends well."

"You're a Tsarusskan!"

"*Da*, Pliny; that's how I know."

"Wha's thar about Da?" rose a voice from somewhere back in the wagon.

Plinius stewed in silence, refusing to talk to Anatoli.

"You need to apologize to me," Plinius finally stated after a few minutes.

"For what?" Anatoli asked, perplexed.

"FOR WHAT!?" Plinius face looked like an overripe tomato. "For ratting me out to the lictors!"

"Ah, you still going on about that?" Here," Anatoli reached into a pouch on his belt and handed Plinius a few imperial loonies, the Emperors Crow & Loon emblem on one side with the Gladia Virgum on the other. "You can have half of the informants fee."

Plinius scowled, but still took the money. *Eh, money is money.* He contemplated their situation, the road ahead, the trials and dangers that surely lay in front of them. His home, even though gone, still felt so close. Their goal felt so very, very far away. "Anatoli," he began quietly, not wanting the others to overhear, "do you think we will truly find Merlin?"

Anatoli nodded. "I do believe it. *Da*, Pliny. I must believe it."

"Good," Pliny said, nodding along. "We will find Merlin, and we will make things right. The Empire will learn the hard way not to mess with Terrastra. We will find Merlin, and then we will show the Magocracy the error of their ways. They will pay. For Terrastra. For Mir. Most of all for burning my home.

This is personal."

Plinius looked over at Anatoli, who had a very pensive look on his face.

Oh, Cronus. I remember now.

Plinius eyes widened, the gears in his head clicking away until his mouth dropped as far as it could and still stay attached.

"No. No." Plinius shook his head fervently. "Anatoli… the lictors were the ones who burned my home. Tell me it was them."

"What?" Anatoli asked sheepishly, shrugging his shoulders." You gave me the idea. I needed a distraction to get away!"

Plinius sunk his head into his hands and whimpered, as the wagons rolled northwards, a shaft of light breaking through the clouds to the west.

Epilogue

The Crow & The Shadow

What is this? Epilogue!? Explain yourself, Tales. This can't be the end of my story!

Remember, Plinius? We're running out of room. Don't worry, we prepared for this. Lots of empty books. All part of the spell.

Running out of room? I find that not in the least bit reassuring, Tales.

Trust me.

I wish I could throttle you every time you say, 'trust me'.

We need to focus. We're still not done here. We need to divert our attention away from the expedition for a moment.

Is it necessary?

To give a full accounting, we decided it was probably a good idea to include the following.

We? My friends, eh. And who are they, exactly?

You already know Plinius. You just need to remember.

Plinius?

Are you there?

I… I can't seem to recall… it's so cold all of a sudden. Why? It's hard to think.

That's ok, Pliny. Please, just relax, listen awhile longer. Everything will make sense when we complete the story. When we complete the spell.

Very well. Let's get on with it.

Centurion Ox'Vacar stormed down the hallway with singular focus, his heavy footfalls shaking the braziers used for lighting in this subterranean part of the Hall of Staffs. The flames quivered in their metal lattice casements as if they feared the goliath's passing, flickering shadows like ripples of water across the walls. The Aurum Circle delegates in the Magistracy had suggested replacing the braziers with glow globes at every quarterly general conclave since Ox'Vacar could recall, and every time he had vetoed the idea. Magi or no magi- in this part of the Hall of Staffs, the Iron Cohort was firmly and undeniably in control. He appreciated the simple, common, non-magical nature of the braziers. He felt that the physically demanding nature of tending to the braziers was a good way to simultaneously discipline the lictors and soldiers under his command while subtly reminding the magi who was in charge in the depths of the Midhill.

Reaching the end of the hallway, the Centurion growled at the two sentries posted in front of the doorway to the surgeon theatre. They stood in front of the doors, and even the centurion's fury could not shake their resolve. The life-long soldier in Ox'Vacar grunted in approval. Both soldiers were Cohort veterans- a woman and a man Ox'Vacar could trust implicitly. They took the growling in stride.

"Necrodrone," snarled Ox'Vacar, supplying today's pass phrase. Necrodrones. Pitiful creatures. I wonder if we will see any up in Tsarusska?

The guards, satisfied, stood aside and let their commanding officer explode through the doors into the theatre.

"Attention. I demand answers immediately," boomed Ox'Vacar to no one in particular. "I am currently commanding a policing action due to the ongoing insurrection. If this summons proves spurious in nature, I will kill every person in this room."

The magus nearly banged his head off the ceiling in surprise at the bombastic entrance of the towering warrior. The blue robes hung off his bony and bruised torso in battle-worn tatters. The magus saluted Ox'Vacar with a tremoring hand. Weasel pushed himself up from the cot he was resting on, desperately trying not to disturb the bandages wrapped around his leg and wincing with continuing failure. He likewise saluted with the Gladia Virgum, an apprehensive look on his face. Venem leaned on a stool against the wall next to Weasel, cleaning her fingernails with a thin stiletto dagger. She did not bother saluting, instead inclining her head in the absolute minimum of deference necessary. Ox'Vacar frowned. Weasel shuddered and flexed whatever muscles he could find to stop from soiling himself- a goliath frowning was a terrifying sight. A face like a broken mirror.

"My annoyance is growing. I will repeat myself to be perfectly clear. I have a city to bring to heel, and the rabid dogs only gain ground while I divert myself with this summons. This better be worth my while, lictor, or you will understand the true extant of my displeasure."

"Ah, Centurion, it was I who noticed first," Weasel piped in, eagerness tinging his voice, "They had brought the body in you see- and I was in here all bored like, so I decided to have a peek."

"I am annoyed now. Edge take you, get to the point, lictor." Ox'Vacar's patience was near snapping point.

"The body- the body of the fugitive, Plutonus, Platoni… the scrivener! Publicanus?"

"Plinius," offered Venem, not bothering to look up from her nails.

"Grrkeill," rumbled Ox'Vacar. It was the closest to a polite acknowledgement that existed in the gravelly language of the goliaths.

"Yes! Plinius, that's it, ser!" Weasel nodded emphatically. "The body was sent up here by special order for an autopsy. At first, I ain't too keen on sittin' here with a dead body like, so I did's my best to ignore it. Yet with nothin' to do here, I'll admit me curiosity got the better of me and-"

"Get to the fucking point, Weasel," Venem drawled.

"Venem's words are correct. I agree. Now, lictor," commanded the Centurion, cracking his knuckles, "Get to the fucking point."

Weasel gulped. "Fine- don't listen to me, see for yourself! Superior, can you show the Centurion what we found?"

The magus nodded with barely concealed apprehension and beckoned for Ox'Vacar to come over to the operating table. A long white sheet had been drawn over the corpse from head to toe, a few dried splotches near the face the only hint as to what had happened to the unfortunate soul underneath. The magus gently pulled back the clothe. Oh, this feels weird.

Plinius Scrivener's corpse lay underneath, an empty vessel of cold, pale flesh. The throat and mouth were a brutal scar of bruised and ruptured ribbons of meat, most of the teeth missing from the unnaturally distended mouth. The dim lifeless eyes stared up at nothing. Ox'Vacar, comfortable companion to death in a thousand different guises, shrugged indifferently.

"I am confused. It looks like the corpse of a traitor to me," Ox'Vacar drawled, his ire reaching a boiling point. "Is this some kind of joke, lictor? We have talked about your humour before. I will now remove your head from your pathetic body with my hands."

Weasel waved his arms in fresh panic. "No! No joke, Centurion! Look- look closer! It was Venem who noticed first- look!"

Ox'Vacar squinted his face in suspicion, turning back towards the corpse. If there was something that needed to be seen, the centurion would see it. If Weasel had been able to see it, then the Edge could take him if he could not. He studied it in closer detail for a minute, then two, then another two. Weasel held his breath nearly the entire time, his eyes switching from the goliath's face to the corpse, then to the blade on the centurion's back. He knew from first-hand experience it was a blade that was always waiting and hungry.

"The eyes," said Ox'Vacar finally, and Weasel dared to release his breath.

"Yes!" Weasel exclaimed, his excitement rising along with the growing possibility of leaving this room alive. "Venem noticed- and we still had the leaflet from the Hall to compare against!" He pulled out a crumpled sheet of paper which he hastily smoothed out and offered to the Centurion.

"I do not need the traitor's description," growled Ox'Vacar, "I remember. The magus' eyes are green, not brown."

Weasel's smile faltered slightly as he turned to the magus. "Show him what you found, Superior!"

Ox'Vacar looked at the magus with what he would consider curiosity, but to the others in the room it came off more like he was threatening spontaneous brutality. The magus placed hands on the corpse and muttered a spell under his breath. As he finished, the tell-tale aura of magic filled the air as the River flooded the room, a crackling sensation that made Ox'Vacar's skin crawl inside his heavy plate every time he felt it. Ox'Vacar had served the magi for literally his entire life and had often wondered what the River looked like while watching his masters practice their craft. The knowledge that he would never get to see the River for himself made him angry. The corpse on the table began to shimmer and vibrate on the table, the face warping and changing. After half a minute the corpse that laid before the Centurion was not the rogue magus, the magus he had spent an entire day hunting down, which happened to be the same magus he had helped personally execute a couple days ago.

In the corpses place lay an old man, wrinkly and scraggly. His teeth were yellow and brown, sores and lesions dotted his skin. Ox'Vacar leaned over the corpse. "An illusion? A trick?"

The magus spoke up in a clipped, nasally voice. "A polymorph spell by the feel of it. A rather strong one as well, at the very least 7th circle but I would hypothesize even higher. The corpse will revert to the imitation momentarily. Whoever cast this spell knew what they were doing and had the power to back it up."

Ox'Vacar chewed on this new information momentarily. A coppery taste flooded his mouth. Is he even aware that he's panting and snarling like a dog?

"This Plinius… he is a grandmagus, correct? 8th circle? He could be responsible."

"Mmm," hummed the magus thoughtfully, stroking the meagre beard on his jawless chin, "Yes, that is most definitely possible. Likely even."

"It gets better," chimed in Venem.

Ox'Vacar growled.

"On a hunch, I recast the tracking spell on the grandmagus when we discovered the trickery this morning," the magus smiled, misreading the unfolding scene. "And I got a hit. Very faint, but sure as gremlin shit."

"Where?" swore Ox'Vacar.

"North. At least a week's ride. He seems to have fooled you, Centurion."

Ox'Vacar went rigid. "Fooled me?"

"Hmmm?" said the magus, bending over the corpse to examine something on his neck, "Yes, fooled you. Us. You know what I mean."

The Centurions shoulders tightened. With catlike grace he cracked his neck and extended to his full height, the top of his bald head brushing the high ceiling. Venem, familiar with the warning signs, got off her stool and backed up into the corner as far as she could. Weasel, having been on the receiving end of what was about to happen, pulled up his blankets around his chin until only his nose and eyes peeked over the top. The magus was intently examining the counterfeit corpse, completely unaware of the imminent jeopardy he was in.

With a deafening roar that shook the flames in their sconces, Ox'Vacar brought both fists down onto the face of the corpse. Chunks of dead flesh rained across the room as he flipped the table upwards, bringing up his foot with preternatural speed and kicking it in a straight line eight metres across the room. The magus found himself in the unfortunate position of being directly in line of the goliath's wrath and before he could utter a word Ox'Vacar snatched the magus by the throat and lifted him savagely off the floor. The magus tried to speak the words of a spell to free himself, but the Centurion gave one sharp squeeze and crushed his windpipe as he smashed his head into the stone ceiling. Completely acting on instinct as his brain leaked out of his skull, the magus lifted his hand up and frantically tried to conjure a defensive charm. The centurion's free hand shot out like a striking viper, catching the terrified man's wrist. In two sharp and deliberate motions, the goliath snapped the magus' forearm in two, followed by ripping the arm off in one screaming motion. Throwing the mutilated body across the room, the magus mercifully died instantly as his already severely mangled head met the stone wall and collapsed in a broken and bloody, blue-robed heap. Ox'vacar heaved in the now silent room, Weasel now completely under his blankets and Venem still working on her nails. His breath pounded in his ears for a minute until he regained his composure.

Ox'Vacar rounded on the lictors. "I am calm now. Good work, lictors. Get this mess cleaned up. Where are the other bodies from the execution?"

Venem shrugged as Weasel, still beaming, answered, "No idea, ser."

Ox'Vacar eyed them murderously. "Find out. Who ordered this special autopsy?"

No answer was forthcoming as the two lictors looked at each other.

"We thought the order came from you, ser,"

Ox'Vacar snarled. "I will look for answers then. The hunt begins again."

Venem and Weasel exchanged glances. "Yes, Centurion," they answered, just quick enough to be acceptable for Ox'Vacar.

Walking across the room, the centurion lifted the broken body of the magus and hefted it over his shoulder. Still holding the magus' arm, he thought about it for a moment before tossing it to Weasel. He walked across the room, kicking the door open and off its hinges with one swift movement.

"Where are you going, centurion? Where can we find you?"

Ox'vacar did not bother to turn around as he answered.

"I am going to see the Hollow Man."

There's that name again! Remember, Tales?

I do remember. The children's song.

I think I heard it in the Exchange as well.

Weasel blanched and Venem clicked her tongue against the roof of her mouth as the centurion ducked through the doorway, storming out of the theatre.

"I guess we'll let him find us," whispered Weasel.

The Hall of Staffs, towering symbol of imperial power, was the tallest building in all Terrastra- taller even than Merlin's tower. What was not as well-known was that the lower levels and dungeons stretched downwards, nearly double the height of the topside building, way down into the dark and secret heart of Midhill. Past the cellars, larders, cold rooms, and torture chambers, where the marble-tiled walls gave way first to fieldstone and then to rough-hewn rock, where the light of day had never shone. The Lyceum and the Wayfarers had always assumed the existence of such hidden levels, even before when the Hall had simply been the Imperial embassy. Numerous attempts had been made in the past to infiltrate the lower levels, but none had ever met with anything that could even be remotely considered a success.

The Iron Cohort referred to it as the Hollows. It was a black hole. Anything that went down there that did not belong never came out again. Despite its secretive nature, or maybe because of it, rumours about it invariably found a way to spread among the people of Terrastra. The more fanciful the tale, the more widely believed. Some swore that a dragon slumbered there on a hoard of gold, others that Merlin had been taken there and imprisoned for the past century. The one truth they all agreed on was that something dangerous resided in the heart of the hill. Those who knew of its existence rarely talked about it for fear that even mentioning it would draw its attention. For that reason the imperials had adopted another name for the terror beneath them, this one used in hushed whispers when the lictors were in their cups.

The Hollow Man. Spooky.

Ox'Vacar squeezed through the steep staircase, a winding tunnel hewn from rock heading down into the heart of the hill. There was no light down here, which was no impediment to the goliath. His enhanced senses, inherited from his hunter-warrior ancestors that had once ruled the Spinebreaker Mountains, made walking in pitch black darkness no more difficult than a midday stroll along a beach. How strange- I'm just a plain old human but I can see just fine here. He had to cradle the corpse against his chest to fit, the dead magus looking like a baby in the goliath's massive arms.

The staircase came to an open landing, a natural cave of crudely smoothed stone walls. No sconces adorned these walls, no carpets along the floor. None of the ostentatious imperial trappings on proud display far above his head. The only decoration was of primitive engravings drawn on the walls. All manner of beasts were depicted in simple lines and circles, from horses, chickens, and cows to blinkcats, rocs, and dragons. Stick figure hunters were shown stalking the beasts, losing many people in the process. A figure brandishing a staff stood above them all. The goliath walked past them, paying them no mind, having lost interest in them years ago.

The tunnel wound around in a circle, the curved left wall carrying on for what felt like more than enough time to double back around on itself, but it never did. Ox'Vacar passed a few ancient oaken doors, spaced every dozen metres or so along the left wall. He counted them off silently as he passed each one, extremely careful not to lose count. A mistake here and he might be trapped down in the Hollows forever. What a dreadful thought.

"Thirteen," he grunted, pulling the door open.

The room he stepped into was, for the first time in its very, very long history, illuminated by a steady candleflame. Ox'Vacar could barely contain his surprise. Oh my god.

The room was not large, nor was it small. It was plainly adorned, a solitary, simple wooden table and chair in the middle of the room. A large, thick red candle burned in a copper candlestick, the large amount of wax pooling on the table below giving an idea for how long it had been burning. Aboard the table sat a chess set, fully prepared in starting positions, waiting for the game to begin. A natural stalagmite, tall as a man, cast the only shadow in the otherwise spherical room- the candle gave neither the table nor Ox'Vacar himself their shadows, some profane trick of magic that made the centurion's skin crawl. Viscous blood oozed and dripped on the stone from the dead magus, tiny plopping sounds magnified in the confines of the cell.

Ox'Vacar had expected one occupant, and was slightly unsettled to find two awaiting his arrival. The first one, the expected one, could barely be seen at all. The darkness behind the stalagmite shifted ever so slightly, and Ox'Vacar could just barely make out the outline of what looked like a man hidden in the shadow. A floating, rigid smile of perfect white teeth materialized as the shadow split, pulling the darkness itself back like dry lips.

My god. What the hell is that thing?

"Good morning, Centurion," said a soft, haunted voice from somewhere in the shadow, the teeth staying perfectly still, "Do you know where my brothers are?"

The goliath did not respond. As strange as the creature hiding in the gloom was, he was not surprised to see it. On the contrary, the Hollow Man was exactly who he had come to see.

"Have you brought me a present? A tasty treat?" asked the Hollow Man, the things empty voice flavoured with childlike anticipation.

The goliath tossed the dead magus into the shadow. No sooner had it passed out of the light it disappeared, the smiling teeth folding back into the darkness. A wet rending, cracking, and sucking could be heard coming from behind the stalagmite, only a couple metres away but sounding as if from a far greater distance. Ox'Vacar paid it no heed, his eyes never leaving the second man in the room. Reflecting on it later, the centurion believed it was the first time in his life he had been truly, completely surprised. The man sitting in front of the chessboard was the last person on Mir that Ox'Vacar had expected to meet that day, in the Hollow of all places.

"I have been waiting for you, Ox'Vacar," said the portly man, his golden robes swishing as he turned in his seat. He snapped his fingers and a chair popped into existence across from him. He motioned towards the open chair, "Please, sit. Do you play chess? I can teach you if you don't."

"Emperor Eternal!" Ox'Vacar fell to one knee.

Alister Crowley, Emperor of the Magocratic Empire, laughed heartily.

"None of that now, my dear fellow. We have much to discuss, and our prey gets further away each moment we waste."

The Emperor leaned over the table, his fingers steepled before his grinning face. The Hollow Man quivered in the shadow. *I don't like the look in his eyes, Tales.*

"Tell me, centurion- what do you know of Plinius Scrivener?"

Author's Note

Wait, was that it?

Just for this book. We're getting the next book prepared right now. It should switch us over once we get through this last page.

Should? You don't sound very confident.

Trust me, Pliny, this will work.

Trust me, it better have. So… Author. That's you, isn't it?

Maybe it's you.

Maybe it's neither of us.

Maybe it's both of us.

So…

Pfft.

When's this ending?

Now.

Now?

Now.

PLINIUS SCRIVENER WILL CONTINUE HIS STORY

IN

BY THE RIVER SO SWORN
BOOK TWO

COMING SOON

ABOUT THE AUTHOR

KR Carnegie is a part-time mythozooologist, witty raconteur, and novelist? who currently resides with his family in the fantastical Niagara Region, Canada. He was infected at a young age with a lifelong passion for reading, pretending, acting, singing, listening, watching, and most importantly telling stories.

During the hour of the wolf, you may just find him walking along the secret paths that connect all worlds.

Who the hell is this guy?

www.ingramcontent.com/pod-product-compliance
Lightning Source LLC
LaVergne TN
LVHW091150150826
845672LV00005B/1102

* 9 7 8 1 7 3 8 1 5 7 1 1 2 *